# THE
# TALKATIVE
# POLICEMAN

# THE
# TALKATIVE
# POLICEMAN

by

Rupert Penny

RAMBLE HOUSE

ISBN 13: 978-1-60543-368-4

ISBN 10: 1-60543-368-3


Cover Art: Gavin L. O'Keefe
Preparation: Fender Tucker

# THE
# TALKATIVE
# POLICEMAN

# FOREWORD

". . . the detective story is a game between two players, the author of the one part and the reader of the other part."

" The true detective fan is constantly asking himself, I take it, the following question : ' Have I now arrived at the point in this story at which I ought to stop, put the book down, light a fresh pipe, take a turn round the garden, and try to solve the mystery for myself before I read on further ? ' "

Father Ronald Knox: Introduction to ' Best Detective Stories of the Year ' —1st Series.

---

*Chapters I to XXXII form the body of the book, and state the problem ; Chapter XXXIII contains such additional facts or hints as will enable a moderately intelligent person to arrive at the correct solution without further help. The maximum of satisfaction will probably be got by whoever succeeds in doing that after an invigorating struggle ; or who, failing, nevertheless admits when he has read the remaining chapters that he ought not to have failed.*

*No claim to originality is made in thus directly challenging the reader. The precedent was created in 1929 by an American detective-story writer, Mr Ellery Queen, in ' The Roman Hat Mystery'. In England it seems to have been ignored, which is surely a pity. A good idea is not less good because somebody else thought of it first ; nor, having everything to recommend it, should it be disdained.*

5

*The detective story is no self-supporting form of literature. It is not, as the works of Blake or Beethoven or Botticelli are, destined for the future equally with the past. By its nature it is for to-day, and possibly for tomorrow ; and perhaps its highest hope is to pass by and by from dustbin to dustman, and back again to bin, until, the day after tomorrow, it begins to smell too strongly of bloater skins and tea leaves for even a dustman's nose, and is allowed to go the inevitable way of all rubbish. The detective shall find his grave at last as surely as the lifeless flesh he theorized upon.*

*The sole undoubted exception within the last fifty years is Sherlock Holmes, who persists not because of his profession or his problems, but because of himself and Dr Watson. They are, first and foremost, characters, and the rest is incidental. At a guess, it is not impossible that Lord Peter Wimsey may one day qualify to keep them company.*

*In general, then, the detective story is nothing ' per se,' because it is impermanent. If it is not written for the present generation, or their very near successors, it should not have been written at all. In other words, the author works neither for himself nor for posterity, but to please a limited number of contemporary readers ; and, being thus dependent upon them for his success, he ought to treat them with all possible consideration. He would be imprudent if he did otherwise, and they dull-witted to put up with him.*

*Since they expect to be set a riddle, and tacitly request as much, they are being badly used if it is not made reasonably clear to them at what point the riddle ends and the explanation begins. They would, indeed, be justified in demanding that information noisily, or even rudely. The lack of it depletes their hope that presently they will have their reward : the satisfaction of being able to say with truth " Your help was not required—I did if for myself ! ".*

*If, in spite of possible past failures, they have not this hope to begin with, then they are no players in the game, but mere idlers, apathetic page-turners torpidly filling up time, as indifferent to detection and the accepted claims of justice as the corpse itself. The best that can be said for them is that they have mistaken their recreation.*

*Finally : in place of a list of characters, which usually confuses as it seeks to help, is the guarantee that Chief-Inspector Beale, Detective-sergeant Matthews, Anthony Purdon, Dickie Donovan, and Bobbie Seccombe are entirely innocent. While this statement does not necessarily mean that the rest of the characters are guilty without exception, it may nevertheless be of some use, not only in relieving a little the minds of the too-suspicious, but also in acquainting the beginner with the need for caution.*

# Contents

# CHAPTER I

CHIEF-INSPECTOR BEALE looked at the clock on the dash-board, and then at his wrist watch.

" Yours is the first car clock I ever saw that wasn't slow " he observed. " We'll get down there in good time, Tony."

" Well, I haven't been crawling exactly " said his companion.

" No " agreed the Inspector. " My conscience is heavy. I've got a feeling that I ought to have arrested you any time during the last twenty miles."

" What for ? The limit doesn't come in till next year. You're ahead of your time."

" If I were to clout your head " mused Beale, " we should probably begin to hit things, instead of just missing them. I suppose I'd better leave you alone."

" Instead of talking nonsense " said Anthony Purdon, avoiding a flustered chicken, " what you ought to be doing is forming theories about how the late Rev. Thingummy met his death."

" ' Death is before me today ' " quoted Beale sententiously " ' Like the recovery of a sick man,'—look out for that bicycle !—' Like going forth into a garden after sickness.' Anyway, how the devil can I form theories without any facts ? "

" Come ! " said his friend. " You can't dismiss a dead clergyman with his head battered in as not being a fact. You mean clues."

" What is a clue ? " enquired Beale.

" You ought to have been a judge. A clue is a sign-post pointing to the highway of truth."

" Sounds all right."

" E.g., a cigar end full of teeth-marks."

" You've been reading too many thrillers. Perhaps

11

you'll be kind enough to find me a clue or two when we get there."

"Certainly" said Tony; "I'll go straight out and look for some. By the way, Ted" he added, more seriously, "it's decent of you to let me come down. I've always wanted to see the great Beale smelling out a murderer : something to tell my children about."

"Bachelors of thirty-five shouldn't have children" declared Beale.

"When I do, I mean. Anyway, officials of forty shouldn't go putting ideas into people's heads. No, but I really am grateful. Of course, you ought to be too. When I've nosed about and found a few handfuls of bloodstained rags, several cigarette stubs with monograms on them, a lady's glove, an undecipherable code message, and the footprint of a heavy boot with two hobnails missing, you'll begin to realize what an ally you've got."

"I don't think you can strictly say that hobnailed boots have feet" objected Beale. "To some extent they are feet; as good as, anyway."

"End of brief lecture on boots" said Tony. "Well, policemen ought to know. And talking of policemen, why aren't all the local Sherlocks running round measuring and magnifying ? They don't usually call in Scotland Yard within an hour of finding the body, do they ? "

"No, but the local man is on sick leave, and the Superintendent got into such a row over the Butterworth case a year or so back for muddling everything on his own that I suppose he's keen to do the right thing this time."

"And what about the Chief Constable ? Or doesn't he count ? "

"Decidedly, I should think. That's who the Super got it in the neck from. Jeffson was all for getting us in before. How much further ? "

"We've done forty-four—just coming into Shale now. It's six miles from there to Wyre."

"Good—we'll be there by 2.0. You'd better drop

me at the police-station, and then run along and book rooms at the local pub. What's it like ? You know this part, don't you ? "

" Not bad. The King's Head, or Arms, or something. Rather a surly bloke, the man who keeps it, but he's got a pretty daughter, and so shall be forgiven."

" Well, I hope he doesn't stand in need of forgiveness over the present case."

" O lord ! " exclaimed Tony. " I was forgetting. You'll go about suspecting everybody, won't you ? How horrible ! I shan't know whether the hand that sells me a stamp, or fills up my tankard, or gives me a packet of Gold Flake, isn't metaphorically dripping with the late Rev.'s blood. I think you ought to be able to tell a murderer instinctively."

" You can't " said Beale. " At least, I can't. I had breakfast with one once every day for a week, and got to like him so much that I told him to look me up if he was ever in London. I was really quite sorry when I had to arrest him."

" By the way, what's the dead man's name ? "

Beale took a deep breath.

" Tatham. The Rev. Arthur Tatham, Rector of Wyre, in the county of Kent, for nineteen years. Age sixty-three, height five foot five, slight build, blue eyes, own teeth, white hair, strictly evangelical, widower, leaves a widowed daughter and grandson, teetotal, non-smoker, body found in Wyre Woods about 11.30 this morning by a gamekeeper, dead approximately twelve hours, head battered in with unknown weapon."

He stopped his recital, exhausted.

" Marvellous ! " said Tony. " Even if you did forget the weight of the man who christened him. Who told you all that ? "

" The Superintendent. I always like to know as much as possible about corpses. Is this Wyre ? "

The car was slowing down to enter the beginnings of a village.

" Yes. I seem to remember the police-station comes

13

before the pub. On the left, I think. Yes—where that bobby's standing."

" By the way " said Beale, as he got out, " you won't go butting in too much, Tony ? "

" No, of course not."

" Thanks. Come back here when you've booked the rooms ; and find out the telephone number, if they've got one. And bring the bloodstained rags with you ! "


## CHAPTER II

It was a somewhat different Chief-Inspector Beale who shook hands with the sergeant inside the police-station. For the moment all trace of flippancy had gone, and his steady grey eyes held no hint of humour. He was on his job now, and eager to get at the facts. Although above the average height he was sparely built, and seemed almost insignificant in bulk by the side of Sergeant Rush, who was explaining why the Superintendent was absent.

" He's had to go back to Shale, sir. There's been another smash-and-grab—the fourth this month. He asked me to say he was sorry he couldn't stop, and he'll try to get over tomorrow or Thursday. He's left a couple of men on duty in the woods where the Rector was found, and wants you to ring him up before five, if you will, sir."

" Very well " said Beale. " I suppose you can tell me all I want to know ? "

The sergeant declared that he could.

" And the Chief Constable will be over tomorrow, sir " he added.

" Right. I'll just ask a few questions before I see the body. Where is it ? "

" Downstairs in one of the cells, sir."

" Who identified it ? "

" Dr Hatherley, sir—the police-surgeon. Very old

14

friends, sir—he's quite cut up about it. He'll be along at half past."

" Good—then I'll ask him about the cause of death, and so on."

" Blunt instrument, sir " said the sergeant, helpfully.

" Yes, quite " replied Beale. " You haven't got a headache, have you ? " he added, maliciously.

" Beg pardon, sir ? No sir—have you ? "

" No, not yet. Now, let's hear something about the Rector. Was he popular ? "

" Oh yes, sir. Everybody liked him. Leastways, that is——"

" Go on, Sergeant."

" Well sir, I don't know how to put it, quite." He scratched his massive head with a large forefinger. " You see, sir, there's been a bit of trouble with Farmer Bassett over the right of way across Pond Meadow."

" Where's that ? "

" Opposite the Rectory, sir. One gate's there, and the other's facing Wyre Woods, where he was found, about a hundred yards from the cross-roads."

" How much does the footpath save ? "

" Best part of five minutes, sir."

The sergeant, with the ghost of a righteous smile, began fumbling in his pocket.

" I made a map out, sir."

" Ah, thanks very much " said Beale, more warmly.

He spread it out on the table. " Yes, I see—you go across there instead of round here."

" That's it, sir."

" Many people use it ? "

" No sir—that's what Bassett said. You see, it's not much help unless you want to get to the Rectory or the church, so it's mostly used of a Sunday. Bassett says he's got a right to close it if he wants to, as it's not in general use. And Mr Tatham said it had always been a footpath while he was at Wyre, and as long as he was alive it always would be."

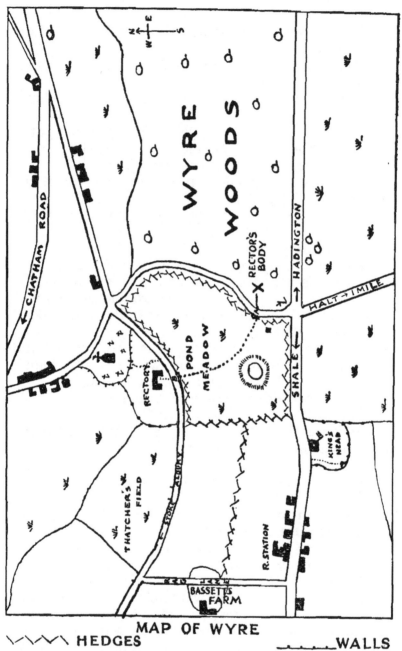

MAP OF WYRE

∨∨∨∨∨ HEDGES          _____ WALLS

ᴓ ᴓ ᴓ TREES          ⅋⅋ ⅋⅋ GRASS

SCALE 6" = 1 MILE

16

" Oh " said Beale : " as long as he was alive, eh ? "

" Yes sir ; but I hope you aren't thinking Bassett did it—I hope not, anyway."

" It wouldn't be a very strong motive, would it ? Come in " as someone tapped lightly on the door. " What sort of man is this Bassett ? "

" Well sir—he's got a bit of a temper."

" Anything else ? "

" Not as far as I know—not now, anyway. He used to be a bit of a lad with the girls, but Ellen looks after that all right."

" Old ? "

" No sir—just over thirty. Not what you might call old at all "—with a look at Beale. " Here's his farm, sir "—pointing on the map. " He's only had it since his father died last Christmas. There wasn't any trouble with the footpath in old Bassett's time, but William—he's got ideas."

" Why did you say you hoped he didn't do it ? Any personal reason, I mean ? "

" Yes, in a way, sir. You see, he married my sister, and it'd be awkward, like."

Beale smiled.

" Very, I should think. Is she the Ellen you mentioned ? "

" Yes sir, that's right." He emphasized this with several nods, licking his moustache.

" It'd be awkward, and no mistake. You don't know my sister."

" Is she nice ? " asked Tony Purdon.

" Well sir " was the answer, after Beale had introduced them, " I don't know about that. No beauty, sir—not but what I gets on all right with her. Mostly, that is " he added, reminiscently. " But " with a sudden burst of confidence " she'd blame me, sir, somehow. If it was William Bassett did it, she won't be able to go for him, so she'll take it out of me."

" Well, I don't think you need start worrying yet " said Beale. " But I must certainly see Bassett. Have you any idea what he was doing last night ? "

"No sir; but he was busy yesterday afternoon all right."

The sergeant smiled again. "You see, the Rector went to London in the morning."

"Yes; the Superintendent told me that on the phone."

"That's right, sir. Well, it wasn't often he was away, and Bassett, he sees his opportunity. I told you one end of the path finishes opposite the Rectory, sir. There's a five-barred gate, usually fastened with a chain. Well sir, about quarter past two yesterday along comes William and three of his farm hands with a drum of barbed wire, and I defy anybody, man woman or child, to get out of Pond Meadow that way. Made a proper job of it, he did."

"What about the other gate?" asked the Inspector. "Did he barricade that too?"

"No sir—William's cunning. He knows the Rector's gone to London, and he knows he'll be coming back that night, and'll go along the footpath for sure instead of round by the road."

"I see" said Beale. "And when he got to the second gate he'd either have to risk tearing himself to pieces on it, or go all the way back and round."

"That's it, sir—only, of course, he never came."

"It's quite definite that he didn't return home after he left in the morning?"

"Quite, sir. I saw Mrs Seccombe myself—that's his daughter. And we couldn't find any footprints in Pond Meadow. It's pretty sure he never got to the second gate."

"How has Mrs Seccombe taken it?"

"Very upset, sir—but quietly. She's a nice lady, not one to make a fuss over what's done. Saw me at once, but I think she'd been crying. There won't be any trouble if you want to see her."

"Good. I'll go up there presently. Now, just one or two more questions. Have any strangers been seen round here lately?"

"No sir, not that I've heard of. Weather's not much
18

good for visitors. I was out of doors most of the night myself, and I saw nothing."

" Oh—why was that ? "

" Well sir, Mondays I go on duty at 12.30, and I always have a look round the church. I went by Pond Meadow at quarter to one, and came back about half past. Everything was quiet enough then. When I got back here I was rung up from Shale and told to watch the cross-roads for a stolen car. I was there from 2.0 till after 4.30, with a few minutes' break about 3.0, and I never saw or heard a thing—worse luck."

" Why ? "

" It seems the car came this way after all, sir. Leastways, that's what the Superintendent says. I don't see how it could have done, but there you are. I wasn't away ten minutes all told, and I kept my ears open too, and couldn't have helped but hear it."

" I see. Did you get told off ? "

" Well, yes, sir." The sergeant smiled rather shame-facedly.

" Bad luck. Now, which train did the Rector come down by ? "

" Don't know that he came by train, sir " was the cautious answer, at which Tony smiled.

" Yes " admitted Beale. " I suppose he might have been brought down by car."

" I might be able to find out " suggested Rush. " Tickets for Wyre Halt are collected at Shale Junction. There's no train between the 4.32 and the 9.13, and nobody got off the afternoon one, because I was there to meet it."

" Disappointing for you " said Tony.

" No sir, begging your pardon. I wasn't meeting anybody. There was something on it for me—new bicycle, sir."

" Ah, so you'll be able to live up to your name now."

" Yes sir. Well "—to Beale, " as I was saying, there's two evening trains : the 7.44, which arrives at 9.13, and the 8.56, getting in at 10.21. I could telephone Shale and ask how many people got off each train by

19

the tickets given up. Though of course somebody may have travelled without one " he added as an after-thought.

" It doesn't seem a very good plan " said Tony. " Collecting tickets at Shale, I mean. I'm sure if I lived here I'd never buy one at all."

" Ah, sir " returned the sergeant, " but you see, not many people from here travel up and down at all regularly ; and they're locals, and mostly pretty honest. And, sir, a stranger coming from London wouldn't know he didn't have to give his ticket up at the Halt itself, would he ? "

" No " agreed Beale. " Well thought out."

" Thank you sir." Sergeant Rush was obviously gratified.

" Well, I can't think of much else. You don't know of anybody but Bassett who had any sort of grudge against the Rector ? "

" No sir. I don't think there was anyone. He was a very harmless sort of man."

" Oh yes, one more : can you think of anything which would have made him go into the woods where his body was found ? "

" No sir, I can't—unless he'd gone across the foot-path, found the gate barred, and come back and round by the road. But even then, he was found some way in. And he couldn't have got to the second gate without leaving tracks, because the grass is long that end of the field."

" Let's see " said Beale, turning to the map again : " he was found about here."

" Then you must mark it with a cross " declared Tony, looking over the Inspector's shoulder, while the sergeant stood eyeing them benignantly, as one who has produced a toy to soothe two fractious children.

" What's all this path business about ? " he added.

At that moment there was a knock at the door, and Dr Hatherley came in. He was a small energetic man of middle age, and his face bore signs of strain

20

and tiredness. After the introductions had been completed, Beale turned to Rush.

"Suppose you tell Mr Purdon about the path" he suggested, "while I see the body."

"Very good, sir" said the sergeant, not displeased. The dead clergyman was no pleasant sight with his head battered in, and he was not sorry to miss looking at it again.

"You don't mind, Tony? I don't expect it'll be much in your line. Did you fix up the rooms all right?"

"Yes, quite, and the telephone number's Stoke Albury 97."

## CHAPTER III

### 2.30 PM—3.30 PM

"THIS way, Inspector" said the doctor, leading the way out of the room. "Private detective?" he asked, as they made their way down the stairs.

"Who? Tony Purdon? Good lord no! Friend of mine—he did me a good turn once, and I promised I'd let him see me investigate a crime, as he calls it."

"Ah" said the doctor; and then: "This is a bad business, Inspector. My oldest friend—it hits hard when you find him brutally murdered. Count on me for any help I can give you."

Beale murmured thanks and sympathy as they reached the cell which was acting as a mortuary. Dr Hatherley drew back the sheet which covered the body. It was still unclothed; the face wore a startled expression, and down one cheek stretched a thin dry bloodstain. Beale stood looking for some moments in silence. Then he turned to the doctor.

"Weapon?" he asked briefly.

"Some kind of blunt instrument" was the reply, no less terse.

"That might mean anything from a rolling-pin upwards."

" It's hard to be precise. I can only give you sur-
mises ; but I should say it was something with a large
surface, and perhaps an edge. You see that gash above
the ear—yet the left temple is smashed in all of a piece.
I can give it you technically——"

" Don't bother " said Beale. " Death instan-
taneous ? "

" Undoubtedly."

" Much strength needed for the blows ? "

" It depends. If it was a short weapon—the rolling-
pin you mentioned—, then the murderer would have
had to be a powerful man ; but if it was a long one—
on a long handle, say—, then the extra leverage would
have helped, and almost anybody but a child could
have done it."

" A woman ? "

" If she was rather more than averagely strong, yes."

" Flat, with an edge, possibly on a handle " said
Beale, half to himself. " I deduce a spade."

" Yes, that would do."

" Now " he went on, looking at the corpse again,
" can you help me any more here ? "

" Only guess-work. I should say he was standing
almost facing the man who hit him—unless the
murderer was left-handed. All the blows are on the
left side of the head. Some of the damage was done
after he was dead. Poor old Arthur " he added.

" Yes " said Beale, not paying much attention to
the last remark : he was staring at the feet of the corpse.

" What sort of man was Tatham ? " he asked.
" Tidy ? I mean, neat in his personal appearance ? "

" Most particular."

" Likely, for instance, to go about with a knot in
his shoe-lace ? "

The doctor bent his head.

" That's curious " he admitted. " I'd have said not
—but it's there all right. You've got sharp eyes."

" Did he always tie his laces in these double knots,
do you know ? "

" Yes—sort of habit. He ragged me once when my

22

own shoe kept coming undone, I remember. Oh yes, and that reminds me : another time, double knot and all, his lace got loose, and when he went to do it up it broke. We were in Shale, and he went straight into a shop and bought a new pair."

" Oh " said Beale, " that's interesting. I think we'll have the shoes off. " No " as Dr Hatherley put out his hand, " I'll do it myself, if you don't mind."

He took out his handkerchief, carefully held the sole of one shoe by the edges between finger and thumb, and after unlacing drew it off.

" Fingerprints ? " asked the doctor.

" Possibly."

" Whose ? The murderer's ? "

" There's a chance."

He held the left shoe up, and examined it closely. " Cow dung " he decided, pointing to a round patch on the instep. " Not on the knot, though. Curious— there's nothing on the other one."

He went to the door and called to Rush, who came down immediately.

" Is Mr Matthews here yet ? " asked Beale.

" Yes sir, just come." Then, in a hoarse whisper : " Is he really a Yard man ? "

" Yes—why ? "

" Oh, nothing, sir. I wondered. He looks like a— well, meaning no disrespect, sir, more like a jockey."

" Yes. Detective-sergeant ' Horsey ' Matthews, one of Scotland Yard's handymen ; hot stuff on finger-prints and photography. Now, take these shoes care-fully—hold them by the edges with the handkerchief, like this—, and tell him I want them examined. And talking of photographs, I hope someone had the sense to take the body before it was touched ? "

" Yes sir " with pardonable pride : " I did."

" Good man. I can see you're going to be useful. Are they ready ? "

" Not yet, sir—another few minutes. Sawyer's doing them—Constable Sawyer, I should say " as Beale raised his eyebrows.

" He won't mess them ? "

" Not him, sir—won hundreds of prizes."

" And I suppose there was nothing worth having in the way of footprints ? "

" No sir. Superintendent Bowman went over the ground pretty thoroughly."

" Ah yes, and tell me : when did it last rain here ? "

Rush thought for a moment. " Not since Friday midday, sir."

" Thanks. Be careful with the shoes."

" May I say something ? " asked Dr Hatherley, as Beale turned his attention to the body again.

" Of course, Doctor."

" Well then, I'd swear he wasn't murdered where he was found."

" Ah, that's worth knowing. I was just going to ask. Not enough blood ? "

" Not nearly enough " said the other definitely. " And another thing : I knew him forty years, and in the last twenty I've never seen him out of doors without his walking-stick, except at funerals. Where is it ? "

" I don't know. What's it like ? "

" Ebony, with a biggish silver knob for a handle, and a band with his initials on. It had a bone ferrule —a screw-on affair. He kept a stock of them."

" We must look for it " said Beale. " Now, this is worth a little attention, don't you think ? " He slowly took off one of the dead man's black socks. The foot beneath was stained with dye.

" Got his feet wet " declared the doctor. " Walked in a puddle."

" No rain since Friday, and it's been fine in London."

" Was that why you asked about the weather ? "

" Yes—I spotted the dye had run when I took the shoe off."

" Trod in a ditch."

" His shoes weren't stained."

" Perspiration, then."

" Very few people perspire immediately above the ankle."

Dr Hatherley thought again. " Dew " he said at last. " The body was out all night."

" A phenomenal fall, then, Doctor. Even the soles of his feet are marked—through strong shoes—with wide tongues."

" Yes, you're right. What do you make of it ? "

" I can't tell you definitely yet. Now, let's see what's in the pockets."

There proved to be little unusual in their contents : a leather wallet, a half-filled card-case, a small calendar, a black fountain-pen and a silver pencil whose lead was broken, four and twopence in change, two rubber bands, a piece of string, and a bunch of keys.

" I think we can go upstairs now " declared Beale. " I've seen all I want to here."

He led the way out of the cell, carrying the wallet. The rest of the things he left on the table by the door, placed there for the use of the doctor. They found the sergeant talking to Tony.

" The photos aren't quite ready, sir " he said, " but I've been on the phone to Shale. Two persons, as far as they know by the tickets, got off the 9.13, and one off the 10.21, which was twenty minutes late—the first time for months. I spoke to the man who collected the tickets. One of the first two was a stranger, and the other was Mr Ralph Curtis."

" And who's he ? "

" Lives at Wyre Place, sir—nephew of Miss Frankes that owns it. The woods where the Rector was found belong to her, too."

" What's Mr Curtis like ? Old ? Young ? "

" Youngish, sir—under thirty. Great friends with Mrs Seccombe up at the Rectory Bit of a lad once, too, so I've heard."

" And what time did he get home last night ? "

" I don't know, sir " answered the sergeant, with the accent on the pronoun, as who should say : " Am I a magician ? ".

" Daft young fool ! " said Dr Hatherley unexpectedly. " Went out rabbit-shooting this morning, and sprained his ankle. Started his shooting before he went, too—tripped up coming downstairs, and nearly polished off one of the maids. Didn't you hear about it, Sergeant ? "

Rush shook his head. " I took a bit of a sleep this morning " he explained. " Where did it happen—his ankle, I mean ? "

" Near the cross-roads. Parker picked him up in a cart and brought him along to the pub. Anybody who goes about with a loaded gun indoors deserves to be shot with it. Ouch ! "—as he broke off to do something to the inside of his mouth with a handkerchief. " Damn this tooth—been aching since Sunday."

" And off the last train, Sergeant ? " enquired Beale, anxious to get on.

" The Rector, sir."

" I see. Now, let's look in this wallet."

" I must be getting on " said Dr Hatherley. " Busy man, you know. See you again soon."

" How about dropping in tonight for a chat ? " suggested Beale. " About 9.0 at the King's Head ? "

" Well, I'll come if I can " replied the doctor, " but I won't promise. I may be called out. Mrs Dawson's expecting again " he added to the sergeant, who nodded.

" So I heard. That makes five, doesn't it ? "

" Yes, will do, if all goes well."

" All right, Doctor " said Beale ; " then come if you can manage it. Good-bye, and many thanks for your help. Perhaps you'll be able to give me some more later on."

" Yes, perhaps " agreed the doctor. " Good-day, everybody."

Beale looked after him abstractedly for a moment, and then turned his attention again to the wallet. He was just arranging the contents when Tony spoke.

" Have you found any fingerprints yet ? " he asked.

" No—unfortunately this is the wrong kind of leather. People ought to be made to have shiny wallets. I don't know how Matthews is getting on."

The only thing that aroused his attention was a letter. He read it aloud.

" Tovey & Tovey, Ltd.,

November 16th, 1934      15 Elkin Street,
London, W.C.2.

Rev. Arthur Tatham,
   Wyre Rectory,
    Wyre,
     Kent.

Dear Sir,
      With reference to your book, ' Further Light on St Augustine of Hippo ', which you recently submitted to us : we are prepared to buy the work outright from you for the sum of fifty guineas (£52. 10. 0) cash. As you are doubtless aware, it is likely to appeal only to a very limited public. We think it an excellent treatise on the subject, and of value to scholars and theologians ; but we do not consider that it will be to the advantage of either you or ourselves to undertake its publication except on the terms we have mentioned. In this way you will be sure of a definite sum of money, namely, fifty guineas ; and although of course we hope that eventually the sales will total more than this amount over and above the costs of printing, etc., it is certain to take a period of years. In these circumstances we feel that a royalty would be both an unsatisfactory and a tedious method of business.
    We shall be glad to have your answer as soon as possible.
We are,<br>Yours faithfully,<br>pp Tovey & Tovey, Ltd.,<br>P. JELKS (Director)."

When he had finished reading he put the letter away. Tony struggled with speech for a moment.

" Well " he said at last, " quite frankly, I don't
believe it."

" Why not ? "

" For several reasons. In the first place, it's going
to take at least ten years for the sales on a book about
St Hippo to cover the cost of carriage from the printers
to the bookshops. Some centuries later you might
possibly begin to get a small percentage of the price
of the paper back—but it's doubtful. And you mean
to say there's a publisher in England who'll *buy* the
thing for fifty pounds odd, spot cash ? It's incredible.
I repeat, I don't believe it. If I thought for half a
second that it was true I'd sit straight down, borrow
your fountain-pen, and write a Critical Commentary
on the life of St James the Less in the sergeant's note-
book."

Beale smiled. " All publishers aren't necessarily
rogues, you know."

" All lions aren't wild, prowling through the jungles,
seeking whom they may devour " retorted his friend,
and growled realistically. " A few, I believe, languish
in zoos and circuses and such-like places, tame and
toothless. I imagine the proportions are about the
same."

" All the same, if it's similitude you want " insisted
Beale, " I think you'll find this letter's genuine. I've
heard of Tovey & Tovey before. But ' spot cash ' is
interesting. Did he go to see them ? If so, did he get
the money ? If so, where is it ? "

" You mean, sir " put in the sergeant, " he may
have been knocked on the head for it ? "

" Barely possible. Whoever knew he was carrying
so much wouldn't be very likely to follow him all the
way back to Wyre. No, what's more probable is that
if he had the £50 in his pocket, whoever did him in
took it. I'll find out if he was paid, anyway. I'm
beginning to be sorrier than ever that the wallet
didn't have any fingerprints on it."

" Yes " said Tony. " I suppose it's not even likely
that many people did know he had it with him—if he

did. Unless—ah! wait now : I'm beginning to see light."

He paused a moment, and then pointed a finger dramatically at the other two.

"Tovey & Tovey!" he exclaimed. "Don't you see? They buy his miserable book for a preposterous sum, follow him here, club him on the head in the dark, and hop off back to town."

Beale gave his friend a smile of pity.

"I hate to mention it" he murmured, "but on your own reckoning they could at best hope to make about two bob on it after several years. The motive is, well, unconvincing."

He got up, walked over to an ordnance survey map which hung on the wall, and studied it for a moment. Tony sighed.

"I shan't help you any more" he threatened. At that moment the sergeant, who had gone out of the room a short while before, returned with 'Horsey' Matthews.

"Hullo" said Beale. "Anything doing?"

"Not a thing, sir—not a smell of a print anywhere."

"I thought there mightn't be" replied the Inspector equably.

Matthews sighed. "It's a hard life. Fingerprints are to me pretty nearly what a babe is to the mother who bore it."

"Yes, quite" said Beale. "No doubt. Don't bore me, that's all."

"The photographs, sir" interposed the sergeant, handing Beale an envelope.

"Ah, thanks." He took out the six three-quarter plates, and examined them carefully. "Nobody had touched the body when you took these?"

"Not that I know of, sir. Underwood swore he hadn't."

"I'll take them with me" said Beale. "We'll go along there in a few minutes, but I must telephone first. Will you get Scotland Yard for me, please? And I shall want to see Underwood."

29

"I'll send the constable for him, sir" promised Rush as he went out.

As the Inspector got up he saw Matthews looking enquiringly at him. "I don't think I shall want you any more" he said. "You'd better get back to town. Hepworth's coming down this evening. By the way, aren't you due for a week's holiday?"

"Yes, sir."

"Then what are you doing here? Simpson would have done."

Matthews looked pained. "Simpson's a good lad, sir" he agreed. "He tries hard, but——"

It was implied that there might be occasions, such as the present, when Simpson would fall short of requirements.

"I thought I'd better come along myself, sir. And to tell you the truth, too" he added, "I had another reason. Do you know, it's four years since I got a look in at a decent murder—being actually on the spot, I mean, seeing what's happening. I was wondering if I could stay on. I can do everything that Hepworth can do, and his mother's dying, and it'd be a holiday for me all right, and——"

He tailed off into mute entreaty. Beale looked severe.

"This is a put-up job—but I didn't know about his mother. Anyway, what would your wife say?"

"Not guilty—thank God."

"Marriage is life's crowning joy" murmured Tony. "Or is it motherhood? It seems that we are all uncrowned, either way. Dear dear!"

"I can do without you" said Beale. "There'll be a man at Shale if I wanted anything urgently, or I might even do it myself, but I'd be glad of your company if you'd care to stay. I'm phoning the Yard, and I'll put Hepworth off."

Matthews expressed satisfaction and thanks.

"I hoped you'd make it all right, sir. I brought my bike, in case." And then, to no one in particular: "Which was just as well, really". Beale started guiltily.

" Yes, that was bad " he admitted. " I ought to have had you met."

" That's all right, sir " said Matthews with a grin. " I'd have got out at Shale and had a taxi otherwise."

" You'd better fix yourself up at the pub " suggested Tony. " Then we can all drink beer together. The Three Musketeers. Something sinister somewhere : now, what is it ? Yes, I know—but not in this case, I hope."

" What ? " asked Beale.

" The sequel : twenty years after—solution of the crime. ' The venerable Commissioner staggered upright in his bath chair. " I see it all now " he quavered, in his excitement getting his beard caught up in the front wheel. . . ." ' "

" Come on—enough of this pessimism. I must be back by Saturday."

Matthews, without warning, began to laugh.

" Share the joke " said Tony.

" Concert in aid of the Police Orphanage Fund. ' Chief-Inspector Beale has kindly consented to render " Drink to Me Only ".' "

" Hell ! " cried his superior. " I'd clean forgotten all about it—and I've booked seats at the theatre, too ! "

Sergeant Rush came back while they were still laughing.

" Scotland Yard on the phone, sir. And the keeper will meet us where he found the body."

" Oh, thanks."

He got up, and turned to Matthews. " Take the Rector's fingerprints " he said, " and then book yourself a room. Get the sergeant to show you on a map about where we shall be leaving the car, and meet us there.

" Hullo ! " he called, when he got to the telephone. " Scotland Yard ? Is that Superintendent Vinney ? This is Beale, sir. Will you please send someone round straight away to Messrs Tovey & Tovey, the publishers ? Tatham called there yesterday, I believe, about a book he'd written for which they offered him fifty guineas. I want to know whether he was paid that amount, and if so, how. I shall be at Stoke Albury 97 from half past six onwards. It's quite important. . . ."

Before joining the others he rang up the Shale police-station, assured Superintendent Bowman that his absence made no difference, and agreed that it would be unnecessary for both men to remain in the woods all night. " But I'd like one there " he said. " Can I leave that to you ? Thanks. If you'll send him along to the King's Head about 10.0 I'll have a word with him first. Yes, that's splendid—a relief about 4.0 in the morning. Thanks very much, sir—good-bye."

Outside by the car he found Tony and Sergeant Rush trying to ignore half a dozen reporters. He interrupted authoritatively.

" You all newshounds ? "

" Yes—Shale Gazette."

" West Kent Recorder."

" Evening World."

" Metropolitan News Agency."

" The one and only Rag-Bag or Garbage-Bin. How's yourself ? "

" Hullo, Dickie—didn't notice you. Well, sorry, but there's nothing much yet. The body of the Rev. Arthur Tatham, Rector of Wyre, was found dead this morning in Wyre Woods by a gamekeeper. Head bashed in. Dead some time. Scotland Yard hard on the trail owing to prompt action by local authorities and Chief Constable. Go away and write that up."

A volley of questions smote his ears.

" Clues ? "

" Motive ? "

" Time of death ? "

" Gamekeeper's name ? "

" Whereabouts in the woods ? "

" Any arrest coming off ? "

" Who d'you think did it ? "

" Weapon ? "

Beale sighed. " ' The Police are reluctant to discuss the matter at this stage ' " he said. " If you like to call at the station later—about 10.0, but not before—I might have something for you. In the meantime don't go making a blasted nuisance of yourselves. And for heaven's sake, Dickie, don't use the word ' poignant ' more than eleven times in five lines."

Dickie Donovan, young, tall, and untidy, looked offended.

" I'll see what you've got for us tonight before I promise " he declared. " It's a good word, if unpronounceable, and the public loves it. Pognant, po-ee-nant, and pyongyong are the favourites."

" God save us ! " exclaimed the Inspector. " Anyway, keep these chaps quiet till then, there's a good fellow."

" Righto ! Come on, you rabble ! "

The gentlemen of the press moved off in a body to their respective conveyances.

" And the King's Head's full up ! " shouted Beale after them.

The answer was barely audible. It appeared to refer to the Maid-in-Waiting, which Rush said was the name of a hotel in Shale. Tony suspected that it was a rude answer, but said nothing.


## CHAPTER IV

### 3.50 PM—4.25 PM

" TELL me your story in your own words " suggested Beale. He and the others were standing near the spot where the Rector's body had been found. The ground had already been thoroughly examined again, but had yielded little beyond a few dry bloodstains.

The head gamekeeper at Wyre Place cleared his throat. He was a weather-beaten man of middle age whose double-barrelled gun, tucked snugly under his arm, seemed to be part of him ; one could imagine, thought Tony, that he had been born with it there, much diminished in size, and that they had grown up together. His face was seasoned by years of outdoor life, and his voice was calmly deliberate.

" Folks sometimes come into these woods of a night-time " he said. " Courting couples, and so on ; not poachers—there aren't many of them round these parts nowadays. I have a look round pretty often in the day-time, and when I see their marks I wait about the next night or two with Rex "—he indicated the brown spaniel at his heel, " and if they come again I give them something to remember it by."

He smiled slowly.

" Ask young Dodge down at Wyre Farm " he suggested. " At all events, I was prowling about this morning when Rex spotted the Rector's body. I saw he'd found something, and went over, and there it was, lying in amongst the bracken and bushes. Time, 11.26. I didn't touch anything—I thought Sergeant Rush here would rather I didn't, so I left Rex to look after it, and went down to the police-station. I think that's all."

" Thank you " said Beale. " How long did you take fetching the sergeant ? "

" We were back by ten to twelve."

Rush corroborated this with a nod.

" And have you any reason to think that anybody disturbed the body while you were away ? "

" No sir. I should have known if they had—Rex can't keep secrets." He looked down at the dog affectionately, and rubbed his foot gently against it.

" Does your watch keep good time ? "

" It loses two minutes a week. I puts it right of a Sunday night by the wireless."

" And one more question : did you find any traces of people in the woods ? I mean, the kind you were originally looking for."

Underwood considered the matter.

" No sir, not that sort. There's little enough that I could show anyone, but I could take you the way the body was brought in, all the same. I see things in a

34

wood like this that others mightn't notice perhaps—my job."

"And mine" said Beale with a smile, "if you leave out the woods, and make it general. For instance, why do you say 'the way the body was brought in'? How do you know it was brought—or that it was a body?"

The gamekeeper regarded him almost admiringly.

"Smart" he remarked, quite disinterestedly. "Well sir, first of all, Mr. Tatham wasn't killed here. There's no blood about to speak of—not anywhere near enough. Second, he didn't come here of his own accord unless he got someone to carry him. He never went anywhere without his stick, and he didn't carry it for show, either; he walked with it—left marks all over the place. I spent a whole afternoon once, for a bet, tracking him just by following the little holes it made. He'd use it at night all right, wood and all, but there aren't any signs of it."

"Surely he might have left it behind" suggested Tony.

"He might" agreed Underwood, very doubtfully. "What do you say, Sergeant?"

"I never saw him out of doors without it."

"Well then" said Beale thoughtfully, "leaving the stick out of it altogether, it still doesn't seem to me conclusive. Suppose the tracks you saw were made by the murderer, who'd arranged to meet the Rector in the woods; and suppose the Rector came in another way?"

The keeper shook his head.

"I don't think so, sir. There's nothing near here for a meeting-place. I mean, if I wanted to meet you here I wouldn't know where to tell you to come—and I know these woods pretty well. And another thing, it couldn't be done, at night: not come straight to this place for an appointment; and the tracks I found do come straight."

"Suppose" said Beale, unwilling to give up his argument, "that you'd found here this morning, not

35

the Rector's body, but traces of a courting couple. If you'd decided to catch them tonight, how would you come yourself—which way ? "

" Ask Rex, sir. He's more than a dog : he's human, except he's the wrong shape and can't talk properly. And yet he's a dog, and knows his way better than a man. I'd make him know I wanted to come here, and he'd take me straight as an arrow."

" Really ? I might find Rex useful one day. Anyhow, I think you've proved your point."

He took the photographs from his pocket, and stared at them thoughtfully.

" Who will be a body ? " he asked. " Do you mind, keeper ? The sergeant might find it difficult "—at which Rush smiled ; he was used to covert remarks about his bulk.

" Right, sir." Underwood prepared to simulate the dead clergyman.

" I tell you what " said Beale, pointing to a spot a few feet from where Rex had made his discovery : " get down there and take up your position as nearly as you can remember. Then you rearrange him Sergeant, and I'll check by the photos."

" What's the idea ? " asked Tony. " Or mayn't one know ? "

" Just that if two different people look at the same thing, they're quite likely to see it in different ways. What strikes one as the most important aspect may not be noticed by the other at all. Ready, Underwood ? "

" Yes sir."

The gamekeeper lay down among the bushes—old dying whortleberries and brittle dead bracken—and twisted himself a little to his left side, his legs drawn up and his arms hanging loosely across his stomach. His head was almost hidden in the undergrowth.

" Now Sergeant, do your bit " said Beale, consulting the photographs. Rush gazed contemplatively at the prostrate form.

" Hands a little more this way " he decided,

36

arranging them to his satisfaction, " and the feet hidden. I think that's about it, sir."

" Almost exact, as far as I can tell " agreed the Inspector. " Are you sure about the feet? It's an important point, and they don't come out too well in the photos."

" Quite sure, sir."

" All right, Underwood, you can get up."

" Well? " enquired Tony. " Any results? "

" Yes, I think so " said Beale. " Underwood gave the impression of someone who's been chucked down, not just fallen, and the sergeant cleared up the feet part splendidly."

He turned to the gamekeeper, who was brushing himself.

" Now, if you'll take us out the way you think the Rector was brought in, I needn't bother you any longer. By the way, in view of the difficulty of going straight to a particular place in these woods at night, it's unlikely that whoever brought the body in went out the same way? "

Underwood nodded approvingly.

" He'd go very carefully " he said. " He'd have nothing to carry, and he wouldn't want to make a noise. I looked this morning, but I couldn't see anything."

When at last they stood on the road, Beale called the constable standing nearby and told him to mark the spot.

" Almost opposite the gate into Pond Meadow " he remarked, " and as near a straight line through the woods as possible. About seventy yards, I think. Well, good-bye keeper. You'll be wanted for the inquest, of course, though I don't know when it will be yet—Thursday, probably. And that reminds me, Sergeant: who's the coroner? "

" Mr. Rattan from Shale, sir—a lawyer " was the reply.

' Is he a good man? "

Sergeant Rush looked puzzled.

37

" I don't mean, does he say his prayers. I mean, if I want it, will he give me an adjournment after evidence of finding the body, and identification, or does he spread himself ? I might want it cut very short."

" Oh no, sir—most obliging. Did a fourteen-minute one once."

" Good ! That's the kind of coroner I like. I hate inquests—we'll see if we can't knock a minute off the record. Now I must get along to the Rectory. Come on, Tony."

As the car engine started up a voice hailed them from behind, and Matthews appeared.

" Found this at the side of the road " he announced, a little breathlessly, holding out a well-worn cherry-wood pipe.

" Two feet off, actually " he added.

" How far back ? "

" About a hundred yards. From where it was lying I should think it might have been dropped by someone coming out of the woods. No fingerprints worse luck."

" It may not have anything to do with the case " said Beale, " but I'll hang on to it, all the same. And there's been two men on duty since midday ! Is the sergeant still there ? Do you recognize this ? "

Sergeant Rush looked at the pipe glumly.

" Yes sir. William Bassett's, that is."

" Thanks. But don't look so downhearted—it probably doesn't mean anything, you know."

" I hope not, sir."

" Anything for me to do ? " asked Matthews.

" Yes, you can go on to Bassett's farm " said Beale. " Tell him I'll be along in about half an hour. Try to find out what he was up to last night, but be careful —I don't want him frightened."

" I'll have a go " promised Matthews. " Shall I wait for you ? "

" Yes, and keep on the right side of Mrs. Bassett."

" Talk to her about chickens " advised Rush. " She's never tired of arguing about how they ought to be fed."

" Right " said Matthews. " Thanks for the tip. And what do you feed chickens on, anyway ? "

" Bran " suggested Tony.

" Potato peel " declared Beale.

" Worms " said the sergeant.

## CHAPTER V

### 4.25 PM—5.20 PM

THEY drove next to look at the wired-up gate in the last of the daylight, and agreed that it and the neighbouring hedge were both impassable. Then they turned into the Rectory drive, short and curved, leading between well-kept lawns to the house itself, which was old-fashioned and low-built.

" I'm afraid you'll have to stop here, Tony " said Beale. " I won't be longer than I can help."

He got out, and rang the bell in the porch. A moment later a maid appeared, and he vanished into the interior of the house. Tony took out his case, lit a cigarette, and prepared to pass the time thinking about the events which had occurred so far that day, and making what he could of them. But Bobbie Seccombe had other views.

" Hullo ! " he said, standing on tiptoe to put his head in at the open window. " Is this your car ? "

" Every bit of it " agreed Tony gravely.

" Does it go fast ? Will it do more than sixty ? "

Its owner proudly asserted that it would do considerably more than that.

" Can I get in and see how it works ? "

" Yes, rather—hop round the other side." And, once Bobbie was in, the conversation became for a time strictly technical.

" Bottom—second—third—top—reverse. Pull it out in cold weather—half-charge in summer——"

Meanwhile Beale was talking to Mary Seccombe. She was an attractive woman of about thirty-one with a calm intelligent face, and dark brown hair and eyes

39

that emphasized her paleness. She assured her visitor that his apologies for intruding were unnecessary.

" Naturally my father's death—I suppose I should say murder—has come as a great shock. We seemed to be so remote from tragedy here ; it's hard to realize what has happened, or that we're not imagining it all. You seem to make it more real. I thought you'd be in uniform " she added, with a brave attempt at a smile. " Please ask any questions you want to."

" Thank you " said Beale. " First of all, what time did your father go to London yesterday, and why ? "

" He caught the 10.17, getting in at 12.05, I think. He'd just written a book about St Augustine of Hippo. The publishers made him an offer, and he went up to see them about it. I forget their name, but I can find out ; or you can. All his papers are in his desk, and I'll give you the key."

" Thank you " said Beale again. " As a matter of fact, I know about the publishers—their letter was in his pocket-book."

Mary Seccombe frowned at this information.

" Yes, I expect you're wondering why I asked you the reason for his journey if I knew already " he went on. " I really wanted to know if he intended doing anything else. I mean, he wouldn't be going to London frequently, I take it, and might have made out a list of things to do."

" He said something about going round to his tailors, and also I think he was going to buy Bobbie—my little boy—a birthday present : he's nine tomorrow. But he wouldn't tell me what. He said he wanted it to be a complete surprise, and he was afraid I might give it away." She smiled rather sadly.

" Was there anything else ? "

" Not that I can remember.

" Now, here's rather an important point. Could your father have possibly spent over fifty pounds between the time he left the publishers yesterday—I don't know yet exactly when it was, but say 2.30—and 8.55, when he caught his train home ? "

40

" Good heavens, no ! I'm sure he couldn't have done. He wasn't at all extravagant, and he ran no accounts in London."

" Could he have bought and paid for anything, and made arrangements for it to be sent ? Books ? pictures ? jewelry ? "

" I really don't think so, Inspector. I've never known him do anything like that. He spent very little money, on the whole. I don't mean he was a miser, of course—he used to give a lot away to different charities."

She saw Beale raise his eyebrows, and smiled.

" No " she said, " not that way either. He always said that the best place for what he could spare was at home."

" Did he tell you if he expected to receive a cheque from the publishers ? "

" No, but I rather think he'd take the money in cash. He didn't have much on him when he went, I know. And another thing : today he was to have presented a purse to the Matron of the Cottage Hospital at Hadington, who's retiring soon. He offered to make up whatever was collected to the next multiple of £5, and I happen to know that the amount he received from the treasurer was just over £37. 10. 0."

" So you think he intended to bring back at least £40 to use in that way ? "

" Yes. How much——? "

" Only four and twopence, I'm afraid " said Beale gently, and saw Mary Seccombe turn a little paler.

" Do you think he was murdered for it ? " she asked in a low voice. " But I don't see how anybody would know he'd be bringing it back. I'm not even absolutely sure that he was going to."

" I don't know " answered Beale. " It's possible, of course. Was he the sort of man who'd confide in strangers ? "

" No, I'm sure he wouldn't. He was rather talkative with people he knew, but not otherwise."

Before he could continue she spoke again.

" I'd be very grateful, Inspector " she said, " if
you'd not talk more about this than you can help
when Bobbie's near. He knows that something's
happened, but you can understand that I don't want
him to get hold of the details."

" Yes, quite—I'll be careful."

He was rewarded with a smile, and a request to
smoke if he wanted to. He gratefully took out his
pipe and began to fill it.

" In a way I wish now we'd stuck to the original
plan " Mary Seccombe went on, more to herself than
to him.

" What was that ? "

" Sending him to school. He was to have gone in
the spring, and then it was put off till September, and
now he's supposed to be going after the New Year.
I think I shall send him to stay with my cousin at
Canterbury."

" Yes " Beale agreed, " it might be as well. By the
way, were there any letters for your father this
morning ? "

" Oh yes—I'm sorry." She got up, and handed him
two unopened envelopes from the mantelpiece. With
a muttered apology he glanced through their contents,
and then returned them.

" I'm afraid they don't help " he said, and began to
light his pipe, while his hostess waited expectantly.

" You must understand " he went on presently
" that to get at things that may matter, one has to
ask a lot of questions that don't. Some may seem
quite beside the point—idle curiosity, or even imperti-
nence—, and of course you're not bound to answer
any you don't want to. I'd like to say, though, that
I shan't ask you anything that—to me—has no bearing
on the problem in hand. I intend to do my best to
clear up the mystery of your father's death, and I can
only ask you to be patient, and help me, if you will,
by letting me get as much information from you as I
can. It's not the most pleasant part of my job by a
long way " he finished, half apologetically.

" I'll try to make it as easy as possible " she promised, as he took out his note-book.

" Don't let this frighten you " he said. " I just jot down points here and there. It makes it simpler when I come to the hardest part of the day's work : sorting out what I've learnt, and trying to find what's got any value and what hasn't."

Then, with a change of tone :

" I say, I'm talking an awful lot—do forgive me. Here goes ; no special order—just as I think of them."

Mary Seccombe smiled. " You're human, anyway " she said.

Somewhat amplified, the Inspector's note-book read thus :

Q : Was your father well off ?

A : Yes : income of £1200 p.a., half from living, half private.

Q : He didn't return here after leaving in the morning ?

A : No (positively).

Q : Can you think of any reason for his having been murdered ?

A : None whatever.

Q : Or of anyone who may have done it ?

A : No.

Q : I take it he knew most of the people in the neighbourhood ?

A : Yes.

Q : Who were his especial friends ?

A : Dr Hatherley, and Miss Frankes to a lesser degree. Two of his most intimate friends recently dead.

Q : What about William Bassett ?

A : Does not consider disagreement serious enough for motive. B. has bad temper but is not kind of person to do murder, as far as can be judged.

Q : Have there been any strangers in the house lately ?

A : Only the new curate from Shale, who came to lunch last Saturday.

Q : How many servants have you ?
A : Two : cook and housemaid. Gardener from village twice a week—over 70.
Q : Who inherits the Rector's private income ?
A : I do.
Q : Will it make much difference to you ?
A : No. I already have £1000 a year which my husband left me.
Q : Are you contemplating marrying again ?
A : No (decisively). ?*
Q : Can you give me a summary of your father's life ?
A : Born Cambridge 1867, where father a don. Eton and King's, Cambridge (1886–89) ; rowed for college ; B.A. 1889. Took orders 1895 ; curate in Cheltenham till 1898 ; M.A. 1896. Vicar of St Mary's nr Stratford-on-Avon 1898–1915. Married 1899 ; wife died 1910. Rector of Wyre 1915–1934.
Q : Had he appeared depressed lately ?
A : Not at all ; no reason to suppose he anticipated anything happening to him.
Q : Was he insured ?
A : Only for a small sum—£500, I think.
Q : Who are his solicitors ?
A : Williamson & Borgate, Ely Place E.C. (*Williams & B* ?)
Q : Have you a car ?
A : Yes : Morris-Oxford saloon now being repainted in Shale.
Q : What puzzles you most about the case ?
A : The complete lack of motive. Not the sort of man one could hate. Revenge out of the question altogether.
Q : What are the people at Wyre Place like ?
A : *Miss Frankes* : maiden lady about 65 ; blind for several years.

* The precise meaning of this question-mark is obscure. It may perhaps best be taken as expressing Beale's sudden doubts as to the truth of his oft-repeated statement that he is not a marrying man ; but he is probably unaware of this.

44

*Janet Elder*, her companion : not been there long—2 months or so. (Mrs Seccombe's own words) : " If I may be catty, Inspector, I don't think she likes me much. It's pretty common knowledge that she has her eye on Ralph Curtis, Miss Frankes' nephew ; he got her the post. I've been fairly friendly with Ralph for some time. We often go out riding together, and so on, and I believe she thinks I'm queering her pitch—which of course is ridiculous."

*Ralph Curtis* : son of Miss Frankes' dead sister. Born and lived in U.S.A. until he was 10, when his parents died in earthquake ; then came to his aunt. Not the most satisfactory of nephews. Was going to be a surgeon ; at St Philip's for a year, but drank too much. Was in last few months of war—joined up under age. Has not settled to anything since. Plays the violin extremely well, but Miss F. will not hear of his doing it professionally.

Q : Can you tell me anything about Dr Hatherley ?

A : A great friend of father—at Cambridge together. A constant visitor here ; Bobbie's godfather ; a widower ; lives at Stoke Albury, 6 miles away. " The Doctor was father's best friend, I think. I've only known them to quarrel once—some years ago—and they soon made it up." (Cause of quarrel, in confidence) : Hatherley's only son married against his wishes, and later died at home of consumption contracted abroad. H. refused to communicate with him in any way after the marriage, and would not attend funeral. Rector went for him for being too hard. H. did not go to funeral.

Beale shut his note-book. " I think that's all, Mrs Seccombe " he said. " Thank you for being so patient ; if I think of anything else perhaps you won't mind if I come along and ask you ? "

" Of course not : I want to give you all the help I can. By the way, where are you staying ? "

" At the King's Head. I've brought a friend down —or rather, he brought me in his car. My sergeant's there too."

" I could put two of you up, if you liked."

" That's exceedingly kind, but I don't think we need bother you. Oh, may I have a recent photograph of your father ? Thank you."

Mary Seccombe went to the front door with her visitor, and they found Bobbie still deep in conversation with Tony Purdon, though it was now dark.

" Bobbie ! " exclaimed his mother. " Why didn't you ask the gentleman to come in ? "

" He did " said Tony, " but I was showing him how the car works, and we couldn't very well do that indoors."

" Won't you both stay to tea ? "

" I'm afraid we mustn't " answered Beale, before his friend could accept. " I've sent word to Bassett to expect me along for a talk with him."

Mrs Seccombe smiled.

" Talking isn't one of Bassett's star turns " she said.


## CHAPTER VI

### 5.30 PM—6.45 PM

WILLIAM BASSETT was dark and slim, and would have been handsome but for his sullen expression, and the obvious fact that he had not shaved. Before Beale had been with him five minutes he realized that what he had heard was true. It was only with the greatest difficulty that he could induce the farmer to say anything ; and what he did manage to drag out was mostly non-committal, and not worth the trouble of getting. About his relations with the dead clergyman Bassett was extremely vague.

" We weren't friends " he said with a scowl.

" Why did you wire the gate ? " demanded Beale.

" It was my path " was the surly answer. " He hadn't no right to use it."

" What time did you finish the job ? "

" About three o'clock."

He made a note of the time and then, looking the

46

farmer straight in the face, asked his most important question.

" What were you doing from ten o'clock onwards last night ? "

He watched Bassett intently as he spoke, and thought he detected a slight change of colour. As he expected, the reply was an attempt at bluster.

" That's my business. What do you want to come nosing into it for ? "

" Because it's my job " said Beale. He leant forward, and emphasized his words.

" I'm here to enquire into the movements of anyone that I think may have had anything to do with last night's murder. When I find somebody behaving suspiciously by being reluctant to answer questions or give me any kind of help, I make it my business to find out whether he's concealing anything, and if so, what it is. I advise you to tell the truth, Bassett."

The farmer stared at him in silence for a moment.

" I don't mind " he said at last. " I was at Stoke Albury."

" How did you go ? "

" Walked."

" What time did you start ? "

" Half past nine."

" And what time did you get back ? "

" Half past eleven."

" What did you do there ? "—casually.

" I saw a man about some pigs I thought of buying."

" I see. Now, Stoke Albury's about five and a half miles from here, I believe. You walked there, which would take you an hour even if you hurried. You didn't start till 9.30, so that you couldn't have got there before 10.30. To arrive back here at 11.30 you'd have had to start returning straight away—and hurried again as well : yet you managed to see a man about some pigs in no time at all. Pigs in a poke, I suspect. Listen, Bassett : you'll find it doesn't pay to be funny with me. I don't believe a word of your story ; I'd bet a fiver you were never anywhere near Stoke

Albury last night. Of course, I could ask you to give me the name of the man you saw——"

He waited expectantly, but there was no response.

"But I won't press you. Mr Nobody takes a deal of looking for, and I can't spare the time. I'm too busy looking for Mr. Somebody—a murderer, Bassett : Mr. Somebody, a murderer. Remember that."

The farmer shifted uneasily. One of his hands was playing with his collar, and he seemed to find it even more difficult than usual to break into speech. Beale assisted him.

"Anything further to say ? " he asked.

"No ! " declared Bassett vehemently, suddenly freed from his inhibition. "If you don't believe me you can find out for yourself, Mr Clever ! Because me and the Rector didn't get on overmuch isn't fit reason for behaving as if I'd killed him. I didn't."

"Don't deny what you haven't been accused of " advised the Inspector, as he rose to go. "It's always unwise."

"Where now ? " asked Tony. Beale looked at his watch.

"The pub " he decided. "It's nearly 6.0, and I don't think there's much else we can do out of doors. I suggest supper, and then a discussion."

"Don't forget the doctor may be coming " Tony reminded him.

"I haven't " he replied. "Does that suit you ? "—turning to Matthews.

"Anything'll suit me that hasn't got to do with chickens " was the answer. "God, how that woman talked ! "

"That's more than her husband did, then."

"I don't wonder, if he lives with her."

"Did she mention him at all ? "

"She said ' William simply ruins the fowls ' about ten times."

"It doesn't help. What's she like ? "

"Plain—older than he is—glassy look in her eye—

48

shouldn't like to jog her arm when she was drinking."

It was just opening time as they reached the King's Head, but no customers had come, and the spacious bar was deserted.

"I'll play you darts" volunteered Tony, but Beale refused.

"I want to get my notes in order" he said. "But I'd like a drink—don't they sell beer here?"

As he spoke the door behind the bar opened, and the landlord came in.

"Good evening, gentlemen" he greeted them. "What time would you like supper?"

"As soon as possible" Beale told him. "And three pints of bitter now—four, if you'll join us."

"Thank you sir—that's very kind of you. I'll just tell my daughter to get on with the meal."

He opened the door again, and put his head round it.

"Lucy!" he shouted. "Get the gentlemen's supper ready right away."

For a few moments, chiefly from habit, Beale studied the landlord of the King's Head unobtrusively in the intervals of sipping his beer. John Tate was about fifty, thickset, slightly above medium height, almost completely bald, and very solemn and precise in all his movements. His face did not look over-kindly in repose : the eyes were rather too close together, and the mouth showed signs of ill temper.

"Jolly lot down here!" thought the Inspector, remembering Bassett. He turned to watch Tony Purdon vainly trying to get started on a double, but a second later, rather to his surprise, Tate addressed him.

"Shocking business, about the Rector" he observed.

"Very" agreed Beale, wondering if the other could give him any information. "Did you know him?"

"Lor yes, sir—everybody knew him. It ain't a big place, I mean, Wyre isn't, and he took a bit more interest in what went on than some parsons do."

He paused to lift his tankard.

"Good health, sir" he murmured. Then, after he

had wiped his mouth on a coloured handkerchief, there came the inevitable question.

" Any idea who done it yet, sir, if I may ask ? "

Beale laughed.

" I'm not a magician, you know " he said. " I haven't been down here long enough to form any opinions, but I don't doubt we shall find the person all right."

" Well, I'm sure I hope so, sir."

" Any ideas yourself ? " Beale went on pleasantly. If the man wanted to talk, all the better : something might come out. Tate appeared a little surprised at the question.

" No, I'm afraid not " he replied, after a pause. " I can't see why anybody'd want to kill Tatham. He wasn't the sort of man who made enemies—he never did anybody a bad turn. He was just the Rector " he finished, rather weakly.

" You're probably right " agreed Beale. " But I gather that at least one person didn't always see eye to eye with him."

The landlord's face hardened.

" I don't like William Bassett, and I never have done " he declared with a finality which implied that he never expected to. " But give the man his due, I don't think he'd do murder."

" What makes you say that ? "

" Well sir, for one thing, that quarrel about Pond Meadow wasn't as important as all that. He'd got his remedy—take the matter to court; and many's the time I've heard him threaten to—in this very room, too. And for another thing, he hasn't got the guts. For all his bad temper and black looks, he's a coward. I had a few words with him myself once, and I didn't wrap 'em up much, but he never so much as took his hand out of his pocket."

At this moment a village ancient came in for a pint of cider, and was so long in finding the necessary fourpence that Beale began to despair of any further conversation before supper. His fears were soon set

50

at rest, however, though not in the way he would have chosen. The door behind the bar opened again, and a girl's face looked round. Its expression was rather scared.

"Dad!" she said, and Tate turned. "Dad, I had everything ready, and that blessed cat knocked dish and all off the table. Whatever shall I do?"

Tony Purdon, pausing in his quest for the double six, groaned.

"Catch the something brute" he said, "and cook it as a punishment. I could eat anything."

"Clumsy little idiot!" growled Tate. "No business to have the cat in the kitchen. I'll get rid of it to-morrow."

"Oh no!" cried his daughter. "You can't—it didn't mean to do it."

"Well, we'll hope not" said Beale with a laugh. "Is there any more food?"

The girl reflected.

"I could do you some bacon and eggs, sir" she suggested. "Only there's no more meat left."

"Bacon and eggs will do."

"Oh thank you sir! I'm very sorry——"

She closed the door before her father could speak again. He expressed his feelings to Beale instead.

"Always doing something or other, she is. I'd rather have a dozen boys than one dratted girl. I'm sorry you've got to wait for supper, sir. Perhaps you'll all have a drink along of me—help to make the time pass."

When at last Beale was able to resume the talk he found it impossible to return to the point where it had left off. The landlord seemed to have lost interest in William Bassett, and accordingly he started a new subject.

"How big is Wyre?" he asked.

"Well sir, that's hard to say. It's straggly-like; pretty near two miles from end to end, must be. I suppose you might say it begins just the other side of Wyre Place, really, on the Hadington road, and I don't quite know where it does stop."

51

" T'other side the big gate " said the ancient, to
no one in particular. " Just t'other side, see ? Mile
and a quarter along."

" And where does it stop ? "

" Ah, now—where does it stop, eh ? You tell me
that now, see ? "

" It's out of all proportion " Tate went on. " Take
this place, for instance : close on two hundred years
old, and big enough for a town like Shale. And then
the church : hold four or five hundred, easy, and never
gets above fifty. Proper police-station, too—more
than any of the villages round have got. Miss Frankes'
father built it—out of gratitude, they say. There was
a big burglary up at the Place years ago, and a lot of
valuables taken : paintings, and fancy china, and
such-like. The police caught the men, and got everything back, and old Sir Henry was so pleased he gave
them that. So we've got a sergeant and a constable,
not that they're both needed. Nothing ever happens
here nowadays."

" Don't you count murder as out of the ordinary,
then ? " enquired Beale, with a quiet smile.

" Oh lor yes, sir ! I was forgetting. Doesn't seem
somehow as though it could have happened, really—
not here. But it did."

By this time the bar was beginning to fill up. Tony
and Matthews, seeing several eyes turned longingly
towards the dartboard, relinquished their weapons to
those likely to make better use of them ; and almost
at once the supper was declared to be ready at last.

## CHAPTER VII

THEIR sitting-room was large and not very comfortably furnished. In front of the window was a sofa, old-fashioned and, as Tony said, probably dangerous. There were, however, three not impossible arm-chairs, and the fireplace was filled with blazing logs.

" It might be worse " decided Beale. " The pictures are quite foul, of course, but you needn't look at them."

" How about that for the weapon, sir ? " asked Matthews with a grin, pointing to a sword hanging on the wall to the left of the window. " But I'm afraid it's not going to be as easy as that. I wonder where it went to."

Just as they finished their meal Lucy Tate came in to say that the Inspector was wanted on the telephone. At a closer view she proved to be a pretty dark-haired girl inclined to plumpness. She showed him where the telephone was kept, in a little room she called the office, and when she had gone he shut the door.

" Hullo ! " said the voice the other end. " Is that you, Beale? Superintendent Vinney speaking. Plenty to tell you. Tatham went to see Tovey & Tovey all right. They offered him a cheque, but he said he'd rather have cash, so they sent some one round to the bank with him. He left there about three o'clock with £50 in fivers—numbers $^{118}_{H}$ 69735–44 inclusive—and the odd £2.10.0 in smaller stuff. Got that down ? Then where's the £50 ? "

" That's what I'd like to know, sir."

" No sign of it your end ? "

" No sir."

" What are you going to do ? "

" I'd like the numbers circulated to the press."

" Do you think that's wise ? "

" Well sir, if they've not been stolen, it doesn't do any harm. If they have, whoever took them will have got rid of them by now, unless he's an idiot, and we might get a line on him. Of course, if he's hanging on to them we can't very well warn everybody else without warning him too, but I think it's worth taking a chance."

"Very well. I'll see to this end—you cover the local rags. Anything else to report ? "

"Not at present, sir."

"Anything else we can do ? "

Beale thought for a moment.

"Will you check up on a Dr Hatherley ? " he asked. "And find out anything you can about a Ralph Curtis who was a student at St Philip's Hospital for a year, just after the war. There's Tatham's solicitors, too : Williams & Borgate, Ely Place. I think that's all, sir."

"Right you are. Well, good luck. Send me a report tomorrow night if you've got time. Good-bye."

When Beale returned to the sitting-room he found that the table had been cleared. The other two were chatting, but Tony now got up.

"Look here " he said, " you professional sleuths probably want to roll up your sleeves and get down to it. I'll go into the bar and see if I can't pick up something about darts. There's an awful lot I don't know."

Beale pulled at his coat as he went by.

"Don't go if you'd rather stay. You're not half such an ass as you look ; and even if you were, gems of wisdom come from the most unexpected sources. And anyway, it's not fair to Matthews."

"That man doesn't need practice—he's a dead shot already. He couldn't do better if he put his dart in first and threw it afterwards. But I'd like to stay—thanks. I'll try to be extremely wise."

"Good man. Well, what about some beer ? Matthews, you look thirsty——"

The detective-sergeant deftly caught the half-crown that Beale flicked at him. " Three pints ? " he asked.

" Yes."

The Inspector watched him go out, and then,

immediately the door shut, called after him in a fairly loud voice to get a packet of Gold Flake as well. There was no reply, and when Matthews returned he denied having heard the request.

" Then we ought to be all right if we don't shout " said Beale. He took a long drink, and then lit his pipe.

" Now " he observed, " we may as well start at scratch. I didn't have time to get my notes sorted out before, so I'll do it now. Turn the lamp up a bit, will you ? "

The next few minutes he devoted to his notebook. Matthews did the same, and Tony frowned over the financial page of a newspaper.

" All ready ? " asked Beale presently. " Good. Here's what I know.

" Tatham, who'd just written a book, went to London yesterday to see the publishers about it. He also intended, so he said, to get his grandson a birthday present, but we don't know what, or whether he actually bought anything. Tovey & Tovey sent a man round to the bank with him to cash the cheque for fifty guineas. He left there with £50 in £5 notes, and the rest in small stuff. He arrived at Wyre Halt— as far as we know—at about 10.40 last night, and was found dead in Wyre Woods at 11.26 this morning by the gamekeeper at Wyre Place. He'd been dead about twelve hours, and had only four and twopence in his pockets. He did not return to the Rectory after leaving in the morning—unless Mrs Seccombe is telling lies, and I'm sure she isn't. The woods are pretty dry, and there were no footprints worth having.

" Now, here's the sergeant's map. The Rector and William Bassett are known to have disagreed about this path across Pond Meadow, which leads to the Rectory and the church. While Tatham was in London yesterday Bassett wired up this gate, B, so that anybody crossing the field at night from gate A would have to turn back and go round by the road.

" Dr Hatherley says that Tatham was not killed where his body was found—not enough blood. His walking-stick, which it is said he always carried out of doors, is missing. Bassett's story is that he went to Stoke Albury last night, a five-and-a-half-mile walk each way, starting at 9.30 and getting back at 11.30. I don't believe him for a minute ; in fact, you can count on his not having done that. His pipe—or what is believed to be his pipe—was found by the side of the road not far from where we think the body was taken into the woods. It's not known how or when it got there. It is said to be unlikely that if Tatham went into Pond Meadow at all he got to the second gate, B, because the grass there is long, and would leave marks."

Here Tony interrupted.

" Apart from your English, which is appalling " he said, " you wouldn't expect him to leave tracks if he walked on the path, would you ? "

" No " returned Beale mildly ; " but then, I shouldn't expect him to walk on the path, you see. You try going across a field at night. The thing isn't a Roman road—it's only about two feet wide. And anyway, why is my English appalling ? "

" Marks might be left on grass " said Tony : " but the grass itself would leave none."

" All right, nuisance. To go on : two people got off the first evening train, which reached Wyre Halt at 9.13. One was Ralph Curtis, the nephew of Miss Frankes at Wyre Place ; the other was a stranger to the ticket-collector at Shale Junction. At least, we suppose he got off ; he certainly gave up his ticket.

" There is no motive known for killing the Rector apart from Bassett's quarrel with him."

Beale put down his note-book, got up, and walked over to a writing-desk which stood between the fire-place and the head of the sofa. Finding no paper in any of the pigeon-holes, he attempted to open the top drawer, but without success. He wrestled with it for some moments, while Tony offered suitable advice.

" Remember Bruce and the spider " he said encouragingly. Beale turned round to glare.

56

" Come and do it yourself " he suggested.

" Certainly : let me demonstrate."

He went across, seized the central handle firmly, and pulled. After a moment's resistance the handle came off, and Tony staggered back to collide heavily with the door.

" Remember Bruce and the spider, sir " murmured Matthews.

Eventually Beale solved this minor problem by opening the second drawer, which gave no trouble, and finding a writing-pad. He tore off three sheets.

" Make a list of questions that you think could bear to be answered " he said. As he began to make his own he noticed approvingly that Matthews at once consulted his note-book.

Beale's questions were :

" Who was the stranger ? Did Curtis see or recognize him ? Where was Bassett last night ? Where is the £50 ? Where is Tatham's walking-stick ? Where was Tatham killed ? Where is, and what was, the weapon ? Did Tatham buy anything for his grandson ? If so, what ? And where is it ? Who killed him ? Why ? "

When the others had finished he read his list out.

" Rotter ! " exclaimed Tony. " You've cribbed nearly all my best ones. I hoped you'd forget about Curtis recognizing the stranger."

" Well, have you got any extras ? "

" Yes "—mildly triumphant : " four. First : what fiend out of hell made that desk ? No good ? All right. Second : why did Tatham prefer cash to a cheque ? Answer—maybe : because he was going on the bust. Ergo, the money wasn't stolen. Ergo again, you won't get much help from tracing the notes."

Beale looked guilty.

" Sorry to disappoint you " he said, " but his daughter told me that he'd almost certainly be bringing back at least £40, because today he was to have presented a purse with that amount in to some hospital-matron at Hadington."

Tony objected strongly.

"How can I ask intelligent questions without knowing all the facts?" he demanded. "It's really my turn for drinks, but I think you ought to be fined another round. Don't you, Matthews?"

The detective-sergeant indicated that so long as the beer was forthcoming it made little difference to him who provided it.

"All right" agreed Beale, and duly paid up.

"Well, what's your second question?" he asked, when the drinks had been brought. Tony consulted his paper.

"Was the Rector insured?"

"Yes—£500. Is that another round?"

"No—I'm a fair-minded man."

"You mean you can't hold any more at present."

"Much you know! Anyway, the third one isn't so much a question as a suggested answer to one of yours, but I'll put it interrogatively. Is it not possible —nay, even probable—that Bassett was waiting about near the wired-up gate last night to observe effects of barricade upon the late Rev.'s face and temper? I know I should have been, in his place."

'Horsey' Matthews nodded agreement, but Beale frowned.

"Very good, Tony. That's a perfect answer, except for one thing: why doesn't Bassett admit it? Why tell me a cock-and-bull story about walking eleven miles to see a man about some pigs, all in two hours? As he admits to wiring the gate, why not say he was hanging about to see what happened? Unless, of course, he did the murder; but then, that washes out your answer."

"But it's so good, it ought to be right" Matthews broke in. "Suppose Bassett did that—waited about—, and then saw somebody else doing the killing. He gets frightened, legs it off home, and naturally says he was anywhere else in the world."

"Yes, that's reasonable; the landlord here tells me that Bassett's a coward. I wonder if that's what

58

happened. But it still doesn't explain the pipe, though that may have been dropped some time before. I must find out how many pipes like that he's got, and when he was last seen smoking one. Anyway, Tony, you've certainly given us an idea. Now Matthews, have you got any questions ? "

" Yes sir, but not as good, I'm afraid. Could Tatham have got to where he was found without passing the cross-roads ? "

Beale consulted the map, and shook his head.

" I don't think so " he said.

" Well then, sir : was anybody in the village at or near those cross-roads between, say, 10.30 and 11.30 last night, and did they see or hear anything ? "

Beale smiled. " On your own head " he declared. " That's something for you to find out tomorrow. Any more ? "

" One : did the Rector walk fast ? "

" I haven't the slightest idea, but I'll soon get a local opinion. Drink up, and I'll do that too. Come on, Tony—one and sixpence."

He was soon back.

" Tate says he didn't walk fast and he didn't walk slow ; just ordinary-like, if you get his meaning. About twenty other people agree."

Matthews looked at some figures written on his sheet of paper, and then at the map.

" He arrives at Wyre Halt at 10.41 " he said. " Give him a minute or so to get out and stretch his legs. That means he starts walking ' ordinary-like ' at about 10.44. How long to do a mile ? "

" Quarter of an hour " said Beale.

" Or a bit longer " suggested Tony. " He was an elderly man, you know.

" 'The way was dark, the night was cold ;
The Rector's feet were pretty old.
He reached the cross-roads, and was passin',
When out there leapt a bold assassin.'

59

" Anyway, it's safe enough to say he got to the cross-roads as near eleven o'clock as dammit. Sorry, Matthews—I seem to be telling your story for you."

" That's all right, sir. Say 11.0. Rush says there's no trace of a car having stopped anywhere between the Halt and the Rectory recently, so it seems to me, sir "—to Beale—" that it's all right to count on him still being alive then."

The Inspector nodded, his eyebrows raised a little.

" Well, suppose somebody, for reasons we don't know of, wants Tatham out of the way. He knows about the gate being wired up—the whole village seems to. He also knows—assuming Mr Purdon's guess is right—that Bassett's waiting near it. Suppose this Mr Somebody kindly waits for the Rector, to tell him about the gate, so that he'll go round by the road instead, Mr Somebody kindly offering to keep him company in case there's trouble with Bassett the other end. Only they never get there."

Beale looked interested.

" I see what you mean—shove it all on to Bassett. The only thing is that Mr Somebody's taking a pretty big risk that Bassett can't produce witnesses to prove he was by the gate all the time."

" Do you mean that somebody might have seen him from the Rectory ? " asked Tony.

" That wouldn't be very satisfactory evidence—too far away at night. No, I mean that, as you said just now, Matthews, the whole village knew about the gate : how can Mr Somebody be sure that Bassett will be the only person waiting about to see what happens ? We must try to find out about that, by the way ; but I don't think I'd have chanced it.

" Well Matthews, it's an interesting theory, but it's got too many snags for my liking. Anyway, who is this Mr Somebody ? He must be devilish smart, for he's got to think it all out between the wiring of the gate and the arrival of the first evening train. I suppose he might have heard beforehand about what Bassett intended to do, but he couldn't be sure of it, any more than of what time Tatham would turn up."

" What does Mr Somebody do " enquired Tony " if, while he's by the cross-roads inviting the Rector into his little trap, a second somebody barges along ? "

Beale turned to Matthews with a grin.

" He's your creation " he said : " what does he do ? "

They found the reply eminently satisfactory.

" He just says ' Thought I'd better come along and tell you, sir—save you a journey, don't you know, what ?   Oh, not at all—pleasure, I'm sure—good-night', raises his hat, and slopes off home chewing his moustache."

Beale laughed.

" At all events, we'll keep him in mind " he promised. " Now, it seems to me that there are three possibilities. (1) :  the murder was done by a local ; (2) :  by a stranger passing through the village ; (3) : by a stranger coming here deliberately—either following Tatham, or getting there first and waiting for him. (1) sounds very much like premeditation, though it mightn't be ; (2) most like murder for robbery by a tramp or someone like that ;  and (3), almost without doubt, very carefully planned.   There you are, gents—back your fancy."

" (1) for me " said Matthews unhesitatingly.

" I'll have (3) " guessed Tony. " That leaves you number (2)."

" Thanks very much, but I don't think I want it. I'm inclined to agree with Matthews."

" Why so down on the sinister stranger ? "

" Well, I'm not forgetting that there is—or is supposed to be—a stranger ;  but look at it this way. First, what a place to choose !  Think of all the better ones.   Why, he can't even be certain he'll get any chance at all : someone else might get off the same train, and walk all the way home with the old boy. Again, apart from that, he still doesn't do it in the quietest part—between the Halt and the cross-roads ; he waits until Tatham gets into the built-up area. No ;  if he'd got any sense he'd do it in the train—

always provided he was in it, of course ; open the door, push the body out, and light a cigarette.

"I wonder sometimes that there aren't more murders in trains. It's almost the ideal place—on this railway, anyhow, where only the best ones have corridors. You've got no possible witnesses, an easy way of disposing of the corpse, plenty of time to choose just where to make your get-away, and scores of other people to confuse the scent."

"The next time anyone's killed in a train" declared Tony, "I shall suspect you."

Beale laughed.

"Suppose you were the victim !" he suggested darkly. "By the way, how's the time ? After 9.0— if Hatherley's coming he ought to be along soon. Well, I don't think we can do much more at this stage. As Sherlock Holmes says, it's a capital mistake to theorize ahead of your facts. Let's borrow some cards and play cut-throat."

"What a nasty mind you must have !" said Tony sadly. "First you threaten to murder me, and now cut-throat ! "

"What about tomorrow's programme, sir ?" asked Matthews. Beale smiled at him.

"You haven't worked with me before, or you wouldn't ask. I think it out in bed when I wake up. Will one of you get the cards ? I must phone the sergeant what to say to the newshounds—they're besieging him at 10.0."

Soon afterwards a constable from Shale arrived on his bicycle.

"The Superintendent sends his compliments, sir, and says I'm to take orders from you."

"Yes. I want you to keep your eyes and ears open, and if you hear anybody in the woods, let him come up before you challenge him. I'm afraid you won't be able to have a light—can you manage ?"

"Yes sir."

"Got everything you want ? "

"Yes thank you sir."

" I know it's a rotten job, and probably nothing will happen, but we can't afford to leave the place unguarded. Well, good-night, and don't sleep well."

The doctor failed to turn up, and they went to bed just before 11.0, Tony having won two and elevenpence.

" If we play every night " he said hopefully, " I ought to be able to cover my petrol, at any rate."

" This case isn't going to last a year " countered Beale.

## CHAPTER VIII

WEDNESDAY    NOVEMBER 21ST    6.20 AM—9.0 AM

BEALE awoke at 6.20, and could not get to sleep again. He turned over this way ; changed back ; doubled his legs up ; put them out straight ; but in all these attempts he failed to find that perfect position in which his mind could slip away once more from the harsh realities of sheet and pillow, and the sound of chickens clucking outside, and the cold air blowing on to his face.

He gave up the struggle at last, got out of bed, lit the lamp—it was still dark—, and filled his pipe. Then, when it was burning evenly, he looked at his watch.

' Half past six ' he thought : ' three quarters of an hour before I need get up. I ought to be asleep instead of sitting up shivering.'

He reached for his note-book and a pencil.

" Why, how, when, and where, did Tatham get his feet wet ? " he wrote, and then sat staring at the words until they became meaningless marks on a white background.

' It was not the dew ' he told himself. ' His feet were hidden in the undergrowth, and anyway dew wouldn't reach the soles. How ? '

" He took his shoes off " he added at last. " Why ? "

Why should an elderly clergyman take his shoes off late at night, and get his feet wet ?

Presently he put down two more questions.

" When did his shoe-lace break ?

" Did he take his socks off as well ? "

Against the first he wrote " When he took his shoes off, or when he put them on again (?) " ; and against the second " Probably—the dye had run in patches only, even on the soles of his feet".

Five minutes later he propounded yet another question.

" What did T. kick, shortly before he removed his shoes and broke a lace, so that the impact left a small patch of cow dung round, but not on, the knot ? "

And that one he could not answer satisfactorily. At the end of ten minutes the only attempts he had made were " A cow "—heavily crossed out—and " Something to which cow dung was adhering."

Then another idea broke in upon his mind, and he seized the pencil again.

" Why didn't he wipe his feet before putting his socks on ? " he wrote, and quickly turned back half a dozen pages.

" Contents of deceased's pockets " he read : " 1 pigskin wallet (see below) ; 1 pigskin card-case, half full (own cards) ; 1 small calendar, current year (June 5th, July 18th, Sept. 2nd, Nov. 21st, marked with crosses)."

('Forgot to make sure from Mrs Seccombe that those *are* all birthdays, didn't you ? ' he admonished himself.)

" 1 Blackbird fountain-pen, pre-war type ; 1 silver pencil with broken lead ; 2 rubber bands ; 1 piece of good-quality string (2' 4") ; 1 steel ring holding 5 keys, various ; 1 florin, 1 shilling, 2 sixpences, 1 penny, 2 halfpennies—total 4/2 ; 1 watch, gold hunter, no. 24776, initialled A.T., and corresponding gold chain, bloodstone seal and silver sovereign-case attached."

With something akin to excitement he added, underneath his last question :

" Because, for reasons unknown, he had no handkerchief".

64

'But' he told himself 'Tatham could have got one out of a machine at Charing Cross if the shops weren't open. Therefore it seems reasonable to suppose that he didn't notice he hadn't one until after he left there. A man who's so particular about his shoe-laces as Dr Hatherley suggests isn't likely to go about voluntarily for long without a handkerchief.

'If the feet-wetting incident occurred before he left London he would surely have been able to dry his feet somehow; therefore it probably happened later. The fact that apparently he wasn't able to get a fresh shoe-lace bears that idea out. Query: can one get one's feet wet in a train? Answer: possible, but improbable, especially for a clergyman. Therefore, again, he probably arrived at Wyre Halt dry-shod, but without a handkerchief.'

Having got so far, he made one or two notes.

" Investigate Pond Meadow thoroughly, particularly pond. Handkerchief? walking-stick? cow dung?

" Make sure about marked dates.

" Have Pond Meadow closed."

At that moment there was a gentle knock on the door.

" Come in " he said, looking up, and Lucy Tate entered with a can of hot water.

" Oh! " she exclaimed. " I didn't think you'd be awake."

" I don't usually talk in my sleep " he retorted, a trifle sharply. He was displeased at having his reflections terminated.

" No sir " agreed Lucy meekly, colouring a little at his tone. She put the can on the wash-stand, covering it with a towel.

" Breakfast's at 8.0 " she informed him, and prepared to go out.

" Wait a minute " he said, looking at her with some interest. He had noticed that her eyes were red; she had obviously been crying recently.

" What's the matter? " he asked.

" Nothing " she muttered unconvincingly. " Father's been going for me."

As she said this he had the impression that she was quite willing to confide in him. But immediately he asked " Oh—what about ? ", her expression changed. She hesitated, and then replied " The cat". Beale's mind instantly registered : ' That's a lie'.

" He says he's going to do away with it " she went on hastily, opening the door.

" Perhaps he doesn't mean it " he said kindly, wondering all the time at her sudden change of manner. A moment ago, he would have sworn, she either wanted to ask him something, or tell him the real reason for her tears : and now she as plainly wanted to be gone.

" I hope not, sir " she replied, and went out.

' Did Tate go for her this morning ? ' he wondered. ' If so, why ? Not about the cat, and probably nothing to do with anything—but it was queer how she seemed to think better of telling me. Maidenly reserve ? Or did she suddenly remember that as well as being a rather grumpy middle-aged man in green pyjamas, I am also the Law ? '

He arrived downstairs just before 8.0 to find Tony talking earnestly to a strange young man with flaming red hair.

" Hullo ! " cried his friend. " Do you two know each other ? Beale, this is Mr Ambrose McFeish— the poet, you know ; Chief-Inspector Beale of New Scotland Yard."

They shook hands, and Beale prepared his ears to withstand a torrent of Scotch, if not of Gaelic itself.

" How do you do ? " enquired the red-headed one, in a voice that would have done credit to a B.B.C. announcer but for the faintest cockney twang. He stared hard at the detective for perhaps three seconds, and then turned towards Tony again, inviting him to continue. Beale began to move away, assuming that he was not wanted, but the surprising voice stopped him.

66

" Please don't go " it said.

This time it was his turn to stare, but McFeish was again intent on what Tony was saying.

". . . really neither one thing nor the other. It's not prose, and it's certainly not what I understand by poetry. Rhyme, I suppose. I believe he calls it narrative verse—a sort of mis-begotten thrice-removed epicene relation of epic, as much like the real thing as a paragraph about a jumble sale in a church magazine is like the Sermon on the Mount.

" The trouble is, of course, that he's trying to be a poetical free-lance journalist, choosing his own subjects and ' hammering out ' so many lines a day, as he puts it. You can't write poetry that way—the gods don't allow it. The man who says ' Now, what shall I make a poem about today ? ' is half damned already , and wholly unless by some almighty fluke he manages to get his heart interested as well as his head. Good verse is not to be written in cold blood.

" Poetry has been defined in a hundred different ways, and nobody's ever explained it fully. But one thing's certain : whatever else it may be, at the actual moment of putting-down it's got to be a conviction ; a passion ; the utterance of a man who's so worked up that he's literally possessed—not to say literarily as well. Most of the later Masefield, to my mind, has about as much urgency of expression as a policeman's evidence about a tramp he found in a ditch."

He broke off as the breakfast gong sounded.

" We must go now " he said. " Might see you this evening, perhaps."

In silence he and Beale departed to their sitting-room before McFeish could speak again. Once the door was shut the Inspector went across to a book-shelf in the far corner, took down a thin paper-covered volume, and presented it to his friend.

" First prize " he said " for Oratory. The candidate has passed with unexpected credit."

Tony looked at the book, and then laughed. " ' How to Talk Convincingly on Anything : A Handbook for

67

Commercial Travellers ' " he read. " I think you might
have dusted it first. I'm afraid little Lucy isn't much
cop at housework."

Beale sat down, and began helping the bacon and
sausages.

" Where did you find the late audience ? " he asked.
" And what on earth is it ? "

" It's one Ian Duncan Alistair Ambrose McFeish "
declared Tony. " It's believed to be descended from
an old Scottish family—hence the names. I fancy the
descent was somewhat steep in places. Its mother's
dead, and its father made a fortune in the war—
vacuum cleaners, or soap flakes, or aeroplane wheels,
or something. It's been disinherited for disgracing
the aforesaid family by going all arty, but its grand-
mother makes it an allowance. It has occasionally
been guilty of offensively modern ' poetry,' and on
the whole is pretty bogus. At present it's staying
here—for peace and quietness !—while it writes its
' Gospel for Psycho-Furamagists '."

Beale permitted a large portion of sausage to transfer
itself from his fork to his waistcoat. " What the hell's
a Furamagist ? " he asked. Tony drank a cup of tea.

" Now I feel better " he said, grinning broadly.
" Psycho-Furamagism is the one hope of the next
generations. Unless they embrace it they may as
well not be born. It is—as you, being a detective,
ought to have guessed—a compound of Psychology
and/or Psycho-Analysis, Futurism, and Imagism.
Dear Ian Duncan Whatnot is its arch-priest—and
also, incidentally, its inventor. Anyway, so people
say."

Beale shook his head.

" I thought creatures like that were only possible
in the imaginations of creatures like you " he murmured. " Anyway, ' furamagism ' is a rotten port-
manteau. I could give you a much more appropriate
one."

" Go on, then."

" Well : ' Ima ', from Imagist ; ' turist ', from

68

Futurist ; result, ' Immaturist '. Definition : one who isn't likely to grow up on you."

" Pretty good " agreed Tony ; " but don't go telling him."

" How did you get talking ? "

" It seems that in order to find out what his own generation thinks about everything done nowadays in what he calls ' the outworn mode ', he goes round asking it whenever he gets the chance. He picks on people who look as if they know the difference between an ode and an anode, and demands to have their opinion of Kipling, or Drinkwater, or—in my case— de la Mare and Masefield. The gong saved you just in time.

" As a matter of fact, I'd heard about him before, though I never expected to meet him here. I rather suspect his curiosity's just a cheap way of getting hold of readers. You see, he says he's going to quote from all the intelligent answers he gets, and a certain amount of people will buy the book simply to find out if they're considered intelligent. He ought to give me a share of the royalties—I was talking for a good ten minutes before you came down."

" What good is that to him ? He can't remember anything except a phrase here and there, and the general drift."

" Well, I don't know so much. As I told you, this isn't the first time I've heard of him. From all accounts he seems to be one of those blokes with a flypaper memory ; Macaulay's line, though not so pronounced. It's said that once, for a bet, he repeated the full score of a cricket match, names and everything, after it had been read to him, and made only one mistake."

" Gosh ! " exclaimed Beale. " I wish I could do that. How long has he been staying here ? "

" Couldn't say—some time, I think. He said something about going soon—I expect the murder's rather spoilt the peace-and-quietness effect."

" I wonder if he was about on Monday night."

" Useful if he was—provided he happened to be paying attention, and not composing his gospel."

" Does he really call it ' Psycho-whatever-you-said ' ? I don't believe it."

" Well, I won't swear to it. That's what a friend told me : it may or may not be true. But he really is doing something on similar lines, and he really does write poetry—so he says. I mean, he's in more than one modern anthology. Where's our horsey friend, by the way ? "

" I don't know—nosing round, probably."

" I rather like him."

" Yes, he's a decent little chap, and quite smart at times."

Matthews came in just as they were finishing.

" Good morning, sir " he said to Beale, and included Tony in his greeting. " Sorry I'm late. Lunatic outside."

His superior stared, but said nothing.

" I've been out to have a look round " he went on. " Oh, by the way, sir, there's a bit of news for you. I saw the old girl in the general shop. It's post-office as well, in case you want any stamps. Her name's Mrs Bull ; she's had her shop for forty-two years, and she's going on with it till she dies. But she admits she isn't as young as she was, and she has a young girl in to help her. Guess who."

Beale shook his head.

" Bassett's young sister, sir."

" Well, what of it ? "

Matthews smiled amiably.

" Long-winded, I know, but I get there in the end. Mrs Bull's is the only shop in the village that sells cherry-wood pipes. I found that out by buying her last one, so that Bassett shouldn't get hold of it. One and threepence, sir."

He produced it from his pocket, and they saw that it was the twin of the one already found.

" Not many of the young men round here smoke

70

pipes, apparently, and the older ones don't fancy this kind, so it's not worth her while getting a big stock. She sold the last one three months ago to Nancy Bassett, to give to her brother. He hadn't had one before, and she doesn't think anybody else in the village still uses one like it. She doesn't realise I wanted to know all that."

"Good work" said Beale, giving the detective-sergeant one and threepence, and Tony agreed. "But 'Nancy' already?" he asked. Matthews grinned even wider.

"I ain't ever set eyes on her" he said, "but from what the old lady says, she isn't quite all there."

"If she's Bassett's sister" murmured Tony, "she's also Sergeant Rush's step-niece-in-law."

"Is she the lunatic?" asked Beale.

"Lor no sir—I was forgetting him! I was a bit longer talking to Mrs Bull than I meant to be, and I was hurrying to get back here when a big red-haired chap steps right in front. 'Pardon me' he says, 'but I should be greatly obliged if you'd give me your frank opinion of the Sitwells' latest work'."

His imitation of McFeish's voice was life-like, and much appreciated.

"And what did you say?" asked Beale.

"Well sir, having no idea who the Sitwells might be, I wasn't sure what'd be best. I said I thought they'd do much better if they forgot they were the Sitwells."

Tony began to clap vigorously.

"Oh, good!" he cried—"damn good! That's the snappiest bit of criticism I've heard for years."

Matthews looked pleased, but still puzzled.

"Who is the red-headed chap, sir?" he asked. "You seem to know something about him. And who or what are the Sitwells?"

Both matters were made clear to him, and then Beale looked at his watch.

"Hullo!" he said. "It's nearly 9.0. This won't do at all. I'm going down to see Rush. You'd better come too, Matthews—you might find out who's most

71

likely to have been near the cross-roads Monday night. And some time today I want you to see to one or two other things. Find out how long McFeish has been here, whether he knew the Rector, and if he can tell you anything. Ask Mrs Seccombe at the Rectory the meaning of the dates marked in the little calendar I found in Tatham's pocket—I'll give it to you presently. I think they're birthdays. Try and discover where Bassett really was ; Mrs B. might know, if you can bear to see her again. Have a look in the woods. You might find something, especially a handkerchief. Oh yes : and tell Bassett that on no account is anyone to go inside Pond Meadow. Frighten the life out of him if necessary ; put up a blood-curdling notice ; do anything you like, but I want it shut. Do that first—it's important."

He turned to Tony.

" You coming along ? " he asked.

" Yes, rather—car ? "

" If you don't mind having to leave it standing about. It'll be very useful : I must go up to Wyre Place and see Curtis."

" Right—I'll get it out."

While he was doing this Beale glanced at the newspaper, noting with approval the prominence given to the numbers of the missing £5 notes, and the general vagueness as to his own activities ; and with great displeasure at the extremely bad photograph of himself which occupied the centre of the second page. " ' Not a bloody bit like the man ! ' " he quoted.


## CHAPTER IX

### 9.0 AM—11.15 AM

WHEN they reached the police-station Beale proceeded to give Sergeant Rush his instructions.

"See if you can find traces of anyone's having waited about within a hundred yards of the wired-up gate " he said. " Likewise make enquiries about the

72

stranger off the first train. Oh yes, and I want a complete list of everybody who was at the King's Head on Monday night ; if possible with the times they arrived and left. Don't take one person's word—check as often as you can."

At exactly ten minutes past nine the telephone bell rang. Rush went out to take the call, and returned inside a minute, his face flushed with excitement.

" Hullo ! " exclaimed Beale. " Anything up ? "

" Yes sir—I should say so ! Call from the police at Shale. The missing notes were paid in to Messrs Lomond & Travers, the brewers, at Shale yesterday morning by John Tate."

Beale leapt to his feet, and was out of the door in the same second.

" Lumme ! " said Matthews.

" Our good landlord, eh ? " murmured Tony. " I wonder what's going to happen now."

" Inspector'll be off to Shale as quick as you can drive " prophesied Matthews, " and leave me here to keep watch on the King's Head. And when he comes back I shouldn't like to be Tate for the next hour. Ah, here he is ! "

Beale entered, and immediately fulfilled the detective-sergeant's forecast. He spoke rapidly, and for a moment Tony failed to recognize the quiet humorous man of a few minutes before.

" Matthews, stay in the pub and see that Tate stays too. No funny business or I'll have you sacked.

" Rush, get Matthews to tell you what I want done, especially about closing Pond Meadow : have the constable keep watch if you can spare him.

" Tony, drive me to Shale—come on ! "

He hustled his friend out, and paused at the door.

" Don't anybody start asking Tate anything " he commanded. " I'll do that myself."

They departed in a whirl of dust, leaving Matthews and the sergeant to smile knowingly at one another.

Tony covered the six miles to Shale in something under nine minutes. A policeman on point-duty directed them to the brewers', and as they drew up outside Beale turned to his friend.

" Shorthand ? "he demanded, briefly but unhopefully.

" Yes—bit rusty, though."

" Doesn't matter—come in if you like."

He thrust a note-book into the other's hand, and they went through the glass door together.

Five minutes later they were closeted with Mr Sidney Lomond, one of the partners, and a cashier named Pell. Lomond was obviously inclined to tell his employee's story for him, but Beale intervened at once.

" I'm afraid I haven't much time to spare " he said. " I must ask you to let Mr Pell use his own words."

The Inspector said afterwards that Francis Pell was one of the most satisfactory witnesses he had ever been lucky enough to meet.

" I am the chief cashier here " he began. " I have been employed by this firm for fifteen years."

Mr Lomond, still frowning a little, corroborated this.

" We have been trying for the last two months to get John Tate, the licensee of the King's Head at Wyre, to settle his account for goods received from us. The amount was £30. 6. 0. Repeated letters secured nothing from him but promises to pay. Last Friday he was informed that unless the account was settled by midday on Tuesday of this week—yesterday—we should put the matter in the hands of our solicitors. At about 10.30 yesterday morning Tate came here in person, paid his bill with ten £5 notes, and gave instructions that the balance of the money should be used to pay for further supplies, as and when he required them, until it was exhausted. His is not a tied house, and that sum—£19. 14. 0—will cover his purchases from us for several weeks.

" I dealt with the matter myself. The numbers of the notes were $\frac{118}{H}$ 69735—69744. As is usual in this firm, I got him to sign the first and last notes, since they were in sequence. Naturally both Tate and myself handled them yesterday, but I have taken care that they have not been touched today. These are they."

He suddenly opened a small tin cash-box lying on the table, and held out a wad of bank-notes wrapped in tissue paper and kept together by a rubber band.

" I have something of a memory for figures " he went on, after Beale had examined the money, first slipping on a pair of thin rubber gloves. " At breakfast this morning I noticed in the newspaper that the police required information about these particular notes. I was almost sure they had passed through my hands yesterday, and accordingly came here rather earlier than usual to make certain. We bank on Wednesdays and Saturdays, so that I knew they would still be on the premises. Having verified my suspicions I at once telephoned to the police-station, acting on my own initiative, as Mr Lomond was not yet here. It seemed probable to me that you would like to be informed without delay."

" Most certainly " agreed Beale warmly. " You've saved me a good deal of trouble. Your firm should be proud of having such an alert member of its staff. Is there any objection to my taking these notes with me ? I'll give you an official receipt for them, of course. And I must have your fingerprints, Mr Pell. Will it be convenient for you to call round at the police-station in an hour's time ? Thank you. I'll make arrangements so that you won't be kept waiting."

Meanwhile Tony had been reading through what he had written. He looked up now.

" May I ask a question ? " he said. " Did Tate make any reference to how he got this money ? I mean, you'd been dunning him for it for some time, and he might have tried to explain how he became able to pay so suddenly."

" He offered no information on the matter " replied Pell.

75

' Now " said Beale, outside, " I'd better see the coroner while I'm here. Ask the nearest cop."

When he came out of Mr Rattan's office he found Tony gazing abstractedly at the steering-wheel.

" What's up ? " he asked. " Pain in the tummy, or the birth of an idea ? "

" Yes. I've just remembered it's that kid's birth-day—what about getting him something ? "

Beale readily agreed, and ten minutes later they were the temporary possessors of a magnificent model of Bluebird II.

" I fixed the inquest all right " said the Inspector. " Tomorrow at the police-station, as short as possible. Now I must see the people here about taking Pell's prints. We could do with another man, too."

This visit took them quarter of an hour. At the police-station they met Major Jeffson, the Chief Constable. He was a quiet scholarly-looking man who spoke in a very soft voice.

" I'm glad to see you, Inspector " he said, " and I'm sure the case will get on better in your hands than in ours."

Tony, standing by, saw the Superintendent wriggle at this.

" As a matter of fact " Jeffson went on, " I don't propose to interfere at all for a day or two. I've got a conference at Maidstone, starting tomorrow. Super-intendent Bowman here will help you all he can, I'm sure, and I'll leave a telephone number in case you want me."

He listened to the story of the bank-notes, agreed that the matter might be of the greatest importance, and promised to have the cashier's fingerprints taken immediately he arrived. He would send them to Wyre by a plain-clothes man, who would then put himself at Beale's disposal.

They drove back at a somewhat safer speed.

" What's the next move ? " asked Tony. " Half an hour with Tate ? "

Beale nodded.

" I wonder what line he'll take " he mused. " Anyway, we shan't be troubled with Bowman : he can't think of anything but smash-and-grab at the moment."

" Do you think he did it ? "

" I don't know. It looks possible at present, but I'm not at all sure. He'll have to give a pretty good account of himself, though."

" If he did, you know, he's behaved like a nit-wit ever since. Can you understand anyone who's not a lunatic getting rid of such incriminating evidence so casually ? "

" No " answered Beale ; " that's partly what's worrying me. And the other thing's this : how did Tate know for sure that the Rector would have anything like enough money on him ? It's all very well to say he'd been told about the visit to the publishers, and so on. But nobody does a murder for money unless he's reasonably certain the money's there ; and short of having seen Tatham put the notes in his pocket at the bank, and then followed him home to make sure he didn't get rid of 'em, I don't see how he could have known. The only possibility seems to be a pre-arranged meeting ; but is it likely ? What could there have been between a clergyman and a pub-keeper that couldn't be settled in daylight at one or other of their homes ? Anyway, I'll do my best to find out."

" Am I in on this ? "

" Yes, I should think so ; probably a bit irregular, but you've got the notes of what Pell said. Matthews will have to be there as well. Stop at the station first —I want to be quite sure that Pond Meadow's closed."

## CHAPTER X

### 11.15 AM—12.05 PM

Tony noticed that John Tate went suddenly pale at Beale's request to see him in private. Without speaking he invited them into the small room where the telephone was kept, and after Matthews had entered last

77

he closed the door. They sat down one by one in silence, and there was an apparent tenseness in the atmosphere. All seemed to be waiting for something to happen ; for someone to begin, and make an end of the uncomfortable hush. A moment later Beale did this bluntly enough.

" I want to ask you some questions, Mr Tate. Did you go into Shale yesterday morning ? "

" Yes, I did " answered the landlord in a quiet voice. He was plainly distressed, and as plainly striving not to show it.

" And did you visit Messrs Lomond & Travers, the brewers, in order to settle an account you owed them ? "

" Yes."

" Will you please tell me the amount of that account?"

" It was £30. 6. 0."

" In what way did you pay ? "

Tate hesitated a little.

" I mean " Beale prompted him, " by cheque or in cash ? "

" Cash."

" With what sum of money did you do this ? "

" Fifty pounds."

" Did you receive the balance of that amount from them ? "

" No—I paid for more stuff with it."

" So that you handed them a lump sum of £50 in cash, all of which they retained ? "

" Yes."

Beale leant forward.

" Am I correct " he asked " in saying that that sum was made up of ten £5 notes ? "

Again Tate hesitated.

" Yes " he admitted after a moment. " Yes, that's right."

" Did you make any record of their numbers ? "

" No."

" Did you identify yourself with those notes in any way ? "

The landlord looked puzzled.

78

" Identify myself ? " he asked. " Oh, I see what you mean. Yes, I signed two of 'em. The clerk asked me to—said it was usual."

As Beale put on his gloves again, and then took the bundle of money from his pocket, Tate for a moment stiffened a little in his chair.

" Are those the two notes in question ? "

The landlord gave them only a brief glance.

" That's my writing " he said. " They must be the ones—I never signed any money before."

" Now " continued Beale : " if you'll look again you'll see that these ten notes are in sequence. They go from 69735 to 69744 in the same series. You signed the first and the last. Have you any doubt that these are the same ten notes with which you did business yesterday morning with Lomond & Travers ? "

" No—they're them all right."

Beale nodded, and put the money carefully away. When he spoke again his voice was a shade less harsh.

" Will you please tell me how these notes came into your possession, Mr. Tate ? "

The landlord considered the question.

" Why ? " he asked at last. " What do you want to know for ? "

Beale said nothing for a moment, but began to fill his pipe. Then, without looking up, he remarked quietly but definitely :

" It'll be very much better for you to tell me yourself, instead of making me have to find out ".

When he had lit his pipe he turned to Tate again. " Well ? " he queried.

After another minute's silence, during which the landlord was plainly making up his mind about something, he began to speak, rather more quickly and far less convincingly.

" I'd owed 'em that bill for some time now—two or three months—and I didn't know how I was ever going to settle it. Business is bad here this last year, since they opened the bus service to Shale regular. Folk don't come in so much of an evening.

" I hadn't got the money, and I didn't rightly know what to do. Lomond's said they'd prosecute if I didn't pay by midday yesterday, and I was fair at my wits' end."

He paused, and everyone, especially Tony, looked expectantly at him to continue.

" Yes ? " said Beale.

" Well, I'm a funny man some ways. I forgets things at times ; I put 'em down and never think about 'em again till they turn up a week or maybe a month later.

" I tell you, I was pretty desperate, and all the while I'd got it fixed in the back o' my mind that somewhere in this house was a tidy sum of money, if only I could lay hands on it.

" Monday night I was pretty depressed—Lucy was out, over at her aunt's. I couldn't stop thinking I'd be all right if I could only find it, so I went upstairs and had another search, but I never found nothing. I'd already looked everywhere I could think of down-stairs, though it wasn't no good. Mr McFeish'll tell you I spent pretty near the whole of Sunday morning routing round your sitting-room. Well, in the middle of the night—Monday, that is—I woke up and remembered somewhere I hadn't looked.

" Six months or so back I threw out an old suit I had when I was a gamekeeper. Didn't seem much good expecting to find anything in the pockets, and I wasn't rightly sure where the suit was, but I couldn't afford to let any chance go by, so I lit a candle, and started looking.

" I found it stuffed on top of a wardrobe in one of the spare rooms—yours, sir " turning to Matthews, " and my luck had turned at last, for snug in a waist-coat pocket I come on them notes.

" Of course, the minute I sees them I remembers how they got there. Early last year I was in London for the day. I was walking along the Strand when I see a little kiddie just stepping off the pavement in front of a bus, so I moves across and pulls her back.

80

The bus cut my arm a bit, but otherwise we was both all right. I was just going to tell the kid to be a bit more careful in future—she was only a nipper, 'bout ten—when a posh-looking chap comes running up. ' God bless you sir ! ' he says, all excited. ' She'd have been dead for a cert if you hadn't done that. I don't know how to thank you—here, buy yourself a drink and a new suit.'

" Well, I was a bit shook myself, and the next thing I knows is, I'm standing there holding a great packet of bank-notes, and he's walking off jawing the little girl like hell. Sixty-four blessed pounds there was in that bundle, and by the time I'd done counting 'em I began to think maybe he'd made a mistake, so I went after him. But he must have gone into a shop or something, for I never saw him again.

" Well, that evening I bought a paper, and there I sees half a column about unknown hero saving child. Felt a bit of a fool, I did, 'cause I hadn't done nothing, really, and got paid over sixty quid for it. I could see myself the laughing-stock of the village if anybody here got to know, so I never let on.

" How I come to leave them notes in the pocket like that I don't know, but there it is, I did it right enough. Tell you, I'm funny sometimes that way."

He stopped, rather out of breath, and sat looking at Beale with as composed an expression as he could assume.

" In fact " said the Inspector, " you're asking us to believe that for over a year those notes have remained in the pocket of an old suit of yours ? "

" Yes, that's right."

Beale looked at the landlord of the King's Head very steadily.

" Would it surprise you " he asked " to learn that without any possible doubt these very notes were handed to the late Rector of this parish by one of the cashiers in a London bank on Monday afternoon of this week ? "

Tate gasped.

" Tatham ? " he cried. " Monday ? The day he was killed ? Oh my God ! "

There seemed to be genuine amazement in his voice, and he sat staring at them in bewilderment.

" Tatham ! " he repeated. " Monday ! "

" Without any doubt."

" God almighty ! "

And then, after a moment, a new idea seemed to strike him, for he leant out of his chair as if it had suddenly burnt him.

" You don't think I done it, do you ? " he asked in horror-stricken tones. " I never—I give you my oath ! "

" Sit down " said Beale calmly, " and don't get flustered. Have a cigarette, and perhaps a drink wouldn't hurt you. Can I send Mr Purdon for a bottle of whisky and some glasses ? "

Tate nodded without speaking, and passed his hand over his head dazedly.

" Now " suggested the Inspector five minutes later : " what about telling us where you really got the money from ? "

The landlord still appeared unable to grasp the whole import of what he had just been told, but he was no longer so agitated. Instead he seemed to Tony, who was watching him covertly but closely, to be in some way resigned to his position. He shook his head now stubbornly.

" I'm not saying any more but this " he declared : " I never killed Tatham, and I don't know who did. That's the truth, believe it or not."

Beale, contrary to his friend's expectation, took this statement calmly enough.

" Ah well " he said, " let the money go for a bit. You say you didn't kill Tatham. Now I've not formally charged you with having done it, mind you. I'm trying to be as considerate as possible, Mr Tate. If you can give me a satisfactory account of what you were doing between, say, half past ten and half past eleven on Monday night, it'll clear things up a lot.

82

You see, Tate, my first job is to find out who did this murder. Until that's settled, other things are only of secondary importance. I shall naturally have to keep an eye on you for a bit : but it seems to me that you'd prefer it done without all the bother of being arrested. I could do that, you know, but I'd rather hear what you've got to say—if you feel like telling me."

Tate looked as grateful as might be expected in the circumstances. " I'll tell you what I can " he offered, " but it isn't much."

" I said before that Lucy was out on Monday night. She was over to see her aunt—my sister—at Stoke Albury. I closed here half past ten, same as usual, and sat about waiting for her to come in. To tell you the truth, I don't get on too well with my sister, but I was sort of hoping that she might help.

" Well, I began to get worried when it got to 11.0 and there was no sign of her. I went to the door, and just outside to see if I could see her coming—she rides a bike, and generally gets back soon after closing-time—, but there wasn't no sign of her. Then I thought I'd phone up Stoke Albury to see what time she left. I must have done that about ten minutes or quarter past eleven. Ruth—that's my sister—said she'd left before 10.0. We talked a bit, but she said she couldn't lend me anything, and then Lucy came in just before I hung up, and said good-night to her aunt—about twenty past, I suppose.

" I tell you, I fair blinded at her—she's a bit too fond of her own way sometimes. But it seems she got a puncture, and had to walk home, and that's why she was late. That's all I know."

Beale thought for a moment or two, and then took the sergeant's map out of his pocket. " Show me which way she'd come " he said.

Tate regarded the sheet of paper.

" Ordinary, riding, she'd go along here past the Rectory, turn right, down to the cross-roads, and along here. But she didn't do that, because if you're walking

83

it's quicker to come down Rag Lane, through Bassett's yard, and on to the road here."

" Why only if you're walking ? "

" Rag Lane's no good for riding a bike down ; terrible bit of road, all narrow and rutty, and it's quicker to ride round than walk through."

" But actually, on Monday night, she wheeled the bike down it, and didn't go near the cross-roads ? "

" Yes, that's right."

" And you say she got back here about twenty past eleven ? "

" Yes."

" And she really did have a puncture ? "

" Oh yes. I went out to make sure the next morning early—I was still cross. Just before Mr Curtis was brought in, I did that."

" Why ? "

" Thought she might have been having me on— playing the fool with some fellow or other, maybe. There's tramps in Rag Lane sometimes, too."

" And one more question : where was Mr McFeish all this time ? "

" I don't know, sir. He went off Monday morning, and never turned up again till last evening about quarter past ten."

" How did he go ? "

" Motor bike."

" And how did you go into Shale yesterday morning ? "

" Push bike, sir—my own."

" What time did you leave here ? "

" Just on 10.0."

" I see. Well, naturally I'm going to check your story where I can. Mr Matthews will stay here with instructions not to interfere unless you give him cause to. I must ask you not to use the telephone, or talk to anyone in private."

" That'll be all right, sir—I won't give you no trouble. You'll be wanting my sister's address ? "

" Yes, please."

" Mrs Binner, High Street, Stoke Albury. You can't make a mistake—it's a butcher's shop in the left-hand side."

He seemed about to add something more, but Beale forestalled him.

" I won't tell her anything that isn't absolutely necessary " he promised, and Tate's drawn face contrived a smile of sorts.


## CHAPTER XI

### 12.05 PM—2.55 PM

BEFORE going to Stoke Albury Beale sent Matthews to look at Lucy Tate's bicycle, himself remaining with her father. The detective-sergeant returned from the shed at the bottom of the garden within five minutes to report that the back wheel was undoubtedly punctured.

" It looks genuine enough " he said.

" Let's hope it is " answered Beale. " This case is quite complicated enough already. Well, we'll clear off now. Keep an eye on Tate, though I don't think he'll bother you. Get the girl's story with times, too, and don't let her talk to him first. And tell somebody to have lunch ready at 1.0, and keep it hot if necessary."

They arrived back actually at ten minutes past.

" Did he do it, sir ? " asked Matthews. Beale shook his head.

" I don't see how he could possibly have got back in time " he said. " His sister agrees about the phone call, the exchange puts the time as 11.12, and the girl on duty recognized his voice."

" Is she reliable ? "

" I think so. She seems to spend her time listening in to conversations. I'll check on her accuracy when I see the nephew at Wyre Place, though. She says he rang up a friend called Ridgeway about some rabbit-shooting on Monday night at 10.28."

" Then where did he get the money from ? "

All three agreed that they had no idea.

" Could the wench have done it ? " asked Tony.

" What, Lucy ? She might be strong enough to do the killing, but she certainly couldn't have carried the body into the woods."

" What time did her aunt say she left ? " enquired Matthews.

" Just before 10.0—how does that agree ? "

" She said five to. She told her aunt why she was late, too, when she said good-night on the phone."

" Yes—it all seems all right."

" Suppose somebody else did the carrying ? " Tony continued.

" Then why does she need to be there at all ? It doesn't make much sense. A and B wait to kill C. A's just strong enough to do the murder, but can't dispose of the body, so she scuttles off home and leaves the rest to B. Why not leave it all to him ? He'd have probably made a better job of it."

" But " said Tony obstinately " suppose B didn't come on the scene until after the murder ? "

" Then in that case there was no arrangement beforehand between A and B. She wouldn't have done it without him if there had been. And that being so, it all falls very flat. She was back here in time to get in on the end of the telephone conversation, which leaves her next to no time to explain to B what's happened, and persuade him to tidy up. Where murder's concerned people don't just say ' Yes, right you are certainly—any particular place you'd like the corpse parked ? ' when you ask them to become an accessory."

" No, I suppose not. And yet the fact remains that at eleven o'clock on Monday night those notes were in Tatham's pocket, and at half past ten the next morning he's dead, and Tate's paying his bill with them. You say that neither he nor his daughter can have done it : then kindly tell me how the blazes he got hold of the money. That's all I want to know."

86

" Tatham sent them by post to Tate from London " said Matthews. The other two looked at him.

" Why not wait till the next day, and give them to him ? " demanded Beale.

" Because " Tony broke in excitedly " he doesn't want him to know where the money comes from. He's a kind-hearted old thing, he knows Tate's broke, and he prefers to do good in secret."

" Yes, that's possible. We'll see the postman. If he delivered any letters here yesterday morning, you may be right. If he didn't, you aren't."

" Unless Tate bribed him to say there weren't any " said Tony.

Beale groaned.

" But you've just said yourself that Tate wouldn't know what was in the letter " he grumbled. " Why should he ? "

" He might have bribed him afterwards " declared his friend stoutly.

" Again, why ? Much simpler to say it was a catalogue or something, and he'd destroyed it. And anyway, I don't like your theory. It doesn't explain why Tate spins that fairy-tale about his old suit, and little girls falling under buses. It'd be far less trouble to tell the truth : he received the money anonymously."

" Anyway, we'll wait and see. Are you going to ask him again where he got the money from ? "

" No. I have asked him, and you heard what he said. If I could take a red-hot poker, or a pair of thumb-screws, I might get at the truth ; but since I can't, I prefer not to waste my time until I've got a bit more to go on. After this morning I shouldn't believe him whatever he said. He might pitch me a dozen different stories in succession, and I might spend a week disproving them, and still be no nearer finding out who killed Tatham. I can't third-degree the man, so I'm going to leave the money alone for a bit.

" It's like a big jig-saw puzzle. You don't get any idea of the general design by sweating away at one corner. This particular bit will fall into place

87

presently, though at the moment I admit I don't understand it."

" All right—you probably know best. Just as a matter of interest, what are you going to do ? "

At this, Matthews sat forward to listen.

" Go up to Wyre Place, for one thing " said Beale. " I want to know what Curtis can tell me about the other man on the early train. And have a look round Pond Meadow, for another. Matthews, this afternoon you're going to do the woods. Then talk to Bassett, or better still, Mrs B."

" Yes sir " agreed the detective-sergeant despondently. " What about Tate ? "

" There's a plain-clothes man coming over from Shale—he can stay here."

" Idea ! " announced Tony a minute or two later.

" What, two in one day ? " asked Beale rudely.

" All right, I shan't tell you."

" Oh, go on—do ! "

" Well, wouldn't it be a good plan to get Sergeant Rush to find out from Mrs B. where her husband was on Monday night ? She might tell him—he's her brother. Always providing she knows, of course."

Beale considered this suggestion.

" Yes " he said, " that might work better. Get on the phone, Matthews, and ask him to come up."

' Horsey ' Matthews beamed gratefully at his saviour, and departed.

" He'll be your friend for life " remarked Beale.

When Sergeant Rush arrived the Inspector had just sent the reporters away.

" Hullo Rush—come in " he said. " I've got something I want you to do. Have a drink ? "

The sergeant looked dubiously at his armlet.

" Oh, forget it ! Pint ? "

" Yes please sir."

After listening to what was required of him, Rush agreed to ask his sister as tactfully as possible if she knew where her husband was on Monday night. He

88

stayed for a further five minutes while Matthews gave him a rapid account of all that had happened that morning. Meanwhile Beale had been called out to speak to Dr Hatherley, and Tony was enquiring the present whereabouts of Ambrose McFeish. Soon Beale came running in, almost colliding with the departing sergeant.

" Sorry ! " he grunted. " Going ? I'll drop in at the station later. Oh, by the way—what's the postman like ? "

" Well sir, all right—sort of cousin of mine."

" Good. Where's he likely to be now ? "

" At home, I should think. I could take a message——"

" Thanks. What time's the post delivered at the Rectory ? "

" About quarter to five, sir."

" Then tell him to ask for me there, and if there's a letter for me, to bring it with him. I suppose he's the only one ? "

" Yes sir—I'll tell him."

" Oh, and while you're seeing your sister you might ask her again about the times her husband went out and came in ; and find out too whether there were any lights on at the farm between, say, 10.15 and 11.15. And have a look in Rag Lane for the mark of a bicycle that's been wheeled."

" Yes sir " said Rush with a smile : " but there won't be any."

" Why not ? "

" Couple of dozen cows went right up it this morning, over the Stoke Albury road, and into Thatcher's Field. That's on the other side—Bassett bought it last month."

" Well, look—there might be something. Is the postman reliable, by the way ? "

" Oh yes sir. Not too clever, but you can trust him."

" Now " Beale went on, turning to Matthews and Tony, who had just returned with the information that McFeish was upstairs in his room writing : " the doctor's going up to Wyre Place, and I think I'll go with him.

" You two had better stick together—you'll do the woods quicker that way. Get the man there to help. And before you start ring up Mrs Seccombe and make sure it's all right for us to go along there for tea at half past four. I don't know what time I'll get away— could you come for me about quarter past three, Tony ? That's roughly an hour from now. Thanks. Now Matthews, instead of seeing Mrs B., when you've done the woods have a go at the red-haired chap. Ask him where he got to Monday and Tuesday, and especially if he knew Tatham. Then go up to the Rectory and meet us there. Ah, here's the man from Shale, I think. Tell him what to do : keep an eye on Tate and not talk to anybody—and not let Tate use the phone. He's to take all calls that come, and if they're all right the girl can answer. And make sure he gives you the cashier's fingerprints. I must dash now— Hatherley won't wait much longer—see you later."

" How're you getting on ? " asked the doctor, as they drove the mile and a half to Wyre Place in his small two-seater.

" Oh, so-so—nothing startling at present. There's one little mystery that's rather puzzling me, but I'm afraid I can't tell you about it now."

" No, quite. I wasn't trying to be nosy, but naturally I'm interested. What about the inquest, by the way ? I haven't heard from the coroner."

" Half past ten tomorrow morning at the police-station. It's going to be very short : evidence of finding the body, a short statement from you as to cause of death, approximate time, etc., and then adjournment. Oh, while I think of it, Doctor : there's a red-headed fellow staying at the pub by the name of McFeish. I believe he's a poet of sorts. Do you know him ? "

" No " said Hatherley. " Seen him about, that's all."

" Did the Rector know him ? "

" No idea—Mary could probably say."

At that moment they turned into the drive leading up to Wyre Place. The house, invisible from the road, proved to be a big ugly building, tall and square and white.

" A bit better inside " volunteered the doctor. " Too much furniture, of course, and not nearly enough windows open. Fad of mine, that—hate stuffiness. Will you want to see Miss Frankes ? "

" Not unless she wants to see me."

" She probably will. She's a decent sort—stone-blind, but quite a power in the village for all that. You don't want to be frightened of her."

Beale wondered at the need for this advice, but he began to understand five minutes later, when they were shown into Miss Frankes' drawing-room. The lady of Wyre Place seemed to him very old and very small, and, as far as he could see, dressed entirely in black, even to her woollen mittens. Dr Hatherley introduced him, and she acknowledged his presence with a stiff nod, turning her sightless eyes towards him. He was not quite sure what kind of a voice he expected her to have, but it was certainly not the one she used : when she spoke her tone was as deep and firm as a man's.

" Inspector " she said, " this is a tragic business, and it must be cleared up. Are you doing your best ? "

He assured her that he was, feeling extraordinarily like a small boy being examined by a headmistress.

" Have you formed any opinion yet as to who is responsible ? "

" No, not yet."

" No—I suppose you've hardly had time. The very idea of anybody wanting to kill Tatham is ridiculous. A more kindly creature never lived. We didn't always agree about questions of doctrine, but he was my good friend for all that, Athanasian creed or no Athanasian creed.

" I understand you wish to see my nephew. Do you expect any help from him ? "

" I'm hoping so " answered Beale. " Naturally I'm interested in the movements of any strangers in the neighbourhood on Monday night, and I understand that two people got off the 9.13 train."

" How do you know the other was a stranger ? "

" I've received information to that effect."

" I see. Yes, that appears sensible enough, though I doubt if you'll get anything out of him. But then, you haven't seen Ralph when he's been drinking. Nor, you might justly retort, have I ; but I've listened to him, and smelt him, and that's quite enough. I shall be surprised if he was in a fit state to notice anything. He got home soon after 10.0, and I could tell at once when he came to say good-night that he'd had too much. Something must be done about him, but I don't know what. That draught of yours isn't the slightest use, by the way, Doctor. I didn't close an eye that night until three o'clock, and consequently overslept till nearly 10.0. I didn't even hear the gun go off, and I sleep very lightly.

" You heard about that, Inspector ? Ralph apparently tripped over a loose stair-rod, and frightened one of the maids out of her life. Very fortunately he didn't hit her, but he smashed a vase instead. It all comes of drinking. How can anybody expect to have steady hands—or feet ? The last time he went to London, in June, he nearly got put in prison for assaulting a policeman, and I threatened to stop him going again, only he couldn't, because he was ill.

" And then poor Tatham, on top of everything."

She sighed, and Beale suspected that the Rector's murder had touched her more nearly than she cared to admit.

" However, I expect you think I'm a selfish old woman, bothering about my own troubles. You'll get like that too, when you're old, if you don't take care."

She sighed again, shook her head, and then said suddenly :

" Do you drink, Inspector ? "

Beale stared, and Dr Hatherley repressed a chuckle.

" Well, Miss Frankes, I'm not a teetotaller."

" I see. You drink in what is called moderation, I believe. Anyway, I'm sure I hope so. Would you care for a glass of ginger wine ? "

Before answering he glanced for a fraction of a second at Hatherley, who energetically nodded his head.

" Thank you—that's very kind of you."

" And of course you would, Doctor. Ring the bell, one of you."

She relapsed into silence until the maid had departed. Then she turned once more to the Inspector.

" You have a sensible voice " she said. " I wish you good luck in your task. Please let me know if I can help in any way. I have several gardeners and game-keepers who might make themselves useful for once. For instance, you might want somebody watched."

" Thank you. If necessary I shan't hesitate to borrow them."

When he had finished his wine he rose to go. Miss Frankes bowed stiffly once more, and then, as he got to the door, called him back.

" You come from New Scotland Yard, don't you ? " she asked. " I thought so. It controls a big organization, I believe ? "

" One of the biggest of its kind in the world."

" Are you an important person there ? "

" Fairly—a chief-inspector, if you know what that is."

" It sounds most imposing. But you'd have to be some good, or they'd hardly put you in charge of a murder case, would they ? Inspector, I'm going to ask you to do something for me. If you can't, or don't want to, say so, but please do if you can. Dr Hatherley, suppose you look at Ralph's ankle ? And I understand he has some sort of a chill. You'd better give him a bottle of something—non-alcoholic, if you please."

The doctor accepted his dismissal good-humouredly, and Beale was left alone with the old lady.

" I won't waste more of your time than I can help "

93

she said. " Twenty years ago I quarrelled with my brother, and I've seen nothing of him from that day to this. I'm getting old now, and I feel I don't want to die without making the quarrel up. After all, he is my brother. For the last three years I've advertised regularly once a month in all the important papers, English and colonial, but with no result. Can you use your influence at Scotland Yard to try to find his whereabouts ? Herbert Frankes, fifty-nine, blue eyes, about five feet seven inches tall, last seen twenty years ago in London, since believed to have gone to Australia. It doesn't sound much to go on, and I may be wanting the impossible, but as Janet said, it's worth asking you."

" I'll have enquiries made when I get back " Beale promised.

" Do you mean that ? Thank you. I once spoke to my solicitor about it, but he said that the police wouldn't be bothered, as it was so long ago."

Beale raised his eyebrows.

" I think he was taking rather a lot upon himself " he observed.

" Really ? I never liked the man, but he's dead now. At all events, I was advised to employ a private enquiry agent. I engaged one, who sent me endless reports which worked out at about sixpence a word, but contained nothing of the slightest importance. I shall be glad to know that somebody responsible is dealing with the matter. You're quite sure that Scotland Yard won't mind ? "

" Quite sure. If there's anything to be found out, I'll see that you're informed."

" Thank you very much indeed. Before you go, will you please fetch the brown photograph album from on top of the piano ? "

Beale got up, but could see no sign of it.

" I'm afraid it isn't there " he said.

" Not there ? But it ought to be. The new parlour-maid, I suppose. I'll get my companion to send you a photograph of Herbert, then. Now I think you'd

94

better get on. Good-bye, and I'm very grateful. Don't forget to send for my gardeners if you want them. Ring the bell as you go out, and ask the maid to show you my nephew's room. And don't bother Mary Seccombe more than you need—she's had enough to put up with these last few years. That husband of hers was most unpleasant—but he died. It's the penalty for being alive, and we all have to pay. Tut ! "

## CHAPTER XII

### 2.55 PM—3.45 PM

WHEN Beale entered the bedroom, which overlooked the drive, Ralph Curtis sat up and held out his hand.

" How d'you do ? Sit down, won't you. The doctor's just gone. He's sorry he couldn't wait for you."

His voice was thick, and he had an obvious cold.

" Oh, that's all right—I've got a friend coming for me presently. How's the ankle ? "

" Not so bad. Damn silly thing to do, what ? You here on business ? "

" Well, in a way, yes. I want to ask you one or two questions, if you don't mind."

" No, rather not—carry on."

" Can I smoke ? "

" Yes, of course. Sorry—have a cigarette ? "

" No thanks, I'll stick to a pipe."

As he filled it he took the opportunity to observe the man in bed more closely. There were unmistakable signs on his face that he drank fairly heavily and regularly, but otherwise he looked pleasant enough and bore an oddly striking resemblance to his aunt.

" You spent the day in London on Monday ? " Beale asked, a moment later.

" Yes. I went up with Tatham, as a matter of fact."

" Oh, that's interesting. Did he mention his plans ? "

" Nothing definite. He was talking a lot about St somebody or other—apparently he'd just written a book about him, and was going to see the publishers.

95

He seemed very bucked, but I'm afraid I was a bit bored, and didn't listen much."

Beale nodded philosophically. In his experience people never did listen when, afterwards, it proved at all desirable that they should have done. The world, he had long ago decided, was full of busy tongues and inattentive ears. He hesitated for a moment about putting his next question, but thought there could be no harm in it.

" Do you remember if he said anything about expecting to be paid for it ? "

" No, I don't think so—why ? "

" Oh, nothing much. He's supposed to have been, but we can't find the money."

" Probably spent it on his lunch."

" Have you got a down on publishers too ? " asked Beale, laughing.

" No, but I know one or two chappies who write, and they're always grumbling. Why, who else has ? "

" A friend of mine—the one who brought me down ; but I don't know why."

He took out his note-book, and made one or two entries.

" Did he say anything else ? " he went on presently.

" No, I don't think so. Oh, wait a bit : I'm practically certain he mentioned the British Museum, but I can't remember if he said he was going there or not."

" I see. Now, you came down from London by the 7.44 from Charing Cross, arriving at Wyre Halt at 9.13 ? "

" Yes."

" Was it on time ? "

" I don't know—yes, I think so."

" Now, what I particularly want to ask about is this.: did anyone else get out of the train ? "

" Yes, there was another chap. I banged into him, as a matter of fact. Nobody I knew."

" Can you describe him ? "

Curtis thought deeply for a moment.

" I don't remember much " he said. " I think he

96

was fairly tall—but that may have been the dark. And he had a dark coat of some kind on. I believe he wore glasses, too."

" Suit-case ? "

" I don't think so."

" Hat ? "

" Yes, I believe so. The only thing I can tell you definitely is that he didn't have a beard. I always notice—used to play beaver a lot years ago. Funny how things like that stick."

" Yes, very. Which way did he go ? "

" Ahead of me, but I don't know what happened when he got to the cross-roads. I don't think he came this way, or I'd have seen him."

" Then that means he either turned left, or went straight on."

" Yes, that's roughly about it."

" Unless, of course, he didn't mean to go any further."

Curtis looked interested.

" I don't quite see—oh, wait a bit, though. Hanging about for Tatham, you mean ? That's an idea. At least, it is to me. You probably thought of it ages ago. Do you think it was him ? "

Beale smiled.

" I can't tell—I don't know anything about him except what you've just told me, and that isn't much."

" No—I'm sorry. If I'd known I'd have had a good look."

" He didn't say anything when you banged into him ? "

" No—just grunted."

" Did he seem in a hurry ? "

" Yes, he might have been, now I come to think of it. But maybe I'm imagining that. It's so hard to be sure afterwards, when you weren't paying attention at the time."

" Yes, but think about him. Some people would say that your sub-conscious memory holds a picture of him, even though you don't remember noticing him much."

" For a policeman you seem quite up to date "
remarked Curtis with a laugh, though not offensively.
" One gets used to thinking of Scotland Yard as full
of men with big feet and square heads like bulldogs."

" There are some like that " Beale admitted, " but
not so many nowadays. Well, I think that's about all.
Oh—what time was it when you sprained your ankle ? "

" About 7.0, I should think, or just before. I left
here about quarter to—not without a little excitement."

" Yes, I heard about that."

" From my aunt ? "

" Yes."

Curtis leant forward.

" Is she cross with me ? " he asked bluntly, taking
Beale a little off his guard.

" Yes, I think she is, rather. But not so much about
the shooting."

" Not ? Then what ? "

" She seems to think you drank too much on
Monday."

" Oh but I say ! " expostulated the man in bed.
" That's a bit thick. Dammit all, I didn't come home
tight or anything. I admit I'd had something, but I
was perfectly sober. She's always rather touchy about
drink, though—nose like a hawk. But I'm sorry she
thinks that. Is my tripping up due to the same
reason ? "

" She did suggest the possibility, combined with
stair-rods—and a loaded gun, of course."

" Yes, that was careless " agreed Curtis. " Why did
you want to know what time, by the way ? "

" Oh, in case it was early enough to be any use as
a check on people's movements. You didn't notice
anything ? "

" Not a soul till Parker picked me up."

" Who's Parker ? "

Covertly Beale had consulted his watch, and since
the time was only five past three decided not to leave
for another few minutes. He could not reasonably
expect Tony to come for him before quarter past.

"He's got a small farm half a mile down towards Hadington. I was damned glad when he came along, I can tell you. My foot was hurting like blazes, and I don't remember much till I found myself lying on a couch at the pub drinking hot milk and brandy and staring at a picture of Moses."

"Had you been waiting long?"

"No—about quarter of an hour. It was twenty past seven when I got to the King's Head, so they told me."

"How did you get home eventually?"

"Tate rang up for the car."

"Why didn't Parker take you straight back?"

"Well, for one thing he and my aunt don't like each other much. One of the keepers caught him poaching about two years ago. And for another, he told Tate's girl that he'd got a load for Bassett, and daren't waste the time. I can't say I really cared what he did, and I know Bassett's got a bit of a temper—oh lord!" He broke off abruptly.

"What's up?"

"Oh, nothing—I just remembered something."

"What?"

"Well—I don't think I want to tell you."

Beale smiled.

"You needn't be afraid of swearing away Bassett's life" he said. "Everybody seems to know he's got a temper, and also that he and the Rector didn't always agree."

"Oh, then that's all right. But I don't honestly think he'd do murder, and I shouldn't like to put him in bad with you."

Beale nodded understandingly as he rose.

"It's quarter past three" he said. "I must get on."

"Is it? Then would you switch the wireless on for me? Over in that corner—the right-hand knob. There's a concert from Bournemouth practically due."

"Anything good?"

"Rather Saturday-night. All the old favourites: Finlandia, the Unfinished, Bolero. But they're doing

99

Dvorak's 'cello concerto as well. Do you know it ? "

" Only vaguely. I remember thinking it didn't come up to Elgar's. Mrs Seccombe tells me you're pretty good on the violin yourself."

" Good second-rate. I'd like to take it up seriously, but the idea isn't encouraged."

As he finished speaking the first bars of Finlandia arrested Beale's attention. He was about to pick up his hat, but instead he sat down again with a smile and a shrug. When the last note had faded he rose quickly.

" I simply must go now, before they start something else. Good-bye."

At the door he paused.

" Do you happen to know the red-haired man who's staying at the King's Head ? " he asked.

" No. He started talking to me once, but I shut him up. Poisonous-looking creature, I thought."

" And one other thing. Don't think I'm being impertinent, but did you make a phone call on Monday night after you got in ? "

" Yes, to the man I was going shooting with."

" Can you tell me the exact time ? "

" Well, not to a minute. Yes I can, though. The grandfather struck half past while I was talking."

" Splendid ! You might like to know—but for goodness' sake don't say I told you—that one of the telephone exchange girls listens in. I saw her this morning about another call I wanted to trace, and she mentioned yours. I asked you just to test her accuracy. You don't mind ? "

" Not a bit."

" Not my style at all " said Beale afterwards, describing Janet Elder.

" Mine, do you think ? " enquired Tony hopefully.

" Not unless you like them dark-haired and willowy and slightly pre-Raphaelite and extremely intense."

" Thanks—I don't think I'll bother."

He encountered her on the landing, and guessed at once who she was from her obtrusive air of gentility. " Oh, are you the Inspector ? Oh, how do you do ? I'm Janet Elder, Miss Frankes' companion. I do hope you'll be able to settle this terrible business, Inspector. The murderer must be brought to justice."

Beale shuddered slightly. There was an arty-crafty gushing insincerity in the tone of her voice which repelled him. ' If the old lady could get her sight back for just five minutes ' he thought, ' I bet you'd be out on your ear at the end of three. Horrible—purrs like a cat.'

" Poor Mrs Seccombe ! " she went on, giving him no chance to escape. " I feel so sorry for her."

" Yes, doubtless it was a great shock."

" Yes, indeed ! If my duties had permitted I should certainly have visited her to express my sympathy. Such a nice gel, Inspector ! And such a dear little boy ! "

' Hey, what's this ? ' demanded Beale of himself. ' I thought she didn't like her.'

" Yes, I met him " he said. " Seems a decent little chap."

" Yes, truly. Bobbie has been very well brought up —extremely well brought up. It must be a comfort for poor Mary to have him with her at a time like this. How is she taking it, Inspector ? "

" Very well, I thought."

" Ah yes, she would—a strong character, you know. It counts in times of crisis. Poor Mary ! And then this other misfortune at the same time, Inspector ! I mean poor Ralph. Troubles never come singly, do they ? "

Beale repressed a desire to scream : one should remain silent and abashed before those capable of equating murders and sprained ankles. He said nothing, staring fixedly at a pile of books and papers she was holding. She followed his glance, and began again.

" For Ralph " she explained. " From his room—so awkward not having a fireplace when one is in bed all day, and naturally I don't need one in my room, so we have exchanged. These are his treasures. . . ."

# CHAPTER XIII

HE got away as quickly as he could, and half way down the longish drive met Tony in the car.

"Good man—I'm glad you've come" he said. "Better go up and turn, unless you can back down a bit and do it by the garage——"

"Listen!" broke in his friend. "I've got two bits of news. With my usual acuteness I've found a most important clue. I told you I would."

"Well?"

Tony grinned.

"Don't get too hopeful" he said. "As a matter of fact, I don't think it is very important. Half way up a tree within fifty yards of where Tatham was found, only nearer the road, I saw an object lodged among the branches."

"What?"

"A football."

Beale stared at him.

"Say that again" he commanded, and the seriousness of his expression astonished his friend.

"A football—one of them round things. As far as I could tell, rather a small one—what the devil's the matter?"

Beale was suddenly possessed by a fit of laughter.

"A football!" he cried. "Of course—a football! And all I could think of was a cow. What a fool!"

"Well, I won't contradict that. If you'll get in I'll see if we can't find a nice quiet nursing-home."

Then, looking more closely, his tone changed.

"I say, Ted, is it really important?"

"It certainly is. You've kept your promise with a vengeance. Where is it?"

"We left it there. Matthews thought you'd like to see exactly where it was."

" Yes, good. What's the time ? Quarter to four. When does it get dark ? "

" Pretty soon, I'm afraid " said Tony. " Not much more decent light left."

" No, confound it ! Won't I ever get to Pond Meadow ? Oh, you said two things. What's the other ? "

" Well, it's Matthew's idea. Just as we were coming out of the woods he looked down the road and saw Bassett."

" What doing ? Not going into the field ? "

" No—posting a letter."

"Well? Lots of people post letters. It's not criminal."

" I know—I'm telling the story badly. Rush came along on his bike earlier to say that he'd seen his sister, and that Bassett was sticking to Stoke Albury. He told her that he was going to nip over there and arrange with a man to say he'd been to see him on Monday. Mrs. B. wasn't having any of that. She's a bit of a shrew, and she gave Rush to understand that she'd flatly forbidden her husband to do anything of the sort. Matthews thinks it's suspicious that Bassett's next move is to post a letter. He suggests that you get the postman to let you have a look inside the box."

" Yes, it might be advisable. Why's Mrs. B. so down on her husband ? "

" Rush says because she doesn't know where he was on Monday night. She's positive he didn't kill Tatham, but just as certain that he wasn't at Stoke Albury, and she doesn't want him to make a fool of himself pretending he was. Apparently she's been at him hammer and tongs to tell her where he did get to, but he wouldn't."

" I see. When is the post-box cleared ? "

" Half past six."

" Then there's bags of time. I shall have to leave Pond Meadow over till to-morrow. Is it all right about tea ? "

" Yes. I've got the car in the back, by the way, for the kid. Oh yes—I knew there was something else :

103

Tatham's solicitor is there, but wants to push off before 5.0, though he'll stay if you particularly want to see him."

"Oh, thanks. I don't think it's necessary—a word or two should be enough."

At the King's Head Beale found ' Horsey ' Matthews chatting to the plain-clothes man from Shale.

"Hullo!" he said. "Is this what a generous government pays you for? "

"Generous! " snorted Matthews. "I've seen McFeish, sir. He didn't know the Rector except for talking to him for five minutes once, and he didn't want to; the Church of England is the last refuge of the mentally decrepit—does that sound right?—and the emotionally unbalanced; God is a myth; the Holy Ghost, or Life-Force, abides within us all; and he spent last Monday and Tuesday in Chatham."

Beale absorbed this varied information.

"Why did he go to Chatham? " he asked.

"To visit his mother, sir."

"His mother? But he hasn't got one! "

"Well sir, that's what he told me."

At that moment Tony came into the room.

"Didn't you tell me McFeish's mother was dead? " demanded Beale accusingly.

"Yes—why? "

"Red-head tells Matthews he visited her Monday."

"Then maybe he's a spiritualist as well as a furamagist."

"Are you sure she's dead? "

"Well, I wasn't actually holding her hand when she passed over, but there's not much doubt. Pa created quite a stir by marrying his secretary two months after the funeral."

"Dear dear! Then what's little Ambrose playing at? "

"Is Tate giving any trouble? " he went on.

"No sir. He's asleep in the kitchen now. What about tonight, sir? I suppose he'll be serving in the bar, and I don't quite see how I'm to keep a check on everything he says."

" No, you can't. Just stick close. I want to get him rattled. Any phone calls ? "

" No sir."

" You can get off about 9.0—I'll take charge from then."

" Thank you sir. Will you want me tomorrow ? "

" No, I don't think so. If I do, I'll ring up in the morning."

He turned to Matthews and Tony.

" We'll go along and look at the famous clue now " he said. " There's just time before tea."

It was dusk when they stood beside the pine tree in which reposed the football. Beale released the constable on duty for a cigarette.

" Can you see it ? " asked Tony anxiously. " Up there, just above that big crooked branch. Hullo, who's this ? "

His question was speedily answered by the appearance of Rex, growling a little, followed almost immediately by Underwood.

" You're just in time to do the dirty work again " said Beale. " There's a football in this tree—could you get it for us ? Be very careful to hold it by the lace."

" A football ? Up there ? Yes sir."

He was soon back on firm ground, regarding the ball suspiciously, as if it were a bomb which might explode at any moment.

" Ah, football right enough " he said, handing it to Matthews. " Not much of a size, neither."

" No " agreed Beale. " Hardly big enough to be worth talking about, in fact."

The keeper nodded solemnly, and pocketed half a crown.

" That'll be all right, sir " he promised ; and then added reflectively : " First time I ever see a leather egg. Anything else, sir ? "

" Yes. I saw Miss Frankes this afternoon, and she gave me leave to borrow any of her outdoor staff if necessary. I've just remembered that the same constable's been in Pond Meadow for hours. Can you put a trustworthy man on guard there ? "

" Yes sir—how long for ? "

" Until 9.0 or 10.0—somebody from Shale will be over then. Can you do that ? "

" Yes sir. I'll get one now. Good-day."

" Don't forget the inquest tomorrow morning " Beale called after him : " half past ten at the station."

" What's going to happen to my clue ? " asked Tony, when they were by the car again.

" Oh, we'll have it stuffed, and present you with a silver-paper replica."

" Inscribed ' Seek and ye shall find ' " added Matthews unexpectedly. " I wonder how it got up there." He cocked his eye enquiringly at Tony, who was indignant.

" What a low suggestion ! The man's jealous."

" We'll have a look at it presently " said Beale. " Treat it carefully, and don't go rubbing any mud off. There might be fingerprints, too. And that reminds me : tonight you must have a go at those bank-notes."

They arrived at the Rectory just as Mr Henry Borgate was preparing to depart, and Beale had a short talk with him. The solicitor, young but efficient-looking, was shocked that anybody should have murdered one of his firm's clients, but had no helpful suggestions to make.

" There's nothing I can think of at all " he said. " Mr Tatham's affairs were apparently in perfect order. To be quite honest, we hadn't seen or heard from him for some years."

" When did he make his will ? "

" A considerable time ago—before I joined the firm. I have a copy of it here."

There was little of interest in its contents. The date was July 1911, and all the late Rector's property, apart from £1000 to various charities, and £500 to Dr Hatherley, was left unconditionally to his daughter, except for a request that in the event of her marrying and having children she should make ' suitable and inalienable provision for them at the first opportunity '.

" This was made shortly after the death of his wife,

106

I believe " said Mr. Borgate. " I've looked through his papers here, but there's nothing out of the ordinary. I was careful not to disturb them more than I could help."

" Thank you. Roughly speaking, what does his estate amount to ? "

" About twenty-four thousand pounds."

" And this is undoubtedly the only will in existence ? "

" There's no reason to suppose otherwise."

## CHAPTER XIV

### 4.50 PM—6.45 PM

TEA was a more cheerful meal than might have been expected. This was chiefly due to Bobbie's delight in the toy motor car, and to the fact that his presence precluded any conversation about the murder.

Beale had informed Mrs Seccombe on arrival that the postman would be wanting to see him, and just before five o'clock the maid came in to say that he was waiting outside. He turned to his hostess as he got up.

" I may be a few minutes " he said. " I hope you'll excuse me."

" Yes, of course—tell Hetty to show you into the library."

" Do you want me, sir ? " asked Matthews.

" Yes, you'd better come along."

As he had thought likely, there was a letter for him from Superintendent Vinney. After a hasty glance he handed it to Matthews.

" Nothing much there " he said. " Now " turning to the postman : " I understand you're a sort of cousin of the sergeant."

" Yes sir—he said you wanted to see me."

" I do. Can I trust you to hold your tongue ? "

" Oh yes sir ! "

" Good. Just by way of making things clear, there'll be a most almighty row if you don't."

The postman, whose eyes at the best of times were inclined to protrude, fairly goggled.

" I won't say nothing " he asserted.

" First of all, then, did you deliver any letters at the King's Head on Tuesday morning ? "

" Only one, sir—for the red-haired man that's staying there."

" What sort of letter was it ? "

" Yellow one, sir—fancy affair. Lady, I should think."

" Not registered ? "

" No sir."

" Postmark ? "

" London, sir."

" How do you know ? "

" Well sir, I always look, somehow." The postman appeared a little uncomfortable.

" And there was nothing else for anyone there ? "

" No sir."

" And you're sure it was addressed to the man with the red hair ? "

" Oh yes, sir—McFish his name is."

" Did you give it to anyone, or put it in the letter-box ? "

" I gave it to Tate, sir—he was at the door. It had a message on the back " he added, hopefully.

" What kind of message ? "

" Queer, sir, but I don't rightly remember the words. Something about bones I think it was."

" Bones ? "

" Yes sir, bones."

" And did you deliver any letters at Bassett's farm ? "

" No sir."

" Where else, then ? "

" Let me see now. There were ten all told—at least, nine and a postcard. Two for the Rector, and four to the Place—three for the old lady and a foreigner for the butler. And then there was that yellow one. That makes six—no, seven. Oh yes, and one for the ser-geant, and one for Mrs Bull. I see her open that."

" Oh—anything in it ? "

" No sir."

" What, nothing at all ? "

" Oh yes sir."

Here Matthews refrained from laughing.

" Well, which is it ? "

" There was a letter in it, sir, if you know what I mean, but nothing else, like."

" I see. Now, what I'm going to ask you to do is probably irregular, but I'll see you don't get into trouble. What time do you clear the post-box near the cross-roads ? In the afternoon, I mean."

The postman looked pained.

" Half past six, sir—same as it says."

" Well, suppose you did it at six o'clock today, instead ? Could you manage it ? Where are the keys ? "

" In my pocket, sir. You see, it's early-closing day, and Mrs Bull, she doesn't like to be upset of a Wed-nesday afternoon, so I takes the keys with me."

" That's splendid—we'll leave the good lady in peace. What happens to the letters after you've collected them ? "

" I takes them along to the office after I've done the other box up past the Place, and then after they've been stamped I takes 'em to the Halt for the 7.49 for Shale."

" Who'll do the stamping today ? "

" Mrs Bull, sir."

" Will anyone else be there ? "

" No sir—the girl's off Wednesdays."

" Better and better. Then I'd like you to collect them at 6.0, give them to me, and I'll re-post them in time for you to clear the box again in the ordinary way. Oh, just a minute——"

He got up and went over to the window, where Matthews had been beckoning frantically behind the postman's back.

" What's the matter ? " he asked in a whisper. The detective-sergeant put his mouth very close to Beale's ear.

" If Bassett's really written to anyone at Stoke Albury, and Mrs B. finds out, she might make him try to get the letter back. Then there'd be a fuss if it wasn't in the box. Wouldn't it be better if the box was cleared only once, as near the right time as possible ? Say twenty past, and then the postman can get the letters back from us at the station."

" And if Bassett's there waiting at twenty past, or stops him on his way to the station, or wants to know afterwards why the letters were collected early ? "

Matthews replied to these objections briefly.

" (1) : the postman says he can't have his letter back ; (2) : postman pelts by on his bike ; (3) : postman's very sorry, but his watch must have been fast."

" All right." Beale turned back to the man with the prominent eyes.

" Wash out that plan " he said, " and start again. You're to collect the letters at twenty past six, cycle down to the cross-roads, give them to me, clear the other box, and then come back to the police-station, where we'll return them to you. If anybody should be waiting there at twenty past, and asks for a letter back, you're very sorry, but you're not allowed to give it him. If anybody tries to stop you, ride on. And if you're asked why you were early, say your watch was wrong. Just to make sure, put it ten minutes fast now, will you ? And don't alter it again till you go to bed.

" It all sounds very exciting " he went on, as the postman produced an old-fashioned turnip watch. " I don't suppose for a minute that you'll meet anybody, but I've told you what to do just in case. Is it plain enough ? "

" Yes sir."

" Then repeat the instructions."

The postman did so to Beale's satisfaction, and departed greatly mystified and slightly richer.

" I'm sure your tea's stone-cold " said Mary Seccombe when they re-entered the drawing-room. " I'll
have some fresh made."

" No, please don't bother—there's no need " Beale
told her. He looked round the room, but saw no sign
of Bobbie.

" He's gone up to the nursery " explained his mother.
" Thank you for not saying anything while he was
here ; and especially for the present. It was extraordinarily good of you both."

" Mr Purdon's idea, I'm afraid " admitted Beale.

" Proving that kind hearts can flourish under the
most forbidding exteriors " added Tony cheerfully.
" That includes yours as well, Ted."

Matthews grinned widely, but abstained from
speech.

" Now " Beale went on : " may we look at the
study ? "

" Yes, certainly—I'll take you up." As he moved
to open the door she turned to him. " Have you found
anything out, Inspector ? " she asked.

Beale looked at her steadily.

" Several things " he said, " but not enough to know
what they mean yet. Try not to worry."

Mary Seccombe nodded her head silently, and passed
into the hall.

" The keys are on the desk " she told him, when they
had climbed the stairs. " I won't come in, if you don't
mind. Yes, the lamp is lit."

Matthews shut the door, and for a few moments all
three were very quiet. It was uncomfortable to realize
so forcibly that an event which interested them simply
because it propounded the problem of who killed a
clergyman, and why, might for another consist only of
grief at the sudden death of someone she had loved.

The room at first glance seemed to contain little but
ecclesiastical books, relieved by a few novels. It was
obviously a clergyman's study, and as obviously had
been much used. On the mantelpiece were all the little
things a man collects from year to year : a worn-out

golf ball, several score cards, an old sparking-plug, three snapshots of Bobbie, the programme for the last promenade concert that year, a wireless valve, a tin of butter-scotch, and a half-finished cardboard aeroplane.

"Get the football" said Beale at last to Matthews. "Without letting anyone see it, if possible. I'll go through this desk. Tony, have a look at the groups on the wall. Here's a recent photo of Tatham ; see if you can spot him anywhere."

"I'm afraid your letter theory's a washout" he added. "There was nothing for Tate yesterday morning."

When Matthews returned with the football he got up.

"As I thought" he said, looking at it through his magnifying-glass. "What do you make of that ? "

"Manure, sir" declared the detective-sergeant.

"Well, that's a polite way of putting it. Cow ? "

"Yes sir, I think so."

"Right. Don't disturb it on any account."

Twenty minutes later he rose from the desk.

"Tidy man" he said. "Nothing of interest. I wonder if he kept a diary. Oh, and those dates—I simply must ask about them. Well, Tony ? "

He stared hard at the face which his friend alleged to be the dead man's.

"Yes, I believe you're right—let's have it down."

On the back, to their satisfaction, was written proof.

"So he played for Cambridge in 1888 " murmured Beale. "And an old soccer Blue's always good for a kick, even in the dark."

"Eh ? "

"Nothing—show you later."

"No prints of any kind, sir " said Matthews.

"Positive ? "

"Yes sir. Picked up by the lace, I guess. If you really want this manure you'd better let me take it, sir. Otherwise it'll drop off."

"All right—get an envelope out of the desk."

Matthews did so, labelled it, signed his name, put the date, gave it to Beale to initial, and then filled it.

By now it was five minutes to six, and as there seemed nothing else to do in the study they went downstairs. A few minutes' conversation with Mary Seccombe confirmed the Inspector's suspicion that the marked dates were merely birthdays, and drew from her the information that her father had not kept a diary, but had most certainly possessed a handkerchief when he set out for London. As far as she knew, he had had nothing to do with McFeish.

They drove to the King's Head, where they left Matthews.

" Take Tate's fingerprints first " Beale told him, " and get things ready for the bank-notes. You might order supper for 7.0 sharp as well ; there's a lot to do this evening. And don't drink too much beer."

From there Tony drove to the police-station. Sergeant Rush, when questioned, said that he would be able to recognize Bassett's handwriting. He had comparatively little to report. There were no bicycle marks in Rag Lane ; the cows had churned up the ground too thoroughly. There had been a light on downstairs at Bassett's farm continuously from five o'clock until midnight, and Mrs. Bassett verified the times of her husband's departure and return again as 9.30 and 11.30. No one had been able to give any information about the stranger ; and no other residents in the district admitted to having travelled by that train.

" And the people at the pub ? "

" Here, sir "—taking out his note-book.

" Just tell me if any of them would be going home past the cross-roads towards Wyre Place."

" Not one, sir " said Sergeant Rush, studying the list. " There's only Parker, and the butler and footman and chauffeur up at the Place, as use it all from that side, and none of 'em was there that night."

" I see—thanks for finding out."

Beale spent the next few minutes in removing a little of the manure from the dead man's shoe. This he placed in another envelope, duly labelled. He also telephoned to Shale to make arrangements for that night's watch in Pond Meadow and the woods.

The contents of the post-box disappointed Tony exceedingly. There were only seven letters.

" Well, what did you expect ? " asked Beale. " This isn't London. I'm rather surprised there's so many."

The postman informed them that no one had been waiting near the box, and they arranged to meet him at the station at quarter to seven. When they arrived there Beale was told that Dr Hatherley had just come, and was down in the mortuary making a final examination of the body.

" I'll have a word with him " he said. " Here, Sergeant, look through these letters."

Not long afterwards he came upstairs smiling broadly.

" Matthews is going to stand me the biggest pint of beer anybody ever saw " he told Tony.

" Why ? "

" Because you've found nothing — have you, Sergeant ? "

" No sir. Nothing here in Bassett's writing."

" Of course not ; and do you know why ? "

" No " said Tony.

" Because he didn't write a letter."

" But dammit, I saw him post it."

" Seeing's believing " agreed Beale, with a grin.

" What on earth are you talking about ? "

" Today's simple story : once there was a clerk who was sent to post seventy-nine letters. A large ugly man in a soup-coloured suit jumped straight to the conclusion that the only person who could possibly have written those letters was the clerk himself. Amen."

Tony stared, and then laughed.

" You mean somebody gave it to him to post ? "

" Brilliant ! "

" Who ? The doctor ? "

" Yes—you're positively scintillating."

" How did you find out ? "

" He happened to mention that Bassett isn't liking
me much because I shut up Pond Meadow without
asking permission. I asked him how he knew, and he
said that on his way to visit a patient he remembered
he had a letter to post, and then saw Bassett, and gave
it to him."

" Well, it was worth taking a chance, anyway."

" Oh yes, I don't say it wasn't—but Matthews shall
still stand me that pint."

" And my suit is not soup-coloured."

" There are soups and soups, you know. How about
a mixture of oxtail and tomato ? "

" What's cheered you up so suddenly ? " asked
Tony, looking at him keenly. Beale shrugged his
shoulders.

" Don't know : violent wave of optimism, or something."

He took the letters which Sergeant Rush was
holding out, and with barely a glance stuffed them into
his pocket.

" Well, good-night Sergeant " he said. " I think
we'll be getting on now."

" Good-night, sir—good-night."

Outside they encountered the postman again,
learnt that nobody had tried to stop him, returned
the letters, and set off for the King's Head and supper.


## CHAPTER XV

### 7.30 PM—9.0 PM

AFTER the meal was finished Beale wrote his report,
while Tony watched Matthews examining the bank-
notes. Half an hour passed mostly in silence, broken
only by the scratching of a pen and an occasional
grunt from the detective-sergeant, doing the job he
liked best, utterly oblivious of Tony's presence.

" Five fairly decent ones " he said at last, " and

several smudges." Then, rather shyly : " Thanks for not talking, Mr Purdon ".

Beale, just signing his name, looked up.

" That, Tony, is a genuine compliment : and quite deserved, too—which is another ! "

Meanwhile Matthews had taken out a small leather case, from which he produced two magnifying-glasses carefully wrapped up ; each was mounted in a frame with adjustable feet worked by a screw.

" They look neat " said Beale admiringly, walking over. " Not part of the official outfit, I know."

" No sir—I had 'em made."

After comparing each print in turn with Pell's, Tate's, and the dead man's, the expert sat back.

" Only five are clear enough to be any use " he said. " One of them is Pell's, three Tate's, and one I can't place."

" Quite sure it doesn't belong to any of them ? "

" Quite sure, sir."

" And there aren't any of Tatham's ? "

" Not unless he made some of the smudges. He probably wore gloves at the bank."

" Or else the money was given to him in an envelope. I wonder who the other man is."

" One Murderer by name " suggested Tony.

" Possibly—or one of the bank people. Good print ? "

" Fairly good, what there is of it " replied Matthews. " Looks like the tip of his finger. This is the one."

He indicated the smallest impression of all, on the back of the last note.

" I see. Well, that's done, and it's quarter past eight. Put your toys away, and then we'll work out the evening's programme."

He described his visit to Wyre Place briefly, emphasizing his dislike of Janet Elder. Then Tony suddenly produced a piece of paper from his inside pocket.

" Do you know what I think ? " he asked.

" No—how should I ? Do you ? "

" Yes, I do—lots. I think, Mr Blooming Inspector,

116

that you aren't paying nearly enough attention to John Tate.

"Wait a bit "—as Beale was about to interrupt. " I know you're going to say he didn't have time. Well, don't ; let me show you instead that he did.

" The train arrives at 10.41. Tatham gets out and finds it's beastly nippy, and accordingly he doesn't walk ' ordinary like', but gets a move on. While you two were out with the postman I asked Mrs Seccombe when her father usually got in. She said that if the weather was cold—which it was—she wouldn't expect him to take more than twenty minutes from the Halt."

By now the other two were intent on what he was saying.

" That puts his time at the cross-roads as about five to eleven, and he'd reach the gate a minute later. Tate could have killed him in a couple more, and got hold of the money in another couple, which makes it the hour. It wouldn't take him more than six minutes to carry the body into the woods and creep out again quietly ; I know that, because Matthews and I tried it this afternoon. I took five, and I've stuck one on because he'd have to do it in the dark. He could then get back here in another five minutes, hurrying, which makes it eleven minutes past eleven. He goes straight to the telephone, and there you are."

Beale's face was serious now.

" In that case " he said, " Lucy's in on it too."

" I don't see why, quite."

" Because he's got to have a reason for phoning."

" Oh yes, of course. She might even have been keeping watch for him."

" You haven't left much time to get rid of the hat and stick " objected Matthews. " And the football " he added.

" They've not been really searched for, you know " rejoined Tony. " He could have brought them back here, if it comes to that. Sticks burn, and so will hats."

" But why bring them back ? " asked Beale. The theorist considered for a moment.

117

" The hat fell off just as he was starting to carry the body into the woods " he began.

" Pardon me : the hat was off before he was killed. If you'd seen the state of his head you wouldn't doubt that."

" Well then, it fell off before. Tate leaves it, together with the stick—I defy anybody to carry a body in one hand and a walking-stick in the other. When he comes out of the woods he realizes that the sooner he's home making an alibi the better, so he just grabs them, takes a flying kick at the ball, and trundles off."

Beale got up, went out, and returned shortly with three pints of beer. " I've told the plain-clothes man to hang on for a bit " he said. " Here's to you, Tony ! But the trouble is—from my point of view, anyway— that I'm sure you're wrong."

He smiled as his friend's face fell.

" Your theory appeals to my mind, but my instinct's all against it. You see, I think I know where the hat and stick are ; and for them to be there adds at least five minutes, which your story won't stand. You've stretched the time to the absolute limit, and it just can't be stretched any farther."

" Where are they, then ? "

" In the pond in Pond Meadow.—Do you remember I suddenly went all cheerful at the police-station ? "

" Yes—was that why ? " Beale nodded.

" I'd fitted everything together : birthday present ; manure, as Matthews calls it, on both ball and shoe, but only round the knot ; black socks ; dye on feet ; old Soccer Blue ; broken shoe-lace ; no handkerchief ; well, everything."

" You'll be finding yourself paying for a couple of barrels in a minute " said Tony severely. " What's all this about dye, and socks, and knots ? "

Beale explained.

" Now here's my reading. Perhaps it's foolish to tell you before I've looked in the pond, but I'll take the risk.

" Tatham goes to London with the intention of

118

buying a birthday present for Bobbie. Next term he was to have gone away to school; so what more natural than that his uncle, an old Blue, should buy him a football? The kid's got to learn the game some time.

"He gets to the gate leading into Pond Meadow about eleven o'clock; as far as my story's concerned the exact time doesn't matter much. It's a starry night, but there's no moon. As he goes across the field he drops the ball, which bounces in a patch of manure. On the spur of the moment he does what I'd probably have done myself, without nearly so good a reason, because I never played the game seriously: namely, he takes a good hefty kick at it."

"An extremely hefty kick!" Tony broke in. "Sending it, in fact, some hundreds of yards to rest peacefully in a fir tree. I rather doubt if a football bought by anyone but a man of God would possess such resilience."

Beale glared at him. "'Who is this that darkeneth counsel by words without knowledge?'" he demanded. "Kindly wait till you've heard the whole story. The ball didn't behave like a minor miracle; it merely disappeared from the Rector's immediate view. Upon looking for it he finds it floating in the pond.

"Tatham is determined not to leave the ball there. For one thing, if Bassett finds it he'll collar it for certain; and for another, he probably wants to sneak into the kid's room and hang it on the bed. It doesn't take him long to decide that he'll have to wade in after it. He removes his shoes and socks, rolls up his trousers, takes off his hat in case it should fall into the water, and then proceeds to fetch the ball with the help of his walking-stick.

"Back on dry land he puts it down and starts looking for his handkerchief to wipe his feet with. He then discovers that he's lost it, and therefore has to put his socks on while he's still wet: hence the stains. While he's doing up the shoe with which he kicked the ball—the left one, and according to that photo he used to play outside-left—the lace breaks. That's why the manure was round the knot, but not actually on it.

" Now comes a gap. We leave him standing by the pond with shoes and socks on again, but feet still wet ; ball, stick and hat are on the ground nearby. We next find him dead in Wyre Woods, with every indication of having been brutally murdered in some other place. What happened ?

" The nearest I can get at present is this. As he was standing there something aroused his attention. I can't tell you what ; if I could I'd be a sight nearer knowing who killed him. It must have been something pretty startling, though, or at any rate unexpected, or he wouldn't have gone straight off, leaving the things by the pond. But that's what I'm convinced he did ; and got murdered for his trouble. X, the murderer, having disposed of the body, then looks round for the hat, and finds it with the stick and the football. He probably wraps it—the hat—round a stone, and chucks it into the water ; and the stick too, which was heavy, and wouldn't float. But he can't get rid of the ball that way, so he boots it into the woods as he leaves the field."

Beale stopped abruptly, and the other two relaxed their attention.

" I like it " said Matthews at last, as though he were praising a work of art.

" So do I " agreed Tony. " Of course, it washes my theory out completely, but that can't be helped. There doesn't seem to be any way of combining them. If you're right, then Tate's out. The problem is : what made Tatham leave the pond ? And who did he meet on the way that upped and killed him ? "

They discussed the matter for some minutes, but decided that they could do nothing until the next day, when a search of the pond would reveal whether Beale's theory must be treated seriously or not.

" Meanwhile " said its author " we mustn't forget yours, Tony. If I'm wrong, then it's possible that you're right. I think the first person we ought to see is Lucy. By the way, Matthews, did she know where the money was supposed to have come from ? "

" Yes sir—the old suit. You'd better read my notes." Just as Beale had finished there was a knock at the door, and Lucy herself came in.

" Please sir, the butler from the Place wants to see you " she informed him.

" Oh, thanks—ask him to come in, will you ? "

The butler, a stout elderly man with a twinkle in his eye, accepted a chair and a whisky and soda, and handed Beale an envelope.

" Miss Frankes sent me along with this, sir " he explained. It contained two photographs and a single sheet of note-paper. Except that the writing on this last was widely spaced between the lines, and not always straight, there was no indication that it had been done by someone who was blind. The words themselves were clear and firm.

" Wyre Place,<br>
Wyre,<br>
Kent.

Wednesday November 21st

Dear Chief-Inspector,

I am sending the butler down with two photographs of my brother. Doubtless he has changed considerably in twenty years, but they may give you something to go on. He probably went abroad, to Australia or South Africa, or possibly Canada, and may have taken up mining or sheep farming ; in fact, any outdoor work. My solicitors are Messrs Grayson, Dean, & Grayson, of Temple Chambers, E.C., in case you may need to communicate with them.

I sincerely trust you are making progress with your present investigation.

Yours gratefully,<br>
Edith Frankes."

" That's what I call courage " said Beale, as he finished reading.

" Yes sir " agreed the butler. " She's a wonderful old lady."

" By the way, can you tell me—in confidence, of course—how many letters were delivered at Wyre Place on Tuesday morning ? "

" Four, sir—three for Miss Frankes and one for me from my son in Ireland."

" I see—thanks very much. What time does the postman get to you ? "

" About 8.30."

The butler departed soon afterwards, and when they had looked at the photographs—one three-quarter face, and one full-length standing between Miss Frankes and an unknown woman—Beale sent Matthews to summon Lucy Tate.


## CHAPTER XVI

### 9.0 PM—9.45 PM

THE girl was obviously nervous, and hesitated a moment before complying with Beale's invitation to sit down.

" There's no need to be frightened " he told her. " I just want to ask you a few questions."

She shifted uncomfortably in her chair, but said nothing, continuing to look expectantly at him, while Matthews sucked his pencil.

" First of all, what time did you leave your aunt on Monday night ? "

" Five minutes to ten, sir."

" And how far had you gone when you got the puncture ? "

" I don't know exactly—not very far. About half a mile, I should think."

" I see. Then what did you do ? "

" Well sir, I got off and walked."

Tony grinned to himself at the unhelpfulness of the answer, and then frowned. Was the girl deliberately trying to say as little as possible ?

" Yes, quite " agreed Beale. " I mean, didn't you

think of going back and perhaps borrowing another bicycle ? It would have been much quicker, and saved you a long walk."

" No sir—I never thought of it."

" Would you have done that if you had thought ? "

" Yes sir, I expect so."

Her questioner sighed, and drank half of his pint.

" Did you meet anybody you knew on the way home ? " he asked.

" No sir."

" You came down Rag Lane ? "

" Yes sir."

" And you saw no one ? "

" No sir—that is, nobody I knew. Before I got to the lane I met a tramp."

" Did he speak to you ? "

" Yes sir, but I couldn't hear what he said. I don't think it was very nice."

" You didn't stop ? "

" Oh no, sir."

" Which way was he going ? "

" Towards Stoke Albury."

" What time would that be ? "

" Between half past ten and eleven "—after thinking for a minute. " About quarter to."

" Did he follow you ? "

" No sir—at least, I didn't see him again."

" I suppose you hurried a bit ? "

" Yes sir."

" Do you think you'd recognize him again ? "

" I don't know—I don't think so."

Beale nodded, and leant forward.

" Now answer this carefully " he said : " did you notice anybody waiting about when you passed the Rectory ? "

Although he was paying particular attention he could not make up his mind if the girl hesitated before replying.

" I didn't go that way "·she reminded him. " I told you, I went down Rag Lane."

" Oh yes, of course—sorry. Was there any sign of life at Bassett's farm ? "

" There was a light on, but I didn't see anyone."

" Upstairs or downstairs ? "

" Downstairs, sir."

" And you got back here—when ? "

" About twenty past eleven. Dad was just finishing phoning, and I told auntie why I was late."

Beale thought for a moment before putting his next question. Then he asked it sharply.

" Can you tell me where your father really got that money from ? "

Lucy immediately looked frightened.

" No sir—I don't know at all."

" But he told you he found it in an old suit."

" Yes sir."

" Well, don't you believe him ? "

She moved abruptly, crossing her legs.

" I don't know, sir " she said at last. " It doesn't seem likely."

" But you told Sergeant Matthews this morning that if he said he found it there, then he must have done."

" Well sir, I didn't know——"

" Didn't know what ? "

She began to cry a little.

" You're all saying he's stolen it " she muttered. " And it's funny where it could have come from so suddenly."

" How do you know we're saying that ? "

" Well, you must be—look at the way he's being watched. And I asked him what was the matter, and he said money."

" And you don't know where it really came from ? "

" No sir."

" Did you actually see it on Tuesday morning before he went into Shale ? "

" No sir."

" What time did he start ? "

" Just about 10.0."

124

" Do you know how much he ' found ' ? "

" He said £50."

" When did he say that ? "

" Yesterday morning after breakfast. He said :
' It's all right—I've found £50 in that old green suit '."

" Did you know the suit he meant ? "

" Yes sir—it's one he threw out some time ago."

" How long ago ? "

" Oh, about the end of last winter."

" And did you believe him ? "

" Yes sir—then."

" And you're not sure now ? "

" No sir."

" Would he really leave a lot of money in a pocket,
and forget about it for a year ? "

" Well, he's very forgetful sometimes.—Do you
think he stole it, sir ? "

Beale looked at her for a moment.

" Had he ever told you how it got into the green
suit in the first place ? " he asked.

" No sir."

" Well, I know for certain that the actual money
with which he paid the brewers' bill wasn't in this
part of the country a week ago " he told her. " It
was in bank-notes, you see, and they've been traced."

She received this information with a little cry.

" Oh dear—then he'll go to prison this time ! "

" Possibly. What do you mean by ' this time ' ? "

Lucy suddenly flushed.

" Much better tell me."

" He kept a watch he found a long time ago when I
was a little girl " she answered reluctantly, " but they
found out, and the man said he'd let him off, but if
he was caught again he'd have to go to prison."

" You mean he was bound over ? "

" Yes, I think that was it."

" And you truthfully don't know where your father
got this money ? "

" No sir, truthfully."

" Well, I hope you don't ; because if you do, you

125

may be getting him into a lot of trouble by not telling me—very serious trouble, Lucy."

He was just about to give her some indication of how serious when Tony interrupted.

" You know " he said quietly, " I'm pretty certain you've got an idea about it, haven't you ? "

She turned to look at him, and then nodded before bursting into tears.

After a minute or two she recovered somewhat, and her first act, to their secret amusement, was to pull up her skirt and extract her handkerchief from the elastic knee-band of her knickers.

" Don't bother to put it back " advised Beale with a smile. " You'll completely demoralize Mr Purdon."

She stared at him in surprise for a moment, and then blushed deeply.

" Now, suppose you give us your idea."

Once she got started the words came easily enough.

" I think he stole it from Mr McFeish, sir " she said, leaning forward and almost whispering. " You know this morning "—to Beale—" you asked me why I'd been crying, and I told you because dad said he was going to get rid of the cat ? "

" Yes—but I didn't believe you."

" Well, it wasn't the truth anyway. You see, Mr McFeish likes to be woken early—quarter to seven. When I took him his water this morning he started asking about a wallet he said he'd lost. I told him I hadn't seen one, and that I'd speak to father. He said there was a lot of money in it, and he wasn't certain that he'd left it here—it might have been lost at Chatham, he said. Well, I went downstairs and asked dad, and he said no, he hadn't seen it, and what was I such a long time in Mr McFeish's room for ? I told him it was because he'd been asking me about the wallet, and then he went for me, and said it wasn't right for me to go into a gentleman's bedroom at all. I asked him who'd take the hot water round if I didn't, and he told me not to be saucy.

" Well, I looked everywhere, but I couldn't see the
126

wallet, and Mr McFeish was very rude about it latei. He said he'd rung up the hotel in Chatham, and they hadn't found it, and he couldn't afford to lose so much. Then I was a bit rude, and said he ought to take more care of his things, and it served him right. I don't like him anyway " she finished.

" Why not ? "

" Well, I don't know——"

She blushed again, and none of them found it difficult to understand the reason.

" Why don't you tell your father, if he's been annoying you ? "

" Oh no sir—he'd say I started it."

" He seems a bit down on you " observed Tony, and she nodded.

" It's mother, really, I think " she said. " She ran away with another man, you know, and then came back, and then ran away with someone else."

" How old are you ? " asked Beale. " Twenty ? " Lucy smiled.

" Dear no ! " she answered. " Just eighteen."

" Really ?  You look more.  Are you—well, walking out with anyone ? "

" No sir.  Dad says I'm too young."

" I see.  Well, I think that's all now, Lucy.  I'm to understand that you think your father may have taken Mr McFeish's wallet, and paid his bills with the money he found inside it ? "

" Well sir, he was very worried, and you say he couldn't have found it in the old suit—and the wallet hasn't turned up."

" Did Mr McFeish mention any particular sum of money ? "

" No sir.  Well, yes, forty or fifty pounds, he said."

She got up, started to put her handkerchief back where it had come from, remembered Beale's warning, tried not to look flustered, and stood waiting.

" Bring three pints of beer, will you please ? " he asked.  " In about five minutes."

" Yes sir."

" Now Matthews " said Beale, the minute she was out of the room : " I think we'd better take McFeish next, provided he's in. What do you say ? "

" Yes sir. There'll be a thing or two to ask him."

" What about this fresh lot of money ? " asked Tony. " Coincidence ? "

" It may be. 'Forty or fifty pounds '—it can't very well be the same lot. At least, it could be, but would anyone in his right mind make a fuss if he lost it ? "

" No, hardly. What about the rest of the girl's story ? "

" It seems genuine enough, and checks with what she told Matthews this morning. By the way, Tony, I'm very glad you butted in. I was just going to tell her the money was Tatham's ! "

" Oh lord ! Then she probably wouldn't have said anything about McFeish. But even now I don't quite see it. If she's right, then Tate pinched one lot of money from red-head—presumably in order to pay his brewers' bill ; but somehow or other he mysteriously gets hold of Tatham's notes as well, and does actually pay the bill with them. There's no doubt about that having happened, is there ? "

" None whatever. But another thing I'm almost as certain of is that Tate didn't know it was Tatham's money."

" Then that lets him out of the murder."

" Yes—I suppose so. Maybe he did know—but he must be a damn fine actor."

" Well, anyway, let me get on with my own particular muddle. If the girl's suspicion is right, Tate stole two lots of money—unless they were the same lot : that is, unless the money he took from McFeish was one and the same lot as Tatham's ; in which case McFeish presumably murdered him for it. But then, why in heaven's name, having killed a man, pinched his dough, and then either lost it or had it re-pinched from him—*why* go and tell the world he's lost it ? Just doesn't make sense."

Matthews broke in with a suggestion.

" Supposing that happened, sir " he said, " but that before it passed out of his possession McFeish did really put it in his wallet. Then, for all he knows, somebody may find it with the incriminating money inside. His only hope is to get hold of it again quick."

" But it's very risky " Beale pointed out. " Whoever finds it is pretty sure to look inside, and if in the meantime anything's been said about the notes, then the game's up. And in that case, too, why doesn't Tate come straight along and say : ' I took this wallet from McFeish, with the money which you say belonged to Tatham inside it'. It looks very much to me as if they can't be the same lot."

" Then that lets McFeish out."

" Not necessarily—presuming he was ever in. *If* he killed Tatham, and took the £50, he may have lost it, *and* his own wallet as well ; separately, I mean. Tate, we'll say, finds one—Tatham's—, and there you are."

" Then, again, why doesn't Tate come along and say : ' Look here, I found this under the dining-room table ' —or wherever it was ? " asked Tony.

" Perhaps " suggested Matthews " because it sounds so thin."

" But if he knew it was Tatham's money " Beale objected, " it'd be a much better tale than the one he did spin us. That seems to bear out my feeling that he didn't know. Hush ! " He broke off as Lucy entered.

" Will you see if Mr McFeish is in ? " he asked. " And if he is, ask if he'd be kind enough to come down for a few minutes ? "

" Yes sir—I think he's in."

" Now " he continued, when she was gone : " leaving all that aside, here's something I want your opinion about. When I asked her if she saw anybody near the Rectory, did she hesitate before saying she didn't go home that way ? "

" I don't think so " said Matthews, " but I've been wondering." He turned to Tony, who shook his head doubtfully.

" I don't know. It's hard to say. You see, the minute you asked her that I was waiting for a slip, and I'm hanged if I'm sure whether she answered straight off or not. I was listening too carefully."

Beale nodded understanding.

" Yes, it was the same with me. But why were you waiting for a slip ? "

" I don't quite know, really."

" Because of something she said earlier ? "

" Yes, I suppose so. Oh yes, I remember. It's probably nothing : but first she told you she didn't know what the tramp said, and then in the same breath she said she didn't think it was very nice. To me that seemed very much like an afterthought— touch of local colour to lend conviction, and so on. I may be wrong."

" I didn't notice that " admitted his friend.

" Nor did I " agreed Matthews. " What did seem a bit fishy was not thinking of going back for another bike ; but I don't see "—as the other two nodded— " how we're to disprove her story about the puncture unless we can definitely show that she was somewhere else. She was right enough about the light at Bassett's place."

" Yes : but let's work times out, all the same " said Beale. " Suppose she didn't have a puncture. Then she leaves Stoke Albury at five to ten—there doesn't seem to be much doubt about that ; the aunt backs her up—, and arrives here at twenty past eleven. If she hurried she could have got to the cross-roads, say, at half past ten, or a little before. But I still don't think she had anything to do with the murder. I mean, she's such a kid, and if she did she's a remarkably good actress."

" Inherited from her father " observed Tony. " But I don't think she's a murderess either. Anyone who's eighteen, and still keeps her handkerchief where

130

she puts hers, doesn't seem likely to be, well, sophisticated enough to kill a man ; unless it was a 'crime passionelle', and that seems even less likely.—Here's his lordship. I think."

## CHAPTER XVII

### 9.45 PM—10.15 PM

IT was just after quarter to ten when Ambrose McFeish entered their sitting-room. He was smoking a pungent Brazilian cigaratte, and wore a black silk dressing-gown decorated with small gold parrots.

" I understand you want to see me " he said.

" Yes, if you don't mind—sit down."

" Very well, but please don't be long ; I've got work to do."

" I'll try not to be " promised Beale. " I'm in the same position myself. First of all, as a matter of form, I must ask you to account for your movements from midday on Monday until last night."

McFeish blew a leisurely smoke-ring.

" On Monday I went to Chatham " he told them. " I left here about eleven o'clock by motor-cycle, and arrived there at 1.0. I had lunch at the Railway Hotel, and then afterwards, when I went to start the bike, it refused to go. I took it to a garage, and was told that the magneto had gone wrong. The engine hadn't been running very well, by the way. The repairs were not finished until 4.15, and as I'd just run into some friends, and didn't anyway fancy driving back at night, I decided to remain until Tuesday. I spent the rest of that day with my friends, saw them again yesterday, left Chatham at 8.0, and was back here by about quarter past ten. I stopped for a drink on the way. I think that's all."

Beale looked at Matthews, who nodded to indicate that he had it all down. Then he turned to the poet.

" Now, Mr McFeish " he said, " I'm going to speak

131

very plainly, and I hope you won't take unnecessary offence."

" No—please say what you want to. It's generally the best way."

" Thank you : then I will. Your account sounds reasonable as far as it goes ; but there are noticeable gaps in it. For instance, you say nothing about what you did from the time you left the garage after lunch until you returned there at 4.15."

McFeish nodded, but kept silent.

" I must ask you to fill up that gap."

The other regarded the ceiling for a moment, and then smiled.

" I spent part of the time in a tea-shop writing " he said, " and the rest wandering about the local grave-yard : both quite harmless occupations."

" Possibly " agreed Beale. " This morning you told Sergeant Matthews that you went to Chatham to visit your mother. I'm sorry to be blunt, but I have reason to believe that your mother is dead. Will you please explain ? "

" Certainly " was the cool reply. " I'm surprised that a man of your profession can't see the connection. Of course, the trouble with you people is that nine times out of ten you don't recognize the truth when you do hear it. Because something doesn't sound right you immediately conclude it must be wrong. What were my words ? ' To visit my mother', which is precisely what I did ; or her grave, if you prefer it. She happens to be buried in St Stephen's cemetery."

" Then I must apologize."

" Don't bother—it isn't your fault she's dead. Anything else ? "

" Yes. You decided to stay over Monday night because you didn't fancy driving back in the dark : so instead you returned on Tuesday night."

" I told you I met some friends. I was with them most of the day."

" I see. When did you meet them ? "

" As I was coming out of the tea-shop."

132

" Thank you. Now, will you please give me the name of the hotel, the garage, the tea-shop, and the names and addresses of your friends ? "

" The first two with pleasure : the Railway Hotel again, and Craven's Garage in Main Street. I don't know the name of the shop—it was a little place near the cemetery. And as for my friends, I'm afraid you'll have to take my word there. I'm not prepared to tell you anything about them except that they're no longer in Chatham."

Beale sat forward.

" Why not ? " he demanded.

McFeish thought for a moment.

" You're a policeman " he said, " and my friends don't like policemen. Can I be clearer ? "

" Considerably : you can tell me why they don't like policemen."

" I could " agreed the other : " but I'm not going to."

" Very well ; but don't expect me to be satisfied with your attitude—or, until I've checked it, with your story. Am I to take it that you prefer not to fill up the other gap, between 4.15 and the time you went to bed on Monday ? "

The poet nodded.

" I was back at the Railway Hotel by half past twelve, or soon after, if that's any help " he said.

" I see. Now, what was the primary reason for your journey to Chatham : to visit your mother's grave, or to meet these friends ? Or did you go just for the ride ? "

McFeish smiled sardonically, his red hair glinting in the lamplight.

" The first " he answered. " The second happened by accident, as I've told you, and the third was too cold to be enjoyable."

" There's such a thing as a railway, sir " interposed Matthews quietly. The poet dismissed this suggestion in a single sentence.

133

" Trains always make me sick " he said, and then turned to Beale.

" You know, I haven't even asked why you should think it necessary to question me " he remarked. " I wonder if you've any right to ? Is it just curiosity ? Because I'm a somewhat startling-looking person staying in the neighbourhood when a murder's committed ? "

" Not altogether " Beale told him, rather to Tony's surprise. He could think of no other adequate reason.

" And as for your description of yourself, perhaps you know best ; but you don't go about in that dressing-gown all the time : and I've seen people with red hair before. There was Terence Dolan, for instance. He got ten years for attempted murder, if you remember."

McFeish grinned openly, until the reminiscence was completed.

" But his hair wasn't as red as yours."

Matthews made an uncertain noise which might have been a stifled sneeze, and the poet coloured a little.

" Anyway, I'll ask you now " he said. " Why are you questioning me ? "

" Tell me something first : did you know Mr Tatham ? Had you ever spoken to him ? "

" Yes, once. I asked him his opinion of Drinkwater's verse. He said he thought some of it undoubtedly showed——"

Beale broke in abruptly.

" You asked me not to take up too much of your time " he reminded him. " I must make the same request of you. When did you meet him, and where ? "

" Near the church about a week ago " answered McFeish, rather shortly.

" Thank you. Now I'll tackle your question. I'm interested in you because your behaviour during the last fourteen hours strikes me as rather peculiar."

At this both Tony and Matthews sat forward, wondering what was coming.

" Peculiar ? In what way ? " asked McFeish.

"I'll tell you" replied Beale, speaking slowly. "Between your departure for Chatham on Monday morning, and your official return last night, a murder was first committed, and then discovered. One direct result of that discovery is that we three have temporarily taken up residence here. That event occurred during the same period of time : namely, your absence."

McFeish interrupted with a somewhat sarcastic smile.

"I should hardly describe the arrival of two policemen and the undistinguished-looking owner of an expensive car as an event" he observed. Beale treated the digression amiably.

"It probably is from the village point of view" he retorted ; "and, when I've caught him, the murderer's opinion might be interesting. And as for my friend : whatever his looks may be, in his own line he's really quite distinguished."

"And what is his line ?" asked the other, whose attitude was steadily growing less friendly, and whose voice now held more than a suspicion of cockney twang : "travelling salesman ?"

"No. As a matter of fact I help to edit a paper" said Tony. "The 'Stockbroker', in case you're interested."

McFeish's manner underwent a considerable change.

"Do you really ?" he asked, in more respectful tones. "Then can you tell me whether Stimson's Consolidated will ever come up again ? What's their scrip worth ?"

"About sixpence a hundredweight—I believe that's what a rag-and-bone man would give you. But I think the Inspector wants to get on."

"I do" agreed Beale, a little impatiently. "I was saying that you returned last night to find us here. Between your arrival and quarter to seven this morning you discovered that you'd lost a wallet containing forty or fifty pounds. It seems to me remarkable that you haven't bothered to ask us if we've seen it. As a matter of fact, we haven't, but I'd very much like

to know why you didn't enquire. Unless of course
you're a millionaire."

McFeish frowned at him.

" I don't see what the devil it's got to do with you "
he declared. " Mayn't one even lose money in peace
nowadays ? "

" When a murder's being investigated " Beale told
him, no less sharply, " it doesn't pay anybody to do
anything that attracts attention. If he does he'll get
it, and he may not like it—as apparently you don't."

For a moment it seemed likely that the red-haired
man would lose his temper. Then with an obvious
effort he controlled himself.

" Oh, I don't mind much " he said. " What do you
want to know ? Why I didn't say anything to you ?
I'm not sure exactly. For one thing I've got too much
else to think about. Tate's girl knew I'd lost it, and
she was supposed to be looking. And then again, I
wasn't certain I hadn't lost it in Chatham, or on the
way there or back. The last time I actually remember
seeing the wallet was on Saturday evening in my
room."

" What's it like ? "

" Black leather—fastens with a strap."

" Marked with your name ? "

" No."

" Anything else inside ? "

" No."

" And what was the exact amount it contained ? "

" I don't know to a pound : forty-seven or forty-
eight."

" What kind of notes ? "

" Pounds and ten-shillings."

" New ones ? "

" No, all old stuff, I think."

" And how long had it been in the wallet ? "

" Since I came here three weeks ago."

" Do you suspect anyone in particular of having
stolen it ? "

" Good lord no ! I don't expect it's been stolen at

all. I probably just dropped it, or put it down somewhere, and it hasn't turned up yet. Possibly stolen
by finding " he added.

" So you've really no clear idea when or where the
wallet left your possession ? "

" Between Saturday evening and late last night—I
know I hadn't got it when I went to bed. But I don't
know where."

" But surely you needed money in Chatham ?
Don't you know if you had it then or not ? "

" No. You see, I've got two wallets."

He took from his inside pocket a case made of
crocodile skin.

" There's a certain amount of money in here " he
said, " but I spent some in Chatham, as you cleverly
surmised. Last night I found I was getting short, so
I looked for the other one, but with no result."

" Have you looked again today ? "

" Yes—it's definitely not in my possession."

" H'm. You seem very casual about money."

" Yes, possibly—does that matter ? "

" No—it's your loss, not mine. Does anyone here
know the lost wallet by sight ? "

" I don't suppose so. I've used this one for the last
few weeks."

" Thank you. I don't think there's anything else.
Oh yes, just a moment : I understand that a letter was
delivered here for you on Tuesday morning. Did you
receive it all right ? "

" Yes, perfectly, thanks."

" I mean, it hadn't been tampered with ? "

" Not as far as I know. The envelope's upstairs—·
would you care to see it ? "

" Yes please."

McFeish went out of the room, and returned shortly
with one which fitted the postman's description. It
was large and yellow, and had plainly been addressed
by a woman. On the back, in the same writing, was
a message : ' Drive your cart and your plow over the
bones of the dead '. Beale repeated it aloud.

" That's a queer piece of advice " he remarked. " Is it a quotation ? "

" I don't know. It's not one I recognize. I imagine it refers to the book I'm writing. I'm afraid I'm being rather harsh on certain dead versifiers."

" Really ? Is it indiscreet to ask who wrote this ? "

" My cousin."

" I see."

He regarded the words again, and then, to Tony's surprise, licked the tip of his finger, and rubbed it against the final letter, smudging it.

" That seems quite satisfactory " he said, handing the envelope back. " Thank you. You're sure you won't tell me why your friends don't like policemen ? "

" Quite sure—I know they wouldn't like me to."

" That's a pity. By the way, I suppose they're alive ? "

" They were when I last saw them. Is that really all ? Then I'll say good-night."

He included them all in his salutation, and went out.

" Well, really ! " exclaimed Tony. " Travelling salesman, indeed ! Do I really look like one ? "

As Beale merely grinned he turned to Matthews, who shook his head, not trusting to speech.

" That reason you gave him was rather smart " Tony went on, after a mock-ferocious glance at the detective-sergeant's heaving shoulders. " I mean, for asking all those questions. I thought he'd got you there."

" So did I at first " agreed his friend. " It really was sheer curiosity, to begin with. The man's a freak, and you naturally wonder what he's been up to. What are Stimson's Consolidated ? "

" A second-rate industrial that went bust years ago. But what about the bones of the dead ? They make one think. For 'cart' read 'motor-cycle', and for 'plow', 'side-car' : does that help ? "

" The money seems genuine enough, sir " remarked Matthews, keeping to the business in hand.

" Yes, I'm inclined to agree " said Beale slowly.

" Don't think there's much doubt, sir. If he didn't lose it at all, I can't see any point in saying he did ; and if he lost a different lot he wouldn't dare describe it wrong in case it was found."

" Yes, that seems sense. But I'm going to phone Chatham—or you can. Ask them to check his story where possible, and ring up when they've any news."

## CHAPTER XVIII

### 10.15 PM—11.10 PM

The detective-sergeant was back within ten minutes.

" They'll call us either before midnight, or in the morning " he said. " And Bassett's outside, sir, asking to speak to you. It'll soon be closing-time, so if you want to see him——"

" Yes, just as well " Beale decided. " Perhaps he'll tell us where he got to Monday night."

But the farmer's attitude held out little hope of that. He came into the room carrying his cap, stared rudely at the two occupants of the arm-chairs, moved to let Matthews shut the door, and then addressed Beale.

" See here, mister ! " he began roughly. " It's coming to something when a man can't go into his own field. What's the idea of putting a cop in charge there without so much as a by-your-leave ? "

Beale smiled amiably.

" Won't you sit down ? " he asked.

" No—I'm all right standing."

" Very well. The idea, Mr Bassett, is to keep people out of Pond Meadow. I've got my own reasons for doing that, and they're pretty good ones. If you have any complaints, make them in the right quarter. Sergeant Rush would be the best person ; or you might see the Superintendent at Shale, if he's not too busy. If yesterday you'd shown any willingness to help me, I might have consulted you. As you didn't, it seemed unreasonable to waste time asking for

139

permission to do something that you'd probably object to."

The farmer broke in angrily.

"You 'aven't got no right——" he began, and then stopped at the sudden sharpness of Beale's voice.

"Shut up! I'm not going to argue about it. If you don't like it you can do the other thing. And if you interfere in any way I'll have you arrested for obstructing a police-officer in the execution of his duty."

"All right" said Bassett gruffly, and turned to go.

"Wait a bit, please—I haven't finished yet. You'd really better sit down, you know."

After hesitating, the farmer did so.

"Well?" he grunted. "More of your poking and prying?"

"Precisely. First of all I'm going to ask you again what you did on Monday night between half past nine and midnight."

"Find out!"

Beale took no apparent notice.

"It's occurred to me that you might have been waiting near the wired-up gate to see what happened when the Rector came back."

"Well, suppose I was? Nothing wrong in that, is there?"

"So that's what you did?"

Bassett's face remained unsmiling and hostile.

"It might have been, and again it might not" he said.

"True, if not profound" agreed Beale. "But from the fact that there are no signs of anybody's having stood in one place for a long time, or walked up and down, or sat smoking, I'm inclined to think you didn't. The same question then arises : what were you doing? You didn't go to Stoke Albury, and you didn't wait about to see Mr Tatham come home—not, anyway, near the Rectory ; and you obviously don't want us to know what you did do. It looks to me as if it was something you oughtn't to have been doing."

140

From the tone of his voice he might now almost have been thinking aloud : but his eyes were fixed unwaveringly on Bassett's face.

" My first thought " he went on " is naturally this : did you have a hand in the murder ? "

" No I didn't ! " interrupted the other fiercely : but again he was ignored.

" So I begin to look for traces of you elsewhere."

Bassett's face twisted itself into a sneer.

" And you didn't, Mr Clever ! "

" On the contrary : I did."

The farmer's expression changed abruptly.

" Oh, you did, did you ?  What ? "

" This " said Beale, producing the pipe from his pocket with a swift movement.  Bassett was clearly taken by surprise, and for a moment could do little but stare at his property.  Then he attempted to laugh.

" Where'd you find that ? " he asked.

" At just about the place where Mr Tatham's dead body was carried into the woods.  Can you give me any explanation of how it came to be there ? "

" I suppose that's where I dropped it—I lost it Sunday."

" That's what you would say, of course."

Bassett, apparently less sure of himself now spoke more politely.

" If you're thinking I killed the parson, and dropped that Monday night " he said, " you're making a mistake.  I can give you the names of half a dozen chaps who were in the bar here Sunday evening when I found I'd lost it."

" Very well : who are they ? "

" Jem King, the road-mender, for one ; and Bert Armitage, one of the keepers up at the Place ; and Tate, and Collins the postman.  Want any more ? "

" No, I don't think so.  Matthews, it's barely half past.  Just see if any of those gentlemen are still here.

" You know " he went on, turning to Bassett again, " even though these people agree that you said you lost the pipe on Sunday, that still doesn't make it impossible for you to have been at the same place again on Monday. What were you doing, by the way, when you dropped it ? "

" I was taking a walk round, like, Sunday afternoon."

" Alone ? "

" Yes."

" In the woods ? "

" No, along by the road. You couldn't have found it in Wyre Woods, 'cause I never went inside 'em Sunday. I was trying to make up my mind which gate I'd wire up."

" So you knew the Rector was going to London the next day ? "

" Yes."

" Oh, that's interesting : how ? "

" Because he told me."

" But I thought you weren't on speaking terms."

" Nor we weren't ; but he stopped me one day last week. ' Bassett ' he says, ' I'm going to London next Monday, and I'll get a legal opinion about this right of way while I'm up there.' "

" Did he say from whom ? "

" No. His lawyers, I guess."

" Yes, perhaps. Now, here's a point where you could help. Can you tell me of anyone else who knew he was going to London on Monday ? Barring the people at the Rectory, of course. For instance, did you tell anyone ? "

Tony expected some rude suggestion that he could find out for himself, but the farmer answered readily enough.

" I told the missus " he said, " and the men who did the gate. No, that's wrong—I didn't tell them till Monday morning, in case they gave the show away I didn't want Tatham to get wind of the idea."

" No, I suppose not. And you don't think your wife told anyone ? "

" Not her. She ain't got many friends—too sharp a tongue."

Matthews came back in time to hear the last remark, and smiled broadly.

" Well ? " Beale asked.

" Collins and Armitage remember Mr Bassett saying on Sunday evening that he'd lost his pipe in the afternoon. Tate's not sure, and the other man isn't there."

" Thanks. Well then, if you've nothing else to tell me I don't think I need keep you. I'd just like you to give me the times again—when you went out and when you returned."

" Half past nine and half past eleven."

" Thanks. About Pond Meadow : as soon as possible I'll have it opened. Until then I shall be much obliged if you can put up with the inconvenience."

" Oh, all right. It's only grass land, so you can't do much harm. Well, good-night."

When he reached the door he turned.

" Are you satisfied now I didn't kill Tatham ? " he asked. Beale temporized.

" I'm very much more satisfied than I was before you came in " he said. " And I'm not sure that that isn't true " he added, when the door had closed. " What do you think, Matthews ? "

His subordinate countered this with another question.

" Did he tell you anything while I was out, sir ? "

Beale recounted what Bassett had said.

" Then I don't think he had anything to do with it himself, sir, though he may know more than he lets on. He's open enough about some things, and neither of 'em's at all shaky about the times. Whatever he was doing, I think he really did do it between 9.30 and 11.30. The pipe seems all right, too. I'm sure Tate remembered as well, but wouldn't say so because it was Bassett. They don't like each other much. If he was the one, sir, then he's either very very clever, or a perishing fool ; and I don't think either fits."

Beale smiled encouragingly.

" Let me see if I know what you mean " he said. " Bassett's present behaviour appears to be either that of an innocent man acting perhaps unwisely, but quite

143

in keeping with his character ; or else that of a guilty man being not merely unwise, but positively stupid. Now, if he really is innocent, the first is what we might expect. But if, on the other hand, he's not, then he's either so clever that he's behaving just as he would if he hadn't done it ; or so dense that he doesn't realize that his refusal to say where he was Monday night automatically draws attention to him."

"Making him almost incredibly thick" declared Tony.

" Yes, I agree ; and the way he went about wiring up the gate goes towards disproving that. Still, let's consider the possibilities.

" (1) : Innocent man acting unwisely.

" (2) : Guilty man acting like a fool.

" (3) : Guilty man pretending to be (1).

" (4) : Guilty man pretending to be (2). That last is a subtler difference still."

" But what's the point ? "

" Simply that, as you said yourself, it appears incredible that he would behave like that if he were guilty."

" All right : what about this ? Bassett is innocent : Bassett doesn't like your face. Therefore Bassett says to himself : ' Instead of being innocent, suppose I weren't : then, to mislead this pestering cop I should try to pretend I was. If, now, I do that anyway, just for fun, then old flat-foot will think I'm guilt masquerading as blundering virtue, whereas actually I'm just laughing at him '.

" As you may perceive, it's apt to get a bit complicated after a time. You'd quite likely finish up in a mad-house pretending you were pretending to be an unwise innocent man deceiving yourself about yourself to yourself in order to make the other bloke think he was somebody he wasn't."

" Harmless for the most part " explained Beale to Matthews. " And anyway, his brain won't stand much of that. Put his face inside a tankard and leave him. To go back : we've agreed to wash out the stupid dolt —that's (2). Both (3) and (4) postulate a considerable

144

amount of cunning, which presumably incorporates some degree of intelligence. Why don't you think he's capable of that ? "

After a moment's thought ' Horsey ' Matthews gave his reasons.

" First, general impression. Second, I'm sure he couldn't keep it up with Mrs B. He might refuse to say anything, but I bet he couldn't tell her many lies. Third, if he's as clever as all that he's not going to commit a murder anywhere near where he might have dropped his pipe the day before. If you say that that's the crowning-point of intelligence, sir, I'm afraid I just shan't believe you. I don't see it could do him a ha'porth of good.

" As a matter of fact " he went on, " I don't much fancy this super-cleverness. Push it to the limit, and what do you get ? The Arch-Criminal murders the baronet in the library, and then proceeds to sign his name on the dead man's forehead, leave fingerprints right left and centre, tear off his buttons and scatter them round, with his hat gloves and coat—all plainly marked ; and finally ring up the police and confess. Then he sits back and waits for the Super-Detective to say : ' Well, my dear Watson, this man is so obviously guilty that I'm convinced he's innocent. We must look elsewhere : these are deep waters '."

" Finish the story " requested Tony : " does he get away with it ? "

" Well sir, it just depends on whether the Super-Detective's bright enough to spot the flaw in all the super-cleverness."

" And that is ? "

" That the Arch-Criminal was the only person who could have left all that evidence about."

" Well " said Beale, " for the time being I'm inclined to take your view. I really believe we can leave Bassett out—though I'd like to know what he was up to."

Tony nodded : he had vague ideas of his own about that, but hoped to obtain some sort of proof that he was right before speaking.

" Do you want Tate in now, sir ? " asked Matthews.

" Yes, I think so, if he hasn't gone to bed."

The minute they saw the landlord's expression all three realized that he was still determined to keep silent. He answered Beale's questions civilly enough, but added nothing to his statement of the morning.

"You're being very awkward, you know " he was told.

" Sorry, sir. I can only say I hadn't anything to do with the murder."

" And you've no idea who did ? "

" No sir—none."

" Very well : I can't make you talk if you're unwilling to, but don't be surprised if you should find yourself arrested."

At this Tate went pale, though he still said nothing.

" And now we come to another matter, also to do with money. Do you know anything about the disappearance of Mr McFeish's wallet ? "

There was no apparent change in the landlord's attitude at this question.

" I know he says he lost it " he answered ; " but whether that's true or not's best known to himself."

" What exactly do you mean ? "

" Nothing much. But it isn't the first time he's done that—complained of things being missing, and then have 'em turn up again."

" But the wallet hasn't turned up again."

" No—but it will. He's just plain careless."

" Have you seen it about anywhere ? "

" No."

" Would you recognize it if you did ? "

" Only from what he says—shiny black leather, ain't it ? "

" There was a considerable sum of money in it, you know."

" Yes. I hope he finds it : wouldn't hurt if he paid his bill."

" How much does he owe you ? "

" Ten days."

" Well, I think that's all now, Mr Tate. Bear in

146

mind what I said about the other business. Good-night."

"Good-night, gentlemen."

"And still we have the same old stumbling-block" remarked Tony : "where, how, when, and why, did Tate get hold of Tatham's fifty quid ? That seems to me to be the most important point of the whole blessed business."

"Well, don't worry about it" said his friend. "Tomorrow morning I want you two up good and early : ready to go out, say, by half past seven. It'll just about be light enough by then. We'll poke round the pond, and if I don't find the hat and stick I'll feel extraordinarily like arresting Tate before breakfast. But if they're there, then you must admit that it definitely seems to let him out."

"Yes, it seems to. In a way, I hope they aren't there ; it'll be much simpler. Not that I bear the man any grudge—he sells damn good beer : but he's so confoundedly mysterious."

"So's everybody" Matthews pointed out. "Bassett won't say where he was, and McFeish has friends who don't like policemen—though I can't imagine why."

"Perhaps he hasn't" said Beale. "Friends are easy enough to invent, though his reason for not telling us is certainly better than the usual guff about their having been called away to the continent unexpectedly, or not being really friends, you know, but just people he met, and he's sorry, but he doesn't quite remember their names. And if he sticks to his own rules, then that again may not mean quite what it seems to. Listen ! That's the phone—probably Chatham. Come along, Matthews."

## CHAPTER XIX

### 11.10 PM WEDNESDAY—12.15 AM THURSDAY

THEY returned five minutes later.

"Well ? " asked Tony, almost before they were inside the door. "Ah, splendid fellow ! " he added to Matthews, who was carrying still another round of drinks.

" Now don't be impatient " said Beale. " We'll tell
you if you're good."

" Which means ? "

" Not letting your left hand know whose pocket
your right hand's robbing : if you want to be a good
pickpocket, that is. I really mean, are you prepared
to sit up a bit discussing things ? "

" Yes, rather—but I've just thought of something.
What about your report ? "

" Oh, that can go from Shale tomorrow. I'll get you
to run me in before the inquest. There are two things
I haven't told you, by the way. First, the Yard confirms what we know of Hatherley and Curtis, and
Tatham went to the British Museum on Monday, as
Curtis said. He knew one of the curators there, but the
man was out. Second, the funeral's on Friday, and the
doctor's making the arrangements.

" Well, what of it ? "

Beale grinned.

" Last night " he said " you made offensive remarks
about my withholding vital information."

" Ass ! What about red-head ? "

Matthews, at a nod from his superior, began to read
from his note-book.

" McFeish stayed at the Railway Hotel, Chatham,
on Monday night, as stated, booking his room by
telephone at 4.25 pm. He did not return at night until
12.50 am. He made no special arrangements at the
garage with regard to the time his motor-cycle was to
be ready, but called for it about 4.15. No information
about the tea-shop or his friends. He rang up the
Railway Hotel from here this morning at ten o'clock,
the manager says, to enquire about his wallet. They
had not seen it."

" Now " said Beale, " I just want to draw up a list
of possible suspects. We might learn something
from it."

He wrote rapidly, and within ten minutes held it
out for their inspection.

148

| Suspect | Opportunity | Motive | Remarks |
|---|---|---|---|
| **A** <br> John Tate | Just time before he returns here at 11.11 (?) to phone his sister at 11.12. <br><br> (Unless there is anything in the pond, when apparently none.) | Money ? | Time stretched to limit. Motive weak, unless he knew for certain Tatham would have money: but how ? But he got hold of it within 12 hours. Again, how ? Was telephone call an alibi ? |
| **B** <br> William Bassett | Apparently unlimited. <br> Left home at (?) <br> 9.30 <br> Returned at (?) <br> 11.30 <br><br> (N.B.—Times depend on Mr & Mrs B.'s word.) | Trouble over right of way ? | Motive weak in itself, and known to whole village. Pipe found near body's prob. entry to woods (poss. dropped Sun.). Will not say what he was doing between 9.30 pm & 11.30 pm Monday. First story clearly untrue. He knew Tatham was going to London. |
| **C** <br> Lucy Tate | If the puncture was faked, then from approximately 10.30 pm to 11.20 pm unaccounted for. | Knowing her father was in debt ? | Almost certain she could not have carried body into the woods unaided. Her story appears to be genuine. Tramp ? Downstairs light at B.'s farm might be safe bet. |

| Suspect | Opportunity | Motive | Remarks |
|---------|-------------|--------|---------|
| D<br><br>Ambrose McFeish | Collected motor-cycle from gar-age in Chatham 4.15pm. Finally returned to Rail-way Hotel 12.50 am Tuesday. | ? | Says he spent Monday from about 4.0 pm with friends who don't like police-men ; part of Tuesday also. Another money-loser (£47–£48). Wyre-Chatham 36 m. Contra-dictory state-ment about night driving. |

" Any additions ? " he asked, when they had examined it. " No ? Well then, tell me what you think sticks out farthest."

He agreed that both deserved full marks.

" That's it " he said : " the weakness of the motive everywhere. In one case we don't know of any at all. In another it's a piffling squabble about a right of way. And in the other two, where it's money, it presupposes practical certainty of knowledge that Tate and/or Lucy could obtain enough to make murder worth while. Pretty feeble all round ; it makes you wonder."

" Wonder what ? "

" Just how long-standing the motive was."

" You mean, whether the crime was deliberately planned or not ? "

" No, I don't—not quite, anyway. You can have an adequate motive for murdering a man—as adequate as any motive ever is—, and yet not decide to do it until a few minutes, or even seconds, beforehand. When the opportunity you've been hoping for presents itself unexpectedly, you seize it. On the other hand, of course, if you've any motive at all then it must originate earlier than the determination to kill."

150

At this point Tony became excited.

" Suppose there wasn't any motive ! " he cried. " A what-d'you-call-it maniac ! Homicidal, I mean. What about it ? "

Beale smiled at his friend's excitement.

" Sit down " he suggested. " I was beginning to wonder when the idea would strike you. Well, Matthews, what's your opinion ? "

The detective-sergeant shook his head.

" Bogey ! bogey ! " he said, lifting his tankard.

Tony looked puzzled.

" What do you mean, ' Bogey ! bogey ! ' ? " he asked.

" I'll tell you " answered Beale. " If you take any hundred murders, and look at them without knowing all the facts, in about ninety of them the most satisfactory explanation will be that they're the work of your protégé the homicidal maniac. All the rough places are made smooth, and so on. Unfortunately— from your point of view, not ours—, when you go on you'll find that in at least 95% of those ninety cases you're hopelessly wrong. Just as a matter of interest, what is a homicidal maniac ? "

Tony opened his mouth, closed it, thought for a moment, and then frowned.

" I don't know that I can give you a proper definition " he said, rather apologetically. " Someone who kills just for the sake of killing, I suppose, or under the influence of a delusion ; or somebody who's insane in the sense that he no longer recognizes what the newspapers call the ' sacredness of human life '."

" Not bad " admitted Beale. " Well, in general it's a pretty good rule to be extremely chary of attributing a murder to a maniac until every other theory's failed. But we can spare a couple of minutes to look at the present case.

" This so-called ' motiveless ' killing isn't really motiveless at all, of course. The psychologists have taught us that, and also that a person who's mad may be as capable of premeditation and cunning and prudent calculation as one who's sane. Broadly speaking, the difference between the motives is this : the normal person says ' I did it for a revenge, or money, or because so-and-so stood in my way ...'; and the homicidal maniac simply ' I wanted to do it '. The madman is satisfying the urgings of his instincts, the sane man those of his reason.

" As a matter of fact, that's a very bad dividing line, too. The point to make is that the chief difference between sanity and insanity, anyway as applied to crime, is one of control. We're nearly all potential thieves, or cheats, or even murderers. Most of us have thought at one time or another how pleasant or advantageous it would be to kill A, or B. But by a sane man that idea can be brought under control before it becomes a desire : and if he kills, he does so because he deliberately permits himself to, and not because he can't stop himself. That's the danger of a maniac : not that he wants to do a certain thing, but that he won't be able to hold out against the impulse if it's capable of being gratified.

" The chief instinctive reason of all doesn't apply here. This is obviously not a sex-murder, which about 70% of that class are. Again, in general there are two characteristics of your friend's handiwork : he takes his own weapon, and the identity of the victim doesn't seem to matter much.

" You may ask how I can possibly tell that whoever killed Tatham didn't bring his own weapon. You'll hear what Hatherley says tomorrow—that it was a spade, or something very similar ; but the maniac's usual way of killing is by stabbing or strangling. Anybody might have a knife, and everybody's got hands, or can wear a scarf. A spade is a clumsy weapon, and a very puzzling one. Admittedly a maniac might pick up the nearest heavy object : but spades don't lie about waiting to be picked up.

" Secondly, by saying that the identity of the victim isn't of any great importance, I mean that in this kind of crime it nearly always seems that anyone else of a similar class would have done just as well. Jack the

Ripper, for instance : he didn't care who the girl was as long as she was a street-walker ; and, incidentally, he used his own knife. X may have had a clergyman-complex, but it's far more likely—if he was mad—that he killed Tatham because there wasn't any other choice of victim. However, I obviously daren't waste time thinking about that until I'm convinced the Rector wasn't killed because he was a particular person named Arthur Tatham.

"Leaving the homicidal maniac, then, let's turn to motives for murder by a sane person. I'm going to speak generally ; don't expect a detailed account of every possible reason for killing, or we'd never get to bed at all.

"In general, then, all murders of this class are murders for gain, which can be of two kinds, material or abstract. Call them (A) and (B), and take (A) first.

"Here the murderer kills for two main reasons : either to regain his own property, or to possess himself of the victim's. The most usual objects in both cases are (1) money ; (2) valuables—jewelry and so on ; (3) documents, compromising or otherwise ; and (4) persons. By the last I mean, for instance, a seduced wife, or a lover, or hoped-for lover, who was being attracted away from the murderer by the victim.

"These two kinds of murder for material gain may be roughly headed 'Murder for restitution', and 'Murder for greed'. I don't think we need pay much attention to the first. Tatham doesn't seem to have been the kind of man to hold on to something that wasn't his so tenaciously that the only way it could be got back was by killing him. Against that we'll put 'Possible, but highly improbable'.

"The second, murder for greed—here practically synonymous with robbery—, looks more feasible. We know that Tatham had in his possession something worth taking : namely, £50. We also know at least two people who badly needed £50. What we don't know is whether they were aware that he had it. Of course, it's always possible that something else has

153

been taken that we haven't heard about—a something that was the real reason for his being killed; but personally I doubt it. I think that against murder for robbery it'll do to put 'Quite possible'.

"Now we come to murder for abstract gain, which is really satisfaction, whether mental or emotional, and here there are more sub-divisions. The main motive-headings are revenge, hatred, anger, jealousy, and fear. But instead of going into those separately I want to approach things from another angle: that of time.

"There are three conditions of time: the past, the present, and the future. That fact is one of the unassailable laws of existence. And, correspondingly, a man may be killed for three reasons: because of what he did in the past, because of what he's doing now, or because of what it seems likely that he'll do in the future. I include under that heading not only his actual conduct, but also what he stands for. I think I'd better explain that, though, because I don't want you to get muddled.

"Three men wish to kill the Archbishop of Christmas Island. The first man because the reverend gentleman once knocked him down and kicked all his front teeth out; the second—a native of Christmas Island—because the Archbishop is an archbishop; that is, the representative of an opposing religion; the third man in order to prevent the Archbishop from carrying out a threat to expose him for what he is—a blackmailer, or wife-beater, or what you will. The only point to remember is that the Archbishop's having knocked a man down, being opposed to another man's religion, and intention to denounce a third man, are all to be considered as his conduct, past present and future respectively. Do you see?"

The other two nodded.

"Well then, let's deal first with conduct in the past.

"Here the motive, for all practical purposes, is always revenge. There are just two things that ought to be emphasized. First, I'm making no attempt to cover combinations of past present and future. If you kill Matthews because he insulted you yesterday and today, and will pretty certainly do it tomorrow, I should only take notice of today. Second, the murderer is always at liberty to act on another person's behalf."

" You mean " Tony broke in, " he may revenge an injury done, say, to his aged mother, who was a widow woman, and blind in one eye ? "

" Yes, exactly. It's also possible for the actual victim not to be the person meant to suffer. Constance Kent killed her step-brother not because she hated him, but because she wanted to strike at her step-mother, who loved him. Anyway, to get back to Tatham's death : the only pointer to revenge that we know of is Bassett's row about the right of way, which is pretty thin. There may be other reasons, but it seems unlikely, judging from the man's apparent character, and his undoubted position. ' Possible but improbable' will meet the case for revenge, I think.

" Next, the present, where it's anger at, or hatred or jealousy of, the victim's conduct, position, or attitude with regard to a particular matter, or matters. The first, of course, includes most murders done on the spur of the moment as the result of a flare-up. That may have happened here, but I doubt it."

" What about Bassett ? " asked Tony. Beale shook his head.

" If there were any marks in Pond Meadow by the wired-up gate, perhaps ; but everything points to the fact that Tatham never got there, and Bassett wouldn't give the game away in advance. In any case, if it was a row, with him or with anyone else, it's more likely to have been the continuation of a previous disagreement than an entirely fresh one. Bassett's is the only one we've heard about, and, as I say, I don't think we need bother about that."

" Why a previous one, necessarily ? "

" Because people don't go about picking quarrels at eleven o'clock on a winter's night."

" They could, if they did it purposely."

" Then in that case it would hardly be done on the

spur of the moment. But I'll give quarrels ' Just possible ' if you like.

"The second, hatred, doesn't seem very hopeful, either. From what Miss Frankes said I gather that she didn't agree with him about the Athanasian Creed. That would do as a motive—admittedly a weak one—if it were possible for her to have killed him. Apart from that I don't know of anything. Again, we've heard nothing about any jealousy, professional or otherwise, and everybody says what a kindly old man he was. Until appropriate information turns up I'm going to leave jealousy out of it too.

"And that brings us to the future—the plum of the pie. In this case it's hatred or fear of what the victim is expected to do, or could do. A great number of political assassinations come under the first heading, but I can't see anything that fits this business at all Under the second—fear—come most murders of black-mailers and pregnant women. Tatham certainly wasn't a woman, and almost as certainly not a blackmailer, but we haven't yet exhausted the possibilities.

"Now, what do we actually know that he was going to do ? "

"Have a book published " said Tony, " and present some woman with a purse. Also preach a sermon next Sunday, probably."

"And give his grandson a birthday present " added Matthews. "Continue the row about Pond Meadow, too, perhaps. I don't think much of any of them."

"Nor do I " admitted Beale ; " but we mustn't forget the last altogether. Call it plain ' possible '. Well, any more suggestions ? "

"You don't know " pursued the detective-sergeant " that he hadn't discovered facts about somebody which, if published—and he was a clergyman, and might think it his duty to—, would seriously injure that person, socially or otherwise."

"No, we don't ; though we couldn't be expected to, because he'd have been killed just so that people shouldn't know. But you're on the right track, I think.

156

X was afraid of something that Tatham could do in the future—and probably would do. With regard to what in particular ? "

After a little thought Tony answered.

" Whatever he found when he hurried away from the pond " he said decisively. " I mean, the motive was fear of his being a witness of something, or at any rate knowing about it. In other words, he knew too much."

Beale beamed on him.

" I shall just sit down and scream if there isn't anything in the pond " he declared, " now you've taken my theory on trust. Let's see what we've got for our trouble.

" (A—1) —Restitution: possible, but highly improbable.

" (A—2) —Robbery: quite possible.

" (B—1) —Revenge: possible, but improbable.

" (B—2) —Quarrel: just possible.

" (B—3) (a)—Fear of future conduct about Pond Meadow: possible.

" (B—3) (b)—Fear of future conduct with regard to knowledge obtained Monday night: probable.

" I don't mind telling you that I'm going to wash out (A—1) and (B—1) until we get some evidence to support them.

" Now, leaving that for a moment: the crime was either premeditated or not ; and the more I think about it the more I become convinced that it wasn't. X made only the scantest attempt to hide the body, and anyway the killing itself must have been a messy brutal affair—not the kind anyone would choose deliberately. And there's the probable weapon, too."

" But, as you said yourself, spades don't lie about waiting to be used for killing people."

" No ; but people can have spades for some other purpose, and then decide to use them for murder because they've nothing better. Will you agree for the moment that it probably wasn't premeditated ? "

" Yes " said Matthews ; " unless his plans went wrong at the last moment, and he did it this way instead."

" Then he'd have been far more likely to drop the idea for the time being than blunder into a fresh plan, extemporizing as he went along."

" Unless time was vitally important " put in Tony. " But we've got no reason to suppose it was, except in Tate's case, and I've got something to say about that when we come to him. Carry on as if we agreed."

" Very well ; then how does that fit in with what we've left ourselves ?  The first thing that's plain is that the fear-of-future-conduct one with regard to the right of way was almost certainly premeditated. As we've temporarily decided that the crime wasn't, let's wash out (B—3) (a).

" We're then left with three motives. Tatham was killed in order to be robbed, as the result of a sudden quarrel, or because he knew too much. I don't think much of the middle one, either."

" Then let's give it the push " said Tony. " As you say, it's not likely to have been Bassett, because he'd wait to see the effect of his trap, and anyway it's making X extremely hot-blooded. It doesn't seem probable that he'd have had much provocation. Now, here's my objection to the robbery one.".

" Good—I'd like that out of the way."

" Well then : Tatham's a smallish man, it's late at night, and as far as we can tell nobody could have been dead sure he'd got anything worth stealing. Now, suppose for a moment that Tate goes up to the cross-roads, waits for Tatham, and asks for a loan. Rector says ' Very sorry, my man—nothing doing ', and clutches his coat about him protectively, so that Tate suspects he's got some money in his pocket. That's well enough ; but to find out for sure he doesn't kill first, and look afterwards for what mayn't be there : he jumps on his back, shoves a sack or something over his head, sits on it to stop him shouting, and goes through his clothes. That holds good for anybody

158

else, too, except a very feeble specimen. ' The Criminal's Handbook ', paragraph 84, section 2 : ' When committing robbery with violence the aggressor is strongly advised to use only so much violence as will render the other party incapable of interfering on his own behalf. It is entirely opposed to the criminal's best interests to kill unnecessarily. Liquid ammonia may be recommended for beginners, though the direction of the wind should then be taken into account '."

" Dammit ! " cried his friend. " The man's a genius ! We can leave out dear old robbery with violence. Then, as far as three reasonably intelligent men can get by sitting in arm-chairs, drinking beer, and talking imaginatively, it boils down to this : the chances appear to favour the probability of Tatham's having been killed because on his way from Wyre Halt to the Rectory on Monday night he saw or heard something, his possession of the knowledge of which rendered it inexpedient from somebody's point of view for him to be left alive. Gents, after a sentence like that I'm going to bed. See you on the door-step at half past seven."


## CHAPTER XX

THURSDAY    NOVEMBER 22ND    12.35 AM—1.10 AM

As soon as he had blown his candle out, however, Beale realized, to his annoyance, that he was not going to fall asleep yet. His mind was too alert ; there were too many half-formed questions and speculations with which it was busying itself.

This was no unusual condition when he was working on a case, and he knew from past experience that it would be useless to wait hopefully for sleep to come. It was wiser, he decided, to try to set his thoughts in order ; control, at any rate to some extent, their subject and direction. If anything came of it, so much the better ; and if he only succeeded in tiring himself out, then he would be the more likely to drop off into oblivion.

He determined to go through briefly the events of the day, and smiled a little as he made the decision. He was sufficiently familiar with himself to know that it was people and not things which chiefly interested him : action only in so far as it illuminated character.

He turned first to McFeish.

Was the man just a freak, or was he something else : for instance, a murderer ? At present, he seemed in the position of having had opportunity but no motive. Of course, there might be reasons why he should wish to kill Tatham : revenge, or fear of exposure, for example. But leaving out motive, how could the thing have been done ? ' Use your imagination ' he told himself. ' Put yourself in his place.' And having accepted his own challenge, he endeavoured for a few minutes to become Ambrose McFeish.

' The first point ' he began ' is this : do I know what train the Rector's coming back by ? Suppose not ; then I leave Chatham soon after half past seven, and make for Wyre. The journey shouldn't take more than an hour and a quarter—it's only thirty-six miles. But motor-bikes are noisy things, and I don't want people to hear me—or see me, for that matter. Therefore I leave it in some place where it's unlikely to be noticed, and walk the last part. It's taking a risk, even then ; but I've probably been out beforehand prospecting for a quiet hiding-place. Maybe I'm using a false number-plate as well.

' I then have to decide just where I'm going to do the murder. Oh, wait a bit ! Which way do I approach Wyre from Chatham ? Normally, along the road that goes past the church. Yes, that's all right : I can approach the cross-roads through the woods, keeping close to the edge. I then squat down and wait ; I ought to be there easily by ten past nine. When Tatham doesn't come on the first train I grouse a bit and go on waiting.

' But when he does appear, just before eleven, the

160

whole business oughtn't to take me more than twenty minutes. Allow another fifteen, say, to get back to the bike, and that makes it 11.30. I've just got comfortable time for the return journey. Well, that seems all right, even though it makes the murder premeditated, and doesn't attempt to explain why I use a spade, or where I got it from. What's the snag ? '

He soon discovered it.

' What about the bank-notes ? ' he demanded. ' If I took them, it doesn't seem humanly possible that Tate can have them by ten o'clock the next morning, unless he's in on it too. And quite frankly I shouldn't like him to be in on it. He wouldn't make a very inspiring accomplice.

' There's only two ways out if I do take the money. Before I leave the neighbourhood, either I drop it— and apparently I'm supposed to be rather good at that—, and Tate or Lucy finds it ; or I meet one or both of them, they become suspicious, and only agree to hold their tongues at a price—which I pay them. There's no other means that I can see. I didn't post the money to myself, and Tate pinch the letter, because the only one delivered at the King's Head on Tuesday morning, although it was for me, was postmarked London.'

He considered the possibilities for a short while, but was not greatly attracted by them.

' I really think ' he mused ' that if the Tates butted in I'd feel more inclined to settle them as I'd just settled Tatham. It'd be far safer, and the extra time wouldn't matter much. Things might be a bit difficult, of course, if they were both there, but I think I'd have risked it : knocked the girl out first, and then let the father have it when he went for me. Not the other way round, because she might run away ; but a man wouldn't be so likely to.

' Well then, as that didn't happen, and as I don't think much of the bribery business, the alternatives seem to lie between dropping the money or not taking it at all. In that last case, somebody else did : but who ? And when ? What, for instance, would Tate be doing in the woods in the middle of the night, or early the next morning ? And how likely is it that he'd hit on the exact spot where the body was ? Not very.

'One or two possibilities have emerged, though. If Red-head did it, he may have taken the notes, and then either lost them, or bribed one or both of the Tates with them ; or he may have left them there to be found by the Tates, or by someone else who immediately took them round to the King's Head. So much for McFeish, apart from his mysterious friends, who simply don't exist if either of those theories is true. I'm glad I asked for all possible information about him in my report, though. Of course, I haven't allowed for Tatham's getting as far as the pond, and that's a big drawback ; but I may be wrong about the football.

' Now, who shall I take next ? Oh lord, I've forgotten the man's wallet ! Presuming it *is* missing. I wonder if there's anything in the girl's idea that her father took it ? Personally I wouldn't put it past him. But then, as Tony says, why not pay his bill with McFeish's money ? Can't imagine. And once more, how the *devil* did Tate get hold of the £50, unless he was bribed with it, or found it, or did the murder himself ? And there again, as Tony says, why murder the man ? And if he did, then Lucy's in the know ; and she doesn't seem to me to be a strong enough character to be able to keep a secret like that.

' Wait a bit, though ; I'd better make sure I'm right in saying she *must* know.

' For Tate to have killed Tatham, and then made that particular alibi, means that he knew he could rely on Lucy's lateness to give him an excuse for telephoning ; which means pre-arrangement about the time she should get home. Or else it means that without pre-arrangement she came in before he telephoned, and was somehow persuaded to say good-night to her aunt, and so support his false grounds for ringing up unnecessarily. The call wasn't to find out why she was late, but where she was. In either case, if the girl didn't know what it was all about on Monday night, she must certainly have guessed on Tuesday. That means she was an accessory after the fact, in which event she'd have backed her father's story about the money through thick and thin, and not have started another one about McFeish's wallet.

' That makes it look as if he didn't do it : but if he did, then she must know, unless she came in by a fluke while he was actually phoning. But dammit ! That's what they both say did happen ! Then why does her arrival at the right moment seem to be more of a fluke if he did the murder than if he didn't ? Ah yes : because in the first case he couldn't be sure that she hadn't come in while he was out killing Tatham. He wouldn't have time to look in the bicycle shed. He could only give a hasty shout as he picked up the phone. But between the echo of that shout and the putting through of the call—perhaps forty-five seconds—he's got to decide not only that she isn't in, though she may be asleep, or in the bath-room, but also that he's going to make his alibi with an enquiry about where she is. It's hopelessly risky, not to say careless : but does he come unstuck ? No blessed fear ! His guess turns out right, and along the missing daughter comes at precisely the best moment to save his bacon by emphasizing the apparent innocence of his call. It really does seem a bit thick.

' But that doesn't help much. I want to know how Tate got the money by Tuesday morning.

' What possible ways are there of becoming possessed of a thing ? By stealing it ; by finding it ; by having it sent or given to you. None of them gets me much farther. From what the postman says, it couldn't have been sent here. If it was a gift, then it was almost certainly received from the murderer, whether McFeish or another : either out of pure kindness, which doesn't seem likely ; in settlement of a debt ; or in return for a solemn promise to say nothing. I don't think Tate's the sort of man to lend anybody more than half a crown, and I can't see him risking his neck for the sake of his promise ; nor, incidentally, other people trusting him with theirs. That makes it seem probable that if he didn't do the murder himself he doesn't know who did, and therefore must have found the money.

' Then why the blazes doesn't he tell us when and where he found it ? Maybe, as Matthews suggests, because, though true, it sounds feeble. To which I still reply : not half as feeble as the story he did tell. Anybody with a grain of common sense ought to realize that £5 notes are traceable, and that to say they'd been tucked away in an old suit for over a year wouldn't take a lot of disproving. That tale doesn't make me think much of Mr Tate's intelligence. He did the actual telling pretty well, admittedly ; but after all, lots of performers in every branch of art waste good talent on poor material. It's really lack of taste, which amounts to the same thing as judgment, and therefore as intelligence. Golly, have I made a philosophical discovery, or an aphorism, or some-thing ? " Taste is the application—no, the choice— of intelligence " ; or, better : " Poor taste is the judgment of a poor intelligence ". Edward Beale, the English Rochefoucauld. Come back to earth, my boy—you're supposed to be a detective, not a motto merchant.

' Well then, did Tate do the murder ? But I'm not going to think about that until I know if there's any-thing in the pond. He's a queer chap, all the same. What the girl said about his wife is illuminating. I imagine he would be damned difficult to live with. And there again, it denotes a narrow mind to take it out of his daughter. Visiting the sins of the mothers upon the children, I suppose.

' I wonder if she's as simple as she makes out ? But the trouble is that she doesn't seem to be trying to make anything out in particular. I'm not absolutely satisfied with her story, but I really can't see her having a hand in a murder ; not that kind of one.

164

anyway. I don't say she couldn't slip a dose of arsenic into a cup of tea along with the best of them. It's hard to believe that poisoners can fully realize they're actually killing people until their victims die : it might so easily have been a lump of sugar.

'Going back to little Lucy, however : I can't imagine her keeping quiet for long if she did know anything. In her case it all depends on the puncture. If it was genuine, then there's no need to worry about her. But if it was faked, why did she do it, and need it have been to do with Tatham's death ? I don't think so. She might simply have wanted an hour with one of the village boys. "Father thinks I'm too young "; no doubt ; but she didn't say what she thought about it herself, and any girl who wears purple knickers with a green dress ought to be capable of anything short of murder.

'There might be something in that idea. If she's been deceiving her father for some time, then she'd have had enough practice to take us all in. Over that one point alone, or over anything ? I'm inclined to say the first. Lots of people can tell convincing lies when it comes to their love affairs, or anything else they've got used to lying about ; but give them something fresh to put across, and they make an awful hash.

'Now, if she was really with a boy friend from, say, 10.30 to 11.0, or a bit later, where were they ? There seems nothing to have stopped her from staying in or near Stoke Albury till just before 11.0, cycled home fast, and punctured the tyre outside the door. That means she'd have probably passed Pond Meadow about quarter past, and might very well have seen or heard something that would help us enormously.

'On the other hand, if the boy's a local, she needn't have gone near the cross-roads at all. They could have parked themselves in Rag Lane, for instance— pity there weren't any marks—, and she could have walked the rest of the way home just as she says she did. I must try to find out if she's suspected of having any particular attachment. Rush or Underwood or that butler chap might know—you can't hide much in a small village.

'Who are the usual sources of information? Vicars' wives, doctors' wives, maiden ladies. Mary Seccombe might be able to tell me, but I don't want to worry her more than I can help. She's been decent enough as it is. Miss Frankes probably wouldn't know, and Hatherley's a widower. The ideal person, of course, would be that companion creature—she looks as if she'd have her nose into everything ; but I doubt if she's been here long enough. Three months isn't much—and the lord only knows how she's lasted as long. I like the old lady, but I can't understand her putting up with that as a household pet for more than a minute and a half. Maybe there are private reasons. The nephew's supposed to have got her the job, though I doubt if that would carry much weight.

'There's a silly young fool ; but perhaps it's not entirely his fault. The last six months of the war played the devil with many an unformed character. I wish he'd been able to tell me a bit more about the disappearing stranger. I'm rather surprised his aunt's so anxious to make it up with her brother. Of course, it might be because of Curtis. She can't be exactly overjoyed at the thought of having him as an heir. I wonder if Mary's got any influence with him ? But she seemed definite enough about not intending to marry again.'

Here Inspector Beale's thoughts for the next few minutes or so need not be followed. They were more concerned with the Rector's daughter than with the problem of how her father met his death. Presently, however, he succeeded in wrenching his mind back to Wyre Place, and Janet Elder.

'I still can't make out why she was so sugary ' he told himself. 'Why go out of her way to be nice about someone she doesn't like ? At least, assuming what Mary says is true, and I don't see why it shouldn't be. And anyway, it was a sickly unconvincing sort of niceness. There might be half a dozen reasons, really :

166

trying to make a good impression in the hope that Curtis will hear of it, perhaps—she's supposed to be sweet on him. If he doesn't fancy her—and who would ?—, why get her the job ?

' But all this isn't getting me far, though I think I'll find out where dear Janet was on Monday night. Who else is there ? Hatherley ? He seems all right : old family friend, and all that. Just for fun, what can I find against him ? He seemed very ready to handle the shoes in the mortuary, though there was no real need ; he came out very pat with his tale about the way the laces were always tied ; he once quarrelled rather seriously with Tatham ; he didn't turn up last night ; he could—if he wanted to—mislead us over the medical evidence, or even fake some of it ; he knows Bassett well enough to give him a letter to post, and Bassett's behaving suspiciously. It doesn't seem enough to bother about, but it may be worth while to find out about his movements on Monday night, too.

' As for Bassett, I believe he's innocent of the actual crime ; but, as Matthews says, he may know more than he pretends. I wish we could check his times independently.

' Just suppose for a moment that he did it. Then you'd expect the murder to be the ultimate result of the row when Tatham found the gate wired up. But Rush says it's out of the question for anyone to have got as far across the field as that : which agrees with my theory about the football and the pond. Bassett knew the old boy was going to London, though, and he won't say what he was doing. I wish I knew where the actual killing took place. It would help. Yes, it would undoubtedly help. It would be very helpful.'

# CHAPTER XXI

THEY left the King's Head at 7.25 the next morning, Matthews rather self-consciously carrying an ancient butterfly net which Lucy had found for him. As they walked towards Pond Meadow Beale discussed his probable plans for the day.

"Of course, everything depends on what we find" he said. "But anyway I'll get the Shale people on to that tramp, and find out what I can about the wretched companion woman."

"You've certainly got a down on her" remarked Tony; "nearly as bad as Tate's on Lucy."

"Yes" admitted Beale, smiling a little, "though I don't quite know why, except that she's so horribly oily. It would give me the greatest pleasure to pull her in for something, but I don't suppose there's a chance. She's probably much too genteel. Oh yes, and that reminds me, Matthews: I want you to make very tactful enquiries about Dr Hatherley's movements on Monday night."

The other two looked at him in surprise.

"Hatherley?" said Tony. "But surely you don't suspect him?"

"No, not actively; but I'd like to know, all the same. Call it sheer vulgar curiosity, if you like—it's a good quality for a detective to have. Stick your nose far enough into other people's business, and you're apt to come across the most surprising things. And you might ask Rush if he knows whether Tate's girl has got any particular boy in tow. Here we are."

He noted with satisfaction that the gate was fastened with a padlock and chain, and also decorated with several strands of barbed wire.

"All very nice and obstructive" he murmured; "but how do we get in without tearing our pants?"

At the sound of his voice a helmeted head appeared round the corner of the hedge.

" Now then ! " it rebuked them. " What's all this ?
Oh, sorry sir—beg pardon. I'll unlock it."

" Tired ? " asked Beale, as the constable took out
his key.

" No sir—I only took over at 4.0."

" Well, anyway, here's something to warm you up."
He pulled from his overcoat pocket a large vacuum
flask which Lucy had filled with tea.

" Oh, thank you sir—thank you ! "

" Go and share it with the fellow in the woods—
and I expect you'd both like a smoke." He handed
the policeman a packet of cigarettes, and they watched
him depart in a glow of gratitude.

" And now comes the great test " said Tony, as
they moved towards the pond. " The secret of the
sunken stick. I don't think much of the weather."

It was cold, and inclined to be misty, and the grass
underfoot glistened with dew. There seemed every
likelihood that rain would set in later.

The pond proved to be, as Matthews said, ' just a
tidy size '. The water was dark and muddy, and gave
no indication of what might be concealed beneath it.

" Try the bottom with the other end first " suggested
Beale. " If it's slimy you'll have to be careful." But
the detective-sergeant declared that it felt reasonably
firm, and was soon industriously dredging. After a
few minutes he announced the presence of something
hard and heavy.

" The hat wrapped up in a stone " prophesied Tony
hopefully, but the obstacle turned out to be only a
biscuit-tin full of water. They all sighed, and at
Beale's request Matthews handed over the butterfly
net. At first the Inspector was equally unsuccessful,
and then he looked up with a smile.

" I think I've got the stick " he said. " Anyway, it
feels like it. One end's in a hollow, or something."

After a little careful manœuvring he brought it to
the surface.

" Good man ! " cried Tony. " Yes, as per description,
too—one up to you."

169

After a few minutes of fruitless searching for the hat, they decided to give up.

"At any rate, I've justified my theory" said Beale.

"Yes" agreed his friend. "We might do it in verse :

> "'The stick within the pond was hid ;
> The corpse lay in the wood :
> The landlord need not fear the rope ;
> So far, my boy, so good '.

"What are you looking for ? "—to the detective-sergeant, who was staring about him.

> "'We walked along, while bright and red
> Uprose the morning sun ;
> And Matthews stopp'd, he look'd, and said,
> " The will of God be done ! "

> "'A second time did Matthews stop ;
> And fixing still his eye
> Upon the outskirts of the pond,
> To me he made reply : ' ? "

"Stones, sir. There aren't any. Therefore maybe there never were any, and the hat's probably some-where else all the time."

They sat down to breakfast in good spirits. Matthews gobbled his share in so short a time that the other two foretold a violent attack of indigestion about midday, but the fingerprint-expert only smiled.

"I want to look at the stick" he explained. The result of his examination was disappointing, however.

"Not a blessed thing !" he exclaimed in disgust. "He wore gloves—must have done. This knob would show up the slightest touch, unless he wiped it, and even then he'd have left something if he wasn't extra-ordinarily careful."

"Wouldn't the water have any effect ? " asked Tony.

" No sir.  You see, it's the natural grease of the fingers that makes prints on a smooth surface.  The water wouldn't matter on silver."

At quarter to nine Tony drove the Inspector into Shale.  They left Matthews to make discreet enquiries of the butler at Wyre Place about Janet Elder's movements on Monday night.

" It's a very faint chance " Beale told him, " but worth trying.  Make the excuse for going up there that you want to know if we could borrow a man this evening if necessary."

In Shale they visited the post-office, where Beale made arrangements for his report to be sent off promptly, and the police-station.  Here he left instructions about the tramp, and commiserated with Superintendent Bowman over his lack of success in tracing the smash-and-grab raiders.

They returned to the King's Head at quarter to ten. and were immediately set upon by Dickie Donovan and three companions.

" Now, we've been extremely good " declared the reporter.  " We haven't poked our noses in, or interviewed people—at least, not much ;  and we haven't— anyway, I haven't—used the word ' poignant ' more than six times to the square yard.  What about letting us each stand you a beer in return for something a bit more spicy ?  The public's getting restive, you know. People are muttering.  One man turns to another in the street, and says :  ' Friend, what think you of the manner in which Chief-Inspector Beale investigates the mysterious death at Wyre a week ago come next Monday night ? '.  And friend replies :  ' As silent as a starfish basking '."

" All right " agreed Beale, laughing.  " But why not wait and see what happens at the inquest ? "

" Don't try to come it over me " said Dickie. " Nothing's going to happen."

" What makes you think that ? "

" Oh—information received.  It's going to be adjourned almost before it's begun."

" Really ! You're quite right, but I can't imagine how you found out."

The reporter winked at his companions.

" ' Beale is Baffled ! " he murmured.

" Bribery, presumably. How much did it cost you ? "

" Twopence. Look here, I'll satisfy your curiosity if you'll satisfy mine—ours, I mean " as he was nudged heavily in the ribs. " One question each—fair ? "

Beale submitted without protest. " I'll answer if I can ; but I won't promise."

" Good enough. Well, don't back out when you hear how simple my mystery is. I merely rang up Rattan, who's a solicitor as well as a coroner, and asked if I could see him on urgent business at half past eleven. His clerk said that I might have to wait a few minutes, but that he'd certainly be back by quarter to twelve."

" Yes, that's very ingenious. Well, what's your question ? "

" This : where's the missing £50 ? "

" That's easy : in my pocket. Like to look ? "

He displayed the notes, being careful not to let them see Tate's signature, and was rewarded with an appreciative buzz.

" Next " he said, turning to Dickie's neighbour. " But I can't say any more about the money at present."

" Oh hell ! " The reporters were disappointed.

" All right then : where did you find the Rector's walking-stick ? " asked the man from the Metropolitan News Agency.

" How do you know I have found it ? "

" I don't ; but if I just ask if you have you'll simply say ' Yes thanks '—if you have—and leave it at that."

Beale smiled at this cautious attitude, and considered.

" I can only answer if you'll promise not to publish till I say you can."

" Of course—where ? "

" In the pond in Pond Meadow."

" Good lord, really ? Then is that where he was done in ? Oh, sorry—but is it ? "

172

" I don't know yet.   Third ? "

" Do you think Tatham was killed by a stranger, or
by someone he knew ? " asked the West Kent Recorder.
Again Beale pondered deeply before replying.

" That's an awkward one " he declared.   " I've
found nothing to suggest it was done by a tramp, or
anyone like that, and I'm certain enough in my own
mind that the murderer was a local.   The weapon
seems to make that pretty definite."

" Weapon ? "   There was an excited chorus.   " What
was it ?   Where'd you find it ? "

" I haven't found it, but the doctor will tell you at
the inquest that it was a spade, or something as near
like one as makes no difference.   Tramps don't have
spades ;   nor do mysterious strangers.   But my
difficulty is that I don't want the murderer scared.

" You see, it's this way.   If I appear to put a certain
amount of faith in the unknown-tramp idea, then he
may think things are going well from his point of view,
and leave them alone.   But if I let out that I'm dead
sure it was a local, he may think I'm getting too warm,
and rack his brains to see if he can't put me off the scent
before I really get on it.   He might succeed, and I
shouldn't like that.

" It's always best for as long as possible to let 'em
think they've done the perfect crime.   Ten to one
they haven't ;   but let 'em think so.   Then even if
afterwards they spot a flaw which could be covered
up with a bit of risk, they won't take it because they
believe it won't be seen.   So if you don't mind I'd
rather you said that the police are seriously considering
the theory that the murder was the work of a stranger
to the district, or something like that.   You can rub
in the brutal-robbery idea, or even suggest that old
red herring the homicidal maniac."

He grinned at Tony as he said this, and was given
a fierce stare in return.

" And last ? " he asked, turning to the reporter
from the Shale Gazette.

" Who inherits ? "

173

Beale frowned.

" I haven't gone into the matter at all thoroughly
yet " he answered, hoping that his friend would keep
quiet. " And now it's time to be getting on."

As they went out he drew Dickie Donovan aside.

" Get rid of the others afterwards " he said, " and
join up—I might be glad of you."

" Rather—thanks."

Just as they were about to enter the police-station
Matthews came up, a little breathless.

" Your lady-friend had a headache Monday night,
sir " he gasped. " Went to bed at nine o'clock. So
she says. Nobody knows if she really did. She sleeps
private, as they say. She could easily have sneaked
out : her room's at the back, and there's a fire-escape
outside the window."


## CHAPTER XXII

### 10.50 AM—12.15 PM

THE inquest, which Tony considered disappointingly
dull, was adjourned at 10.48. As they came out, Beale
was surprised to notice Janet Elder among the crowd.

" That's the creature ! " he whispered to his friend,
pointing her out. " Wait a bit—I don't want to be
seen."

He concealed himself behind a car, watching her
through the back window and the wind-screen. She
was dressed in just the clothes he would have expected :
a grey-and-black coat with fancy fur collar and
sleeves, and a green hat which reminded him of a
tea-cosy.

" Looks thoroughly Edgware Road " he murmured
in Matthews' ear, and was about to look away when
something in her manner caught his attention. For a
second he was puzzled, and then he understood.
Most of the people who had been in court were standing
about in groups chatting, and she was trying to get
past them without appearing to be in a hurry.

Unfortunately for her, a large farmer was blocking the way, and in moving to avoid him she knocked against a propped-up motor-cycle, which fell over with a crash.

Both the watchers laughed, and then began to stare. Tony, whom Beale had thought to be still by his side, suddenly came into sight near Janet Elder. They saw him say something to her, and then both of them stoop to pick up the machine. That done, Tony raised his hat, and began making his way back.

" So you have fallen for her ! " exclaimed Beale, and then stared again.

" What is it ? " he asked, serious now. " Found anything ? "

" Yes, I think so. Didn't she tell you she couldn't call on Mrs Seccombe because of her duties ? "

" Yes, something like that."

" Well, yesterday morning while you were in the coroner's office I saw that woman go by. If she could get to Shale she could have called at the Rectory."

" Not necessarily—the bus-times may have been wrong."

" She didn't go by bus. She was in a big Daimler— Miss Frankes', I expect. But that's not the important thing. You saw me help to pick up that bike ? "

Beale nodded, wondering what was coming.

" Well " said Tony, " I didn't."

" What on earth are you talking about ? "

" I'm just telling you, I didn't. I'm not ragging, Ted. Motor-bikes are heavy things, but my share in lifting that one certainly wasn't more than a quarter. The woman must have muscles like a prize-fighter."

" Yes, that's very interesting " agreed Beale. " I wonder what her present hurry is, and why she came. Curiosity, perhaps—but you never know."

Almost immediately they were joined by Dickie Donovan.

" Dreary " he remarked, referring to the inquest, " terribly dreary."

175

" I meant it to be " was all the answer he got.
" We'll save the fireworks until later."

They moved away towards the car, round which
half a dozen village infants were standing whispering.
It was not of a make with which they were familiar.

" Where to ? " asked its owner. " More beer ? "

" No " said Beale. " Beer can wait. We'll go to
Pond Meadow."

On the way he gave the reporter a brief outline of
his theory about the football and the pond, and told
him what they had done before breakfast.

" Sounds good " was Dickie's verdict. " And now
we've got to use a bit more imagination still."

" How do you mean ? "

" To find out what made Tatham leave so hurriedly."

Within a few minutes they were standing by the
pond.

" The stick was about there " said Matthews,
pointing. " I don't think it's much good looking for
the hat."

" No " answered Beale, passing round his pouch.
" I don't mind admitting that I'll welcome any bright
suggestions. I can think of half a dozen things we
might do, but all of them seem chancy."

By now it was beginning to drizzle, and they turned
their collars up.

" This business is the devil ! " exclaimed the
detective-sergeant suddenly, with unexpected venom.
" When you start you get the idea that it's all been
done in such a hurry that there's bound to be a lot of
clues : but where the dickens are they ? "

He stared round mournfully, while the others kept
silent. They were all near to being disheartened.

" Look here ! " said Beale at last. " This simply
won't do. There's an answer to every riddle if you look
long enough. Tatham was attracted away from the
pond : take that as a starting-point. Now, what by ?
I don't think it was done deliberately—he was probably
killed just for being a perishing nuisance. But the
fact remains—anyway, so I believe—that he saw or

176

heard something so unusual, or startling, that he at once went off to investigate."

"It's more likely to have been something he heard" said Tony. "You can't see far at night."

"And you can hear from any direction, curse it ! But let's take seeing first, just in case. The striking of a match, for instance, would show up, if he was looking that way."

He gazed round thoughtfully.

"I can only see three things that mightn't be in any field" he decided. "First, the wired-up gate; well, as there weren't any footprints near it, we'll leave that out. Second, the pond; but as he definitely seems to have gone away from there, we'll leave that out too. There remains only that old shed over by the hedge. I'm going over to look. It's better than doing nothing, and it's in roughly the same direction as the gate."

They followed him across, and looked over his shoulder as he peered inside.

"Full of thingummys" he said. "Mangolds, or wurzels, or whatever they are."

Matthews began to frown. "Why ? " he asked.

"What do you mean, ' why ? ' ? Bassett's a farmer, isn't he ? Oh lord, I'm going dopey. Yes, why ? "

Dickie Donovan, a moment later, agreed that the matter was worthy of interest, and explained to Tony, still bewildered.

"Some farmers keep these things in fields in winter as food for sheep or cattle" he said. "I'm not sure which, but that doesn't matter. The point is : what's the use of animal-food when there aren't any animals ? "

"Well, that's simple enough" was the answer. " You are a lot of mugs. Didn't Bassett say last night that you couldn't do much harm here because it was only grass land ? And didn't he tell everybody he was going to use the field ? And what about the manure the football bounced in ? He's obviously had cows in here. First he shut the place up, by blocking one gate, and then he intended to turn a flock of something in. But you "—addressing Beale—" stopped him, much to his annoyance. Tatham says: 'This has always been a right of way—why do you suddenly want to close it ? '; and Bassett replies : 'Very sorry, old man, but I want it for my cows. Look, I've got their stuff all ready. You don't like me, and I don't like you. If I leave the field open, how do I know you won't go letting them out, just for spite ? '."

" Gosh ! " cried Beale. " That's an idea—two, in fact. I wonder. Tony, be a sport and take Matthews for a run in the car. Ask Bassett when he ordered these things, and when they were delivered. Yes, and see what you can get out of Parker first."

The detective-sergeant looked more pleased.

" That's certainly an idea, sir. The job that was so important there wasn't time to take Curtis back to Wyre Place might have been to dump this lot here."

" And conveniently wipe out traces of footprints, or a struggle, or even bloodstains " added Beale.

" Who's this Curtis, and who's Parker ? " demanded Dickie Donovan. " And why should one take t'other back to Wyre Place ? "

When it was explained to him he whistled softly.

" Then, if I understand " he said, " the important thing to know is exactly when these were ordered. Then you'll be able to tell within limits how long beforehand the murder was planned."

" Don't go jumping to conclusions " Beale warned him. " These turnip things may have been here a day, a week, or a month, and quite possibly they weren't brought with the idea of covering anything up at all. It's only a chance. Bassett isn't hanged yet by a long chalk."

" What's chalk got to do with hanging ? " asked Dickie.

" The connection's obvious. Chalk and cheese have been associated from immemorial times. Cheese can be Dutch, and so can courage. Courage is associated with convictions, and the bloke who's convicted of this murder is going to hang. Let's nose round."

He called over the constable standing nearby, but they found nothing more exciting than a number of wheel- and hoof-marks, a brown woollen glove with the fingers eaten away, and the remains of a starling.

" I don't think they can have been here long " said Dickie : " two or three days at the outside." And shortly afterwards Tony and Matthews returned to bear out his opinion.

" They were both together at Bassett's place " the detective-sergeant informed them. " This was Parker's load on Tuesday morning all right, but they both say it was ordered a fortnight ago."

Beale considered for a moment, and then turned to his companions.

" Come on " he said—" a spot of manual labour won't hurt you. I want to see what the floor of this shed looks like."

" What do you think you're going to find ? " asked the reporter presently.

" All or nothing " replied Beale. " Chiefly burnt matches."

When the floor was clear he took from his pocket a powerful torch, and shone it carefully over the surface of the ground.

" You're unlucky " remarked Tony.

" Unlucky my foot ! " retorted Beale, straightening himself. " Look at that."

He indicated a small patch of earth the size of a dinner-plate, round which he had drawn a circle with his finger. They examined it in turn.

" You're right, sir ! " exclaimed Matthews, with animation. " I don't remember much natural history, but I'm pretty sure grass don't grow upside down. We need a couple of spades."

" Well, there's one up there " answered Tony, reaching for the torch, and shining it on to a ledge just beneath the roof of the shed. The expert leapt forward.

" Don't touch ! " he shouted.

He stood on tip-toe, and with gloved hands very carefully lifted it down. The blade was old and worn,

179

and the handle loose. Next he motioned silently for the torch, while fumbling in his pocket for a magnifying glass ; and then he faced the others with a smile.

" I bet a quid this is the weapon " he declared. " Smart work, Mr Purdon. ' Seek and ye shall find ' still goes."

Tony looked gratified.

" Can I have that stuffed too ? " he enquired, but no one took any notice. Beale was examining the shelf, and Dickie had his note-book out, and was putting down in capital letters the legend : ' THE SPADE OF DEATH '.

" Glad the others aren't here " he remarked. Beale nodded absently.

" Tony " he said, " take Matthews to the station, will you ? Leave this spade there, and get hold of at least two more. Bring a camera as well."

While they waited the reporter made shorthand notes, and his companion re-examined the ground on which the shed was built.

" Here you are " he called presently, holding out two burnt matches before putting them away in an envelope. " Never say I'm a false prophet."

A moment later Dickie paused in his labours, his pencil in the air.

" What made you decide to clear the mangolds out ? " he asked. " Because they were put in between the time of the murder and the finding of the body ? "

" Yes."

" But don't forget that Parker says he ought to have delivered them Monday night."

" I hadn't forgotten—I thought they might have made a yarn up between them."

" Don't you think still so ? "

" No—I'm inclined to believe that Bassett hadn't anything to do with it."

" But good lord, man ! "

Beale smiled.

" Tell you about that some other time " he promised. " I wish they'd hurry."

The reporter frowned.

" I don't get it " he grunted, " but you probably know best.   As I see things, the murderer—whoever he was—must have known the spade was here ; fetched it—that accounts for one match ; waited for Tatham, killed him, disposed of him, and then come back here ; cleaned the spade—hence the topsyturvy grass root ; put it on the shelf, striking the second match to make sure he'd got somewhere near the same place again ; and then cleared off."

Beale regarded him admiringly.

" Very clever ! " he said.   " That's covered most of the points nicely—but of course it's hopelessly wrong. Things are much worse than that."

The car returned just as Dickie began his inevitable question.

" But how can they be worse ?   What do you mean ? "

He understood within quarter of an hour.   Three feet down they came upon the second body ; and after one look at the face Tony was just able to gasp out ' Drive your cart and your plow over the bones of the dead ' before going outside to be very sick.

## CHAPTER XXIII

### 2.0 PM—4.0 PM

THE afternoon was a trying one for Beale.   Although he left the body to Matthews and Dr Hatherley, he found more than enough to occupy his time.   For a start he commandeered all three of Miss Frankes' keepers, and one of her gardeners, and set them to protect Pond Meadow until a regular police guard could take over.

The news of the discovery had spread quickly through the village, and every inhabitant seemed to have left his or her normal occupation in the hope of seeing a bloodstain at least, if not the corpse itself. They were disapproved of officially, but tolerated as long as they kept on the move, and did not attempt to do more than look. When cars from neighbouring places began to arrive, however, Beale's patience gave out. He telephoned to Shale, and in half an hour there were four police pickets on duty on the main roads, and no one was allowed to approach the village without a cast-iron excuse. One baker, undaunted, laid the foundations of a modest fortune by smuggling people through in his van, until his stratagem was discovered.

Beale also rang up Scotland Yard, and had a short talk with Superintendent Vinney.

" Another body, eh ? " exclaimed his superior. " Bloodthirsty lot."

He listened to a brief account of the steps which had led to its discovery, and was liberal with his praise.

" Can you manage all right, or do you want me to come down ? I could, at a pinch."

" I'd rather carry on for a bit, if you don't mind, sir."

" Not at all. I've got a very pretty forgery to look after. Anything I can do ? "

Beale requested any available information about Ambrose McFeish—since his report had not yet arrived ; and a complete list of all railway tickets issued from Charing Cross or intermediate stations to Shale Junction or Wyre Halt during the past ten days. He finally hung up with a feeling of relief that Vinney was not the sort of man to let another corpse, however mutilated, flurry him.

Later he gave the rest of the press a short interview, in the course of which he flatly forbade them to pester him.

Then he and Tony went into Shale, where he interviewed most of the railway staff, from station-master to porter, in the hope that someone would remember a stranger who had either enquired about trains to Wyre recently, or actually bought a ticket, even if he had never used it ; but without success. He also left instructions for a second list to be made out of all tickets for Shale or Wyre given up within the same period of time that Scotland Yard was covering the other end, and had a talk with the ticket-collector. The latter, however, was positive that only three tickets had been given up for the Halt on Monday the 19th.

The head porter was unhelpful.

" Short gent, might 'ave bin alone, brown 'air, big muscles, carryin' 'is own bag as like as not, *if* 'e 'ad one, no tellin' what 'e wore neither—lumme, sir, you wants a fortune-teller. I seen a couple of 'undred like that."

" What's the man wanted for, Inspector ? " asked the station-master. " In connection with the Rector's murder ? "

" No " replied Beale, getting up : " in connection with his own. Good afternoon."

Next they went to the police-station, to start enquiries at all local hotels and lodging-houses. From there Beale telephoned to Maidstone, spoke to the Chief Constable, and was again assured that he had a perfectly free hand. Before returning they also visited Rattan's offices to arrange for another inquest.

Later still Beale went up to Wyre Place. There was some sort of hope in his mind that in spite of what he had previously said Curtis might be inclined to identify the body as that of the stranger who had travelled down with him on the earlier train. But again he was disappointed.

" Five foot four ? " repeated the man in bed.

" Well, say five-five in his shoes."

Curtis shook his head.

" I don't think it could possibly be the same man. The impression I've got is that the chap I saw was pretty big. Of course, I may be wrong—I didn't get much of a look at him : but I don't think so. Damn awkward for you having all his clothes pinched—have a job tracing him, won't you ? "

Beale smiled a little bitterly.

" I'm having it " he answered.

" You can't remember whether he had a case or not ? "

" There again I'm not sure, but I don't think so."

" Pity.—How's the cold ? "

" Not so good. As a matter of fact, I feel pretty grubby. I suppose Hatherley's busy, but you might ask him to come up when he's free."

" Yes, I will " Beale promised. " Oh, by the way, I want to ask you for some information in confidence. I mean, I don't want you to tell anyone I've asked you."

Curtis looked mystified.

" I'll tell you anything I can " he said. " What's the trouble ? "

" I'd like to know something about your aunt's companion."

" Janet ? Good lord, what's she been up to ? "

" Nothing, as far as I know, but I'd like to get hold of a little more about her. For instance, how long has she been here ? "

" About three months—just over. As a matter of fact, I got her the job."

" I see " said Beale, taking out his note-book. " Why ? "

" Oh, I don't know—why not ? I mean, my aunt needed somebody. Old Scraggsy, who'd been with her for about twenty years, died, and I shouldn't think it's much fun being on your own if you're blind. I happened to know that Janet was looking for a post of this sort. I wish you'd tell me why you want to know."

Beale thought quickly.

" My detective-sergeant saw her at the inquest this morning " he explained, " and he thinks he remembers her face in connection with a robbery about three years ago."

" But that's nonsense."

" Yes, quite possibly—but there's still no harm in asking about her. If it was somebody else she's got nothing to worry about."

" No, I suppose not. But I'm sure your man's all wrong."

" Do you know yourself where she was three years ago ? "

Curtis considered.

" No, I can't say I do " he replied. " I met her the summer before last in London, at a friend's house. Tommy Jenkinson, the Army rugger player, if it helps. I don't remember what she was doing there, or why we palled up."

' Drunk again, I expect ' thought Beale to himself.

" I see—thanks " he said aloud. " I don't suppose there's anything in it."

" Positive there isn't."

" And you won't say anything to her ? "

" Good heavens no ! She'd have a fit. By the way " —as Beale rose to go : " I hear you're going to scout round for long-lost uncle Herbert."

" Yes—have you made it up with your aunt, then ? " Curtis shook his head ruefully.

" No—she told Janet to tell me. I don't suppose there's much chance of finding him, but it'd buck the old girl up no end if you could."

" I'll do my best. Did you ever see him ? "

" No. I was born in America, you know. To me he's only a legend—the wicked uncle of the fairy-tale, and all that. I gather he was rather fond of backing his fancy, but not so good at choosing the right one. I believe I'm supposed to take after him in some respects. Oh, I suppose she told you about his toe ? "

" Toe ? No—what about it ? Which toe ? "

" I don't know—never saw it. But I remember in the holidays I was always kicking things about, and always being told off. ' Nice little boys don't do that sort of thing '—you know. When that didn't work I used to be threatened that if I wasn't careful I'd break my toe like uncle Herbert, and have a crooked one for the rest of my life. But that's not much to go on— you can't very well go round asking people to take their shoes off—they might have holes in their socks——"

He broke off, coughing violently, and Beale seized

185

the opportunity to depart with a final promise to send up Hatherley as soon as possible. On his way out he was asked by the maid to speak to Miss Frankes. The old lady did not keep him long.

" Inspector " she said, " forgive me for bothering you, but I feel I can't rest until I've asked you one question. Please tell me the worst if necessary. Is this second dead man my brother ? "

Beale stared at her in amazement.

" Good heavens ! I mean, I beg your pardon. No, Miss Frankes, I'm glad to say he isn't. Your brother was a tall man, wasn't he ? Anyway, about average height, judging from the photograph you sent me."

" Yes—five feet seven or eight."

" And this man was on the short side—certainly not more than five feet five in his shoes. I don't think you need worry at all. As a matter of fact, the possibility hadn't even occurred to me. By the way, your nephew said something just now about a deformed foot."

" Toe " corrected the blind woman, " toe. Yes, Herbert broke it when he was a boy, and it never set properly. Fancy Ralph remembering that ! I meant to tell you myself. I'm very glad you've been able to set my mind at rest—I thought the girl must be wrong. But it's extremely selfish to worry you with my own affairs when there's so much to do. This second murder is appalling. Do you expect to discover any more bodies ? "

" I sincerely hope not " he replied, picking up his hat.

# CHAPTER XXIV

FROM THE 'EVENING SENTINEL' FOR THURSDAY
NOV. 27TH

## SECOND MURDER AT WYRE !

### NAKED BODY UNDER SHED

### THE SPADE OF DEATH

(From Our Own Correspondent, Richard Donovan)

*Wyre, Thursday.*

SHORTLY after noon today, in the presence of Chief-Inspector Edward Beale, of New Scotland Yard, who is investigating the Wyre murder, I witnessed the discovery of a second fatal tragedy in this hitherto peaceful Kentish village.

In one corner of Pond Meadow, the field near which the Rev. Arthur Tatham was found dead on Tuesday morning—see accompanying plan—a yard beneath the floor of a shed, there lay buried the completely nude body of an unknown man.

### TERRIBLE INJURIES

It will be no easy matter to identify the victim. His face has been mutilated beyond possibility of recognition, and both hands have also been disfigured, obliterating any trace of fingerprints. He appears to have been a man of about middle age, of good physique and more than ordinary muscular development.

187

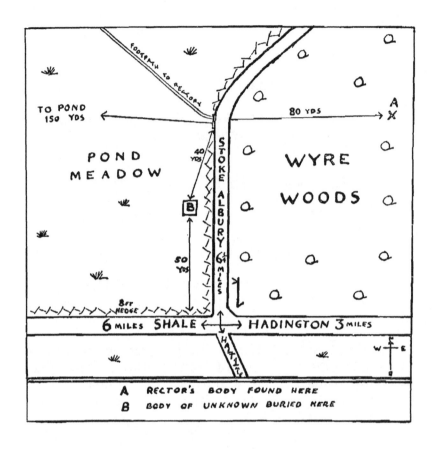

TO POND
150 YDS

80 YDS

A
X

FOOTPATH TO RECTORY

POND
MEADOW

40
YDS

STOKE ALBURY 6¼ MILES

WYRE

WOODS

B

50
YDS

8FT HEDGE

6 MILES SHALE ←→ HADINGTON 3 MILES

HATELY

W—E

A   RECTOR'S  BODY  FOUND  HERE
B   BODY  OF  UNKNOWN  BURIED  HERE

## The Scene of the Discovery

As the direct result of brilliant inferences drawn
from his recent enquiries in the neighbourhood,
Inspector Beale gave special attention to the shed,
whose poignant secret had yet to be unearthed.
Immediately after the adjournment of the inquest on
the late Rector—until Dec. 6th—four of us repaired
thither : namely, Chief-Inspector Beale himself, his
friend Mr Anthony Purdon, the well-known assistant-
editor of the 'Stockbroker', Detective-sergeant
Matthews, also of New Scotland Yard, and myself.
We found the shed to contain 4 cwt of mangolds.

## The Crucial Question

The difference between a great detective and a good one is that both, sooner or later, when faced with an unexpected problem, ask the one question which will elicit information of the first importance ; but the great detective asks it sooner.

I cannot speak for Detective-sergeant Matthews or Mr Purdon, but I know that my own reaction to the mangolds was one of disappointment. ' It's waste of time to stay here any longer ' I thought. But not so Inspector Beale, who immediately seized upon the vital point.

' How long have these mangolds been here ? ' he demanded. When it was learnt that they had been placed in the shed between the time of the Rector's death and the finding of his body, we at once prepared to remove them. Within a short time the ground was cleared.

## The First Clue

The Inspector soon noticed that a tuft of grass appeared to be growing upside-down. Upon declaring that several spades would be required, Mr Purdon drew attention to one lying on a shelf in the far corner of the shed.

*This spade, an old and much used one, is almost certainly the missing weapon.*

An examination is to be made by experts, but it may be taken for granted that its discovery is conclusive proof of the manner in which the Rev. Arthur Tatham was so brutally done to death.

## The Secret of the Shed

There was a still greater shock in store. For reasons which, at the time, I did not altogether grasp, Inspector Beale insisted that the floor of the shed should be dug up. I had put the condition of the grass root down to the murderer's having cleaned his gruesome weapon in the soil.

Mr Purdon drove Detective-sergeant Matthews to the police-station, returning shortly with three spades and a camera. Sergeant Rush, of the Kent Constabulary, accompanied them.

After ten minutes' digging there came slowly into view the body of the second murdered man.

(Here comes an incredibly bad photograph of Beale.)

### BRUTAL DISFIGUREMENT

I have never regarded a more ghastly sight. The face had been literally destroyed by repeated blows, probably with the spade ; and the hands also were cruelly lacerated. There was no shred of clothing by which identification might be effected. Near the remains, however, Inspector Beale, with his remarkable powers of perception, noticed a tangible and definite clue.

*I am not yet at liberty to state the nature of this discovery, to which the police attach the very greatest importance.*

### MEDICAL EVIDENCE

The body is now in the mortuary at the police-station. The local police-surgeon, Dr Reginald Hatherley, states that death took place within from forty-eight to seventy-two hours of its being found.

Exhaustive enquiries are being made into the movements of all tramps and strangers seen in the district recently.

Pond Meadow belongs to Mr William Bassett, a local farmer. It is completely surrounded by high thick hedges.

### WHO IS THE MURDERER ?

There can be little doubt that the same hand was responsible for both outrages. To whom does that hand belong ? What monster has struck down two fellow-creatures with such crude violence ? What was his motive ? Where has he concealed himself ?

There cannot be a right-thinking person who will not rejoice when the perpetrator of these enormities is brought to justice. The public will breathe a sigh of relief at the capture of one who has forfeited his right to live by a double and singularly brutal murder.

## CONFIDENCE IN THE POLICE

But I am certain that the criminal will not long escape. Chief-Inspector Beale, in charge of both enquiries, has a record of success of which any crime-investigator might be proud—even the mythical figure of the great Holmes himself.

It will be remembered that in July of 1932 he was responsible for the arrest of Albert Reddish, the Sussex Strangler, with whom, as he is fond of relating, he breakfasted for a week without being aware of the true identity of his sinister table-companion.

## LATE NEWS

Victim of second Wyre murder found to have had dental plates removed. Body exhibits no outstanding physical peculiarities. Height 5 ft 4 ins without shoes ; dark brown hair.

STOP PRESS   No fingerprints on spade.

# CHAPTER XXV

## 4.45 PM—5.45 PM

THE clock in the hall had just struck eleven, which Tony worked out as meaning quarter to five. For over half an hour the alleged rival of Sherlock Holmes had been sitting in an arm-chair deep in thought. From time to time he jotted something down in his note-book, but more often than not crossed it out a few moments later.

Tony had just finished reading Donovan's story in the ' Evening Sentinel ', a copy of which had arrived from Shale inscribed ' With the author's compliments '.

" Your pal does you proud " he said, seeing that the Inspector was beginning to lose the glassy look in his eye. " Want to see ? "

Beale took the newspaper, and read it with several chuckles.

" It's terribly involved in parts " he remarked, " and the grammar isn't always above suspicion. ' Upon declaring that several spades would be required, Mr Purdon drew our attention . . .', etc. This photo's even worse than the other one, too, and not in the best position. But you get your bit of credit."

" Not enough, though."

" Not enough ? Greedy fellow ! "

Tony regarded him severely.

" According to this " he pointed out, " you no sooner set eyes on the mangolds than you demanded to know how long they'd been there. Whereas according to my memory you'd probably still be gaping if I hadn't explained why they were there at all."

Beale laughed.

" Sorry to steal your thunder " he said.

" Hullo ! Here's Matthews come to cheer us up. I'm afraid the tea's cold."

" Tea ! " repeated Matthews indignantly round the door. " I don't want tea, sir, I want beer—and a bottle of smelling-salts " he added, as an afterthought. " That body was none too fresh. Shall I bring you both some ? "

" If you're talking about beer again, yes."

The detective-sergeant returned shortly with three tankards and the smelling-salts. Tony could not help smiling as he watched the little man sit down, and solemnly take first a long drink, and then a correspondingly long sniff from the small green bottle.

" Well, did you do anything ? " enquired Beale at last. " If you did, you're one up on me. I've just been wasting my breath and wearing out my brains."

Matthews admitted cautiously that he thought his labours might be not entirely without result.

" But it was a filthy job, sir " he said, " and I really can't tell you anything yet. The trouble was that I had to take photographs instead of prints, and goodness knows whether they'll be any good. I'm rather doubtful."

" And if not, does that mean you're stumped ? " asked Tony. The detective-sergeant shook his head.

" Not necessarily, sir."

He looked at Beale, who had closed his eyes.

" Have I got time to explain it to Mr Purdon, sir ? "

" Lord yes! Don't mind me. I'm asleep till they find the next victim. You'll be off to town tonight, I suppose ? "

" Yes sir. I'll go up on the 8.40 from Shale, if that's all right."

" Why not all go up together by car ? " suggested Tony. " It wouldn't take more than an hour and a half each way."

Beale vetoed this idea.

" No, I don't think so, thanks all the same. For one thing, I want some sleep tonight——"

" Which is a reflection on my driving."

" Not at all—merely a reflection on the instability of human life. Today we are, and tomorrow we're being shovelled off the main road so that the rest of the traffic can get by. Also, I might possibly want to prowl round later, and I'd rather like someone with me. Don't mind, do you ? "

" Not a bit."

Meanwhile Matthews had taken out his note-book and a pencil.

" It's like this, sir " he began. " There's four main types of fingerprints : loops, arches, whorls, and composites. I won't waste time explaining the difference ; for purposes of classification, loops include arches, and composites go with whorls. The proportions for the two groups are roughly 65% and 35%

" Now, when a man's prints have been taken, they're split up into five pairs, like this :

$$\left\{\begin{array}{l}\text{Rt thumb}\\ \text{Rt index}\end{array}\right. \left\{\begin{array}{l}\text{Rt mid.}\\ \text{Rt ring}\end{array}\right. \left\{\begin{array}{l}\text{Rt lit.}\\ \text{Lt thumb}\end{array}\right. \left\{\begin{array}{l}\text{Lt index}\\ \text{Lt mid.}\end{array}\right. \left\{\begin{array}{l}\text{Lt ring}\\ \text{Lt lit.}\end{array}\right.$$

Each of those pairs can be one of four different arrangements : $\dfrac{L}{L}$ ; $\dfrac{L}{W}$ ; $\dfrac{W}{L}$ ; or $\dfrac{W}{W}$. Do you see that, sir ? "

" Yes."

" Then with all five pairs the total number of possible arrangements is 4 ; that is, there are 1024 different files.

" The point, of course, with any given set of prints, is to find out quickly which file it belongs to. That's done by giving each arrangement a different numerical value.

" You set the ten prints out as before, in pairs, and give a particular value to the whorls, according to which pair they're in—top or bottom's all the same ; but nothing to the loops. A whorl in the first pair counts 16, in the second 8, in the third 4, in the fourth 2, and in the last 1.

" Take an example at random : $\dfrac{L\ L\ L\ W\ W}{W\ L\ L\ W\ L}$. That comes to $\dfrac{0+0+0+2+1}{16+0+0+2+0}$, which means $\dfrac{3}{18}$. Is that clear ? "

" Yes, rather—then what happens ? "

" You add one each to top and bottom, turn **the** fraction over, and there you are : $\frac{19}{4}$. Then with a filing cabinet of thirty-two squares each way, the one you want is the nineteenth from the left in the fourth row down."

" Just a minute : why add the ones, and why tip it over ? "

Matthews smiled.

" You do the first " he said " because if all ten fingers were loops—which is about the commonest arrangement—you'd get $\frac{0}{0}$. That is, the prints would have to be tucked away in an imaginary file, and even the Yard couldn't deal with a thing like that.

" As for the turning over, that's simply due to the system used for filing. If the cabinets were arranged according to another key, then it wouldn't be necessary. All clear so far ? "

" Yes—carry on. This sounds like genuine inside information. One day I'll tell you how the Stock Exchange works."

" You mean if " put in Beale, somewhat obscurely ; but his remark passed unheeded.

" Well sir " Matthews went on, " as you can guess, some arrangements are more frequent than others. That means that certain files have got to be sub-divided, and then split up again if necessary. We do that in several ways, but I'd better stick to the set of prints in question.

" The doctor and I went over the fingers very carefully, patching them up. They weren't actually as smashed about as I thought, though they all had bits of skin missing here and there, and cuts across the ridges. In seven cases I was able to make pretty sure whether they were loops or whorls. Two of the other three were past help, and the other was too doubtful to be worth making a guess at. Here's the corpse's print-arrangement as far as I can make it out.

$$\left\{\begin{matrix}\text{Rt thumb}\\\text{Rt index}\end{matrix}\right. \quad \left\{\begin{matrix}\text{Rt mid.}\\\text{Rt ring}\end{matrix}\right. \quad \left\{\begin{matrix}\text{Rt lit.}\\\text{Lt thumb}\end{matrix}\right. \quad \left\{\begin{matrix}\text{Lt index}\\\text{Lt mid.}\end{matrix}\right. \quad \left\{\begin{matrix}\text{Lt ring}\\\text{Lt lit.}\end{matrix}\right.$$

$$\frac{L}{W} \qquad \frac{(x)}{W} \qquad \frac{L}{(y)} \qquad \frac{L}{(z)} \qquad \frac{W}{L}$$

" That means that the right middle finger, (x), the left thumb, (y), and the left middle finger, (z), might be either loop or whorl. I think the last one's a loop, but I can't be sure. Now sir, how many possible arrangements do you make that to be ? "

" Eight " said Tony promptly.

" That's right. Here they are, with their values "— displaying a page of his note-book.

$$(1) \cdots \frac{L\ \ L\ \ L\ \ L\ \ W}{W\ \ W\ \ L\ \ L\ \ L} = \frac{1}{24} = \frac{25}{2} \text{ (large)}$$

$$(2) \cdots \frac{L\ \ L\ \ L\ \ L\ \ W}{W\ \ W\ \ L\ \ W\ \ L} = \frac{1}{26} = \frac{27}{2}$$

$$(3) \cdots \frac{L\ \ L\ \ L\ \ L\ \ W}{W\ \ W\ \ W\ \ L\ \ L} = \frac{1}{28} = \frac{29}{2}$$

$$(4) \cdots \frac{L\ \ L\ \ L\ \ L\ \ W}{W\ \ W\ \ W\ \ W\ \ L} = \frac{1}{30} = \frac{31}{2}$$

$$(5) \cdots \frac{L\ \ W\ \ L\ \ L\ \ W}{W\ \ W\ \ L\ \ L\ \ L} = \frac{9}{24} = \frac{25}{10}$$

$$(6) \cdots \frac{L\ \ W\ \ L\ \ L\ \ W}{W\ \ W\ \ L\ \ W\ \ L} = \frac{9}{26} = \frac{27}{10}$$

$$(7) \cdots \frac{L\ \ W\ \ L\ \ L\ \ W}{W\ \ W\ \ W\ \ L\ \ L} = \frac{9}{28} = \frac{29}{10}$$

$$(8) \cdots \frac{L\ \ W\ \ L\ \ L\ \ W}{W\ \ W\ \ W\ \ W\ \ L} = \frac{9}{30} = \frac{31}{10}$$

" Now luckily the only big accumulation there is the first. That one anyway will be sub-divided, and to explain how we do it I shall have to tell you a bit about loops and whorls.

" Generally speaking, all prints have an inner terminus, or point of the core, and at least one outer terminus, or delta. If they're whorls they have two, one either side of the core.

" The delta is either the point nearest to the inner terminus where one ridge bifurcates, or else the ridge or point immediately in front of where two parallel ridges diverge—still taking the nearest to the core."

He held a magnifying-glass over one of his fingers.

" This one's a whorl. There's the left-hand delta, and you can see that from there the ridges go either side of the inner terminus.

" Now, to sub-divide loops, where there's only one delta, you do it by ridge-counting ; that is, you find out how many ridges cut a line drawn from delta to core. Except when all the fingers are loops, anything up to nine in the index finger, or ten in the middle, is classed as I, and anything over those as O. You take notice of those two fingers only, and then not of the middle if it's different to the index.

" With whorls, on the other hand, you don't classify by ridge-counting, because you'd get different results for the two deltas nearly every time, so you use ridge-tracing instead. You take the lower ridge of the left-hand delta, follow it round, going to the one below if it stops short, and see whether it finishes up inside the right-hand delta, meets it, or goes outside. Actually it counts as a meet if there aren't more than two ridges between.

" Then you class it accordingly as I, M, or O. As before, you do that for the index finger anyway, and for the middle if it's a whorl, too.

" Now let's take the first arrangement—the big one.

$$\frac{\text{L L L L W}}{\text{W W L L L}} = \frac{25}{2}$$

197

"The right index is a whorl; but the middle's a loop, so you forget it. If you remember, it might be I, M, or O. I'm fairly sure it's M, so first go off I shall class it as that.

"Next look at the left hand. There index and middle fingers are the same, both loops, and too damaged to tell if they were I or O. That means four possible arrangements : $\frac{M}{II}$; $\frac{M}{IO}$; $\frac{M}{OI}$; $\frac{M}{OO}$. When you're subdividing, the right hand goes on top."

"But if you're wrong about the M" said Tony, "then you'll have twelve possible arrangements instead of four, won't you?"

"Yes sir—exactly. There's just two more things. When either or both index fingers are loops, you take notice of their direction. With the palm of the hand downwards, if they slope towards the thumb they're called radial loops, and if towards the little finger they're ulnar loops. They must do one or the other, unless they're arches being classified as loops, when you can't use that method.

"In this case, the left index is an ulnar loop.

"The last point is this. When the right-hand little finger is a loop you count the ridges from outer to inner terminus as before, but put it down as a number instead of a letter. The corpse's little-finger count is either five or six.

"I'm afraid I haven't made it very clear, sir, but this would be the full formula for case (1), supposing that the right index is M, and the left index and middle fingers both I : $\dfrac{25}{2} \dfrac{M}{U\ II}$ 5 (or 6).

"I've left a space above the U because the right index is a whorl, and not a loop, and so can't be either ulnar or radial.

"Well, sir, you can see that I've got it down from 1024 files to somewhere the right side of 50, even with the two ridge-counts, and if I'm wrong about the right index being M. Luckily I shall have another check, too, when I'm looking through. The corpse's left ring-

198

finger, which I've so far classed as a whorl, is actually a central-pocket loop. It comes under whorls because it really belongs to composites, and not to loops. If a record that seems to be all right otherwise hasn't got a central-pocket loop for that finger, then it's a dud. And when I've got the ones that do seem to fit, I shall compare them with the photos. There shouldn't be many, and with any luck I'll soon know if we've had the man through our hands before."

" Thanks very much " said Tony. " It's certainly a business-like system, and I don't see how you can help spotting them if you've got the prints in stock. Or is there a snag you haven't mentioned ? "

Matthews grinned.

" The only trouble would be, sir, that I may have classed a border-line case as a loop when it ought to be a central-pocket or lateral-pocket loop, and so come under whorls. That would put the whole blessed count out. If I've made that mistake at all, I think it'll be with the left little finger; but I'm hoping I haven't."

Here Beale opened his eyes.

" Very interesting " he declared. " I begin to believe you really do deserve a holiday. But the time's getting on, and we ought to do what we can while we're still together. Let's see where we stand."

# CHAPTER XXVI

" We've found a corpse " he began, " which has been dead between forty-eight and seventy-two hours, reckoning from about 1.0 today. We know that it couldn't have been put in that shed after midday on Tuesday, nor before dusk on Monday, and the probability—almost a certainty—is that the man was killed anything from a couple of minutes to a couple of hours before Tatham."

" I suppose it's quite certain that Tatham *was* killed last ? " asked Tony.

" Yes, I think so. For one thing, if he wasn't, bang goes the theory that he left the pond because of something fishy going on by the shed, and interrupted the burial.

" Now, we can't get much farther with the Rector's death until we know something about this other murder. We've found out how and why Tatham was killed, but that still doesn't tell us who did it. We've got to start again—and with a pretty big handicap, too."

He sighed.

" I wish " he said " that naked faceless corpses were forbidden by law."

" I thought they were " murmured Tony.

" I also wish " Beale went on imperturbably " that a cohort of devils would remove this particular one to the top of a very high mountain, well out of reach. Then I could theorize about it for ever, with no chance of proving myself wrong. It is the body of a foreign anarchist known in political circles as ' The Shadow '. He was disposed of by Lords Beaverbrook and Rothermere, hand in hand, in order that the Empire may go on empirically searching for world supremacy unhindered. On his forehead is written ' So perish all traitors ', but unfortunately it isn't readable because they used invisible ink.

" Or it is the immortal remains of Torquemada, executed by order of the Oxford and Cambridge Crossword Society for carelessly permitting more than two clues in the same puzzle to be solvable without the aid of an honours degree.

" However, returning to earth : there are four or five points that stick out.

" (1) : both murders were done by the same man, or group of men. There's no question that both were committed with a spade, and hardly any that in each case it was the same spade. If there were two independent murderers, then we're faced with either the improbability that both chose the same unusual weapon to kill men on the same evening in approximately the same place ; or the impossibility that the man who killed Tatham used the self-same implement with which the first murderer had just killed and buried the unknown body—presumably so that we should think it was the same person's work."

" Why ' impossibility ' ? " asked Tony. " Call the second murderer Y. He's present when the stranger's done in—hidden behind a bush, of course. He waits until X has finished the burial-service, put the spade back on the shelf, and departed. He then retrieves spade, waits for Tatham, slaughters him, carries second body into the woods, returns to the shed, replaces the spade where *he* found it, and likewise departs. Flourish of trumpets. End of Act II. Interval of twelve hours. Act III : another part of the wood. Enter gamekeeper and dog. Dog: 'Woof!' Gamekeeper: 'Hist!' Dog: 'Woof!' Gamekeeper: 'What is't?' Dog: 'Bow wow!' Gamekeeper: 'How now?'"

This dramatic interlude was cut short with the bottle of smelling-salts.

" You'd make a rotten playwright, but you might do better as a criminal—the first part was certainly ingenious. You and Dickie would make a good pair."

" Well, it's possible, isn't it ? "

" Oh yes, I'll grant you that. But it didn't happen,

all the same. The pond theory's worked so far—it's given us one walking-stick, one spade, and one mutilated body—, and I'm not going to scrap it for something that's only barely possible."

Tony thought rapidly.

"We can combine them" he declared. "What fetched Tatham to his doom was the match that Y struck looking for the spade. Having cut things a bit fine, he meant to tear after the old boy, and bash his head in when he caught up ; and instead of that, along comes his victim, slightly out of breath, to save him the trouble."

"Well, I'll give you a case of whisky if you're right. But you aren't, so let's get on.

"(2) : it's plain that X is a local. If you, for instance, are a stranger in these parts, and just as you've finished burying someone you've killed a man comes up to ask who the something you are, and what the something else you've been doing, you don't need to kill him, because he doesn't know you. You simply knock him out. It's night, remember, when it wouldn't have been easy for Tatham to see an unfamiliar face so clearly that he'd be able to recognize it again. I'm sure he wouldn't have been killed unless it was absolutely necessary—unless he knew who X was.

"It wouldn't matter that he could say it was a short man with a walrus moustache and a pork-pie hat, or a tall thin one with rabbit teeth and button boots : there's a thousand people who'd fit his description, even if it was as accurate as that, which it wouldn't have been. But if he can put a name to the man, then he knows too much to be left alive.

"Another reason, too, is that a stranger simply wouldn't have dared do the burying in a comparatively exposed place like Pond Meadow. He couldn't possibly risk mucking about in that shed for an hour or more, even if he'd come on it by chance, and thought what a handy place it looked.

"There is one case, however, which gets over both those difficulties."

202

" The man who doesn't live here now, but either has done once, or else happens to be known to Tatham by sight, and also to have a fair working knowledge of the village life " said Tony.

" Yes, exactly. Against him seems to be the fact that since he was in the district at all on Monday night, he was here either for the express purpose of committing the first murder, or for some other reason. In the first case the murder was premeditated, which I'm not yet inclined to believe. As well there's the probability that he'd be prepared to prove he was somewhere else, which makes it unnecessary for him to kill Tatham.

" In the second he's here to visit somebody, say, or just happens to be passing through the village. In either case, some means of transport other than feet seems to be involved. That holds good for the premeditated murder too. But there aren't any signs of how he came or went. A car doesn't seem possible. A bicycle localizes him considerably, and it isn't the ideal way of leaving a place if you don't want to be seen. The other possibility would be that he came by train and left on foot, which would presumably make him the man Curtis saw at the Halt ; in which case, where the devil did the corpse come from ?

" (3) : it was of paramount importance to the murder that his first victim should not be found ; and, if that happened, even more vital that he shouldn't be recognized. That's obvious from the fact that so much trouble was taken to avoid both contingencies, especially the recognition one. I think it finally rules out your homicidal maniac, thank goodness ! The hiding of the body came unstuck, but at the moment he's got us guessing over the identity. As I told you earlier, that was my reason for getting Dickie to put in that bit about the ' tangible and definite clue ', well shrouded in mystery. I know it sounds as if I'm contradicting what I said this morning, but I'm not really. As long as I only thought it was a local, I didn't want to let it out. Now that I'm pretty sure, it doesn't matter : X must know that I know.

" This second murder's altered things. His plans have gone astray, because we've found what he hoped we shouldn't find ; and it won't hurt for him to think he's worse off than he really is : he may try to put things right when they aren't wrong. He'll know the ' clue ' was nothing belonging to the corpse—you bet he took good care of that——, so naturally he'll think he must have dropped something out of his own pocket."

" Cruelty to murderers " remarked Tony. " But it sounds a good wheeze."

" Yes, it's worth trying. Anyway, to get back to the destruction of the identity—— All right, don't glare : you understand what I mean. It's so important that X does it with the greatest thoroughness. He takes away everything except the actual corpse ; he batters in the face, removing the false teeth first—people can be traced by peculiar plates or fillings, you know, and have been, especially in detective stories ; and, as a master-stroke, he does his best to stop us from taking fingerprints. It remains to be seen if Matthews has been too clever for him.

" One thing that might be in our favour is the fact that he should have thought the last precaution necessary. It seems to argue that either he had reason to think the man's prints might be already available to the police ; or else that he didn't know him well enough to be sure they weren't."

Here Matthews broke in.

" I've just remembered I've got something to tell you, sir. It struck me this afternoon that you couldn't smash a face in like that without getting splashed. I got Hatherley to pay special attention, and he says it looks as if the head was wrapped up in something— a coat, or a sack. He found one or two shreds of material, but so blood-soaked that he doesn't think they'll be much help, though I'll take them up to the Yard. Whatever it was, it must have been pretty thin, because the character of the weapon was clear enough.

" By the way, sir, Hatherley told me he went to the

pictures in Shale on Monday night. I didn't ask him outright, so you needn't worry. He saw ' The Thin Man '—but I'm getting off the point. What I meant to say was this.

" For X to have done the disfiguring that way seems to show that he knocked the man out first, and then battered him to death when he'd found something to do it with ; first taking care, so as not to get blood all over himself, to cover the head up—probably with the man's own coat. Now that suggests another reason why X must have been a local."

He looked enquiringly at the other two, but they shook their heads.

" Well sir, it puts an interval between the first blow and the actual murder. He hits the man under the jaw as a start-off ; but it's not much good doing that if he doesn't know where to get hold of something to kill him with, and spoil his looks. The shed's tucked away near a hedge you can hardly see through, and you wouldn't go in that direction to get to anywhere else, so anyway he'd have a job to persuade the body to walk across to it. But everything would be all right if he knocked him out by the gate, and then carried him there, providing he knew the spade was inside beforehand. I very much doubt if anybody who didn't live in the village *would* know."

" In other words " said Beale, " you're pointing your finger at Bassett. There I disagree, but the rest seems sensible. X must be a pretty cold-blooded sort of creature, though. Once he's made his plans, it's all so heartless and deliberate.

" (4) : it's not much good taking something in order to get rid of it—especially when it simply mustn't be found—unless you can hide it satisfactorily. From X's point of view it would be more dangerous to take the clothes, and be seen with them in his possession, even by accident, than to leave them. The fact that he did take them makes it obvious that he was desperately afraid of his victim's being traced. He can only have had one reason : because he was certain that if we know who the dead man is we'll be well on the way to finding out who killed him ; or at any rate, what the motive was.

" He did remove the clothes, and the point that concerns us is : what did he do with them ? I see three possibilities : that they've been totally destroyed, partially destroyed, or not destroyed at all."

" Wait a bit " requested Tony : " what exactly do you mean by destroyed ? It's too comprehensive."

Beale acknowledged the rebuke with a smile.

" I was thinking chiefly of fire " he admitted, " but I'll put it differently. X has dealt with the stuff in such a way that either we can't get any of it back ; or we could recover some or all of it if only we knew where to look. If he's sunk the lot off a channel steamer in a fog, for example, I'd call that total destruction ; but if he's put it inside the Lord Chancellor's wool-sack, then we can take it out again."

" Wouldn't that be treason ? Undermining the foundations of a state official, and so on ? "

" Order ! " demanded Beale. " Don't muddle the issue."

" As the duke said when his wife had twins. Sorry —I'll be good now. Let's inspect the three cases. Total loss doesn't interest us much, does it ? "

" No. All we can do is to pray hard there's still something to find. Now, presuming there is, what did he do with it ? "

Matthews, at whom he was looking, answered readily.

" Either he took it away with him to get rid of at leisure, or else he did it then and there."

" Yes, that divides it nicely " agreed Tony. " And if it's the first, then the stuff's as good as gone. He's had two and a half days."

" Well then " said Beale, " let's concentrate on the second—that he hid it somewhere within fairly reasonable distance of Pond Meadow. That means that if we search everything and everywhere we're bound to find it—in theory, anyway. But before we start think-

206

ing about particular places, let's make sure we're not going to be wasting our time. What is there in favour of taking the stuff away ? "

" Easier to get rid of " suggested Tony. " He needn't hurry, and he'll be able to see what he's doing."

" And have time to go through the pockets " added Matthews. " He might want to. Also he can get on making an alibi quicker. I think it's safer, too, on the whole."

" Yes, probably. The objections to taking it away are : risk of being seen carrying it ; of having it found in his possession ; or anticipated difficulties in disposal. He might, for instance, only be able to do so by taking someone else into his confidence."

" I think " said Tony, summing up " he'd take it only if he was certain he could smuggle it indoors without anybody seeing. Otherwise he'd bury it like he buried the body. Anyway, I should have done. It's always possible, too, that he wouldn't be able to take it away : he might have his hands full of parcels."

He looked at Matthews, who hesitated a moment.

" I expect you're right, sir. But I'd be terrified that once the body was found there'd be such a thorough search that it'd be a miracle if the stuff didn't turn up."

" Well " said Beale, taking charge again, " that brings us to ways and means of disposing of things. We'll have to overlook the fact that we don't know exactly what it is we hope to find. It may be just a bundle of clothes, or it may be a suitcase."

" And if that's so " put in Matthews, " the body was probably a stranger. I was wondering about that this afternoon, too. Did Curtis say if the man who got off the train with him had one, sir ? "

" He wasn't sure, but he wouldn't say definitely that he hadn't."

" Problem " said Tony suddenly : " estimate the victim's probable clothing : add—perhaps—one slightly-soiled clerical hat ; and then find the smallest case that could hold them, allowing for possible previous contents of said case."

Beale frowned.

" Yes, ' possible previous contents ' is a snag I hadn't thought of " he admitted.

" But you can get a hell of a lot more into almost any case " remarked Matthews hopefully " than you'd think possible. My mother's a marvel—pack Austin Reed's into a couple of trunks."

Tony smiled. He had not previously realized that for all his equine looks the detective-sergeant must undoubtedly have had human parents.

" Well, I hope you're right " said Beale. " Of course, things can always be tied on to the outside if necessary. Now back to ways of getting rid of things."

He smiled reflectively.

" Last night I was worrying about how to get hold of them " he told the others, in partial explanation.

" Now, you can bury what you want to hide, sink it, or just conceal it."

At this Tony laughed.

" The last way reminds me of the old chestnut : how is it possible to get 30% on an investment ? Answer : find a mug who's both able and willing to pay that much."

" I know, but it can't be helped. At all events, we can safely leave out sinking. Rush says there aren't any wells or quarry shafts in the neighbourhood, and the river's eight miles away. Next, burial, which you seem to favour. I don't, and I'll tell you why. In the first place, it limits me to an area dangerously near where the body is. I've got to use the same spade, you see ; at least, I don't suppose another would be very easy to get hold of at that time of night."

" Except by a farmer " Matthews objected.

" Bassett again ? I'll deal with him presently. The second reason I don't do any more digging is this. I know the clothes won't be looked for unless the body's found ; but immediately that happens, burial is *the* means of disposal that will leap straight to everybody's mind. Consequently I'll have not only the police, but every single person for miles round, staring suspiciously at any bit of ground that looks as if it's ever been touched by a spade.

"In X's place I shouldn't undress the man at all, if I daren't risk taking the clothes away, unless I'd already thought of a safe enough hiding-place near at hand. There are two points to make about the 'safe enough', one in our favour and the other not. First there's the undoubted tendency of most criminals to think they're cleverer than they really are. I know that characteristic applies chiefly to habitual criminals ; but I believe it's quite fair to transfer it to someone who's evidently decided that he's sharp enough to get away with double murder. Against that, however, we've got to put the fact that this man really is clever —anyway, as murderers go. A fool wouldn't have thought of the dental plates, and probably not of the fingers.

"It seems to me that our only real hope is for X to have considered he was being brilliant in hiding the stuff in a certain place that he knew of ; and for us to be even more brilliant by discovering that place without knowing of it."

"A tall order" remarked Tony.

"But not impossible. What one man can hide another can find ; and three heads ought to be better than one, even taking into account the difference in local knowledge. Now, you two be clever, and I'll pick the results to bits. I've already made my own suggestions to Rush, but that doesn't matter, and I shan't tell you what they were. Where ought we to look ? "

"In fact, a hiding-place to suit the case" murmured Tony.

Between them he and Matthews evolved a comprehensive list of places, which Beale annotated during supper.

| | | |
|---|---|---|
| **TO BE SEARCHED** | | |
| T=temporary hiding-place | √ =arranged for | |
| P=permanent  „  „ | ✕ =no good | |
| | * =enquire | |

| | | | |
|---|---|---|---|
| 1 | √ T or P | All local ponds, hedges, ditches, empty houses, garages, barns, and sheds, including digging below where body was found ; hollow trees, railway tunnels, and caves | ⎫<br>⎬ Both<br>⎭ |
| 2 | √ T or P | Cess-pools, drains, and hay-stacks | Matthews |
| 3 | * T or P | Dustbins | Tony |
| 4 | *    P | All houses now being built in neighbourhood | Matthews |
| 5 | √ T or P | The churchyard, especially graves and vaults | Both |
| 6 | ✕ T or P | The church itself, if open | Both |
| 7 | ✕ T ? | Scarecrows | Tony |
| 8 | * T & P | Unlighted bonfires | Matthews |
| 9 | ✕ T | Branches of a tree | Matthews |
| 10 | √ T or P | Enquire at local P.O. and carrier | Both |
| 11 | ✕ T | Unattended cars | Both |
| 12 | ✕ T | Empty railway carriages | Matthews |
| 13 | ✕ T | Empty milk-cans (!) | Tony |
| 14 | ✕ T | Stationary steam-rollers, traction-engines, etc. | Matthews |

# CHAPTER XXVII

JUST before half past seven Lucy cleared the table.

"Can I have these now, sir?" she asked Matthews, indicating the smelling-salts.

"You don't mean to say you like that horrible stink?" demanded Tony incredulously. The girl smiled.

"No sir, but I've got a headache."

"Well, if that doesn't cure it, nothing will."

"Now" said Beale, when she had gone, "I'll go through this with you. There's an hour before you need start getting ready, Matthews.

"I must say you've been very thorough. As a start I'm going to wash out of the list anything that doesn't fulfil two requirements. If the place is temporary, it must be such that X can remove the stuff without difficulty when he wants to, and leave it there meanwhile with a fair degree of safety. If it's permanent, there must be only an outside chance of its being found for a hell of a long time.

"All in the first two are being searched anyway. Incidentally, I'd have been prepared to bet that neither of you would hit on railway tunnels."

"Which shows what a plethora of talent we possess" remarked Tony.

"Possibly. The third one, dustbins, is quite a brainwave. It's a bit on the bold side, but X might have risked it. The only snags are, first, from his point of view, that he'd almost certainly have to split the stuff up, and each division would multiply the chances of discovery; and second, from ours, that all the local bins have probably been cleared since Monday night. But I'll have enquiries made.

"The next is good, too—the foundations of a house would make an ideal place. I'll get Rush on to that.

" The churchyard's being done, and the church itself is no good—it was locked, and nobody could have got in.

" The seventh, Tony, is a credit to your imagination, but not much practical use, I'm afraid. There can't be an awful lot of scarecrows about in winter, for one thing, and any farmer worth the name would spot a comparatively new suit on one. Besides, the body probably wore vest and pants, and I can't see anybody but a professional window-dresser struggling to get them on to a dummy in the middle of the night. Think of the footprints he'd leave, too.

" The next is much better—X would probably be overjoyed to get rid of the stuff by burning. I'll get people on to that as well. There shouldn't be many bonfires about.

" In the branches of a tree isn't safe enough, Matthews. It's all right for a football, but not for a bundle of clothes. You've got to remember that this stuff simply mustn't be found.

" The post-office and carrier are being done, though I don't think there's much hope.

" The last four are all temporary, and they violate the proviso that they must be within X's reach—except possibly the traction-engine, and I thought of that myself. Even if the stuff turned up as far away as Newcastle, say, it's ten to one that somebody would connect it with the present business. One of the garments, at any rate, must be fairly well soaked in blood.

" I'm also having all ploughed fields looked at. If he separated the stuff, it's just possible that he could have disposed of it that way, though unlikely, because of footprints again.

" Well, I think that's as far as we can get in that line at the moment, but don't put it out of your minds, and if either of you gets a really bright idea, let me know.

" And now for suspects."

" Just a minute, sir " put in Matthews, " There's

a point I'd like to discuss. Something's been worrying me every time you said how important it was to X for us not to know who was killed, and I've just found out what."

Beale suddenly smiled.

" That's funny " he remarked. " I'm pretty sure I know what you're going to say, for I've just thought of it myself—a moment before you spoke, as a matter of fact. You want to know what steps X has taken, or is going to take, to keep those people quiet who would otherwise begin to wonder what's happened to the victim."

Matthews grinned good-humoured acknowledgement.

" Just pipped me " he said.

" Oh no—call it a dead-heat. But it's certainly a problem."

" And depends chiefly on why he smashed the hands up : because he knew the man very well, or because he didn't know him well enough."

" Yes. If it's the first, we presume he also knows whom to get in touch with. But if it's the second he may be in a bit of a mess. Of course on the face of it he's more likely to have known the man than not. One doesn't often want to murder a comparative stranger."

" Unless he's a money-lender or a blackmailer " suggested Tony : " in which case it seems to raise X's social position. A working man, for instance, isn't usually able to offer good enough security for a big loan, and you don't kill a man because you owe him a few pounds. And I don't think that working men are very often worth blackmailing."

" We can't take that as certain, I'm afraid " said Beale. " You've withdrawn yourself too high above the common world. It might easily be an affair between equals in the matter of position : one labourer threatening to expose another labourer, possibly to his wife or his employer. And it's not really how much or how little you owe that makes you desperate, but the

213

fact that you do owe, and are being badgered, and can't pay.

"I haven't said much about the victim's identity beyond mentioning about a thousand times that it's been concealed, but we might speculate. He's got to be either another local, or a stranger—unless he's a half-and-half too. If he's a stranger—which I think he was—, then there's more chance that should you be right about money-lending or blackmail you're also right about the social position. He wouldn't have come down here on a little job, and a big one means a biggish man this end, socially speaking."

"I think he was a stranger, too" agreed Matthews. "I mean to say, the more local the bloke was, the quicker people are going to start asking where he's got to, and the less use it is to try and conceal the identity."

"I don't see that the second part follows" objected Tony.

"Well sir, it's like this. If he was a stranger, before he came down here he presumably told his wife or his friends or his landlady he was going away, and so they mightn't worry for a day or two, especially if they didn't know where. But if he was a local, he'd be expected back ; and when he didn't turn up, questions would start being asked. Now the body's been discovered, you'd naturally think that anybody within reach with a friend or relative missing would come along to find out if this is him ; but they haven't. The identification wouldn't be so hard with something definite to go on. Once you get somebody saying that their Alf was five foot four, and that sort of build, and he had false teeth too, and they recognize the shape of his shins—well, there you are, or pretty nearly."

"But a wife in London might think just the same when she read the paper. I mean, she might easily wonder if it could be her husband, especially if she was at all nervous."

"I only hope she does, sir. All I'm saying is that because we've had no local enquiries yet, it doesn't

214

look as if he was a local. I shan't be surprised to hear at the Yard tonight that they've had a dozen people round."

" Whoever he was, I don't think he could have told anyone he was going to Wyre " said Beale, " or we'd have had 'em already.

" Anyway, Tony, thanks for the help. But until we know the name of the corpse, and something about him, I don't see that we can tell what steps X has in mind to stop enquiries. Let's get on to suspects. First of all, I'll deal with Bassett.

" As I told Dickie this morning, when I asked about the mangolds—I mean "—bowing to Tony, " when you so kindly prompted me to ask about them—, I was thinking that Parker and Bassett might have arranged things between them. But the finding of the spade made me doubt if Bassett had anything to do with it, and what I've learnt since confirms that view. There doesn't seem to be anyone round here who knew there ever was a spade in that shed. None of Bassett's men admits to having seen it. There are three of them, and they ought to know, if anybody does, and they aren't likely to be all murderers. From the look of the thing itself, too, and the condition of the shelf, it had obviously been there donkey's years."

" Twelve months come next dung-spreading " murmured Tony.

" Or even longer. Its original position, by the way. seems to have been about a couple of inches from where we found it. Now, if Bassett had used it, I don't think he'd have left it there. He'd know it would never be missed, and therefore he'd feel quite safe in taking it away, which is what he'd naturally prefer to do. Once the weapon's found the body turns up—or is turned up —very soon afterwards.

" No ; I think that while X may or may not have known beforehand that the spade was there, he simply didn't dare take it away afterwards in case its absence should provoke more comment than its continued

215

presence. He probably saw it hadn't been touched for ages, and hoped it would lie on there and get rusted again until even if it were noticed it wouldn't be connected with the murder. He may even have intended to let a reasonable time elapse—say two or three months —, and then remove it himself for good. Does that seem sense ? "

The other two nodded.

" But you're making things very difficult " sighed Tony. " If it wasn't Bassett, and it wasn't Tate or Lucy, who the devil is X ? Red-head ? "

" And that reminds me, sir " Matthews broke in. " You said some time back that it wouldn't matter Tatham being able to say it was a bow-legged man with a cauliflower ear. But it would matter him being able to say it was a man with red hair, if there was one in the district, even though they were strangers to each other. We've only got McFeish's word for it that he'd ever met the Rector. Tatham mightn't ever have seen him, but McFeish couldn't be sure enough of that to risk leaving him alive."

Beale thought out this fresh point of view for some moments.

" There may be something in that " he agreed. " I think I'd better revise the list of suspects I made last night. I've put a few notes down already, so it won't take long. By the way, I suppose there weren't any peculiarities about the body—nothing like a deformed toe, for instance ? No, I thought not."

" Why do you want to know that ? " asked Tony.

" Oh, didn't I tell you ? Apparently Miss Frankes' missing brother has got one, and immediately she heard there was another body she thought it might be his. She seems to have got him on the brain."

The revised list of suspects ran as follows :

| (1) = 1st _murder (of unknown)_ ; (2) = 2nd _murder (Tatham's)_ | | | |
|---|---|---|---|
| _Suspect_ | _Opportunity_ | _Motive_ | _Remarks_ |
| A<br><br>John Tate | (1) Apparently none.<br><br>(2) None, unless he left some one (Lucy ?) to get rid of stick (and hat ? | ?<br><br><br><br>Money ? | It seems imposs. for Tate to have had a hand in disposing of body or clothes, even if he contrived to do murder. Time stretched to limit, and he must have had an accomplice. If he did (2), then nothing in present theory why T. was killed. But: how did Tate get hold of notes ? ? |
| B<br><br>William Bassett | (1) If unknown victim is stranger on 9.13 train, then none if he really left home 9.30, unless pre-arranged meeting, & victim waited for him. Otherwise prob. ample.<br><br>(2) Ample. | ?<br><br><br><br><br><br><br><br><br>Right of way ? | No known motive for (1).<br><br>Presence of spade in shed seems to be in his favour.<br><br>Will not explain his actions Monday night.<br><br>Pipe seems all right. |

| | (1) = 1st murder (of unknown) ; (2) = 2nd murder (Tatham's) | | |
|---|---|---|---|
| *Suspect* | *Opportunity* | *Motive* | *Remarks* |
| C<br>Lucy<br>Tate | (1) None, if she really went to Stoke A<br><br>(2) Could have assisted. | Robbery ?<br><br>Robbery ? | Mutilation of 1st corpse makes her unlikely as murderess ; and doubtful if she could have done digging. Tramp ? Puncture? Could not have carried Tatham's body. Character would seem to rule her out. |
| D<br>Ambrose<br>McFeish | If his story is untrue, ample for both. | ?<br>? | Story suspicious. In best position for disposing of clothes, because of motor-cycle. Red hair ? |
| E<br>Janet<br>Elder | Probably ample for both. | ?<br>? | Extraordinarily strong for a woman : do her nerves match her muscles ? Curious behaviour *re* Mrs Seccombe. Says she went to bed early with headache; fire-escape outside window. |

" You seem to have got it all down " remarked Tony ; and then, with excitement : " Good lord, Ted, I really have got an idea ! Bloodhounds ! "

" Bloodhounds ? " repeated Beale, a little uncertainly.

" Yes—hunt out the missing clothes. What about it ? "

worth trying if we could find his handkerchief or his shirt, say, so the dogs would know what scent they were looking for."

" But what about the body itself ? Hasn't that any scent ? "

" Well, sir, that's hardly the word I'd be using. It smells all right, but not the right kind of smell." He wrinkled his nose reminiscently.

" Bad luck, Tony " said Beale. " It's nice of you to be so keen, though. Now Matthews, it's after 8.0, and if you want to catch that train you'd better start packing."

" Very good, sir. I'm taking up the bank-notes, the scraps of material Hatherley found, and the photographs and fingerprints : is that all right ? "

" Yes, quite; and make 'em busy round a bit—I want you back as soon as possible."

## CHAPTER XXVIII

### 8.45 PM—10.50 PM

AFTER seeing Matthews off, and collecting the list of tickets, they drove round to the Shale police-station for the third time that day. The sergeant in charge could give them only negative information. Enquiries at hotels and boarding-houses had so far drawn blank, and there was no news of the tramp except that he had certainly not called at any of the workhouses within thirty miles, nor been taken up at any of the police-stations.

As they were passing through the town on their way back Tony suddenly drew up.

" What's the matter ? " asked Beale. " Run out of juice ? "

" No—another idea."

" Don't wear yourself out."

" Is that all the thanks I get ? "

" Don't know—what's the idea like ? "

" Pretty lousy, I expect—it's yours, really. You seem to be considering Hatherley as a possible suspect. Well, now we're here, let's find out if he really did go to the pictures on Monday night. They ought to know him at the cinemas—in the country doctors are often called out on a job unexpectedly, and they usually make arrangements of some kind."

" Yes, that seems worth doing. We'll find out where ' The Thin Man ' was on."

" The Playhouse, wherever that is. I saw a placard a minute ago."

" Now " said Beale, when they had found the cinema in question : " you go and ask inside, and I'll talk to the car-park attendant—I know what Hatherley's bus looks like. Be as tactful as you can."

" Couldn't be anything else " Tony assured him. Ten minutes later they compared notes.

" It seems all right " said the Inspector. " The chap remembers him—he arrived about 8.o."

" And when did he leave ? "

" That wasn't noticed. Presumably when the show was over."

" Tripe ! " declared Tony briefly.

" There's something fishy " he added, in explanation. " I saw the girl behind the pay-desk, and two of the attendants. They all know Hatherley, and they're all prepared to swear he didn't go inside the place Monday night : and personally I believe them."

" Why ? "

" Because, dear Chief-Inspector, at approximately 9.20 a telephone message was received from his surgery asking them to tell him he was wanted urgently at Hadington. They duly put the message on the screen —and nothing happened."

" Dear me ! I wonder why not."

" Because he wasn't there, of course. It looks to me as if he left the car as a blind. He parked it some-where near the exit, say, so that he could get away quickly without leaving a noticeable gap, and took care that while he was doing it the attendant was busy elsewhere. Then he drew attention to himself in some way —by giving him an unnecessary tip, or something—, and so established his presence there. He probably hoped that the exact position of his car wouldn't be noticed. Can you find out if he did anything like that ? "

" Yes, I expect so. But if he wanted people to think he was actually inside the cinema, wouldn't he have pushed things a bit further ? "

" How ? "

" By giving them more to go on : asking the man outside what time the big picture started, for instance."

" Yes, I never thought of that. I'll see what the commissionaire's got to say."

" 8.54, ' Thin Man ', sir " declared that much-decorated official. " No sir, 8.54—your friend must 'ave been wrong. What ? Said *I* told 'im 8.24 ? Not me, sir—not likely. What ? The doctor ? Yes, I knows 'im by sight. Yes, 'e did ask me, too, come to think of it. Yes, Tuesday night—no, Monday. What time ? Oh, about half past eight. No sir, I won't say nothing to 'im—touchy gentleman, is 'e ? Oh, thank you, sir ! Good-night, sir—good-night and thank you ! "

" ' Good night, ladies, good night, sweet ladies, good night, good night ' " murmured Tony to himself as he went back to the car. Five minutes later Beale came up smiling.

" O thou soothsayer ! " he began. " In other words, he seems to have done it all just as you said : car near the exit, but not actually seen arriving or departing ; drew attention to himself by borrowing a match ; dumb as a newt about going early. How did you get on ? "

Tony told him, and they returned to Wyre in silence, each trying to work out the problem with the doctor as X.

" Pull up, will you ? " said Beale, when they reached the police-station. " I want to see how Rush has been getting on."

The sergeant appeared glad to see them.

" There's not a lot of news, sir " he informed the Inspector, " and what there is mayn't be much use, but I wrote it out to save you time—when I wasn't telling the reporters to go away."

" Thanks " said Beale. " Just go over the main points, will you ? "

" Yes sir—not that there's many. So far there's no sign of the missing clothes, though they haven't been able to do much looking since it got dark. They'll be on it again first thing in the morning."

" Who's ' they ' ? " asked Tony.

" Three of Miss Frankes' men, sir, two from Shale, and Constable Sawyer."

" And who's looking after Pond Meadow and the woods tonight ? " put in Beale.

" Two more from Shale—is that all right, sir ? "

" Yes, perfectly. Arrange things how you like, as long as they're done properly. I leave that to you. By the way, here's a few more places to search."

He dictated from his list the items he had marked with a star. " Now, have you got anything positive at all ? "

" Yes sir " replied the sergeant. " There was a telephone call from Chatham half an hour ago about Mr McFeish and the tea-shop. It seems he went there right enough, and to the cemetery. Then there's Dr Hatherley's report on the second body, and what I've been able to find out about Tate's girl. I'm afraid that's the lot, sir."

" Well, it's something, anyway. Now I've got a question for you : where exactly does Dr Hatherley live ? "

Sergeant Rush looked puzzled.

" Stoke Albury, sir " he answered. " The second big house on the left past the post-office—' The Gables ', it's called. Did you want him ? Stoke Albury 5."

" No " said Beale. " I just wanted to know where he lives—but you needn't tell him I've been asking."

" No sir " agreed the sergeant, beginning to understand. " But I don't think——" he went on, and then stopped, as if remembering that his thoughts had not been asked for.

" Go on " requested Beale : " what don't you think ? "

" Well sir : the doctor—he's all right. I mean, you aren't thinking he did it ? "

" I don't know, really. I might be."

" I shouldn't, sir " advised Rush, as if he were suggesting to a child that it had better not have any more fancy cakes. " They were great friends " he added.

" Sometimes friendship doesn't count. I suppose I can trust you to hold your tongue ? It seems pretty certain that the Rector was killed because he interrupted the disposal of the first corpse. Anyway, don't go worrying about it—I've really nothing to go on. Now Rush, as man to man, what do you think of Miss Elder ? "

The answer came without hesitation.

" I don't like her, sir, and that's a fact. There's something queer about her."

" To do with the present business ? "

" Oh no, sir—just generally. Of course, I don't really know her at all, but she always seems to be acting sort of suspiciously. For instance, if I'm walking up the village, and she's walking down, and we meet, she won't pass without stopping for a moment, and as like as not she'll tell me what she's just been doing, or what she's just going to do."

Sergeant Rush paused, scratched his chin, and then delivered himself of a weighty reflection.

" It seems to me, sir, that anybody who tells a policeman what they're going to do before they've been asked is trying to hide something."

The other two smiled.

" I think there's a lot of wisdom in that remark, Sergeant " said Beale. " It would be pretty safe as a general rule : but the trouble with general rules is that they always have exceptions. From what I've seen I should think it's quite possible that Miss Elder is the

sort of woman who just can't stop talking about herself. But I'm glad you don't like her, because I don't
either."

"Don't let instinct run away with reason," warned
Tony.

> " ' I do not like you, Janet E.
> The reason why I cannot see ;
> But this at least is clear to me :
> I do not like you, Janet E.' "

"No, I'll try not to. Well, we'd better be getting
along. By the way "—as he reached the door : " don't
you ever go to bed, Rush ? "

"Oh, yes, sir. Don't you worry about me. There's
a camp-bed next door for when I have to spend the
night here. Luckily I'm a light sleeper, so I hear if
the telephone goes."

"Well, so long. If you want me, ring up the King's
Head, but don't start talking till you hear my voice.
Oh yes, wait a bit."

He paused at the door, while Tony started up the
car.

"Didn't you get a letter on Tuesday morning ? "

"A letter ? Yes sir." The sergeant looked surprised.

"Do you mind telling me where from ? "

"No sir. It was from Petters' in Shale, about my
new bike—I could show you——"

"No—it doesn't matter. Forgive my nosiness.
Good-night."

It was twenty minutes past ten by the time the car
was put away.

"What shall we do now ? " asked Beale. "I don't
really think it's much good pottering about Pond
Meadow."

"Thank goodness for that ! " said Tony. "I don't
fancy it either—too blessed cold. Let's go into the bar.
I'm rather curious to find out how the village is taking
this second body. It must be a bit of a shock, you

know. Everything's all quiet and peaceful, like Dickie said, one minute, and the next the Rector's found murdered, real Scotland Yard detectives appear, there's a lot of hurrying and scurrying, and all of a sudden, before there's even been time to get properly used to the first one, up comes a second bloody corpse."

"All right, but I expect they'll shut up like clams the minute we put our heads round the door."

"Yes, I suppose so—but we can try."

One look at the bar-room made it clear that something out of the ordinary had happened in the village. The dart-board, probably for the first week-night since its appearance, was allowed to hang unmolested, and the bagatelle machine, a more recent arrival, was equally ignored. Instead, the occupants of the room were grouped more or less together, though subdivided into twos and threes. The hum of conversation stopped instantly as Beale entered, and a dozen face turned enquiringly towards him. Tony's first glance was towards the bar itself; he saw at once that John Tate was sitting aloof in a corner, apparently deep in thought.

The Inspector felt it his duty to put the villagers as much at their ease as possible.

"Sorry if I'm interrupting" he said. "I suppose it's not much use asking you to take no notice."

He looked rapidly round, and noted with relief that neither Bassett nor McFeish was there.

"The least I can do is to stand drinks" he went on, bringing out a handful of change. For a moment no one spoke, and then an aged labourer broke the spell.

"Thank 'ee, sir" he wheezed. "Pint of mild and bitter, mine is."

There was a general laugh at this.

"Trust old George!" remarked somebody, knowingly, and within a minute or two the atmosphere had grown less strained.

While Tate busied himself supplying demands for beer and cider the company drew noticeably closer, and Tony, standing back, smiled. He could see curiosity on every face : the desire for information, shown here by a tongue softly licking an upper lip, and there, striving timorously to utter itself, by a tentative clearing of the throat.

" Have they found the clothes yet, sir ? " asked one of the younger men at last, and then blushed violently at the sound of his own voice.

" No, I'm afraid not " answered Beale, readily enough. " It's not going to be easy, you know, because more likely than not they were taken away to be got rid of."

" Ah ! " murmured the audience sagely, and relapsed into silence.

" How's the village taking things ? " enquired Tony presently. After some preliminary hesitation, answers were forthcoming without much reluctance.

The village, it appeared, had never known anything like it, not since farmer Tomlin's barns were set afire, and that must be pretty near thirty years back now —well before the war, anyway. Yes, the women were getting a bit scared, but you couldn't blame them, really, could you ? Not really ; not when naked bodies were being dug up like that, with their faces smashed about something cruel. There was simply no telling what Miss Frankes must be thinking of it all. Ah, she was one of the real good sorts. Blind she might be, but she knew when to help them as needed it better than many that had the use of both eyes. Mr Curtis, her nephew—he was a one, too. Where the village cricket team would be sometimes without him the village frankly didn't know.

It appeared also that the chief concern of the inhabitants of Wyre was not that the murderer might be still among them, a possible source of further untimely deaths, but whether any more examples of his past handiwork would be found. When Beale asked the reason for this outlook it was given uncompromisingly.

Nobody that lived round these parts—no, not even the worst of 'em, and that went for old Mossy Face as well—was capable of doing a thing like that ; not of killing two men in cold blood, stripping one of them, cutting him about so that his best friend wouldn't know him, and finally giving him secret and un-authorized burial in a rickety old shed. Therefore the murderer could not be a local man. Therefore, again, it was not more certain that he had ever come than that by this time he was miles away—possibly out of the country altogether. Accordingly, no fresh outrages need be feared, and the only discovery to be made in the future—apart from the detection of the person or persons responsible, for which they confidently looked to the Inspector—was evidence of still further crimes committed at the same time as the other two.

" And how would a stranger know there was a spade in the shed ? " asked Beale ; but that they could not tell him. They had not even been aware themselves that it was there.

" Time, gentlemen, please ! " came Tate's voice, cutting through the talk like a rusty sword.

" Just one more round, landlord " suggested Beale. " I think I can promise there'll be no trouble. Who's ' old Mossy Face ', by the way ? "

It transpired that the person in question was a cer-tain Major-General Mostyn, who lived in a big house the other side of the Place, possessed a large white moustache, was at present in Scotland, and lacked popularity in the neighbourhood for several reasons, chief of which was his habit of addressing all and sundry as ' Hey, dammit, you ! '.


## CHAPTER XXIX

### 10.50 PM THURSDAY—12.40 AM FRIDAY

THE company finally dispersed just before ten minutes to eleven, satisfied that the man from London was a right nice chap, and content to await the results of his investigation.

" And now " said Beale, " I'd be glad if you'd let me have a key, Tate. We might want to stroll down the road presently."

" Very good, sir. Will you bolt the door before you go to bed, please ? "

" Certainly. By the way, how many of these things have you got ? "—as he put the door-key in his pocket.

" Half a dozen, sir " answered the landlord without hesitation. " The girl's got one, Mr McFeish another, there's the one I've just given you, one in my pocket, and the other two I keep on the wall in the office for when visitors want them."

" And was the door bolted on Monday night ? "

" No sir—we didn't know but what Mr McFeish was coming back."

" I see. And is he in now ? "

" Yes sir—been up in his room all evening. All afternoon too, if it comes to that " he added. " Typing, I think."

" And Lucy ? "

Tate looked hard at his questioner.

" She had a headache and went to bed a couple of hours ago " he replied shortly. " Will the other gentleman be here for breakfast in the morning ? "

" Oh no—I forgot to tell you."

" That's all right, sir. And will you be wanting any more to drink tonight ? "

" Well " said Tony, " I shouldn't be surprised. If you'd trust us, you could show me which barrel the bitter lives in, and then we'll be quite happy."

Tate smiled slowly.

" Yes sir, I reckon that'll be all right. It's this one here. Good-night then, gentlemen."

He stood looking at them for a moment, and then departed heavily along the passage leading to the kitchen.

" You know " said Beale, inside their sitting-room, " I feel rather sorry for that chap. He's got something on his mind, and he just can't bring himself to talk. But

228

I'm hanged if I think he's a murderer, all the same."

"Oh, he's got something on his mind all right" agreed Tony : " a little matter of £50 to be explained away. But I admit he doesn't look much like the bird we want. But then, nor does Hatherley, nor McFeish, nor the girl, nor Bassett, nor even your pet aversion, if it comes to that. Shifty, some of 'em, and bad-tempered, but not my idea of a murderer. I should think Bassett would be the best bet. But there again, I've never seen a real live killer, so I don't quite know what I think X ought to look like. The amateur confesses his appalling inexperience."

"They say" remarked his friend pleasantly, as he filled his pipe " that Crippen was the mildest little man you could hope to meet on a day's journey. Man does not kill by looks alone. Plenty of bad eggs have good shells. I think I shall start a correspondence course in maxim-making.

"I'm afraid that lot in there weren't much help" he went on. "They can go on believing that X is over the hills and a thousand miles away, but I don't. I think it would be possible to lay our hands on him —or her—inside half an hour if only we knew who the devil he or she is. I'm beginning to feel we aren't getting on quick enough."

"Rot !" said Tony decisively. " Look before you leap, more haste less speed, slow but sure, and all the rest of it. I will become a sleeping partner in the maxim business, and wake up every seven years to make a brilliant remark, such as ' Time will show '. Actually I think we're doing very well. Tell me, why did you borrow the key ? You haven't changed your mind about Pond Meadow, have you ? If so, my feet ache."

"No, but it's useful to have one, and I wanted to know how many there were. Just see if there really are two more in the office, will you ? And talking about beer——"

He nodded when Tony returned presently to report the presence of two similar keys.

" Then that seems all right " he said ; " unless he's got an extra one up his sleeve."

" What are you suddenly worrying about keys for ? Afraid that X will break in during the night and do some more spade-work ? "

" No—you're forgetting the bolt. I was wondering about McFeish, really. Well, I suppose I'd better go through Rush's packet of news."

He spread out the contents of the sergeant's envelope on the table.

" The girl in the tea-shop says Red-head went in about quarter past three, ordered tea but didn't drink it, did a lot of writing, and left at four o'clock " he remarked, putting the first sheet aside. The second one he grunted over.

" Conscientious chap " he observed : " takes half a page of small writing to say they've found nothing. N.B.G. would have done just as well. Still, I oughtn't to grumble, I suppose."

" Of course you oughtn't. He's a good chap, and I think there's a lot of sense in what he said about people who talk to policemen."

" Yes, he's not a fool by any means " agreed Beale, somewhat absent-mindedly, as he glanced through the doctor's report.

" It seems " he went on " that the victim was well nourished, extraordinarily well-developed muscularly, especially about the shoulders and arms, had had his appendix removed, and was killed with a spade or some similar implement, in the course of which a number of bones with unpronounceable names got broken. I wonder if the last part's first-hand infor-mation—about the spade, I mean. Rush doesn't seem to think much of the idea."

" Well, you can hardly expect him to, really."

" No, probably not ; but I think I'll put Hatherley on the list, all the same, if only because he's a person who appears to have been acting suspiciously."

" Damned suspiciously " agreed Tony, and looked over his friend's shoulder as he wrote.

230

| Suspect | Opportunity | Motive | Remarks |
|---------|-------------|--------|---------|
| F<br><br>Dr Hatherley | Possibly ample for both murders. (Check what time he got home Monday night.) | 1st: ? 2nd: personal quarrel? But where is my theory then? | What is all the funny business *re* cinema and car park? Would surely have no *possible* chance of getting finger-prints. |

That done, Beale turned to Sergeant Rush's enquiries into Lucy Tate's private affairs.

" ' The young person in question . . .' " he read, but could get no further because of Tony's laughter.

" I thought Jeeves was the only man who'd use that phrase " he gasped.

" It's probably just Rush's native cautiousness " said Beale. " He's afraid she might see it, though she'd soon guess it was about her. Anyway, let's see what the young person has been up to. '. . . is believed to have been on friendly terms with a garage assistant at Hadington, William Ashley. Their friendship appears to have broken off some months ago. Since then has been seen on several occasions talking to Mr Curtis of Wyre Place, and once going for a walk with him (daylight). Nothing else is known. Father disapproves of having anything to do with boys.'

" That ought to be framed for the bit about the daylight alone " he added. " Curtis, eh? He's supposed to be a bit of a lad."

" You're as bad as the sergeant. There was probably nothing in it."

" Who the devil said there was? But a man in his position would hardly go out with the local publican's daughter unless he thought there might be. Hang it all, what else would he be thinking twice about the girl for? She's pretty enough, but probably hasn't got an idea between her and heaven. I doubt if she could discuss the respective merits of, say, the Beethoven and the Brahms violin concertos."

" But she might be able to supply him with whisky on the quiet—or the cheap " observed Tony.

" Yes, so she might. I wonder you haven't been making up to her."

" Because I prefer beer."

" So I've noticed, you human reservoir. Anyway, going back to Curtis : heaven knows I try not to be a snob, but he has got some sort of position to keep up, even if only out of consideration for his aunt, who seems to be the female deity of the place. And his friends " he added, thinking suddenly, for almost the first time since midday, of Mary Seccombe.

Tony smiled to himself, but remained silent.

" And what are you looking like a Cheshire Cat about ? "

" Oh, nothing. I just thought of something that amused me."

" Huh ! Anything to do with homicidal maniacs ? "

" No. That subject is closed."

" Well then, maybe bloodhounds ? All right, all right ! I take it back. I don't feel strong enough to argue. Let's be serious—it's less exhausting. As far as we can tell, this information tends to bear out the girl's story. She certainly wasn't out with Curtis, and I really believe she did go to Stoke Albury—the aunt was most convincing. It'll be a job for you tomorrow to find out what Ashley was doing on Monday night.

" Now, is that all ? No—there's the lists of tickets."

" Shall you bother with that until the London lot comes through ? " asked Tony.

" Of course I shall " said Beale. " Don't be so confoundedly lazy."

They examined the ticket-collector's information together ; but the list of tickets given up at Shale within the last ten days was so lengthy that the Inspector decided not to spend long over it. The other, however, was more interesting.

232

## TRAINS STOPPING AT WYRE HALT

| Charing X | Shale Junction | | Wyre Halt | Journey | |
|---|---|---|---|---|---|
| *Dep.* | *Arr.* | *Dep.* | *Arr.* | *Hrs* | *Mins* |
| NS 9.38 am | 10.45 am | 10.51 am | 11.03 am | 1 | 25 |
| 12.55 pm | 2.16 pm | 2.24 pm | 2.37 pm | 1 | 42 |
| 3.01 pm | 4.16 pm | 4.20 pm | 4.32 pm | 1 | 31 |
| NS 7.44 pm | 8.58 pm | 9.02 pm | 9.13 pm | 1 | 29 |
| 8.55 pm | 10.02 pm | 10.10 pm | 10.21 pm | 1 | 26 |

| Wyre Halt | Shale Junction | | Charing X | Journey | |
|---|---|---|---|---|---|
| *Dep.* | *Arr.* | *Dep.* | *Arr.* | *Hrs* | *Mins* |
| NS 10.17 am | 10.29 am | 10.37 am | 12.05 am | 1 | 48 |
| 12.56 pm | 1.09 pm | 1.14 pm | 2.15 pm | 1 | 19 |
| NS 3.34 pm | 3.45 pm | 3.50 pm | 4.56 pm | 1 | 22 |
| NS 7.49 pm | 8.01 pm | 8.07 pm | 9.15 pm | 1 | 26 |
| SO 7.58 pm | 8.12 pm | 8.27 pm | 10.02 pm | 2 | 4 |

NS : Not on Sundays      SO : Sundays only

Tickets for WYRE HALT 12.11.34—22.11.34 inc.
(Collected at Shale Junction)

| Date | St. of Issue | Description | No. | Tr. Arr. W. H. |
|---|---|---|---|---|
| Nov. Thur. 22 Wed. 21 | None | - - - | - | - - |
| Tues. 20 | Charing X | (1) 3rd Single | 1429 | 2.37 pm |
| Mon. 19 | *Wyre Halt | (2) 3rd Ret. Halves | 8672 8673 | 9.13 pm 10.21 pm }† |
| | Charing X | (1) 3rd Single | 1427 | 9.13 pm |
| Sun. 18 | - - - | - - - | - | - - |
| Sat. 17 | Shale Junct. | (1) Outward half of 3rd C.D.Return | 25112 | 11.03 am |

No Tickets for Nov. 16, 15, 14, 13.

| Mon. 12 | *Wyre Halt | (1) 3rd Ret. | 8671 | 10.21 pm |
|---|---|---|---|---|

* Tickets from Wyre Halt issued on the train.
† No information as to which ticket was given up on which train

233

" There you are ! " exclaimed Beale, after a careful scrutiny. "Monday, November 19th : two return halves, consecutive numbers, originally issued on the train as from Wyre Halt ; they belong to Curtis and Tatham, who travelled up together, you remember. And on the same day one third-class single ticket, issued from Charing Cross, for the train arriving at Wyre Halt at 9.13 : obviously that's the mysterious stranger's ticket. Since he took a single, he clearly expected to stay down here that night, if not longer. He couldn't have got back to town by train until the next day even if he'd wanted to, and you don't arrive at a god-forsaken halt a mile from anywhere at quarter past nine in the evening—at least, twenty to ten, actually, but he wouldn't know that in advance—unless you've got somewhere definite to go within reasonable distance. Query : where did he go ? "

" And why hasn't he turned up to tell us all about it ? "

" Well, there isn't really any reason why he should have done. We haven't sent out an appeal, or any-thing. But it's certainly an interesting point. Where *did* he get to ? Why does nobody seem to know any-thing about him ? Wasn't he expected ? It's rather unlikely that he'd come down here without making sure of a bed in advance. If he'd intended to drop in on some friends, and they happened to be away, he'd be in an awkward position. Of course, there's always this place, but he doesn't appear to have called here. and if he came just to meet someone—your blackmail idea, for instance—, then how did he expect to get back ?

" It's all very puzzling, and of course the obvious deduction to make is that he's the battered corpse. In that case it wouldn't matter what he *intended* to do— call on friends, or put up here : it simply boils down to the fact that he was murdered before he could carry his intentions out. But Curtis seems to think he isn't the corpse. Of course, he may easily be making a mistake. In fact, he says as much himself, and I'm inclined to think he must be. All the same, there's a disturbing element of doubt."

"Anyway, I put one over on you there all right. Actually the London list won't help us at all, unless it gives details of tickets that were issued in London, or intermediately, but never collected this end. This cheap-day return, by the way, must have belonged to the curate Mrs Seccombe spoke of, I think."

Tony smiled at this criticism of his detective abilities.

"While we're on the subject" he said, "let me try to prove I'm not quite so dumb. There's something on this page that I don't think you've spotted yet. The mysterious stranger's ticket is number 1427 ; the one on Tuesday afternoon, which was obviously Matthews', is number 1429 : where's number 1428 ? "

Beale stared at the list afresh, and nodded.

"Point to you" he admitted. "Of course, it may be a mistake ; 1429 ought to read 1428, perhaps ; but I rather doubt it. The man who made this out seems to have been pretty thorough."

"How are you going to find out ? "

"Phone Shale first ; and then try Charing Cross. At any rate they'll be able to say if it's been issued or not."

After looking through the list again to make sure that there were no more points to query, he went out to telephone. When he returned twenty minutes later there was a worried expression on his face.

"It's as I thought" he announced. "The Shale people swear blind they haven't had 1428 through their hands, but Charing Cross say it was issued on Monday night. The ticket-office clerk can't remember anything about the person who bought it except that he was a man."

"Well, that's something to be thankful for" said Tony. "I couldn't bear any sinister females in the village melodrama—it's got a big enough cast already. Ten to one she'd be tall and dark and beautiful, and heavily scented, and wear expensive furs, and have a butterfly tattooed on her left shoulder, and carry so many secret-service plans down the front of her dress she'd rustle every time she moved."

Beale smiled.

" Well, she doesn't seem to exist, so I shouldn't worry. But this ticket business is a nuisance ; let's think it out. Start on the assumption that (a) it was bought, and (b) it hasn't been given up. Why then was it bought ? "

" Because honesty is the best policy " answered Tony, remembering his own remarks to the sergeant on the same subject a day or two before. Beale ignored him.

" Presumably, again, because the purchaser intended to use it. Then does the fact that he apparently didn't give it up mean that he couldn't have made the journey ? Of course not.

" Now, let's approach things from another angle. This mysterious traveller may or may not have known beforehand that tickets for Wyre Halt are collected at Shale. If he didn't know, he'd get into the train expecting not to have to part with his until he reached his destination. But that again needn't mean that he didn't come to Wyre. The 8.55 stops at Shale Junction for eight minutes, arriving at 10.02 and departing at 10.10. Our friend may have dashed out for a quick cup of tea, and so have missed the collector. Or he might even have gone to sleep, though I expect they're on the look-out for that sort of thing.

" If, on the other hand, he knew that he could get to Wyre without a ticket if he wanted to——"

" Stop ! " cried Tony. " If you ask yourself any more questions I shall have hysterics. You go on and on like Thingummy's brook. I bet the first thing you did when you were born was to sit up, look carefully round, and start deducing who your parents were by circumstantial evidence. It's time I asked a few questions. How do you know that whoever bought the ticket intended to travel on Monday, or even this week ? It might have been post-dated."

236

" You might have been drowned in water when you were quite small " retorted his friend, " but you weren't. Instead you've grown up—for no other purpose, as far as I can see, than to do it for yourself in beer. Don't let me delay you ; have another pint. Have two. The ticket was issued on Monday, the 19th, for Monday the 19th."

" Well then, how do you know this man didn't come on the earlier train ? "

" Because you can't catch the 7.44 if you don't buy your ticket till eight o'clock."

" Oh, all right ! But you didn't tell me that. Then let me go on where you mercifully left off. You were just about to ask whether the fact that someone knows he doesn't need a ticket, yet buys one, but doesn't give it up, makes him a non-starter. Answer, not at all. He may never have intended to give it up unless he had to.

" Suppose this bloke's a nasty slit-eyed cove, up to any amount of no good. The fact that he probably doesn't want to be noticed, and probably won't need a ticket, won't stop him from buying one. He can't be dead sure he won't need it. If the train was late arriving at Shale, for instance, it mightn't stop there more than a couple of minutes—just time for the collector man to race up and down the platform. Slit-Eye wouldn't have time for his cup of tea then, and that seems to be the only way of avoidance, unless you've got a carriage to yourself, and nip into the lavatory. The innocent chap who didn't know about the tickets might have done that, by the way, but it's not very safe as a method of travelling without paying."

" Why not ? "

" Call yourself a detective ? If that were your plan, what would you do if I got in just as the train was moving off from the last stop, so that you didn't have time to change compartments, and then, as we were running into Shale, nipped in there first ? I might be trying to work the same trick."

" All right " agreed Beale. " Remember, I said

237

you'd got a criminal mind. Then it's your argument that he'd buy a ticket in any case ? "

" Yes."

" Well then, we'll admit that whatever his intentions were, it's quite possible for him to have made the journey. The question is, did he ? If so, either he got out at Wyre or he didn't ; and if not, he doesn't interest us. But if he did, then he's got to be accounted for."

" Yes " said Tony, thoughtfully. " It seems to me that if he came, then he's probably X. He can't be the victim—that's clear enough. Nor can he have evaporated. But nobody owns up to knowing anything about him, which is decidedly fishy whichever way you look at it."

" What do you mean, whichever way ? "

" Well, if he came, and he isn't the corpse, he's presumably still alive. Therefore he must be living somewhere. If he's not in the district, how did he get away ? Decidedly suspicious. If, on the other hand, he was seen, then there's a conspiracy on to keep quiet about him. Equally suspicious. And if he's still in the district, then he's being hidden ; which is more suspicious still."

He hesitated a moment.

" I suppose we shan't have to dig him up as well ? " he asked.

Beale shuddered, remembering that Miss Frankes had put a somewhat similar question.

" I hope not " he answered, " but you never know. There's one bad flaw in your argument, though. I don't see how he can be first murderer, unless my theory's wrong after all, and Tatham was killed before the other man ; and I don't believe that."

" Hang ! I was getting the times muddled. But if you aren't wrong, then he can't be a murderer at all, because it would mean that there were two of them, and the theory won't stand for two. In that case I'm afraid I should back him each way as another victim."

238

Beale regarded the bottom of his tankard with a speculative eye.

"Of the fragments that remained, twelve coffins full" he murmured. "Hullo! Who can that be, I wonder? It's nearly tomorrow."

The telephone bell had begun to ring, and he hurried out.

"Detective-sergeant Matthews speaking" came a tinny voice. "Is that you, sir?"

"Yes, Beale speaking. Any news?"

"Nothing about the fingerprints at present; but I've got two other items for you. First, there hasn't been a single enquiry of any kind about the corpse. It seems a bit queer."

"Yes, decidedly. It may mean that X has taken the necessary steps."

"Yes sir, that's what I thought. The other's not so startling. So far nothing's been discovered about McFeish except that he once knocked a Blackshirt out, and he's got a female cousin who works in Tovey & Tovey's."

Beale chuckled.

"You're just trying to get me muddled" he said. "Neither of those things need count against him."

"No sir—but there seems a sort of connection with the second one."

"Possibly—I'll sleep on it. When do I expect you back?"

"As soon as fingerprints have decided, sir. Some time tomorrow for sure."

"Good—make it as early as you can. There's not much happening down here. A certain M.D. seems to have been acting suspiciously with regard to his alleged examination of a certain thin man, but Rush won't hear of it. I think that's all. Oh no—sorry: I've forgotten the latest puzzle."

He gave a brief account of the missing ticket, and hung up after learning that Matthews had had no brilliant ideas for possible hiding-places.

Tony was not particularly impressed with the news.

239

" I'm afraid the lack of enquiries doesn't seem very significant to me " he said. " It probably only means that the corpse said he was going away for a week or two."

" That's all very well. I know it's the sort of thing you'd do, but luckily most people aren't quite so casual. They do generally give some indication of where they're going."

" Not if there's nobody to give it to. Lots of lonely people about. And the other business ? "

" Tovey & Tovey ? I notice you daren't bring yourself to mention them by name. I don't suppose there's anything in it—just a coincidence ; but you ought to be able to weave a pretty ripe theory."

" Yes, I might try " admitted his friend. " I'd like to make her the sender of the message about carts and bones, but I don't see what good it would do. Anyway, how's this ?

" In a temporary fit of madness Tovey & Tovey— there, I've said it !—buy this unsellable book about St Hippo for fifty quid on Monday afternoon. About tea-time they wake up, and start wondering how to put things right. The female cousin overhears, and bargains with them. 'If I get that book to sell like " Angel Pavement " ' says she, ' what's there in it for me ? ' ' Double your salary ' says Tovey & Tovey, quick as a flash. ' Oke ' says she, and proceeds to phone up Red-head——"

" Who isn't here " interposed Beale.

" Oh well, maybe she knew he'd be in Chatham, and she rang him up there. Don't crab my theory with your beastly details—think big. She persuades him to murder Tatham, and goes out to order herself a fur coat."

" I don't see that she's earnt it."

" Ah, that's the subtle part. She's relying on the inexhaustible curiosity of the public. ' Last Work by the Murdered Rector ! ', and so on—quite irresistible. The only snag is that Tovey & Tovey aren't going to part up unless they're convinced that she was responsible for the murder ; and I don't fancy she'd be very eager to convince them. However, there you are : take it or leave it."

Beale elected to leave it, and Tony yawned.

" Is there anything else tonight ? I'm getting sleepy."

" Only half a dozen questions I'd like answered. Take the list to bed—I know it by heart. Yes, I think we'd better turn in now, in case tomorrow's anything like today."

For quarter of an hour before he put out his light Tony studied the questions, but with no material result.

" 1 : Where are the missing clothes ?

2 : How did Tate get hold of the bank-notes ?

3 : Why won't he say how ?

4 : Why won't Bassett talk either ?

5 : Why was Janet Elder in such a hurry to get away from the inquest ?

6 : Asked to account for his movements (after the discovery of Tatham's murder), McFeish tells a story which, he must know, is unsatisfactory. He is sufficiently interested (and/or implicated) to attend the inquest—I saw him there, at the back. It is inconceivable that he has not heard about the finding of the second body ; and he must realize that there is apparently a direct connection between the two deaths. In view of his manifest interest in the first, is it not worthy of note that since lunch, as far as can be told, he has not left his room ? Or not ? "

# CHAPTER XXX

THE next morning, to their surprise, they found Dickie Donovan seated at the breakfast table, contentedly munching toast and marmalade.

" Morning " he said, somewhat indistinctly. " I was so hungry I thought you'd rather I didn't wait."

" Oh, quite " answered Beale. " I only hope that's not my share you're finishing."

" Nor mine " added Tony.

" Mean blighters " murmured the reporter, helping himself to another piece of toast. " I shan't write any more nice things about either of you."

" Nice things ! " echoed Beale. " And that fearful photograph ! "

" Now, be fair ! That wasn't my fault. As a matter of fact, I thought it was rather good."

" Anyway, where have you been hiding ? " asked Tony, when peace had been restored. Dickie became serious.

" I ran up to town last night—nothing to do with this business—, and had an argument with a lorry on the way back " he said briefly. " The idiot was parked on his wrong side just round a blind corner, and I went smack into him."

" You don't seem any the worse."

" No, but the bike isn't worth much. That was near Sittingbourne, about half past eleven. I did some frantic telephoning from an A.A. box, but Rush said there hadn't been much happening, so I didn't hurry. Now tell me all the news, past as well as present. I hardly know a darned thing."

Beale gave him the main facts shortly.

" And now, my lad " he finished, " you're due out on a job of work. I'm going to phone Hatherley and ask him to come over. While he's out of the way I want you to go to Stoke Albury and find out what time he got home Monday night. It may not be import-

242

ant, but I want to make sure, and obviously neither of us can go. I don't care how you do it so long as he doesn't know it's me asking. Can you manage, do you think ? "

" Leave it to me " said Dickie.

" Good man—here's his address. You might find out as well what time he first went out on Tuesday morning, and if he had any visitors before ten o'clock. And you'll have to take him, I suppose " he added, turning to Tony. " It's a nuisance, though—your car's so confoundedly conspicuous."

" No need " put in the reporter. " You don't suppose I walked here, do you ? I borrowed an old Douglas from a garage. It goes, after its own sweet fashion."

" That's better still. Then maybe you'd find out about Ashley instead, Tony ? "

His friend agreed that he would, and hastily explained for Dickie's benefit who William Ashley was " And what are you going to do, O lord and master ? " he asked.

" Hang about till Matthews comes " replied Beale. " I might take a hand in the search for the clothes."

He sighed, scowling a little.

" The trouble with this business is that I simply don't know what to do next " he said. " There's the money : I could arrest Tate, but I still shouldn't be any nearer finding out about it. There's Bassett and his mystery : ditto with him. There's McFeish and his ' friends ' : same again. And yet I can't help feeling that none of 'em did it. Or else all three together. Anyway, I'll go and phone Hatherley."

He returned five minutes later to say that the doctor was coming straight over. Dickie at once prepared to set out.

" I think I'll push off too " said Tony. " I don't want to miss Matthews. When do we three meet again ? "

" It's quarter to nine now " answered Beale. " I'll be here from half past ten onwards. Can either of you suggest why I should want to see Hatherley ? "

" To find out if it's any good getting a dentist on to the corpse's mouth " suggested Dickie.

" It isn't—I asked him that yesterday."

" Then tell him you're trying to work out how long the whole thing took, and get his opinion about the time required to disfigure the body " said Tony.

" Yes, that sounds better. Well, good-bye, and find out all you can."

Tony was back at the King's Head by quarter past ten. Dickie joined him shortly afterwards, and at twenty minutes to eleven Beale appeared.

" Nothing's happened " he informed them. " I begin to wonder if anything ever will again. How did you get on ? "

" First come first served " said Tony. " Ashley was playing darts on Monday night for the Duke of Cumberland against the Traveller's Rest. The Duke of Cumberland's lot won, if you're interested."

" I'm not. Is that definite ? "

" Hearsay—mere hearsay. I did the hearing, and seven other people did the saying. Some of 'em looked quite honest, too, considering the time of day."

" What's that got to do with it ? "

" No man is at his best until he has beer inside him. Beer is not yet procurable. At least, it wasn't then."

" All right—thanks. That gets rid of him. Now, Dickie, what about you ? "

" Well, I'm afraid I can't quote so many authorities. You'll have to make do with one parlour-maid, and one lidy wot lives next door. The maid—Hatherley's—says he arrived back Monday night soon after half past eleven. She knows because she'd just heard the church clock strike."

" How did she know it was striking half past eleven ? "

" Because she didn't go to bed till quarter to— Monday's her day off ; and then she did a bit of reading. The person next door says not before half past eleven. She remembers because apparently he always makes

244

more noise than she thinks he need do, and she's going to complain again soon. Both agree that they heard him put his car away before quarter to twelve, but definitely not before the half-hour, both seem quite reliable, and the maid is quite pretty."

"Which doesn't affect her evidence. And Tuesday morning?"

"Oh yes: he went out at 10.30 in answer to a phone message from Wyre Place, and nobody called at his place before 10.0."

"How did you explain yourself?" asked Tony, curiously.

"Good morning, madam" replied Dickie, in a fruity voice. "I must apologize for troubling you, but I represent the Ministry of Transport. You would care to see my card, perhaps? The Minister is anxious to compile statistics showing the proportion of owner-drivers in the home counties who regularly use their cars between 10.0 pm and 6.0 am. God knows why" he added, "but I made it all sound very convincing."

"But why the housemaid?" asked Beale.

"Because nobody else was in except the cook. Hatherley lives with his sister, and she's been away for a week."

"Really? That might be interesting—and the time as well, though he'd hardly make a noise if he'd just done the murders. But wait a bit, though—he might. I begin to think that was a pretty good question of yours, Tony. He said the damage couldn't have been done in much under half an hour, and that not to include stripping the body. I wasn't reckoning it would take as long."

"But if he's trying to make you think he couldn't have done it all in the time" said Tony, "surely the delay would be something to do with Tatham."

"Not necessarily. He might be wanting to make me think he couldn't possibly have finished with the other body until after he'd got rid of the Rector; and that as he couldn't go back to the first corpse, and yet

245

arrive home at 11.30, or thereabouts, therefore he can't
be X. Anyway, he's not definitely ruled out yet."

" Which is surely a pity."

" It doesn't follow. I often find that each individual
suspect makes you tackle the thing from one particular
angle, and in doing that you may spot something
which applies equally well to one of the others, once
you've thought of it."

" I'm afraid I don't believe in the Hatherley theory
myself " remarked Dickie.

" Oh—why not ? "

" Oh, I don't know. He looked decent enough ; and
anyway, the doctor's weapon is poison, not a rusty
spade. Remember all the medical murderers : Crippen,
Lamson, Neill Cream, Castaing, Palmer, Pritchard,
de la Pommerais, Cross—poisoners, every one of 'em.
Of course, I know there were a few who used other
methods—Webster and Minor, for instance. But in
general I think practitioners prefer poison."

" If it's alliteration you're after " grunted Beale,
" how about what you've just said for a journalistic
generalization ? "

" All right : I'll give you something a bit more solid.
If Hatherley did the murders, he must have come here
by car, and gone away by car ; and while he was doing
them he had to leave the thing somewhere. Overlook-
ing the fact that nobody could find any marks, there
are two points to make. First, suppose he came here,
met the corpse before it was one, killed it, and then
buried it. That in itself—the burying, I mean—is
dangerous enough : but isn't it a thousand times more
dangerous if your car's parked close by, and it's one
that everybody in the district knows by sight ? It
wasn't late enough for him to count on there being
nobody about. Point the second : if, on the other hand,
Hatherley actually killed the corpse elsewhere, why in
heaven's name choose Pond Meadow as a cemetery ?
There must be dozens of more secluded places."

Beale nodded.

"That seems fair" he admitted. "Ah ! What's that?"

246

" Taxi ! " exclaimed Tony, looking out of the window. " Yes, it's Matthews—quite chirpy, too ! Now we'll know where we are—maybe."

The detective-sergeant came in smiling.

" Good morning, sir " he said to Beale. " Good morning "—to the other two. " Not that I want to raise your hopes too much " he added, seeing how expectant they all were ; " but things aren't so bad. I'll get straight to the point, sir. With the help of the photos I took, we managed to identify the prints with some degree of certainty."

He held out a large envelope.

" We think the dead man is Jacob Welling, *alias* Welsh, *alias* two or three other names. There's a summary of his record. I should say the chances are about five to four in favour, but if the corpse isn't him, then it's nobody we've got any record of. The bits of material from the head were too bloodstained to be any good. By the way, sir, Superintendent Vinney wants to know if you'd like a pathologist down ; but Henderson's in Scotland on the Laurie business."

" I'll think about it " said Beale, withdrawing the contents of the envelope, three typewritten sheets, and putting them in order on the table, so that they could all read at the same time.

DESCRIPTION*

OF

JACOB WELLING, *alias* JACOB WELSH, *alias* FRANKLIN DYER, *alias* VICTOR ' SHORTY ' SALEM, *alias* HENRY CHARLES SAUL

―――――

C.R.O.  No : W/17193

| Date and place of birth, family, etc. | Sheffield, 1873. British subject. Good family. No brothers ; one sister, since deceased. Educated privately. Well-spoken. Looks his age. Unmarried. |
| --- | --- |

247

| | |
|---|---|
| Occupations | Has been : Solicitor's Clerk (1894-1897) ; Schoolmaster (1899-1901) ; Bookmaker ; Mining Prospector ; Company Promoter (1910 : see List of Convictions) ; Commercial Traveller ; Private in South African Fusiliers (1916-1919) ; Farmer (Australia—New Zealand, 1920-1923). |
| Height | 5 feet 4½ inches. |
| Build | Erect, well-developed. |
| Head | Large in proportion to body ; slightly oxycephalic. Size of hat : 7⅜. |
| Hair | Medium brown, turning grey ; fine texture ; going bald on top. |
| Eyebrows | Dark brown ; medium thickness · arched ; well-separated. |
| Forehead | High, sloping, slightly wrinkled. |
| Eyes | Blue-grey, small, widely-spaced ; lashes thin, short, dark. |
| Sight | Normal. |
| Nose | Below average length for size of head ; straight ; broad nostrils. |
| Mouth | Large ; close-shut in repose. |
| Lips | Thin ; upper one long. |
| Teeth | Two central front ones in upper jaw crowned ; plate in lower, not noticeable. |
| Chin | Round, prominent. |
| Ears | Small, close to head ; short lobe ; no peculiarities. |

248

| | |
|---|---|
| Face | Round, clean-shaven ; full cheeks ; lines at outer corners of eyes and mouth, but in general skin remarkably smooth for age. |
| Complexion | Fresh. |
| Expression | Good-natured, smiling ; deceptive. |
| Arms | Short. |
| Hands | Small. |
| Fingers | Long ; broad thick nails, very carefully kept ; no rings or ring-marks ; thumbs double-jointed. |
| Distinguishing marks | Short broad scar on left knee ($\frac{7}{8}''$). Two small moles on left side of back of neck (concealed by hair). Growth of hair on body below normal. Seems to use both hands equally well, even for writing. Has very little sense of smell. |
| Habits | Smokes incessantly (cigarettes and cigars). Drinks heavily (chiefly whisky). Particular about personal appearance. Dresses and walks well. Speaks French reasonably well. Handwriting : right hand—neat, small, upright ; left hand—larger, slight backward slope. Wears watch on right wrist. Spends money freely, but is rarely in debt. Makes acquaintances easily. |
| Interests | All card games ; billiards ; pigeons ; horse-racing ; golf. |

* Details of personal appearance as observed in 1923.

| No. | Sentence | Name of Court at which convicted | Date of conv. | Offence of which found guilty | Name in which conv. | Date of release |
|---|---|---|---|---|---|---|
| (1) | 3 months hard lab. | Woking Petty Sessions | 2.6.97 | Petty theft | JACOB WELLING | 16.8.97 |
| (2) | 6 months hard lab. | Maidstone Qr Sessions | 13.2.01 | Petty theft | JACOB WELSH | 15.7.01 |
| (3) | 18 months hard lab. | Winchester Assizes | 21.11.04 | False pretences | JACOB WELSH | 17.1.06 |
| (4) | 5 years penal s. | Central Criminal Court | 11.3.10 | Fraudulent conversion | FRANKLIN DYER | 28.1.14 |
| (5) | 6 months 2nd div. | Tower Bridge Police Court | 28.10.25 | Drunk in charge of motor car | HENRY CHARLES SAUL | 30.3.26 |
| (6) | 10 years penal s. | Central Criminal Court | 12.10.26 | Forgery : false pretences | VICTOR SALEM | 10.8.34 |

*Remarks* : WELLING has never been sentenced out of England. Is not known to carry firearms. A plausible rogue, familiar with the confidence trick in all its branches. Makes it his chief source of livelihood, although never convicted for this offence. Has several times escaped punishment through the unwillingness of his victims to prosecute, and once through accidental death of prosecutrix. Very little is known of his methods, but it is believed he varies them far more than is usually the case. Prefers when possible to work alone, and seldom fails to exploit a suitable victim. Was released from Dartmoor on licence on July 10th last, and has reported regularly to the Tottenham Court Road police-station up to and including Friday the 16th inst. Present whereabouts unknown.

" Hardly what you'd call a law-abiding citizen "
remarked Tony.

" Plenty worse than him about " said Dickie, " and
still going strong. I name no names, but if he'd got
what he deserved every time he deserved it, there's a
certain gentleman not many miles from Hyde Park
Corner whose record would make that look like a
testimonial for a Sunday-school teacher."

Beale's voice broke in sharply.

" What about the scar on the knee ? " he demanded.

" It's there all right, sir " answered Matthews
promptly. " I took a look as I came by. But it's got
a couple of companions, one nearly an inch and a half,
and they look just as old."

" And the moles ? "

The detective-sergeant shuddered slightly.

" They don't show " he said simply. " But there's
the mark of a watch-strap on the right wrist."

In the meantime Beale had taken out Dr Hatherley's
report.

" Yes, he mentions three scars, but doesn't give
measurements. Well, have you got any more news ?
Elder ? McFeish ? "

" No sir—nothing else so far."

" Right."

He took out his note-book, and wrote rapidly for
some moments.

" Here's something for you to do " he said at last.
" Get on the phone to Wyre Place. Hatherley's gone
up there—see if you can catch him before he leaves.
Say I'm sorry to keep troubling him, but I want to
ask him some more questions : when can he meet me
at the police-station ? "

" Can I help ? " enquired Dickie, as Matthews went
out. Beale looked at him silently for a moment.

" You might be able to " he said slowly, " if you
wanted to. But I don't think you would."

" Why not ? I offered to—I'll buy it."

" Well then, would you consider a journey to
Chatham ? I'm very curious to get to the bottom of

251

McFeish's movements. I know official enquiries are being made, but very often they aren't much good because they're so obviously official. If there's any truth in what he said about being with people who don't like policeman, then an inquisitive bobby isn't likely to find out as much as, say, an inquisitive representative of the Ministry of Transport. And I don't doubt you've got a dozen other temporary occupations —with appropriate cards for same."

Dickie merely smiled knowingly.

" You might even throw discretion to the winds " Beale went on, " and come out in your true colours as a professional assassin of the English language. Will you have a shot ? "

" Yes, rather. What can you give me as a start ? "

He listened to an account of the poet's own story, and made a few notes, together with a description.

" There's just one thing that might be worth bearing in mind " Beale finished. " I remember something he said when I asked him how he could have been visiting his mother if she was dead : ' The trouble with you people is you don't recognize the truth when you do hear it '. Possibly he's giving us another dose."

" In which case " put in Tony, " it would be just as well to remember that he clearly said his friends are no longer in Chatham."

" Well, I'll do what I can " promised Dickie. " But——"

He hesitated, looking at the Inspector, who smiled.

" All right, you needn't worry. I won't let anyone in ahead of you. Phone the station every hour or so, and if anything's turned up you shall have the story first."


## CHAPTER XXXI

### 12.0 NOON—2.20 PM

JUST as the hall clock was striking—someone had put it right—, Matthews returned to report that Dr.

Hatherley could not get to the police-station again before one o'clock.

"That's as well, really" Beale decided. "It gives me time to copy out the description from Welling's record, and then I needn't show him it all."

He thought for a moment.

"You two can do what you like" he said. "I'm going to borrow McFeish's typewriter. Got any ideas?"

Tony answered for both of them.

"Yes, plenty. We'll be quite happy. Come on, Matthews."

Ambrose McFeish consented readily enough to lend the Inspector his machine. He was in his room, sitting at a table by the window, apparently deep in work. There were papers scattered everywhere, on bed, floor, and window-sill, and a dozen books lying close to hand. Among them Beale noticed Robert Bridges' 'Testament of Beauty', and the Nonesuch edition of Blake's poetry. McFeish saw him look at the last, and smiled.

"Here's something that might interest you" he remarked, opening it. He indicated the bottom of a particular page, and Beale laughed.

"So that solves that little mystery!" he said, as the other got up to fetch the typewriter.

"Can you work it all right?" he asked. "It's got one of two patent gadgets, but everything's quite simple when you know how."

"What make is it?"

"A 'Flag'. They haven't been out long. Have you used one?"

"No, but I expect I shall manage all right."

The poet showed him in what particulars the machine differed from most portables, and replaced the cover.

"There you are" he said. "Will you be wanting it for long?"

"No—not more than half an hour. Are you sure you don't mind?"

"Quite sure. I'm always ready to help the police—within reason."

He smiled suddenly, with a flash of white teeth, and Beale nodded slowly, his face sober.

" Very commendable " he said dryly. " How are your friends getting on ? "

McFeish considered the question, and answered obliquely.

" From your point of view they're not worth worrying about. Neither they nor I had anything to do with the murders."

" Well, I'm sure I hope not, for your sake " declared his visitor.

" No doubt about it " averred the other. " By the way, you might tell Mr Purdon I'm sorry I was rude to him the other evening. I'm afraid my temper isn't always all it might be."

" Yes, I'll tell him. You shall have this back immediately I've finished—many thanks for the loan."

It took him twenty-five minutes to copy out as much of Welling's description as he thought necessary. As he typed he wondered to himself just how much nearer the solution of the problem would be if the doctor could definitely identify the body. In a way it would appear to narrow down the possibilities with regard to the reason for the dead man's presence in Wyre. Tony's phrase, ' up to any amount of no good ', came back to him.

When he had returned the machine to McFeish, who scarcely looked up from his book, Beale walked down to the police-station. He arrived there, at ten minutes to one, to find Sergeant Rush listening to Sawyer's report on the progress of the search for the missing clothes.

Nothing had been found, and of the places regarded as possible there remained only hay-stacks and ploughed fields to be inspected. All the rest—bonfires and dustbins included—had proved unprofitable. Bale sighed, and then remembered that if Dr Hatherley's report were favourable he would be no better off with the whole of the dead man's raiment spread out before him. It was quite certain that the murderer would have left nothing in the pockets.

The doctor turned up at five minutes past one, took the typewritten description, and glanced through it.

" I can tell you about the head now " he stated : " it's unidentifiable. Where did you get this ? "

Beale was ready for the question.

" I'm afraid I can't tell you at present " he said, trying to make his voice sound genuinely regretful. Hatherley raised his eyebrows.

" Secretive beggar ! " he grunted. " Anyway, it doesn't matter. Is this all ? "

" No : there's one other very important point. In your previous report you mention three scars on the left knee."

" Yes—what of them ? "

" I want you to look at them again very carefully, one by one, and tell me how long ago you think they were received. I know you can't be exact "—as the doctor began to expostulate, " but you ought to be able to give me some idea. For instance : scar number one, at least two years old, and not more than six ; probably about three. And I'd like the precise length of each, and a rough drawing of the knee, so that I'll know which one you're talking about. I'm sorry to give you so much bother."

The doctor intimated pointedly that no apology was needed.

" If you'd let me talk just now " he said, " you'd have saved yourself a lot of breath. It's quite impossible to tell the age of a scar on a dead body unless it's a very recent one—received within the last six months, say. Otherwise they all look the same, and I wouldn't even make a guess. No, it's my turn to finish. If you care to get a second opinion, by all means do so. Get five hundred if you like, but I don't think any of them would go farther than that. I'm sorry, but there you are. It wouldn't have been easy if the man were still alive. As a matter of fact, I'm rather surprised you haven't had Henderson or somebody down."

255

" Do you think it's advisable ? " asked Beale.

" My dear man, that's not for me to say. I shan't stand in your way if you want to. I'll go and have a look."

He walked away, list in hand, frowning slightly. Beale stared after him thoughtfully, and then went back to the King's Head for lunch. He found Tony and Matthews already arrived, and waiting for him somewhat impatiently.

" Well, what have you two been up to ? " he asked, accepting the tankard of beer that Tony pushed across.

" Just nosing round " said his friend. " I thought it would be nice to know who's going to the funeral this afternoon."

" Oh lord ! Of course, it's today—I was forgetting. I wonder if I ought to go."

" You needn't if you don't want to " Tony informed him graciously. " I saw Mrs Seccombe, and asked if she'd mind if I went, and she said not at all, and how were you getting on ? I told her I thought you weren't doing too badly, all things considered, and then she said you weren't to think of turning up unless you went on business. She suggested you might find it useful to have everybody out of the way for an hour."

Here Matthews created a minor disturbance by swallowing part of a rabbit the wrong way, and had to be slapped on the back many times before he recovered.

" I don't think I shall go " Beale decided. " But why your sudden interest ? Or isn't it sudden ? Maybe you've always had a fancy for funerals. Some people get that way, I know."

" Drivel on, Sherlock " said Tony. " I'm going because I think it may be a useful way of spending the afternoon."

There was something in his tone which made Beale look up.

" What do you mean ? " he asked. " Useful in what way ? "

" Mr Purdon's got a theory, sir " explained Matthews with a smile.

256

" Really ? " Beale was sceptical. " What does he expect ?  Sudden fit of remorse ?  Confession amid hushed horror, and a spectacular suicide in the centre aisle ? "

" Ass ! I don't quite know what I do expect, but I'm going all the same. If I were X, I know I should hate to help bury a man I'd killed—publicly, I mean ; and from that point of view it may be interesting to see who doesn't go. But on the other hand, he might be someone who'd attract more attention by staying away than by being there, in which case I may surprise a guilty look."

Beale still seemed unimpressed.

" Are you in on this ? " he asked Matthews.

" No sir—it's not my theory."

" What are you going to do, then ? "

" I might go into Shale presently, if you don't mind, sir."

" No. And what before that ? "

The detective-sergeant avoided his superior's eye.

" It depends on where you are, sir."

" I shall probably stay here—there's a lot of thinking to be done."

" Then in that case, sir, I shan't be disturbing you."

Dr Hatherley's report was brought up by Constable Sawyer at ten minutes past two. Beale opened it eagerly, and seemed satisfied.

" I'm beginning to think our battered corpse really is Jacob Welling " he observed. " Hullo ! What's this ? "

He had reached the end of the second page, and was staring at a pencilled note.

" What do you make of that ? " he asked the other two. They leant over to read it.

' Don't put all your eggs in one basket, or you might find you've snookered yourself. The body *may* be that of the man whose description you gave me ; but it could equally well belong to thousands of other people. There are no outstanding individual features. The head is past identifying, as I told you, except for the hair and general shape, which seem to correspond.'

" It might mean a lot " said Tony, thoughtfully.

" Or nothing " remarked Matthews. " What did he say about the scars, sir ? "

" Oh yes—I forgot. Apparently it's no good—dead man's scars tell no tales, unless they're very recent. It's disappointing, I must say. I think you'd better phone the Yard, and ask them where Welling did his last stretch, and if he could possibly have injured his left knee there. I don't see why not, if he was at Dartmoor."

" I must be getting ready " said Tony, as Matthews went out. " Choose a good pew, and see the field arrive."

" Oh yes, of course ; you're going to be one of the guests—if that's the right word. Good luck, and don't imagine what you can't see. By the way, McFeish wishes me to convey his apologies for being rude to you the other night."

" Really ? What's the idea ? "

" I don't know—probably wants you to help him get rich quick."

" Yes, perhaps. Anyway, I'll wake you up when I get back."

" Wake me up ! " echoed Beale. " I shall be awake all right. I'm going to do more solid thinking than most people get through in a couple of years."

" Well, everyone to his own taste. Me, I am a man of action ! "

He smote his chest lustily, began to cough, and made an impressive exit by walking backwards into Lucy, who had come to clear away the lunch.

As for the last twenty-four hours both the Tates had noticeably avoided their visitors, the Inspector was a little surprised when a moment later the girl addressed him.

" Please sir, can dad and me go to the funeral ? Mr Matthews said he didn't think you'd mind."

Beale thought quickly. It seemed clear that Matthews

258

was keeping something to himself for the present ; something, perhaps, which made it desirable for the Tates to be absent for an hour.

" Very well " he agreed : " I don't see why not."

The girl thanked him, and went out, and almost at once the detective-sergeant returned to report that Scotland Yard would telephone the police-station as soon as they had any information.

" Thanks. By the way, did you give the Tates your blessing about the funeral ? "

" Yes sir—is it all right ? "

Beale grinned.

" I don't know what you're planning " he said, " and I don't think I want to, but they're going, if that's what you mean."

" Ah, thank you sir—I mean, I thought you wouldn't mind. Mr McFeish will be out, too, but he's coming back for dinner."

Beale studied the ceiling with an expressionless face.

" If I know anything about McFeish " he remarked, " he'll lock his door, and probably set a booby-trap as well."

Matthews managed to introduce a slight tinge of surprise into his rejoinder.

" Now I wonder why he'd think of doing that, sir ? "


## CHAPTER XXXII

### 2.20 PM—7.20 PM

2.20 *pm*

DICKIE DONOVAN is drinking his third cup of black coffee after lunch in the Railway Hotel, Chatham. He is reading through what he has just written.

FACTS (*verified by Chatham Police*) :

A 1 : McFeish writing in a teashop until 4.0 pm Monday.

A 2 : Teashop in question at least 20 minutes by

259

bus from Craven's garage in Main Street, as change necessary.

A 3 : McFeish collected motor-cycle from Garage at 4.15 pm.

A 4 : He booked room for that night at Railway Hotel by telephone at 4.25 pm.

A 5 : He returned to the Railway Hotel 12.50 am Tuesday.

FACTS (*if McFeish is speaking the truth*) :

B 1 : He ' ran into ' some friends coming out of the teashop.

B 2 : These friends ' don't like policemen '. (Because policemen don't like them ?)

B 3 : He met them by accident.

B 4 : They are no longer in Chatham.

DEDUCTIONS (*General*) :

(a) : If friends exist, and B4 is correct, they are either
 (i) normally residents in, or fairly near, Chatham who are (temporarily or permanently) away ;
*or* (ii) visitors to Chatham or district who have since departed ;
*or* (iii) combination of both.

DEDUCTIONS (*Particular*) :

(b) : *From A1, A2, & A3* : that McFeish must have gone from teashop to garage by car ; private or taxi. (Reliable.)

(c) : *From B1 & (b)* : that car belonged to friends. (Fairly reliable ; else no time to say how do.)

(d) : *From B3* : that he didn't know beforehand that friends were in Chatham. (Guesswork.)

(e) : *From (d)* : that very possibly they are *not* normally resident in neighbourhood. (Pure guesswork, not at all reliable ; but chance it's right.)

260

(f) :　　*From* (*e*) : that some or all of friends may have been staying recently in another hotel ; in which case McFeish may have spent some part of time between 4.25 pm Monday and 12.50 am next day in that hotel, when chance somebody will remember him. Hair extremely rememberable.

(N.B.—Against (f), and in favour of (a) (i)—if (c) is correct—is fact that McFeish's first action after meeting friends is to collect motor-cycle ; but would scarcely seem to need it, since they have car, unless all going some place together—e.g., friends' home— but he alone returning. But perhaps car full up, and sat on somebody's knee from teashop to garage. (And got told off by bobby—hence dislike ? Hardly strong enough).

But in favour of (f) : immediately after collecting cycle books room ; but residents could surely put him up. Is not arm-chair of friend better than bed of Railway Hotel ?

But why not same hotel ?)

PLAN (*formed as result of above stupendous labours*) :
Call at all better-class hotels. If no good, have some beer and start again. Amen.

He reads this through, and finds nothing to alter except in the last sentence. Since, he reflects, beer will not be obtainable in the afternoon, he had better have it now, just in case.

*2.30 pm*
Chief-Inspector Beale is sitting in the leather arm-chair by the fire in the sitting-room. His eyes are closed, his feet upon the coal-scuttle. His pipe is drawing evenly. He is thinking.

Detective-sergeant Matthews is on the sofa, smoking a cigarette and making notes. Every two minutes he glances first at his watch and then out of the window. From where he is sitting he can see anyone entering or leaving the King's Head. He appears to be waiting for something to happen. His attitude is a little restive, giving the impression that he would much rather be doing something else.

2.35 *pm*
Anthony Purdon comes into the room, and stands looking at the Inspector, who opens one eye. Then, striking an attitude, he begins to misquote :

> " ' He felt that, in spite of all possible pains,
>  He had somehow contrived to lose count,
>  And the only thing now was to rack his poor brains
>  By reckoning up the amount.

> " ' " Two murdered by one—if that could but be done "
>  He said " with one's fingers and thumbs ! "—' "

2.36½ *pm*
He breaks off sharply at the entry of Ambrose McFeish, attired in a leather coat, and carrying a pair of goggles, who omits the last two lines of that verse, and proceeds to the next.

> " ' " The thing can be done " said the Butcher, " I think.
>  The thing must be done, I am sure.
>  The thing shall be done ! Bring an axe or a spade—
>  The best there is time to procure." '

" However " he continues, as Beale sits up, and they all stare at him, " I didn't come in to tell you how it was done, nor is that a confession. I've just remembered something that might be of interest. Before you people arrived I used to use this room sometimes. You see that desk ? "—pointing to the corner behind the head of the sofa. " Well, the last time I saw my wallet I was sitting there."
" When ? " asks Beale.

" Last Sunday night. I'm fairly certain I left it on the desk, and quite sure I haven't seen it since."

2.42 *pm*
McFeish sets out on his motor-cycle in the direction of Hadington.

Anthony Purdon departs in his car for the funeral.

Beale takes out his note-book, and begins to read.

Matthews gazes out of the window. A cat enters through the half-open door, regards the occupants of the room with momentary curiosity, decides to ignore them, walks daintily over to the fire, and curls up in front of it.

2.45 *pm*
John Tate and his daughter go off on foot to the funeral.

2.50 *pm*
Matthews gets up, looks for half a second at his superior officer, and then goes out. When, a few moments later, Beale hears footsteps overhead, and then, very faintly, the click of a door-handle, he does his best to convince himself that he neither recognizes the sound, nor is at all interested. He deliberately continues to review his notes.

3.01 *pm*   (*Dickie Donovan*) :
" Good afternoon, sir. I'm sorry to trouble you, but I'm looking for my sister's husband. He left home last week, and he hasn't been heard of since. As a matter of fact, they had a few words, and I've got the job of acting as unofficial peace-maker. I'm not very keen on it, but you know what sisters are sometimes. Anyway, I've managed to trace Angus as far as Chatham, and now I've lost him again, and I'm wondering if you can help. He's tall, quite good-looking, and has the most astonishingly red hair. . . No, I really couldn't say what name he'd be using. . . No, I don't think he'd be with a lady, though you never know with a red-headed man, do you ? It's rather a lot to ask, but could you

263

possibly find out if any of your staff remember seeing a red-haired man about the place recently—especially on Monday ? Either as a guest, or a friend of another guest . . . I say, it's most awfully good of you. . . ."

**3.15 *pm***
Beale puts away his note-book, refills his pipe, lights it, and then, closing his eyes, begins to brood.

**3.17 *pm***
" Good afternoon, madam. I'm afraid I'm going to be rather a nuisance. The fact is, I'm looking for my brother-in-law . . ."

**3.29 *pm***
" Hullo ! Is that Sergeant Rush ? Well, you'll do just as well. My name's Donovan. Anything happened ? I see—thank you. Bung ho ! "

**3.35 *pm***
" Good afternoon, madam. You must forgive me for troubling you. No, I'm not trying to sell you any-thing. No, I promise, nothing—no water-softeners, vacuum cleaners, patent brushes, insurance policies . . . No, on my honour, not even one single near-silk stocking. As a matter of fact, I'm looking for a man with red hair . . ."

**3.36 *pm***
Matthews sets off on his bicycle for Shale. He does not disturb Beale, who is deep in thought, and occa-sionally mumbles to himself. The cat sleeps : it has no immediate problems to solve, being comfortably full of mouse.

**3.42 *pm***
" Good afternoon. Can you spare me five minutes ? "

**3.46 *pm***
" Monday evening, you say ? . . . With a party ? . . . Came in about half past ten ? . . . Noisy lot, were they ? Yes, Dougal does get a bit rowdy at times . . . Full right up ? . . . Could I see the paper in question ?
264

... Ah, I can see you're a bright girl. How about getting yourself a new hat or something ? "

3.50 *pm*

John Tate and his daughter return from the funeral.

3.55 *pm*

Dickie Donovan, rather dry in the throat, and five shillings poorer, is drinking a cup of tea, and studying a piece of paper. He seems satisfied.

| | *Articles to be Obtained* | *Marks* |
|---|---|---|
| 1 | One picture post-card of Mae West .. .. .. .. | 1 |
| 2 | One bus ticket from Rochester to Chatham .. .. .. | 1 |
| 3 | One hard-boiled duck's egg | 1 |
| 4 | One seven of spades .. .. | 1 |
| 5 | One pr sugar tongs (need not be silver) .. .. .. | 1 |
| 6 | One horseshoe .. .. | 1 |
| 7 | One last year's copy of ' Punch ' .. .. .. | 2 |
| 8 | One pr goloshes (to be worn) | 2 |
| 9 | Sixpennyworth of dried horse-flesh .. .. .. .. | 2 |
| 10 | One uninhabited lady's vest | 5 |
| 11 | One church (or chapel) hassock | 6 |
| 12 | One unused 2d postage-due stamp .. .. .. | 6 |
| 13 | One red road-lantern .. | 8 |
| 14 | One ' spot ' billiards ball .. | 8 |
| 15 | One Rolls-Royce radiator cap | 10 |
| 16 | One sporran .. .. .. | 10 |
| 17 | One road-sign marked ' Danger ' | 10 |
| 18 | One policeman's truncheon .. | 10 |
| 19 | One live platinum blonde .. | 15 |
| 20 | One large unopened bottle of whisky .. .. | (minus 10 if — not produced) |

Total 100

NOTE: There is nothing to prevent No. 10 from having originally belonged to No. 19—except possibly No. 19. No harm in trying. Faint heart, etc.

MEET Bull & Bush, Littlebury, 7.30 for 8.0.


3.57 *pm*
Ambrose McFeish returns on his motor-cycle.


4.00 *pm*
Beale gets out of his chair, goes upstairs to the poet's room, and knocks.

*McFeish*: Come in.

*Beale*: Sorry to keep bothering you, but I rather need your help. Rightly or wrongly, I've heard that you've got a very good memory.

*McFeish*: Yes, not bad.

*Beale*: Then will you try to recall just what happened when you told Tate—not the girl, but her father—that you'd lost your wallet and money?

*McFeish (after thought)*: I can give you the exact words, I think. He said: Oh, I'm sorry to hear that, sir. Was there much money in it? Myself: Yes, nearly £50. Tate: In notes, sir? Myself: Yes, pounds and ten-shillings. Tate: Pounds and ten-shillings? Myself: Yes. Tate: And what's the wallet like? Myself: A black one with a strap. Tate: Has it got your name in, sir? Myself: No, nothing except the money. Tate: And you're sure it was all small stuff? Myself: Yes, positive—why do you keep asking? Tate: Oh, I only thought a big bundle like that wouldn't be so easy to lose . . .

*Beale (interrupting)*: Thanks—that's splendid. I congratulate you. Now, just one more thing: had you previously complained of any losses?

*McFeish*: Well, yes. I mislaid a book, but it turned up under the bed.

*Beale*: I see. Well, many thanks again. (*He goes downstairs.*)

266

4.08 *pm*

Anthony Purdon returns from the funeral, and enters the sitting-room. Beale takes no notice, and Tony sits down quietly without speaking, produces a pocket-book, and begins to write.

4.15 *pm*

Beale is roused by the arrival of Lucy Tate with the tea. When she has gone he pours out, and then enquires if it was a nice funeral.

*Tony* : Very nice, thanks. Ugh ! You didn't put any sugar in.

*Beale* : Sorry. How many people confessed ?

*Tony* : None.

*Beale* : What ! No confessions ? No suicides ? No excitement ?

*Tony* : None.

*Beale* : Dear me ! How very disappointing !

*Tony* : Stop babbling. (*He reads from his pocket-book*) : " Present at the funeral : John Tate ; Lucy Tate ; Miss Frankes ; Janet Elder ; Mrs Bassett ; Underwood ; Dr Hatherley ; Mrs Seccombe ; Sergeant Rush. Not present at the funeral :—Andrew Parker ; Ambrose McFeish ; William Bassett."

*Beale (grunting)* : Can't imagine Rush in his Sunday best. How did they behave themselves ?

*Tony* : One does not behave at a funeral : one conducts or comports oneself in this or that manner ; one's attitude or bearing is so-and-so or such-and-such. (*He clears his throat, and begins to read again*) : " Demeanour of parties present :

*John Tate* : Attentive, aloof.

*Lucy Tate* : Attentive ; interested ; looked round several times.

*Miss Frankes* : Invisible from where I was sitting.

*Janet Elder* : Too repulsively pious for words. She even sobbed into a snippet of lace which I suppose she imagines is a handkerchief, in the manner of one giving a bad imitation of a second-rate actress simulating sorrow.

*Mrs Bassett*: Looked about her continually with eyes like metal skewers. Stared at Mrs Seccombe; glared at Dr Hatherley; simply glowered at the Tates.

*Underwood*: Appeared to feel partly responsible for the whole business because he found the body.

*Dr Hatherley*: Very serious. Nothing to show that he was anything but extremely upset. I must say I think he genuinely was.

*Mrs Seccombe*: Very pale; very self-controlled.

*Sergeant Rush*: Hidden from view."

*Beale*: In other words, you didn't find out an awful lot.

*Tony (slowly)*: No, I suppose not. As a matter of fact, it was all rather grim. One realized that Tatham was really alive once, and not always just part of a puzzle. He wasn't merely a man who'd be found dead in a wood one day, and give you a job of work discovering who killed him. He was someone with a job of his own, and from all accounts he seems to have done it pretty well.

*Beale*: Yes—I know that feeling. I usually try not to encourage it, if you understand.

(*They relapse into a reflective silence. Both have a second cup of tea. Tony stares into the fire, Beale round the room.*

4.32 pm (*Shale—Sergeant Matthews speaking*):
". . . same with pianists too, if they play—always got a nice touch. Well, many thanks, and all that . . ."

4.35 pm
Beale goes out in search of John Tate. He finds him alone in the kitchen, drinking tea.

*Beale*: I just want to ask you one question, Mr Tate. On Tuesday evening, weren't you under the impression . . . ?

*Tate*: Why, yes, I was, but how the dickens did you—I mean, no, I wasn't. I'm sorry, but I can't tell you anything, sir.

*Beale* : All right—sorry to be a nuisance.
(*He goes back to his arm-chair.*)

4.46 *pm*

Inspector Beale's gaze shifts from window to door ; from there to the writing-desk where McFeish says he last saw his wallet ; then back again towards the window. He appears to regard the sofa with interest. Perhaps he is looking at the cat, now industriously washing itself ; perhaps not. He next closes his eyes for half a minute. Then, re-opening them, he stares at the ceiling with a troubled expression. Turning his eyes from that to the small table opposite the fire-place, he looks upward at the picture of an improbably antlered stag which hangs immediately above. Thence he moves his gaze slowly towards the door, encountering in succession a photograph of a bewhiskered old gentleman in a coat with six buttons ; a crude water-colour of a very large sun setting behind a very small hill ; a faded wedding-group somewhat larger than the ferocity of the bridegroom's expression would seem to render advisable ; and lastly a coloured print of a fat pink baby uncomfortably wedged into what looks for all the world like a perambulator without any wheels, the whole afloat amidst a miniature forest of stair-rods crowned with sausages.

Inspector Beale regards all these works of art unin-telligently. Possibly because he is exhausted by their splendours, he closes his eyes. All is quiet in the room.

4.50 *pm*

Beale once more opens his eyes. They are still staring in the same direction, but their expression is different. They are animated ; they gleam with interest. Their owner has had an idea.

4.53 *pm*

Tony looks up in astonishment : he has just been asked a riddle.

" Where was who when what did what ? "

He finds a suitable retort without much trouble.
" Half way to Bedlam " he says.

269

**4.55 pm**

Ambrose McFeish goes out again on his motor-cycle.

**4.56 pm**

Beale gets up, stretches his legs, which are stiff, and then walks across to the desk to the right of the fire-place. On top of it, in the corner nearest to the window, he puts his pipe. Next, very deliberately, he lifts the cat off the sofa, lies down, screws the upper half of his body round while keeping his legs stretched out, and after one or two unsuccessful attempts manages to get the pipe off the desk. He repeats the manœuvre with the pipe on the floor between sofa and desk, and then, apparently satisfied, returns to his chair.

*Tony (who has been watching)* : Did I say half way ? It was an error. O what a noble mind is here o'er-thrown ! Take him for all in all, he was a man, the cutest copper of the lot. Marcus Aurelius says : ' Mark how fleeting and how paltry is the state of man— yesterday in embryo, tomorrow a mummy or whatnot. So for the hair's breadth of life assigned to thee live rationally——'.

*Beale (mildly)* : The same gentleman also said : ' The controlling Intelligence understands its own nature, and what it does, and whereon it works '. Think that out, and stop talking. I believe I'm beginning to see which way the wind blows.

**5.06 pm**

A message is brought from the police-station. ' Please inform Chief-Inspector Beale that Jacob Welling sustained injuries to left leg in quarrel with fellow prisoner at H.M. Prison, Dartmoor, in 1926. No details available at present.'

**5.25 pm**

After much deep thought, Beale goes out to tele-phone. When the right person has been fetched he asks one question, and the answer he receives, ' No sir, in different ones ', is apparently satisfactory. He returns to the sitting-room, gets out his pen, and begins to make notes.

**5.50 *pm***

Beale again goes out to telephone, this time to New Scotland Yard.

**5.59 *pm***

He finishes his first call, and makes a second one.

**6.14 *pm***

He finishes his second call, and rings up New Scotland Yard again.

**6.27 *pm***

Back in the sitting-room, he continues to write, now more fluently.

**6.30 *pm***

Beale asks Tony where Matthews is. Tony replies that he hasn't the slightest idea. Beale says viciously ' Curse him ! '

He continues to write, now and again pausing to suck his pen, but never for long. His thoughts seem under control. The frown on his face denotes concentration rather than bewilderment.

**6.34 *pm***

Detective-sergeant Matthews returns on his bicycle.

**6.35 *pm***

He enters the sitting-room.

*Beale (looking up sharply) :* Where in God's name have you been ? Don't stop to answer. Find out the name of everybody in this village who's got a typewriter, what make it is, where they usually keep it, and whether they've lent it to anybody recently. Also get a specimen of work. No, wait a bit, dammit—that won't do. Hang ! I wish Dickie was here. He could go prowling round back-doors, but you can't very well —they've all seen you. And I mustn't frighten anyone.

*Matthews (tactfully) :* I'll go and ask Rush, sir—he might know. Or Mrs Bull at the general shop. If that's no good I'll try the stationers at Shale. Ribbons wear out, and I expect most of the people round here would get them locally—and they'd probably be recognized as well. You aren't looking for any special make, sir ?

*Beale* : No. All right, do what you can, only forget what I said at first, and for heaven's sake don't go warning anybody who might have one. Also find out the direction of the wind on Monday night.

### 6.39 *pm*
Tony, who has been listening with unconcealed interest to the last conversation, seems to be struck with a sudden idea. He snaps his fingers excitedly, and begins to mutter to himself.

*Beale* (*without looking up*) : Stop behaving like a lunatic.

*Tony* (*indignantly*) : You're telling me ? Be quiet, O big black pot !

### 6.44 *pm*
The sound of an approaching motor-cycle is heard. Tony rushes to the window, and then returns to his seat disappointed : it is only Ambrose McFeish.

### 6.53 *pm*
A second motor-cycle draws near. This time Tony goes straight out, and grabs hold of Dickie Donovan almost before he has time to dismount. He talks earnestly to him. Dickie nods. Tony returns to the sitting-room, where Beale is still writing.

### 6.58 *pm*
Tony gets up, and saunters into the hall in a leisurely manner. He looks around him, as though wondering where someone or something is most likely to be found, and then walks down the passage leading to the kitchen. As he passes the bar-room he glances in, and notes approvingly that John Tate is reading a paper. He eventually reaches the kitchen door, which is almost shut. He opens it, to find Lucy Tate giggling at some-

thing Dickie Donovan is telling her. Tony coughs discreetly, but does not withdraw.

" The flirtation is at an end " he announces.

*Dickie (innocently)* : Flirtation ? What flirtation ?

*Tony* : Now don't tell me the answer—I know it. Have you no respect for your wife ?

*Dickie (laughing)* : Which one ?

*Tony (as Lucy, who has been smiling, opens her eyes very wide)* : All six : the big blonde one ; the little red-haired thing ; the one with five chins ; the black one ; the Chinese one ; and the bearded lady in the circus. You ought to be ashamed of yourself. Every time you smile at another girl you wrong six loving hearts. And as for you *(turning to Lucy with mock severity)*—such goings-on I never did 'ear of ! *(She giggles again.)* Deplorable ! Something must be done about it. I think *(thoughtfully)*—yes, I think I shall tell William.

*Lucy (surprised, a little embarrassed, blushing)* : William, sir ?

*Tony* : Ah, you thought I didn't know about him —but I do. Yes, William—the dark-haired lad who fills you up with petrol if you run dry. Provided you drink petrol, that is. I prefer beer.

*Lucy (no longer blushing)* : Oh, you mean Bill Ashley, sir ?

*Tony* : Yes. I had quite a chat with him this morning—he cleans a pretty plug. He sent you his kind regards, by the way.

*Lucy (tossing her head)* : Oh, did he ! Then if you're going by that way again you might tell him from me, if they're worth sending they're worth bringing. At least, I mean—it doesn't matter, sir. *(She stops, seeming to become conscious that she may have been rude.)*

*Tony* : The path of true love, etc. Anyway, come along now, Richard : there is work for idle hands to do. Owing to the peculiar law of gravity, a pint of beer will not convey itself to the mouth : it needs to be lifted.

*(They depart. In the passage they solemnly and silently shake hands.)*

7.10 *pm*

They encounter Matthews outside the sitting-room door. All three enter.

*Matthews (to Beale, reading from his note-book)* : Rush says he thinks the Bassetts have a very old type-writer, sir, make unknown. It belonged to Bassett's father. There's also at least three portable machines in the village, all the same make—a ' Flag '. They belong to Dr Hatherley, Miss Elder, and Mrs. Seccombe.

*Beale (eagerly)* : That's quick work—where'd you find out ? "

*Matthews (regretfully)* : Not my doing, sir—message from the Yard. The machine you're looking for, sir, is a ' Flag '. And the wind was north Monday.

*Beale (clapping his hands)* : Marvellous ! A ' Flag ' ! Just fancy that ! But how on earth do they know who's got one down here ?

*Matthews* : It seems that ' Flags ' haven't been out but a few months, sir. It's a new concern, and they're pushing 'em for all they're worth—sending travellers round the country to call on all the likely people, such as doctors and clergymen, and so on. The Yard got in touch with their head office.

*Beale* : Good man ! Now (to them all), give me five minutes on the phone and I'll be with you.


7.19 *pm (Fragment of Beale's telephone call)* :

*Beale* : What time do you think best ?

*Voice* : About half past eight, sir, or just after.

*Veale* : All right. Can you arrange it so that nobody interferes ? . . . What, another ? Big family ! Can you trust him too ?

*Voice* : Oh yes, sir . . . and get a key.

*Beale* : Yes, that seems good enough—he ought to know where to look. I suggest actually in the back of the big . . .

# INTERLUDE

## WHO KILLED TATHAM ?

*At this point the intelligent reader, if he has not already done so, should be able to attempt the solution of the problem with every prospect of success by taking thought, eked out where necessary with a guess or two. He ought not, however, to conjecture further than will permit him to form a reasonable theory, which he should then examine rigorously. The less intelligent reader may perhaps be allowed to guess first and think afterwards, always provided that he does not shirk the thinking.*

*Since nothing can too strongly express condemnation of those who use guesswork alone, making no attempt to exercise their reason upon the product of their imagination, nothing will here be said. The book was not written for them.*

*In passing, a completely satisfactory solution will not only distinguish between sheep and goat, but establish the identity of the former with hardly less certainty than that of the latter.*

*It is plainly impossible to set a time-limit, and make the matter wholly a trial of intelligence. It seems best, therefore, to allow the reader unrestricted liberty, and thus to turn it—for the unalert—into a test of character. They are advised to read on when their patience is exhausted.*

*There may be superior persons who never saw a problem ; to whom it was all perfectly clear ; who, having reckoned with every implication and adjusted every fact, upheld the innocence of the innocent and hanged the guilty with a rope woven of perspicuity and sturdy common sense, are wondering when somebody will write a detective story that shall be worth reading. Of these, after saluting them, there is no request to make but that they will speedily obtain paper and pencil and try their hand at the game from the other side.*

# CHAPTER XXXIII

BEALE returned to the sitting-room just after twenty past seven to find that supper had been laid during his absence. When Lucy was out of the way, and the door shut, he looked at Dickie.

" How did you get on in Chatham ? " he asked genially.

" Pretty well " answered the reporter. " You can count McFeish out."

" Really ? Good man—tell us about it."

Dickie Donovan did so. " And there you are " he said presently. " That's how I worked it out, and this is what I got for my trouble. One of the maids in the hotel found it, and kept it because she thought it was ' ever so funny-like '."

He passed round the sheet of paper enumerating the ' articles to be obtained '.

" A scavenging party " declared Tony immediately. " You hike round and grub up a number of improbable things. The man who made this out seems to have known his job."

He smiled reflectively.

" I wouldn't mind having a stab at it myself " he confessed. " Yes, what with road lanterns and danger signs, I can quite see why McFeish's friends mightn't like policemen."

" Did you find out anything about that ? " enquired Beale.

" Yes " answered Dickie. " I chugged off to the Bull & Bush, and learnt the whole fell story : how a party of gentlemen—one with red hair—had hired a barn for the evening, and made a most disgraceful noise, something awful it was, you wouldn't believe, drunk as lords they must 'ave been ; and how the police had been round the next morning—Tuesday— and taken away a lot of things from the aforesaid barn.

276

I got a list, as a matter of fact : the bobbies gave them a receipt, and I copied it down. Among other things, the spelling is rather instructive."

He gave them a second piece of paper, which provoked some mirth.

"Received from Henry Mallow, licence of the Bull and Bush Littlebury Kent, the articles mentioned herewith depossited on his premises by a party on the evening of the 19th inst as follows :—

| | |
|---|---|
| 4 ducks eggs | 1 pr shugar tongs |
| 5 horse shoes | 4 coppies of Punch |
| 1 hasock | 3 golloshies |
| 4 empty bottles | 3 red lanterns, 1 broke |

2 ladie's vests, 1 blue silk, 1 off-white woolen.
1 motor car ~~rade radd~~ bonnett cap
2 road signs saying DANGER !
1 dented police constable's truncheon
1 ~~brasser brasie~~ boddice (bust) (not damaged)
1 torn blue pettycoat, ~~silk~~ artyfical silk
1 ladys handbag, and contents of same, which being namely : 1 lipstick, 1 puff, 2 shillings, 1 tortushell comb, 1 ivery biliard ball
(Signed) Percy Martin, Police Sergeant
20/11/34."

"Well" said Beale, "that was a good day's work, Dickie—thanks. Now, can anyone tell me who else didn't do it ? "

"Yes" declared Tony. "At least, I think I can. Anyway, I've proved to my own satisfaction that Lucy and Bassett are pretty thick. I got Dickie to help, and he'll bear witness that she blushed when I mentioned the name ' William ', but when I explained who I was talking about she said ' Oh, you mean Bill Ashley '. Inference : she'd thought I meant somebody else."

"William being such an uncommon name" murmured Beale.

"Exactly" agreed Tony. "Common enough as a

277

baptismal name, certainly ; but nine times out of ten it gets corrupted into Bill, or Billy, or Will, or Willie. For instance, ' You mean Bill Ashley ' shows that she's used to thinking about him as ' Bill ' ; but Tate and Rush and Mrs B. all call Bassett ' William '.

"And anyway, that's not all. Consider these points.

" (1) : Lucy was looking round in church this afternoon rather as if she hoped to see somebody who wasn't there : it might have been Bassett.

" (2) : The night we came down here I heard Tate tell you that he'd had occasion to tell Bassett off. Everybody knows that he disapproves of the girl's going about with men. I should think he'd disapprove still more if the man was married, and that might have been the reason for the dust-up.

" (3) : It struck me some time ago that possibly the motive for Bassett's not talking wasn't because he had anything to do with the murders, but because he didn't want his wife to know what he was up to.

" (4) : At the funeral Mrs B. looked as if she'd like to cut the Tates up into a hundred and five slices. She's considerably older than her husband, and by no means a Cleopatra ; what about a mixture of jealousy and suspicion ?

" And finally, (5) : we had the sergeant's word for it that Bassett isn't by any means a woman-hater. I think he and Lucy were together on Monday night ; in which case, of course, the tramp and puncture were bogus. The case for the prosecution rests."

" And I believe you're right, sir " put in Matthews, to their surprise. " This afternoon I happened to come across a letter—I mean "—looking covertly across the table, " I happen to know that Bassett's quite keen on her."

" ' The Mystery of the Furtive Footsteps ', or, ' What the Sergeant Saw ' " murmured Beale, smiling. " Well, as you say, Tony, it seems to fit fairly well. If we accept that explanation, then three of the suspects are cleared. Any more for any more ? "

" Yes sir " continued the detective-sergeant. " You

278

needn't bother about the doctor. He was playing billiards in Shale between quarter past ten and quarter past eleven on Monday night."

" Splendid fellow ! How did you find out ? "

" This way, sir. You remember that note at the end of his last report ? He said you mustn't count on the body being Welling's, or you might find you'd snookered yourself. Now, sir, it's a theory of mine that you can often tell what a man's interests are from the way he puts things. For instance, people who don't play golf won't talk about stymying anyone, and if they aren't keen on racing they won't back someone to do something in a canter. If they don't care for boxing they won't ' scrape home on points ', and if they're not card-players they won't ' draw somebody's last trump '. Because Hatherley used that expression ' snookered yourself ', I thought it was quite likely that he might play snooker. As a matter of fact it was billiards on Monday night, as I said—he plays both.

" If he was innocent, it seemed sense to think he mightn't have left Shale till after eleven. There's only one place I know of in nearly every town of any size that a doctor could expect to get a game at that time, and that's the Conservative Club. I went round there, and found I was right. When I'd done that I thought I'd better clear up the funny business at the pictures. Mr Purdon told me about it this morning, and that was why I wanted to go into Shale, to begin with. I hadn't got much time to spare, though, so I did the only other thing I could think of, and asked Hatherley himself.

" He did go to the pictures all right, but he had a muffler round his face, because he'd got a touch of toothache, so that's why he wasn't recognized, though naturally the commissionaire knew who he was. As for the message on the screen, he never saw it for the simple reason that he fell asleep. When he woke up, and found he couldn't make head or tail of the picture because he'd missed a lot, he went out early.

He told me he kicked himself when he heard next day he'd been wanted."

Beale turned to Tony.

" We're both guilty about that " he said.

" Guilty of what ? " asked his friend.

" The capital mistake that I mentioned the other day : theorizing without any facts. Remember what happened. We didn't collect a bagful, and then try to make a theory out of them : we made the theory first, and then went out to look for something that fitted in with it. You can usually do that without much trouble. By the way "—to Matthews : " did you happen to ' come across ' any other interesting things this afternoon ? "

" No sir, not one : no sign of the wallet."

" Pity, though it's probably just as well, because we shouldn't be able to make use of them."

" Why not ? " asked Dickie. " What's all this hinting about ? "

Beale kept a straight face.

" Ask them as know best " he suggested darkly. " Anyway, at present we've got rid of four suspects, and each of you's done his bit. Now I suppose it's my turn to give an account of myself."

Some shade of meaning in his voice caught Tony's attention.

" Look here " he said, " I believe you're foxing. You know a jolly sight more than you're making out."

" Possibly " admitted Beale—" possibly."

" How far have you got ? "— eagerly.

" Now ! Let me tell my tale my own way. ' Once upon a time there were four men, and they were all as blind as bats. Presently one of them opened his eyes, and then there were three.'

" Has everybody finished stuffing ? Then let's get the mess cleared, and with enough beer in front of me I might be persuaded to tell you the stimulating story of the Clever Policeman and the Coloured Print."

## CHAPTER XXXIV

8.0 PM—8.45 PM

" I SUPPOSE the starting-point was really the old problem about the money : how did Tate get hold of Tatham's bank-notes ? First I asked myself what I knew for certain, and it came to two things : that Tatham received the money about three o'clock on Monday afternoon in London ; and that it was undoubtedly down here, and in Tate's possession, by ten o'clock next morning. That gave an interval of nineteen hours during which the transfer must have taken place. There was absolutely no question that it was the same lot of money.

" Next I asked myself what I could assume. From the moment the money came into the case I couldn't see any reason why Tatham should have sent it on in advance, unless possibly because he was nervous of carrying so much. But in that case he'd scarcely have chosen to take cash, in the first place ; and he wouldn't have been likely to send it anywhere else in Wyre but to the Rectory. However, as it still remained possible for him to have done so, though very improbable, I'd already taken what steps I could to satisfy myself that he didn't. I'm afraid, by the way, that I didn't bother much about the very faint chance that he'd sent it to someone not actually living in Wyre, but near enough for Tate to have got hold of it by ten o'clock in the morning. I was so doubtful about his having sent it at all. Hatherley seemed the only possible person, and Dickie cleared him up.

" There seemed no reason why the postman should have told me anything but the truth. Rush labelled him as being not over-bright, but quite trustworthy, and I must say it seems a very fair description. He said that there had been nine letters for delivery on Tuesday morning. Two were for Tatham—I opened them myself—, and one was left here for McFeish. It was certainly described as being postmarked London,

281

but Red-head assured me that he had received it unopened, and the evidence bore that out. There was a message on the back of the envelope written in the same hand as the address on the front. Tony and I were both interested in it, but for different reasons. The wording intrigued him—it's one of Blake's ' Proverbs of Hell ', by the way ; but I was more concerned with the fact that the ink used would undoubtedly have run if anybody had tried to steam the thing open. As it hadn't run, I believed what McFeish said.

" Mrs Bull, the postmistress, also received a letter—the famous one with nothing in it ; and there was one for Sergeant Rush, who satisfied me about it. The other four were all for Wyre Place : one, with an Irish stamp on it, for the butler, and three for Miss Frankes. When I learnt that on Tuesday morning she slept until nearly 10.0 I felt safe enough in ruling them out and therefore in assuming first that Tatham had not sent the notes at all, and second that accordingly they were still in his possession when he reached Wyre on Monday night. The fact that he had intended the next day to present £40 in cash to the matron of a hospital at Hadington made that conclusion seem likely.

" On that assumption, then, I could narrow down the period during which the notes must have changed hands from nineteen hours to about eleven ; but that still didn't bring me any nearer finding out how Tate got hold of them. I asked myself that question over and over again, until I really hated the very thought of money, but nothing happened. Then I thought it was about time to switch on to another question : why won't Tate say where he got the money ? As it turned out, it was as well I did, for after about quarter of an hour of that one I began to see a glimmer of light."

He broke off to fill his pipe, surveying his audience with a smile. " No " he said, " it's no good scowling, Dickie--I'm not going to hurry."

"I wasn't scowling" protested the reporter. "I'm trying to work it out before you tell us, but I'm darned if I can."

" Well " Beale consoled him, " it took me about three hours, and you said I was a great detective ! Anyway, to go on : you must understand that by this time I was getting pretty desperate. I'd got to the point where I honestly didn't know what to do except sit down and brood, and so I decided that I'd follow anything that was kind enough to show itself, whether it turned out to be a will-o'-the-wisp or not.

" I had a fair number of facts available—as many as there seemed any hope of getting for the moment—, and I felt certain that if only I could find the right point of view to look at them from, then they couldn't help beginning to fit together into some sort of connected whole. Since they quite definitely hadn't been doing that, or anything like it, the view-points must have been at fault.

" Instead of assuming, as I had all along, that Tate was being obstinate for his own ends—in order, that is, to protect himself—, it seemed a good plan to consider the idea that he might have been acting that way for the purpose of protecting someone else. With that for a start, the next step was easy. From what I knew of the man I judged that the only person except himself for whom he'd be likely to take the slightest risk was his daughter.

" In that connection I don't mind admitting that I was considerably influenced by something he told us last night. When I asked where Lucy was, he said she'd gone to bed early because she had a headache. Now, as she'd complained of one when she cleared the supper, he seemed to be telling the truth. From that I persuaded myself that for all his talk about a girl being a dratted nuisance—more trouble than an army of boys, and so on—, he wasn't past being kind to her on occasion. Lucy doesn't strike me as the sort of girl who'd say : ' Like it or lump it, I'm going to bed and be damned to you ! '. She'd stay and help if he told her to. Mind you, I'm not trying to make out that in all things she's the dutiful daughter : simply that she'd only be undutiful over what she could

283

hide from him. She might deceive, but she wouldn't defy.

"Anyway, the fact that he let her go to bed seemed to argue a certain amount of affection on his part, although from his manner towards her in public one wouldn't suppose he had any at all. For the purposes of my theory, therefore, I felt justified not only in completely ignoring his apparent down on her, but in going farther still, and crediting him with something rather stronger in the way of affection than not being awkward about a headache. In other words, I was ready to believe that Tate thought Lucy was in some way connected with the money, and that the reason he shut up the minute I told him it belonged to Tatham was because he immediately jumped to the conclusion that she was also concerned with the murder. I couldn't think of any other motive for his doing that except the money—I mean, anything else that would make him do it.

"That supposition automatically freed him from having had anything to do with either himself; there didn't appear to be the slightest grounds for thinking that he would have had any other reason for killing Tatham than theft; or, if so, that in the financial muddle he was in he wouldn't have gone through Tatham's pockets after what Dickie would call the fatal blow. Anyway, he couldn't have done the first murder, and I was convinced that the same person, or combination of persons, was responsible for both.

"But, all the same, I wasn't going to let this theory upset my whole estimate of the man. He might have a heart of gold, but he was still a pretty rough diamond, and I couldn't see him pushing affection to the limit of getting himself suspected of murder unless he was convinced that it was absolutely necessary; nor, incidentally, unless he was innocent.

"Four questions at once presented themselves. (1): was Lucy in fact mixed up in the murder, but not with the money? Or (2): with the murder *and* the money? Or, (3): with the money alone? And, (4): why

284

was Tate so sure that she was connected with either ?

" All I had to go on to answer the first two was my own impression of the girl's character. I hadn't got anywhere near solving the problem of her exact whereabouts on Monday night. As I said just now, she struck me as the type who'd do wrong by stealth if she did it at all. I couldn't imagine her as a murderess, or even as an accomplice : both attitudes seemed far too positive, not to say brutal. Added to that was the fact that she wasn't physically capable of having carried Tatham's body into the woods, and therefore didn't seem at all necessary to the second murder ; nor could she possibly have been at Pond Meadow in time to do anything but help to dispose of the first body. I decided to let her out of the murders.

" But that conclusion, though it cleared up questions (1) and (2), didn't mean that she mightn't still have been mixed up with the money. I won't go into all the possible ways in which that could have happened, but simply give you my reason for absolving her.

" If she'd had anything to do with the £50, I didn't see how she could help knowing where it came from—if not before ten o'clock on Tuesday morning, then certainly by nine o'clock on Wednesday evening. By that time not only was the murder out, but I, investigating it, was also making the most pointed enquiries about that money. If she didn't know, she must undoubtedly have guessed. And yet on Wednesday evening she told us that she thought Tate had stolen the money from McFeish. Now that would have to mean that although, being concerned in it herself, she must know that he wasn't, she was nevertheless deliberately trying to get him involved in it, and, therefore, in the murder. Quite frankly, that was just as impossible to swallow as that she'd done the actual crime.

" Having now got rid of the first three questions to my own satisfaction, I was free to concentrate on the fourth. In order to make my theory hold water, I had to work on the hypothesis that although Tate's conclusion about Lucy's complicity was wrong in fact, he must, all the same, have had good reason for arriving at it. What was that reason?

"Here again I stuck, but not for long. As I'd told myself in bed the other night, I only know three ways of getting possession of a thing : by taking it, by having it given or sent to you, or by finding it. Since he suspected her at all, the first was no good ; and as I'd decided that she didn't have anything to do with the money, she couldn't have sent or given it to him. That left only one way : Tate must have found it. But in what circumstances? To meet the demands of my theory, they must have been such that in his own mind he had little or no doubt as to who'd left it about : Lucy.

"As far as it went that seemed all very well, but it was too general, and so I became more particular. The circumstances naturally divided themselves into two parts : time and place. Taking place first, I made two subdivisions : (1)—Tate found the money in the King's Head ; (2)—he found it somewhere else.

"Now, from the theory's point of view, if he found it in some other place, why should he immediately think of Lucy? But the facts of the murder seemed to make it extremely unlikely, if not out of the question, that he could possibly have found it here. Those were the two uncomfortable horns of a very annoying dilemma. Well, I bethought myself of all the maxims about people who can't make up their minds which stool to fall between, and finally decided that I was going to chance my arm, and back theory against fact.

"This was what it now involved : that some time between eleven o'clock on Monday night and ten o'clock on Tuesday morning Tate found Tatham's £50 somewhere in the King's Head, and assumed, *not unreasonably*, that Lucy had put it there.

"Well, I don't mind telling you that I thought it sounded damn silly, put that way, and I very nearly packed up. But something made me go on ; after all, it didn't seem quite fair to the theory to drop it until it had been *proved* impossible.

"For the time being I left out of account the mystery of how it could have got there, and concentrated on the other question : why did Tate think that ? Answer—almost at once : because he'd already searched this particular place, and made sure there wasn't any money there. But why then should he look again ? Answer—guessing like blazes : because, in all innocence, the girl advised him to. There, for the first time, you'll notice, the detective's bête noire comes on the scene : coincidence. I steadily ignored it. As a matter of fact, things seemed to be looking a bit brighter. For one thing, a good many places were ruled out, in particular the old green suit. The money couldn't very well have got there unless one or other of the Tates had put it there.

"Then another idea struck me. The fact that Tate only suspected Lucy—he couldn't know, because she hadn't done it—meant that very probably he hadn't even asked her about the money. Was that likely? I thought it might be, as thus : he finds the notes by looking, on her suggestion, in a place where he's already satisfied himself that there isn't any money. He's desperately in need of it, and he knows that she knows that. I tried to put myself in his position, and to think more or less what he must have thought when he found ten nice fivers.

"Says Tate to himself : ' Now, that's funny—she must have known it was there ' ; but she didn't. ' But I couldn't have missed it when I looked before—therefore she put it there since then ' ; but, again, she didn't. ' But why not give it to me, instead of making me find it by accident ? Because, I suppose, she doesn't want me to know where she got it from. Why not ? Perhaps because she thinks I mightn't want to know. Well, am I going to take it, or not ? I need it badly enough, goodness knows, but if I do, then I mustn't ask her any questions . . . Yes, I'll take it, and act as if I'd found it. But I'd better have a yarn ready, in case anybody else starts asking questions. Obviously she's leaving that part to me. Now, what shall the yarn be ? Yes, I know : I'll say I found it in my old green suit. But supposing somebody asks her, and not me ? I'd better tell her where I'm saying I "found" it, so that we shan't have different stories.'

"Which, accordingly, he does : because although they didn't get the chance of saying a word to one another between the time we collared him on Wednesday morning and the time Matthews questioned her, when he asked if Tate had mentioned where he'd found the notes she said ' Yes, in his old suit '.

"Then yet another idea struck me. At 6.45 on Wednesday morning McFeish told Lucy that he'd lost his wallet and ' forty or fifty pounds '. Whether that was true or not I didn't know ; nor, if so, whether it had been lost or stolen. If the latter, however, I felt that I could leave her out as a possible thief, for the same reason as before : I didn't think she'd try to blame her father for something she'd done herself. At all events, that didn't matter much one way or the other. The point was that she'd be bound to tell Tate that McFeish was complaining : otherwise it would at once look as if she was trying to hush it up, and therefore as if she really had pinched the stuff.

"Accordingly, before Tate knows that the £50 had anything to do with Tatham, he hears from Lucy that Red-head has lost approximately the same amount of money as he himself has ' found '. That being so, I don't think it's too much to assume that he immediately jumps to the conclusion that she's stolen it from McFeish ; assuming also, of course, that he himself was innocent.

"Then I remembered that when she brought my shaving-water in the same morning—Wednesday— she'd obviously been crying. I asked her why, and she said, convincingly enough, that her father had been going for her. I then asked her what about, and she said it was to do with the cat—you remember there was a fuss about our supper on Tuesday night. But

her manner in telling me that last bit was anything but
convincing ; in fact, I was quite sure she was lying.
On Wednesday night she admitted as much, and then
said what Tate had gone off the deep end about was
her going into McFeish's bedroom at all. In the light
of what I now believed, that seemed likely to be very
near the truth. It's not pleasant to be in debt, and a
great relief when you're mysteriously enabled to pay
what you owe. It comes with all the bigger shock,
therefore, to find suddenly that—as you think—you've
settled your bills with money that your daughter's
stolen from a man staying in your own pub. There's
also probably an element of self-reproach : you ought
after all, to have asked about the money before using
it, and then this needn't have happened. I don't know
how bluntly he put things, but I expect he was trying
to convey to her the fact that she'd managed to get
him into a worse mess than ever. They probably talked
at cross purposes. Tate wouldn't want to say too much,
in case he was wrong ; and Lucy wouldn't have the
slightest idea what he was talking about at all.

"At that point I thought it might be worth finding
out from McFeish what Tate's attitude had been about
the missing wallet. Luckily the man's got a freak
memory, and he gave me their conversation in what
he assured me were almost the exact words. The thing
that interested me was Tate's apparent reaction to the
description of the money. He didn't, then, profess
doubt that money and a wallet had been lost ; but he
asked twice if McFeish was sure that it had all been
in pounds and ten-shilling notes. He passed the second
time off by saying that he was only thinking a big
packet like that wouldn't be easy to lose ; and people
who ' only think ' are nearly always making reservations.

" I worked out the reason for his curiosity in this
way. To query, not the loss of a thing, but the description of it, isn't the natural attitude of a pub-keeper
towards a guest who's complaining. Tradition demands
that he shall pooh-pooh the very idea of anybody's
being able to lose anything on his premises. ' My dear

sir, it's quite impossible . . . No one has *ever* complained before . . . Perhaps if you were to look again . . .' The correct demeanour, as Tony would call it, is one of inviolable righteousness. If you remember, he reverted to that on Wednesday night. He said it wasn't the first time McFeish had thought he'd lost something, and that it would doubtless turn up. McFeish himself admitted to having previously made a minor fuss about a book which was under his bed all the time, and that incident alone ought to have made Tate instantly dubious, not about the kind of money that was lost, but whether anything had been lost at all.

"Anyway, I won't labour the point. It seemed to me quite on the cards for Tate to have concurred in the loss of money and a wallet because he already knew they were missing ; which could only be if he himself had found them : but to have disagreed about the kind of money that was in the wallet because he knew differently. In other words I was prepared to believe, mad as it seemed, that what Tate had ' found '—thinking Lucy had left it for him to find—was McFeish's wallet with Tatham's bank-notes inside it.

"Incidentally, we had McFeish's word that not only was the wallet unmarked, and empty except for the money, but, as well, it was one he hadn't used since his arrival here. As it's not often that you meet someone with two wallets, and as Tate was accustomed to seeing Red-head with a crocodile-skin one, when he found a black-leather affair he wouldn't necessarily be a fool for not guessing whose it was. And another thing : as you remarked, Tony, Lucy doesn't seem to be over-fond of housework ; and Tate searched this room on Sunday morning. It isn't really surprising, therefore, that the wallet shouldn't have been found before.

"One last point before I get on to the main line again. Between the time he found the money, and quarter to seven on Wednesday morning, when he began to believe it was McFeish's, Tate must have had some particular place in mind as being the one Lucy had got it from. I mean, five-pound notes don't grow on trees. Was there anywhere reasonable? I soon made up an explanation which satisfied me. He must, I thought, have concluded that the girl had stolen the money from her aunt at Stoke Albury on Monday night. That was the only place from which, as far as he knew then, she could possibly have taken it. That seemed to fit in, too, with his not having questioned her. Even if it all came out, it would be a matter between relations and not very likely to lead to a prosecution."

He broke off again, and finished his pint of beer, which by now was rather flat.

" About midday on Wednesday " mused Tony—" if this theory of yours is right—Tate must have felt something like Alice in Wonderland. First he thinks the money came from his sister ; then he decides it wasn't hers, but McFeish's ; next he makes up a charming fairy-tale about it, and probably half believes the thing himself by the time he's finished ; and finally you come along to tell him it really belonged to the Rector."

" Yes " agreed Beale, " and that would account for his dazed look. I've never seen such a stupefied expression.

" As an item of interest " he went on, " I thought I'd see how I was getting on, so I went along to the kitchen and asked him a question. ' On Tuesday evening, Mr Tate ' I said, ' weren't you under the impression that the £50 belonged to your sister ? ' He admitted that he had been, and then contradicted himself in the same breath, and refused to say anything, but it was enough to show me that I might be on the right track.

" And now, not before it was time, I returned to the other part of the circumstances, namely : when did Tate find the money ? And, from that : when did it get into the King's Head ? Who brought it in ? How, short of black magic, could it have finished up in McFeish's wallet ? "

291

At this point Matthews drew in his breath sharply.

" Got it ! " he cried. " But go on, sir—I won't give it away. Lord, what mugs we've been ! "

" And still are, as far as I'm concerned " said Tony. " Yes, go on—lighten our darkness."

" Well, the first person I thought of was obviously McFeish himself. I'd already found out, too, that he could have got into this place on Monday night. He's got a key, and they left the door unbolted because he hadn't said he wouldn't be back. But I really couldn't see any point in his incriminating himself—which is obviously what he would have been doing—, with all due respects to the Arch-Criminal. I got stuck for a few minutes, and then I looked at a particular something in this room, and all my troubles were over —or just starting. There was only one way it could have happened, and one person who could have been the murderer. Let me quote to you.

" ' And the next thing I remember is being given hot milk and brandy at the pub, and looking at a picture of Moses '."

" Well I'll be sunk ! " cried Dickie.

" I don't know about that " said Beale, " but Curtis is."

## CHAPTER XXXV

### 8.45 PM—9.20 PM

" And what did you do then, sir ? " asked Matthews.

" And how could it have been Curtis ? " demanded Tony. " Damn it all, the man was home in bed, wasn't he ? Or wasn't he ? No, I suppose he couldn't have been. Do you mean he never went home at all, or what ? "

" Steady " said Beale ; " I can't answer all those at once."

" Then go on from where you left off, and bring the thing bang slap up to date."

" Very well—if I must, I suppose I must."

There was an unconcealed murmur of satisfaction, and while Dickie attended to the fire Beale took out his note-book.

"In the first place" he said, "I had to go back to the beginning, and re-examine everything that Curtis had said or implied. I also had to get used to thinking of him as X—it was a point of view that hadn't seriously occurred to me before. Then I had to find a motive for the first murder, convince myself that he could have done it by explaining away any apparently conflicting facts, and get hold of at least a minimum of evidence.

"At first sight it was a beast of a thing to tackle, though actually it didn't turn out to be as bad as I expected. I'm afraid I didn't do it very systematically, however—I kept jumping from one thing to another like a grasshopper—, so perhaps that made it harder.

"As I say, I had to get used to not bothering about the Tates, or Hatherley, or Bassett, or McFeish. Instead I had to concentrate on Curtis, always keeping in mind the possibility that Janet Elder might also be implicated. That thought, by the way, didn't in the least discourage me."

"And was she, sir?" asked Matthews. Beale smiled.

"I'll keep to the theories instead of the facts, if you don't mind" he answered. "As a start I got out this note-book, read through everything to do with Curtis, and wished to goodness there was more of it. Then I began brooding again. For some time I didn't get on too well, chiefly because I was trying to answer two questions at once: 'How could he have done it?' and 'Why did he do it?'. The second one seemed the more promising line to take, so I decided to leave the other for the moment. Actually they weren't separable for long, though, as you may notice.

"Why did Curtis murder the naked corpse, who was probably a crook named Jacob Welling? What connection was there between them?

"I was satisfied enough that the body must be that

of the mysterious stranger who gave up his ticket at Shale on Monday night, and then disappeared. Curtis misled me very cleverly there. He didn't say it was impossible for it to be the same man, because the one he'd seen was six foot tall at least, but that he didn't think it was, though he couldn't be sure because it was dark, and he hadn't been noticing. If he'd been at all emphatic I think I might have suspected him : not necessarily of the murders, but—like Hatherley—of not being what he seemed to be.

"Now, I said, you have two men travelling by the same train, and getting out at the same deserted spot at the same time, 9.13. One of them is a resident in the district, and the other apparently a stranger. There's nothing to suggest that any third person was present at the Halt, and every reason to believe that these two men were at least acquainted, since one of them—the resident—later murdered the other. Furthermore, it's quite certain that they must have come into direct contact at the Halt, even if they hadn't met earlier that evening, in the train or before.

"Of course—to branch off for a moment—by contact I don't mean what Curtis said about bumping into one another, though that again was a clever touch. It must have been tempting to say that nobody else got out, and very easy to forget that the man had almost certainly given up his ticket at Shale—presuming, of course, that they didn't meet before quarter past nine. Any enquiries would therefore lead straight to Wyre, and throw suspicion on Curtis for having told an obvious lie. As a matter of fact, when he said that —on Wednesday—I think he was hoping that I might be induced to consider the missing stranger as Tatham's murderer. I didn't know then that there had been more than one killing, and it would be an artistic touch to have the continued absence of your first victim explained by making him appear responsible for the death of your second.

"Anyway, having got to that stage—that their latest time for meeting was about 9.15—I found myself up against two points. The first, which I mentioned the night we got here, though for a different reason, is this. From any sensible murderer's standpoint, if you're already alone in comparative solitude with a man you intend to kill, it seems silly to hold your hand until you come almost within earshot of houses and people, and all the forces hostile to murder. You'd surely do that only if the delay was intentional ; in other words, only if it was more convenient to stage the killing in Pond Meadow at about twenty to ten than or at near the Halt about twenty past nine—*or in any other place within reach.*

" But that postulated a prearranged scheme, which brings me to the second point : that there is reasonable ground for believing that the crime was in fact hastily planned, and not carefully thought out.

" The reason for thinking that is chiefly to do with the inconvenience of Pond Meadow as the scene of action. First there's the general nature of the place, which lacks the privacy desirable for so secret and delicate a job. It lies close to a road, and because of that Curtis wouldn't dare show a light for more than a few seconds at a time—and even that would be risky —however high the hedges, and however confident he might be that nobody would go by. And from that we come to another point.

" It must be extremely difficult to kill someone, undress him, smash up his head and hands, dig a hole, and finally bury him, all in the dark. Curtis would have to tidy up, too, for I'm convinced that he didn't know beforehand about the load of mangolds. In any case, unless Parker was an accomplice—when he'd be laying himself open to blackmail for the rest of his life— their delivery was just as much a risk as a stroke of luck. Suppose the grass root had been noticed earlier, or the condition of the ancient spade. I'm sure as well that it was because he couldn't see what he was doing properly that he didn't mutilate the hands past hope.

" In fact, almost continuous darkness would make the job so hard that for choice Curtis would have done it in some other place where he could safely allow himself more light. Where he'd find such a place I don't know, because I'm not familiar with the district. But he is, and I simply don't believe that if he'd thought the matter out with any attention he could possibly have been content with Pond Meadow.

"But, says the quibbling voice of common sense, it's clear enough that this particular murder was not an end in itself, but merely the best means to another end ; namely, the total disappearance of a certain man. From that point of view, then, is not a spade a necessary part of the proceedings ? And may he not, therefore, *with all due deliberation*, have selected the shed in Pond Meadow because it contained one ?

"I answer : no, he may not. Any spade makes a clumsy enough weapon ; but this one has the added disadvantage of being so old that its handle's liable to come off at any moment. It can't be depended on either to do a decent murder or to dig a decent grave. A cautious man would as soon tie himself into an aeroplane with a couple of yards of frayed bandage, and then loop the loop. Actually, of course, it didn't let him down ; but that's beside the point, which is that forethought would advise not only the choice of a more suitable place, but also the provision of a more suitable weapon, and a better tool for grave-making.

"Anyway, I was satisfied enough myself about that. Just notice that the weapon, the place, and the darkness must all have been very real handicaps to Curtis. They must have hampered him so much, I mean, that we need hardly consider the possibility that he was behaving like Matthews' Arch-Criminal, and purposely committing the crime in such circumstances that we'd be bound to say ' This can't possibly be premeditated ', when in fact it was. Anyway, there seems no sense in it, as Matthews would also tell you.

"Well then, we've got at last to the point I was leading up to. With the absence of forethought, try to combine the fact that Curtis still seems not to have seized upon the best place to do his murder—namely, between the Halt and the cross-roads. Why should this be so ? "

After some moments' thought Dickie proposed an answer.

" Because he could still be delaying purposely, and yet with no longstanding plan " he said. " In other words, having decided to kill the man, and realizing that he'd need a spade, he went to the only place where he could be sure of getting one."

" Yes " agreed Beale, nodding, " that's the obvious reason, but somehow I don't think it's quite the right one. It seems to me that in taking his victim away from solitude into the haunts of men Curtis runs an enormous risk of landing himself in such a position that he can't possibly do the murder. For instance, if they meet anybody at the cross-roads—Mrs Seccombe posting a letter, or the butler going home after a drink— his companion may be seen at such close quarters that a description of him could afterwards be recognized. The point to remember is that because of his ticket it may be easy to trace him as far as Wyre Halt.

" I think that if it had been at all possible Curtis would have preferred to knock the man out while he was still safe from interruption, kill him—by strangling, say—, and then hide him temporarily while he went to fetch a spade. There's not so much danger that way : he can be careful enough, by himself, not to be seen. But to accompany his future victim to Pond Meadow just after half past nine, with the pub still open and the chance of traffic on the roads, is mad : two yards of stamp-paper. It's a crazy hit-or-miss three-shies-a-penny idea ; and yet Curtis, afterwards so clever on most points—false teeth and fingerprints —does just that. The thing seemed to me a plain contradiction in terms of character.

" For a time I almost began to think there must have been two people in it. One, a prize dolt, blunders happily along until he's got the body in the shed, and then makes way for an intelligent reasoning being. Curtis drunk and Curtis sober might have fitted, except

297

that when you're tight your brain doesn't miraculously clear in next to no time at all, even if you have just killed a man.

" But I didn't have to worry long, because I suddenly began to see more clearly myself. There might after all be an adequate reason. The amount of premeditation could be gauged with some degree of accuracy : for it must have started either before or after he and the stranger got out of the train. If I could be sure they hadn't travelled together, then I shouldn't be taking too much for granted in assuming that it needn't have been before.

" Then I really did wake up. All I had to do was to ring up the ticket-collector, and see if he remembered whether they were in the same compartment or not. He assured me that they'd been in separate ones.

" That helped things a lot. It shortened the time for thinking the murder out to twenty minutes at most, and made their meeting at the Halt a cause of the determination to kill, and not a result of it. Curtis met this man unexpectedly as they left the train, and found his presence so unwelcome, or intolerable, that as they were walking along he first decided to kill him, and then started working out ways and means of doing it. Quite probably it wasn't until they'd reached the cross-roads that he was at all clear about what he was going to do—which was why he couldn't do it before, in the safety zone ; and even then one person, merely by his presence, might have saved three lives.

" The connection between these two, therefore, was peculiarly intense—practically kill at sight.

" With this in mind I looked up Welling's record again. By this time, of course, I'd heard that the scars on his knee could be accounted for if necessary. Then I struck what seemed a snag. Miss Frankes—whom I was prepared to believe—had told me that the last time Curtis went to London was in June, and that he hadn't been up since because of illness. But Welling only came out of prison in July, where he'd been for the best part of eight years ; so how the devil could they know one another as intimately as all that ? It was unlikely that they could have met at all since 1926, and I couldn't quite see such strong feeling being kept up for that length of time.

"Well, I won't weary you with everything I considered before I hit on a point of view which gave me the clue. This is the conclusion I wrote down, preparatory to testing it. 'Curtis need never have met Welling in his life until 9.15 on Monday night ; and yet very soon after he does so he can have an excellent reason for wanting to kill him.' It may sound ridiculous—I rather thought so myself ; but after about a couple of minutes I got the explanation. Almost at once I lost it, and laughed at myself for being a fool ; and a few seconds later I got a better one. To be absolutely honest, I guessed, checked, washed out, guessed again, and then started fitting it together—in that order, as thus.

"Welling was Curtis' long-lost uncle, come home to do him out of the old lady's dough. But that was impossible : Welling really was Welling, and anyway he had no broken toe, nor was he tall enough ; I was a fool. But wait a bit—was I ? Suppose Welling was only pretending to be his uncle, *but took Curtis in* ?

"Three points soon struck me as in favour of this idea. Firstly, it gave a fairly strong motive. Secondly, it provided an adequate reason why it was so important that the body should not be found, or ever identified. Anywhere else but in Wyre Curtis need have done no more than get away with the murder ; but the presence of his supposed uncle in the same village as he himself lives in, and the fact that they'd been on the same train, would immediately direct suspicion towards him. He must also do away with the body.

"Thirdly, Welling, judging from his record, seemed a likely sort of man to attempt such an imposture. Let me read you the part that especially impressed me.

"'A plausible rogue, familiar with the confidence trick in all its branches. Makes it his chief source of livelihood, although never convicted for this offence. Has several times escaped punishment through the unwillingness of his victims to prosecute, and once through accidental death of prosecutrix. Very little is known of his methods, but it is believed he varies them far more than is usually the case. Prefers when possible to work alone, and seldom fails to exploit a suitable victim.'

"Note in particular 'prosecutrix'. It shows that he hadn't any scruples about deceiving women, and I don't imagine he'd hesitate about a blind one. At present there's no way of telling whether he'd ever met the real Herbert Frankes, but I expect he knew a fair amount about him. It might be worth bearing in mind that the old lady said her brother probably went abroad, possibly to Australia or South Africa, and that he might have taken up mining or farming : Welling has been to both those places, and done both those things. He was an old hand at the game, anyway, and in the circumstances may have hoped to get away with his lack of inches, at least for long enough to make a bit of easy money.

"Now I must get on to two other points which I thought might be worth examining. (1) : did Curtis yet know that he'd killed the wrong man ? (2) : was Janet Elder implicated ? They're so closely connected that it's going to be rather difficult to make you see how I answered one without first taking the other for granted, and *vice versa*. But I'll try.

"I decided that Curtis had found out, and at latest by Thursday afternoon, because it was then that he told me the story of the broken toe. The purpose of that story, of course, was to make me believe that he wouldn't have the slightest difficulty in knowing who was his uncle and who wasn't. Looking back now, I see that as far as I knew then the subject had nothing to do with what I'd called to question him about. He introduced it purposely, and cleverly enough not to make me wonder what he was up to.

"The thing puzzled me a little, though. If he knew

300

about the toe on Monday night, why do the murder ? The moment Welling says he's Herbert Frankes, Curtis demands to see visible proof. ' Take your shoe off and let's have a look.' A genuine long-lost uncle wouldn't mind doing that, even in a country lane at night, if he could thereby establish himself straight away : and a false one can be proved a fake, and so doesn't need to be killed. Incidentally, Curtis will go up one in auntie's opinion by being spry enough to save her from plots and persecution.

" But if, on the other hand, he didn't know on Monday night, how could he possibly have found out since ? His aunt was the only person in the house who could help : had he asked her, or got Janet Elder to ask her ? The proof that he hadn't was a remark Miss Frankes made when I mentioned that Curtis had told me about the toe. ' Fancy Ralph remembering that ! ' she said ; and now I could fancy it. He must have lain in bed sweating blood to think of something that would serve to show clearly that he wouldn't have done the murder because he'd have known it was unnecessary.

" But it seemed improbable that that alone would have satisfied him. He'd been working in darkness, without paying any particular attention to the feet, and it wasn't likely that he could be absolutely sure about the corpse's toes. He'd need another check before he could start airing his knowledge. The only one I could think of was the man's height, but that meant a similar difficulty : how did he find out, between Monday night and Thursday afternoon, just how tall his real uncle was ?

" That one only took a minute to get over, though. When on Wednesday afternoon Miss Frankes told me about her brother she asked me to fetch a photograph album from on top of the piano. I looked, but it wasn't there. Why not ? Because Curtis had it. By comparing his uncle's height with his aunt's—they're standing next to one another—he could be quite certain that the body in the shed was the wrong one.

301

" Now I come to the other point—about the impli-cation of Janet Elder. I was naturally suspicious of her because Curtis got her the job. I was more suspicious because she seemed to be the only person he'd trust to get the album for him without telling anyone. I gave her another black mark because it was she who sug-gested to Miss Frankes that I should be consulted about Uncle Herbert ; and I was confident when I remembered also that it was she again who put it into the old lady's head that the body we'd just found might be his.

" The motive for the first suggestion, of course, was purely precautionary. I was to get a fairly clear idea of the missing man's description, so that if by bad luck the body turned up I shouldn't dream of con-necting them. The body did turn up, and so the second step was taken. It was now to be suggested to Miss Frankes, and through her to me, that corpse was Uncle Herbert ; and I was then—as in fact I did, playing their game for them in all innocence—to scout the possibility of the idea. In other words, they meant to make a sucker out of me if a certain thing happened, and when it did their plan came off.

" In passing it's interesting to note that apparently the commission of the crimes had finished by midday Wednesday at latest ; but that actually it was still going on secretly all the time. And to underline the fact that Curtis played his hand pretty well, there's this. He proved his mistake to himself by checking on the height with a photograph : but he set out to convince me that he wouldn't have made a mistake by mentioning the toe, which he couldn't have checked on afterwards at all.

# CHAPTER XXXVI

" I THINK I'd better state my exact position at this point. I believed that the corpse was Welling, who was the stranger on the train ; that Curtis had killed Welling because he thought he was his uncle, and that by Thursday afternoon he'd not only taken Janet Elder into his confidence—to some extent at any rate —but also found out that he'd murdered the wrong man. I've left out only two things, which I'll come to later : what made him think he might have made a mistake ?, and why did he tell Janet Elder anything ? In a way they're both results of this imaginative reasoning, or whatever you like to call it, and not causes.

" Well, having built my theory, I now had to see if it would work. I wasn't going to give it up without a struggle ; but, on the other hand, I had no intention of clinging to it if plain facts proved it impossible. I leave that attitude to politicians.

" There was one question that had to be answered immediately : was it possible for Curtis to have done the murders, and yet still to have done the things we know he did do—ring up his friend at 10.28, for instance ?

" In order to answer that, I began by putting down what I knew for certain of his movements that night, and up till 8.0 the next morning.

" (1)  9.04 pm approx.  He gives up his ticket at Shale.

(2)  9.13 pm  He gets out at Wyre Halt.

(3)  10.28 pm approx.  He telephones Ridgeway from Wyre Place confirming Tuesday morning's shooting arrangements.

303

| (4) | 6.30 am Tues. | He 'accidentally' discharges gun coming downstairs at Wyre Place, causing maid to faint and breaking vase. |
| (5) | 7.00 am approx. | He is picked up near cross-roads by Parker, who finds him with a sprained ankle. |
| (6) | 7.15 am approx. | He arrives at the King's Head. |
| (7) | 8.00 am approx. | He returns to Wyre Place in car. |

" I won't comment on any of those for the moment, except to repeat that I considered them all reliable. In dealing with a man in his position, who's telling a story that's different from what actually happened, it's generally safe to assume that he'll keep to the truth whenever possible, and also that there's very little need to query anything he says if it's borne out by independent evidence. The only snag is when you doubt if the evidence really is independent ; but in this case the only person I wasn't prepared to trust was the Elder woman. I couldn't see any reason for disbelieving his aunt, or the servants, or the girl at the exchange.

" I now began filling up the gaps. Wyre Place is about $2\frac{1}{2}$ miles from the Halt. A normal time to do the journey on foot would be 45 minutes ; but in actual fact he took about an hour, or perhaps a minute or two less : his aunt said he got home not long after 10.0. I decided that if I could fill in that hour satisfactorily I'd be justified in thinking I was on the right track. I tried, and I managed it : here's the result.

" 9.13 : Curtis and Welling get off the train. Welling asks the way to Wyre Place, they begin talking, and start off towards the cross-roads, a mile away. By the time they arrive there, approximately 9.30, Curtis believes, as a result of what he has been told, that Welling is his uncle, and has decided to murder him. At half past nine, then, he starts to put his hurriedly thought out plan into action. Most of the times from now on, by the way, are my own guesses, but I don't think I've skimped him too much.

" First he misleads Welling by going straight on towards Pond Meadow, instead of turning right. At the gate (9.33) he knocks the man out, carries him to the shed (9.36), and kills him with the spade (9.39). Whether he knew it was there or not I can't say: perhaps its chance discovery while Welling was unconscious definitely decided him in favour of murder. Then, at once, he undresses the body. The reason for that is because he intends getting home as quickly as he can, and then sneaking out again to bury the body. If he didn't strip it on the spot he might have a job later ; some corpses get stiff surprisingly soon, especially if they died after a struggle, which may have happened. Allow him five minutes for that, and another five to go through Welling's pockets and tie the clothes into a bundle, probably putting in the false teeth as well. That makes the time 9.49. Give him two minutes more to shove the body in a corner out of the way, and he's ready to clear off home. He'd naturally hurry, to make up for lost time, and he ought to reach the bottom of the drive, a mile and a quarter away, by five past ten : that's giving him fourteen minutes.

" And now comes my answer to our problem of what happened to the dead man's clothes. He sprints up the drive, stops at the garage, halfway, unlocks it, hides the clothes, and then dashes up to the front door. He should be able to do all that in six or seven minutes, which makes the whole performance take just under an hour. As a matter of fact, Sergeant Rush is up there now. The chauffeur turns out to be another of his relations. I expect he'll be along soon, and then we'll know whether I'm right or not ; or anyway, whether there's any evidence. You see, he won't have been able to do anything about the clothes himself because of his ankle, and I very much doubt if he'd even tell Janet Elder where they were, in case she made any mistakes and let him down.

"Well, so far was so good, and the only point that worried me was his leaving the body in the shed. I thought about it a bit, but didn't see what else he could have done. It was certainly risky, but not terribly so, I think. The chances were that nobody would go near the place ; it was Bassett's land, remember, and Bassett doesn't encourage people to go into Pond Meadow.

"Now I had to get on with the rest of the night's work, always bearing in mind the fact that Rush said the coast was clear when he went by Pond Meadow at 12.45, and again at 1.30, and that he was on duty near the cross-roads between 2.0 and 4.30, with a short break in the middle. That was useful corroborative evidence for what already seemed obvious : that because I was sure both murders were done by the same man, and because we knew that Tatham must have got to Pond Meadow about 11.0, it followed that Curtis, to be the murderer, must arrive back there before then, or else during the few minutes it took for the ball to be kicked into the pond and got out again.

"There was one other thing, too. Curtis would know that Monday was Rush's night for prowling round, and therefore that he must be away from Pond Meadow by half past twelve, the time the sergeant comes on duty. It's a fairly safe bet that he'd remember that. He's lived in the village for several years, he isn't a fool, as I said before, and he'd have enough time between 9.50 and whenever he sneaked out of the house again to remember it."

He paused, and looked rather anxiously at the clock.

"Rush ought to be here by now " he said. "Anyway, to get on : so far I don't think I've made use of information that nobody else knew about, except perhaps the fact that Curtis was in this room on Tuesday

306

morning. To answer the next thing that worried me, I had to, though.

"I was bothered about how he managed to get out of the house and in again without being noticed, and then I suddenly recalled something which cleared that up, and really made me feel sure that I wasn't imagining things. While I was up at Wyre Place on Wednesday Janet Elder told me that because of Curtis' sprained ankle they'd changed rooms. Apparently hers has a fireplace and his hasn't, and he wants a fire while he's in bed. You see the importance of that, Matthews? It means that the room with the fire-escape—the one you told me about before the inquest yesterday—isn't really hers at all, but his : it's the one he slept in on Monday night, before there was any need to change.

"Knowing that, I could get on filling up his time-table between 10.12 and 6.30. Here's what I think happened, and I shall be surprised if I'm far out.

"The moment he gets home he establishes his presence, saying good-night to his aunt, who was cross with him because she smelt drink, sending the butler to bed, locking up, and probably having a liquid supper. Then, as a final precaution, or perhaps only so that he shall seem to be behaving normally, he rings up this Ridgeway fellow about meeting near the Halt at 7.0 the next morning. After that he goes up to his room and changes into some old clothes—probably those he intended to wear for shooting.

"At or about 10.40 he leaves the house by the fire-escape, taking a torch. I expect he seriously thought of getting hold of another spade as well, but it seems clear enough by the condition of the one we found in the shed that he didn't. Possibly he thought the risk of being seen carrying it too great, or else he was afraid that the gardener would notice it had been used.

"He reaches Pond Meadow again by 10.55. I gave up the idea that he didn't get there until after 11.0 because it wouldn't have left him time to get through by half past twelve. Now the 10.21, if you remember, is hardly ever late. Curtis would be justified,

307

therefore, in expecting Tatham to have been home ten minutes or so by then. The wind on Monday night was blowing towards the Halt from here, so that he wouldn't be able to hear the train.

" Just after five to eleven, then, he begins to dig the hole for the body. A minute or two later Tatham comes along, starts going across the field without noticing anything, and does his business with the football. About 11.10, as he's standing by the pond, something that happens in the shed—either the torch shining, or a noise—attracts his attention, and he goes straight off to investigate. He may not immediately recognize Curtis, but you can bet that Curtis recognizes him, and —possibly in a panic—lets him have the spade as well : he's seen too much.

" Then, of course, he has to start improvising. Tatham's absence will be looked into : therefore he must be found without much difficulty. The last thing Curtis wants is a thoroughly organized search of the neighbourhood. But he certainly mustn't be found in Pond Meadow, for the same reason, and accordingly Curtis carries him into the wood and dumps him.

" Then he makes his first big mistake, by taking the bank-notes. In a way it's understandable, though : fifty pounds is fifty pounds, and his aunt probably keeps him pretty short. Anyway he'd be fairly sure to know about it : they'd travelled up together in the morning, and Tatham was a talkative old man with friends. Curtis himself told me that the Rector had said he was going to see his publishers.

" He gets back to the field about 11.18, remembers the hat and stick, and finds them by the pond, together with the football. As a matter of fact, though, I've changed my mind about the stick. It would be ridiculously careless for Curtis to put it in the pond when his idea is to keep Pond Meadow out of it at all costs. I think Tatham probably dropped the thing in the water himself when he was getting the ball out.

" The hat goes into his pocket, because he can't be sure of finding the body again in the dark, and the ball into the woods, either at once or later. Then he gets on with the digging again, hurrying for all he's worth because he's just lost twenty precious minutes. He finishes the grave by 11.45, which is allowing him roughly half an hour for it, and next begins to deface Welling's body. In spite of Dr Hatherley, I don't think he need take more than quarter of an hour over that, including the mouth and fingers. Burial carries him on to 12.15, tidying up adds another ten minutes, and there you are : all ready to leave by 12.25.

" On his way home he shoves the hat with the rest of the clothes, climbs up the fire-escape, and goes to bed, though probably not to sleep.

" Now we come to Tuesday morning, and the frightening of Sarah Jane, or whatever her name is. I'm quite sure that that was done deliberately, in order to impress on everybody's memory—if it should ever be necessary—that he was in the house on that particular morning. He certainly chose an effective means.

" And now, with no flourish of trumpets, there steps in dear old Fate, alias Nemesis, alias Clotho and Co., thread-spinners. On the way to his shooting appointment he puts his foot in a rabbit hole and does his ankle in.

" That, of course, is another complication that he can't possibly have foreseen, and by the time he gets here I expect he's sweating a bit. He can't now get rid of the clothes, and he's got Welling's papers, and Tatham's £50 on him. He wouldn't risk leaving either of them in his room.

" While he's lying on that couch over there he catches sight of McFeish's wallet, which has dropped off the desk. I demonstrated to Tony this afternoon that it would be quite possible for him to reach it. When he's alone he looks inside, and finds £47 in small stuff. And then the great idea comes to him. He knows that Tate is hellishly hard up, and thinks what a brilliant scheme it would be to plant the £50 on him.

always provided he can make sure that the man hasn't a strong alibi.

" Now remember that at this time—quarter past seven or so on Tuesday morning—Tate would still be annoyed with Lucy for being late the night before. He told us himself that he went out to look at her bike. Remember too that Curtis is at least on speaking terms with the girl—I put things as mildly as possible. One question—' What's the trouble about ? '—is enough to tell him what he wants to know : that Tate was alone in the pub between half past ten and quarter or twenty past eleven. If he knows or remembers that McFeish is staying here, another question settles him.

" Since everything seems all right, he exchanges the money, losing about three quid in the process, but hoping to make sure of saving his neck—surely a profitable deal. But actually it's nothing of the kind ; it's his second big mistake, made in trying to put right his first. I feel sure that by now he'd come to the very sensible conclusion that he'd been mad ever to have touched Tatham's £50. To get rid of it was a sound idea, but all the same he ought to have known better than to follow inspiration so blindly. There's nearly always a snag about sudden dazzling brilliancies ; they need sleeping on, and then usually scrapping.

" It may have occurred to him that the wallet wasn't Tate's at all, but that wouldn't matter. He's still planting stolen money on the premises of a man who's hard up, and hasn't a good alibi, and perhaps throwing suspicion on someone else at the same time. Also, by taking what was in the wallet he's depriving the owner of one line of defence : ' Why should I do murder for fifty pounds when I've already got that much ? '.

" I doubt if Curtis put the wallet back where he found it. His aim would be to leave it in some place apparently out of his reach, crippled as he is : a precaution in case it's ever suggested that he had anything to do with it. How exactly he could have done that I'm not sure ; but I wouldn't put it past him to have made use of that sword on the wall above the couch.

He could reach the handle of the bottom drawer in the desk with it, normally beyond his grasp, and pull it open. It wouldn't take him more than thirty seconds."

Here Tony got up, went quietly over to the desk, and tried the handle in question.

" No " he admitted, " this one doesn't stick, or come to pieces. By the way "—to Matthews : " what about a spot of fingerprinting on the sword ? "

The detective-sergeant nodded, but made no move.

" I'll do it presently " he said, and then turned to his superior.

" And now we come to our dead-heat, sir ? "

Beale smiled.

" Yes : what steps did the murderer take to stop people making enquiries about the victim ? On Tuesday morning Curtis still believes that he really has killed his uncle, remember. He can be reasonably sure, even if he doesn't know it from their conversation, that before coming to Wyre the man had been to see his aunt's solicitors. Very probably Welling mentioned himself that he'd done so as part of his *bona fides* ; and what's more, he would. To stand any chance of deceiving the old lady he's got to deceive Grayson Dean & Grayson first, and to visit them is obviously what the genuine article would do. There can be hardly any doubt that the whole idea of the imper-sonation was suggested to Welling by reading one of Miss Frankes' regular advertisements.

" They'd naturally communicate at once with their client, but Curtis would know that she hadn't heard before he went to town, or she'd have told him. He could also find out when he said good-night to her that evening that no news had arrived while he was away.

" As letters don't get to Wyre Place before half past eight, he was probably relying on being able to get it for himself. Possibly he meant to time his return from the shooting so that he met the postman at the bottom of the drive. He can't do that now he's crocked him-self, though, and this is where I think he begins to realize that he'll need Janet Elder's help. Because

311

Miss Frankes is blind, one of the companion's duties will be to read her correspondence to her.

" I'm not at all sure how much he told Janet then, but I'm certain that by Thursday afternoon she knew nearly all about both murders, because it was she who suggested to the old lady that the second body might belong to Herbert Frankes. On Wednesday, too, I think she knew that Curtis had killed Tatham, though perhaps not why. That's the only way I can explain her curiously oily references to Mrs Seccombe on that day. She didn't like her, and yet she went patently and obviously out of her way to be ' nice ' about her. Why ? Because, I believe, Curtis hadn't told her much about his motive for the murder, and so she'd jumped to a conclusion of her own : namely, that Mrs Seccombe was somehow concerned in it. For instance, she may have thought that Curtis and the daughter did the old man in together, and were going to marry on his money.

" Anyway, from her point of view she couldn't be anything but nice about the woman she didn't like without running the risk of throwing suspicion on the man she did like. It's fairly common knowledge that she's got her eye on Curtis, and she wouldn't try to incriminate him yet, though she might have done later, of course, if she'd been right : ' hell knows no fury ', and so on. But first I think she'd have tried to bargain with him."

" Which will you have, my bed or the gallows ? " put in Dickie, rather crudely.

" The gallows every time " returned Beale, at which the others laughed. " If she'd only known " he went on, " she took quite the wrong attitude. I shouldn't have taken anything detrimental she said at all seriously ; but actually she did start me wondering. Dear Janet was rather a broken reed, really—she muddled the album as well. It ought to have been back on the piano, in case the old lady wanted it.

" Anyway, let's go back to the letter. I worked on the assumption that Grayson's had written to her, and it proved correct. I got their phone number from the Yard, and a stately voice assured me that on Monday afternoon they had been called upon by a gentleman representing himself to be Mr Herbert Frankes, the missing brother of their valued client Miss Edith Frankes. So far no letter had been received from her in answer to theirs informing her of this fact, but instead they had heard from the same gentleman this morning—Friday—that he'd been unexpectedly called away to the Midlands, and might not be able to make his projected visit to his sister for some weeks, or even months.

"I think, by the way, that it was their use of the phrase 'representing himself to be Mr Herbert Frankes', or something similar, which first made Curtis sit up and wonder if the dead man really was his uncle; and from the obsequious way they kept referring to him as 'the gentleman' on the phone to me, I rather think that Welling hadn't altogether taken them in.

"Well, ses I to meself, science is admittedly wonderful, but the dead can't yet write letters, especially if they're lying in a mortuary with no face to speak of and their hands all smashed about. I got the Yard straight on to this epistle, which was typewritten, and had been posted yesterday evening in Nottingham. As you already know, it was done on a 'Flag', and there was no trouble in finding out that half the county owns one, including McFeish, incidentally. The only machine I was interested in was the one at Wyre Place.

"And now" he finished, "we're still waiting for Sergeant Rush. I wish he'd hurry, and I hope you haven't been too bored."

Dickie Donovan put down his pencil.

"Quite honestly" he said, "it's the cleverest mix-up of reasoning and imagination that I ever heard of. You hardly put a foot wrong the whole way."

Beale laughed.

"As a matter of fact" he contradicted, "I did make one very bad mistake. I've been wondering if anybody would notice, but apparently not. Since my final conclusion, which I've pretty well verified, was that Miss Frankes' post had been tampered with on Tuesday morning, it was rather rash of me to take it for granted so easily that Tatham couldn't have sent her the money because she didn't wake up till 10.0."

He paused to light his pipe, which he had been slowly filling.

" As a job done more or less on the spur of the moment " he said, " I don't think Curtis did too badly. He went wrong about the money, admittedly, and quite by accident he reminded me that he was in here on Tuesday morning ; but it wasn't really his fault that Welling's body was found. If my guess is right, he couldn't know that Tatham's stick was in the pond, nor that he'd got his feet wet. He took very reasonable .precautions in case the body should be discovered, and it was sheer bad luck that Welling had been a convict and that Matthews was clever enough to identify the prints. If Welling had been an honest man that couldn't have happened : but nor would the murder, because he wouldn't have tried the impersonation.

" At all events, I don't think Curtis can wriggle out, and the woman will be for it too. I believe penal servitude for life is the maximum sentence for being an accessory after the fact in murder ; but she'll probably get off with two years."

Here Tony suddenly gave an unintelligible cry.

" Sorry, but I've got it ! " he explained.

" You seem to have got something all right " agreed Dickie.

" Rabies : he's been bitten by his bloodhound " said Beale.

" Blast bloodhounds ! I'm serious. I can make or mar your career with a single word."

" Then make it, there's a good chap. The word is ? "

Tony faced his audience.

" The word " he announced solemnly " is ' Prewin '."

There was a howl of amusement, in which he too joined.

" If you mean ' prune ' " said Beale, " then I'm

314

afraid my career's ruined. It's a fruit that has the most astonishing effect on me."

" I don't. I mean what I saw—Prewin."

" Well, what is it ? How do you spell the thing ? Where does it come from ? "

" Nottingham " replied Tony. Beale sat forward.

" Just what do you mean ? " he asked, serious again.

" That Prewin is the name of a lady who lives in Nottingham. I was with Rush on Wednesday evening when he looked through the letters for the one you thought Bassett might have written. There was a typewritten one for Prewin at Nottingham. I remember the name because I made up a limerick about it.

> " ' There was an old lady called Prewin
> Who said " Friends, I shall die very sewin ;
> And when I am dead
> I should like at the head
> Of my grave a pink penny ballewin ".' "

There was no applause.

" Well, if it made you remember——" said Dickie sympathetically.

" Address ? " demanded Beale, but Tony shook his head.

"Who am I to pry into other people's correspondence?" he asked. "I know it was Nottingham, but that's all."

" Oh well, it doesn't matter—there can't be an awful lot of people in the world called Prewin. At least, they may be awful, if they're anything like your limerick, but that doesn't matter either. The times agree, too : the letter gets to Nottingham by the afternoon delivery on Thursday, and arrives in London first post today. Mrs or Miss ? "

" Miss."

" Good : but note the self-righteous attitude of the man. ' Who am I to pry ? ' indeed ! But I'm glad you did. Hullo ! Here's Rush, I think. I wonder whether he's been lucky. If so, I shall get to the theatre tomorrow night after all—forgetting the concert "— as Matthews raised his eyebrows.

315

# CHAPTER XXXVII

THE sergeant came into the room carrying a large bundle.

" The evidence, sir " he said simply, and it was clear both from his manner and his expression that he was by no means happy about the identity of the murderer.

" Thanks—put it on the table and sit down, won't you ? "

Beale too was serious now.

" You're later than I expected—did you have any bother ? "

" No sir, but Miss Frankes was out to dinner, and didn't get back till after 9.0. The stuff was locked in the back of the little car, sir—not the big one. There's two, the Daimler and a small Wolseley that Mr Curtis uses—that is, used, I should say."

Meanwhile Matthews had undone the bundle, and was looking inside.

" It's all here, sir " he said. " Plenty of blood on the clothes, too. Yes, here's Tatham's hat as well, I think. And that reminds me. Before I have a look I'd like to tell you what I'm looking for : the only thing you didn't clear up, sir."

" What's that ? " asked Tony.

" The missing ticket."

" Lord ! " said Beale. " I thought I'd remembered everything. Where is it ? "

" In the hat, I think " answered Matthews. " It's only a guess ; but the Rector lost his handkerchief, so I don't see why he shouldn't have lost his ticket as well, bought a new one, put it there for safety, and then come across the old one."

Dickie took up the hat, and examined the band.

" Full marks " he announced, holding up a slip of green cardboard. " No. 1428. And what's the next step ? "

" Arrest Curtis, I suppose " replied Beale.

Sergeant Rush shifted uncomfortably in his chair.

" It'll kill the old lady " he muttered.

There was a momentary silence, and then Tony spoke, in so serious a tone that they all turned to look at him.

" That may be so " he said, " but it's the lesser of two evils. I know I'm a bit of an ass as a detective, but I've just spotted something very clearly. Until quarter past nine on Monday night Curtis was probably quite convinced that his uncle died years ago. You've seen what limits he was prepared to go to the minute he thought otherwise. I can't see any reason why he should have gone back to his old belief. In fact, I very much doubt if he has, and as long as he's a free man I'd hate to take on the job of insuring Miss Frankes."

Beale sat up sharply.

" You're right " he declared. " The man can't do much because he's in bed, but the woman's still loose. Take me straight up there, will you ? No, wait a minute—I think this had better be done quite officially. Matthews, ring up Superintendent Bowman and get him to come over with a couple of cars and five men."

" What about a warrant ? " asked Dickie. Beale shook his head.

" I haven't got time, and it's not essential."

" And why five men ? "

" Two as drivers, one to look after Curtis, one for Janet Elder, and one to chaperon them. It's part of the regulations—not that anybody would be likely to risk his chance of a pension for her bright eyes. I expect you'd rather have nothing to do with all this, Rush ? "

" That I wouldn't, sir " said the sergeant, definitely. " Thank you, sir " he added.

At 10.40 Tony found himself alone in the King's Head. Dickie had gone with the others, and Rush was back on duty.

For some minutes he sat in front of the fire, staring into it, thinking. This, for Curtis, was the end of the

317

chase. There remained for him now no more than three months or so of life : the remands, the trial, the usual appeals, and then the last few hurrying days, barren alike of hope or promise.

He was glad when Lucy came into rouse him.

" Is there anything else tonight, sir ? " she asked.

He looked at her for a moment.

" Only one thing " he said at last. " You're very young, and you'll be very silly if you make a habit of playing about with married men."

She stared at him in amazement, the colour mounting to her face.

" How—how did you find out, sir ? "

He shook his head.

" It doesn't matter—but I shouldn't go on with it."

" No sir, I shan't."

She hesitated a second, and then went on breathlessly.

" I wouldn't have done then, only he'd been asking me, and I thought maybe he'd lend dad the money."

And then :

" We heard it, you know, sir—right close by ".

" Heard what ? "

" Mr Tatham's body being carried into the woods."

" Good lord ! What did you do ? Couldn't you see who it was ? "

" No sir. We kept still for a bit, thinking it was the keeper, and then I got on my bike and came home. You won't tell dad, will you ? "

" No, of course not. By the way, is your tyre mended yet ? "

" My tyre ? No sir."

" Then why don't you get young Ashley to do it ? I think he'd be glad to, if you gave him the chance. Good-night."

Before the others came back he managed to clear up another point. Somewhat reluctantly he went upstairs and knocked at McFeish's door. When he was bidden to go in he half obeyed, standing in the doorway.

" Sorry to disturb you " he said, " but there's just one thing I'd like to know. How many marks did you score ? "

For a full ten seconds McFeish looked at him steadily before he smiled.

" So you found out, did you ? I got forty-seven, if you must know. It ought to have been fifty-three, only I dropped my hassock on the way. Now you're up here, I wonder if you could advise me about some shares . . ."

" And he really did do it ? "

Beale nodded.

" There's no possible doubt, I'm afraid " he answered. " He practically confessed when we arrested him."

" Just because he was afraid he wouldn't get all the money ? "

" To all intents and purposes, yes. It seems that Miss Frankes always made it clear that her will contained an unsigned codicil making her missing brother the chief beneficiary. If he turned up it would be completed within a few hours, provided they settled their quarrel, and I suppose Curtis lost his head for a moment."

Mary Seccombe frowned.

" And Janet Elder in it too " she said. " Poor Miss Frankes. I must go up there—she'll be all alone. Do you think she might have been the next ? "

" It's more than possible " he agreed. " It would have been the logical step to make quite sure."

There was a short silence, and then she spoke again.

" You know, it makes me wonder whether it's worth while having any friends : or whether perhaps I'm the sort of person whose judgment can't be trusted. This isn't the first mistake I've made."

He picked up his hat, and stood pulling at it, pondering the best way of putting what was in his thoughts. But there seemed no best way, so he branched off to another subject.

319

"About Tate" he said : "it's rather a problem who ought to prosecute. You see, he stole your father's money inside Mr McFeish's wallet. As you inherit, I suppose he was really stealing from you."

She smiled at him.

"And even that's not certain, you know. It was more Sister Tomlin's money than mine. But she's been paid, and as far as I'm concerned the matter can drop. I mean, he'll be in trouble enough already, because the brewer people will be after him again, won't they?"

"Yes. If you do nothing he'll be getting off pretty well on the whole, though. He burnt the wallet, but McFeish will get his money back, and I shouldn't think he'll make much fuss. He's got another one, anyway.

"You must make up your own mind about what you said just now" he added, after another pause. "If you want—I mean, if I can help, you could get in touch with me at the Yard. Telephone if you like : Whitehall 1212, but I expect you know that from the wireless."

She nodded.

"I shan't stay here long" she told him. "If I'm in London, and I lose my way, I'll ring you up. Or perhaps I'd better say, if I find my way. Good-bye, Mr Beale. I'm glad you're still human—but don't spoil the hat entirely."

THE END

# RAMBLE HOUSE's
## HARRY STEPHEN KEELER WEBWORK MYSTERIES
(RH) indicates the title is available ONLY in the RAMBLE HOUSE edition

The Ace of Spades Murder
The Affair of the Bottled Deuce (RH)
The Amazing Web
The Barking Clock
Behind That Mask
The Book with the Orange Leaves
The Bottle with the Green Wax Seal
The Box from Japan
The Case of the Canny Killer
The Case of the Crazy Corpse (RH)
The Case of the Flying Hands (RH)
The Case of the Ivory Arrow
The Case of the Jeweled Ragpicker
The Case of the Lavender Gripsack
The Case of the Mysterious Moll
The Case of the 16 Beans
The Case of the Transparent Nude (RH)
The Case of the Transposed Legs
The Case of the Two-Headed Idiot (RH)
The Case of the Two Strange Ladies
The Circus Stealers (RH)
Cleopatra's Tears
A Copy of Beowulf (RH)
The Crimson Cube (RH)
The Face of the Man From Saturn
Find the Clock
The Five Silver Buddhas
The 4th King
The Gallows Waits, My Lord! (RH)
The Green Jade Hand
Finger! Finger!
Hangman's Nights (RH)
I, Chameleon (RH)
I Killed Lincoln at 10:13! (RH)
The Iron Ring
The Man Who Changed His Skin (RH)
The Man with the Crimson Box
The Man with the Magic Eardrums
The Man with the Wooden Spectacles
The Marceau Case
The Matilda Hunter Murder
The Monocled Monster

The Murder of London Lew
The Murdered Mathematician
The Mysterious Card (RH)
The Mysterious Ivory Ball of Wong Shing
Li (RH)
The Mystery of the Fiddling Cracksman
The Peacock Fan
The Photo of Lady X (RH)
The Portrait of Jirjohn Cobb
Report on Vanessa Hewstone (RH)
Riddle of the Travelling Skull
Riddle of the Wooden Parrakeet (RH)
The Scarlet Mummy (RH)
The Search for X-Y-Z
The Sharkskin Book
Sing Sing Nights
The Six From Nowhere (RH)
The Skull of the Waltzing Clown
The Spectacles of Mr. Cagliostro
Stand By—London Calling!
The Steeltown Strangler
The Stolen Gravestone (RH)
Strange Journey (RH)
The Strange Will
The Straw Hat Murders (RH)
The Street of 1000 Eyes (RH)
Thieves' Nights
Three Novellos (RH)
The Tiger Snake
The Trap (RH)
Vagabond Nights (Defrauded Yeggman)
Vagabond Nights 2 (10 Hours)
The Vanishing Gold Truck
The Voice of the Seven Sparrows
The Washington Square Enigma
When Thief Meets Thief
The White Circle (RH)
The Wonderful Scheme of Mr. Christopher
Thorne
X. Jones—of Scotland Yard
Y. Cheung, Business Detective

## Keeler Related Works

**A To Izzard: A Harry Stephen Keeler Companion** by Fender Tucker — Articles and stories about Harry, by Harry, and in his style. Included is a compleat bibliography.

**Wild About Harry: Reviews of Keeler Novels** — Edited by Richard Polt & Fender Tucker — 22 reviews of works by Harry Stephen Keeler from *Keeler News.* A perfect introduction to the author.

**The Keeler Keyhole Collection:** Annotated newsletter rants from Harry Stephen Keeler, edited by Francis M. Nevins. Over 400 pages of incredibly personal Keeleriana.

**Fakealoo** — Pastiches of the style of Harry Stephen Keeler by selected demented members of the HSK Society. Updated every year with the new winner.

# RAMBLE HOUSE's OTHER LOONS

**The Case of the Little Green Men** — Mack Reynolds wrote this love song to sci-fi fans back in 1951 and it's now back in print.

**Hell Fire** — A new hard-boiled novel by Jack Moskovitz about an arsonist, an arson cop and a Nazi hooker. It isn't pretty.

**Researching American-Made Toy Soldiers** — A 276-page collection of a lifetime of articles by toy soldier expert Richard O'Brien

**Strands of the Web: Short Stories of Harry Stephen Keeler** — Edited and Introduced by Fred Cleaver

**The Sam McCain Novels** — Ed Gorman's terrific series includes *The Day the Music Died, Wake Up Little Susie* and *Will You Still Love Me Tomorrow?*

**A Shot Rang Out** — Three decades of reviews from Jon Breen

**A Roland Daniel Double: The Signal and The Return of Wu** Fang — Classic thrillers from the 30s

**Murder in Shawnee** — Two novels of the Alleghenies by John Douglas: *Shawnee Alley Fire* and *Haunts*.

**Deep Space and other Stories** — A collection of SF gems by Richard A. Lupoff

**Blood Moon** — The first of the Robert Payne series by Ed Gorman

**The Time Armada** — Fox B. Holden's 1953 SF gem.

**Black River Falls** — Suspense from the master, Ed Gorman

**Sideslip** — 1968 SF masterpiece by Ted White and Dave Van Arnam

**The Triune Man** — Mindscrambling science fiction from Richard A. Lupoff

**Detective Duff Unravels It** — Episodic mysteries by Harvey O'Higgins

**Mysterious Martin, the Master of Murder** — Two versions of a strange 1912 novel by Tod Robbins about a man who writes books that can kill.

**The Master of Mysteries** — 1912 novel of supernatural sleuthing by Gelett Burgess

**Dago Red** — 22 tales of dark suspense by Bill Pronzini

**The Night Remembers** — A 1991 Jack Walsh mystery from Ed Gorman

**Rough Cut & New, Improved Murder** — Ed Gorman's first two novels

**Hollywood Dreams** — A novel of the Depression by Richard O'Brien

**Six Gelett Burgess Novels** — *The Master of Mysteries, The White Cat, Two O'Clock Courage, Ladies in Boxes, Find the Woman, The Heart Line*

**The Organ Reader** — A huge compilation of just about everything published in the 1971-1972 radical bay-area newspaper, *THE ORGAN*.

**A Clear Path to Cross** — Sharon Knowles short mystery stories by Ed Lynskey

**Old Times' Sake** — Short stories by James Reasoner from Mike Shayne Magazine

**Freaks and Fantasies** — Eerie tales by Tod Robbins, collaborator of Tod Browning on the film FREAKS.

**Six Jim Harmon Double Novels** — *Vixen Hollow/Celluloid Scandal, The Man Who Made Maniacs/Silent Siren, Ape Rape/Wanton Witch, Sex Burns Like Fire/Twist Session, Sudden Lust/Passion Strip, Sin Unlimited/Harlot Master, Twilight Girls/Sex Institution*. Written in the early 60s.

**Marblehead: A Novel of H.P. Lovecraft** — A long-lost masterpiece from Richard A. Lupoff. Published for the first time!

**The Compleat Ova Hamlet** — Parodies of SF authors by Richard A. Lupoff – A brand new edition with more stories and more illustrations by Trina Robbins.

**The Secret Adventures of Sherlock Holmes** — Three Sherlockian pastiches by the Brooklyn author/publisher, Gary Lovisi.

**The Universal Holmes** — Richard A. Lupoff's 2007 collection of five Holmesian pastiches and a recipe for giant rat stew.

**Four Joel Townsley Rogers Novels** — By the author of *The Red Right Hand: Once In a Red Moon, Lady With the Dice, The Stopped Clock, Never Leave My Bed*

**Two Joel Townsley Rogers Story Collections** — Night of Horror and Killing Time

**Twenty Norman Berrow Novels** — *The Bishop's Sword, Ghost House, Don't Go Out After Dark, Claws of the Cougar, The Smokers of Hashish, The Secret Dancer, Don't Jump Mr. Boland!, The Footprints of Satan, Fingers for Ransom, The Three Tiers of Fantasy, The Spaniard's Thumb, The Eleventh Plague, Words Have Wings, One Thrilling Night, The Lady's in Danger, It Howls at Night, The Terror in the Fog, Oil Under the Window, Murder in the Melody, The Singing Room*

**The N. R. De Mexico Novels** — Robert Bragg presents *Marijuana Girl, Madman on a Drum, Private Chauffeur* in one volume.

**Four Chelsea Quinn Yarbro Novels featuring Charlie Moon** — *Ogilvie, Tallant and Moon, Music When the Sweet Voice Dies, Poisonous Fruit* and *Dead Mice*

**Five Walter S. Masterman Mysteries** — *The Green Toad, The Flying Beast, The Yellow Mistletoe, The Wrong Verdict* and *The Perjured Alibi.* Fantastic impossible plots.

**Two Hake Talbot Novels** — *Rim of the Pit, The Hangman's Handyman.* Classic locked room mysteries.

**Two Alexander Laing Novels** — *The Motives of Nicholas Holtz* and *Dr. Scarlett*, stories of medical mayhem and intrigue from the 30s.

**Four David Hume Novels** — *Corpses Never Argue, Cemetery First Stop, Make Way for the Mourners, Eternity Here I Come*, and more to come.

**Three Wade Wright Novels** — *Echo of Fear, Death At Nostalgia Street* and *It Leads to Murder*, with more to come!

**Six Rupert Penny Novels** — *Policeman's Holiday, Policeman's Evidence, Lucky Policeman, Policeman in Armour, Sealed Room Murder, Sweet Poison*, classic mysteries.

**Five Jack Mann Novels** — Strange murder in the English countryside. *Gees' First Case, Nightmare Farm, Grey Shapes, The Ninth Life, The Glass Too Many.*

**Seven Max Afford Novels** — *Owl of Darkness, Death's Mannikins, Blood on His Hands, The Dead Are Blind, The Sheep and the Wolves, Sinners in Paradise* and *Two Locked Room Mysteries and a Ripping Yarn* by one of Australia's finest novelists.

**Five Joseph Shallit Novels** — *The Case of the Billion Dollar Body, Lady Don't Die on My Doorstep, Kiss the Killer, Yell Bloody Murder, Take Your Last Look.* One of America's best 50's authors.

**Two Crimson Clown Novels** — By Johnston McCulley, author of the Zorro novels, *The Crimson Clown* and *The Crimson Clown Again.*

**The Best of 10-Story Book** — edited by Chris Mikul, over 35 stories from the literary magazine Harry Stephen Keeler edited.

**A Young Man's Heart** — A forgotten early classic by Cornell Woolrich

**The Anthony Boucher Chronicles** — edited by Francis M. Nevins
Book reviews by Anthony Boucher written for the *San Francisco Chronicle,* 1942 – 1947. Essential and fascinating reading.

**Muddled Mind:** Complete Works of Ed Wood, Jr. — David Hayes and Hayden Davis deconstruct the life and works of a mad genius.

**Gadsby** — A lipogram (a novel without the letter E). Ernest Vincent Wright's last work, published in 1939 right before his death.

**My First Time:** The One Experience You Never Forget — Michael Birchwood — 64 true first-person narratives of how they lost it.

**Automaton** — Brilliant treatise on robotics: 1928-style! By H. Stafford Hatfield

**The Incredible Adventures of Rowland Hern** — Rousing 1928 impossible crimes by Nicholas Olde.

**Slammer Days** — Two full-length prison memoirs: *Men into Beasts* (1952) by George Sylvester Viereck and *Home Away From Home* (1962) by Jack Woodford

**Murder in Black and White** — 1931 classic tennis whodunit by Evelyn Elder

**Killer's Caress** — Cary Moran's 1936 hardboiled thriller

**The Golden Dagger** — 1951 Scotland Yard yarn by E. R. Punshon

**Beat Books #1** — Two beatnik classics, *A Sea of Thighs* by Ray Kainen and *Village Hipster* by J.X. Williams

**A Smell of Smoke** — 1951 English countryside thriller by Miles Burton

**Ruled By Radio** — 1925 futuristic novel by Robert L. Hadfield & Frank E. Farncombe

**Murder in Silk** — A 1937 Yellow Peril novel of the silk trade by Ralph Trevor

**The Case of the Withered Hand** — 1936 potboiler by John G. Brandon

**Finger-prints Never Lie** — A 1939 classic detective novel by John G. Brandon

**Inclination to Murder** — 1966 thriller by New Zealand's Harriet Hunter

**Invaders from the Dark** — Classic werewolf tale from Greye La Spina

**Fatal Accident** — Murder by automobile, a 1936 mystery by Cecil M. Wills

**The Devil Drives** — A prison and lost treasure novel by Virgil Markham

**Dr. Odin** — Douglas Newton's 1933 potboiler comes back to life.

**The Chinese Jar Mystery** — Murder in the manor by John Stephen Strange, 1934

**The Julius Caesar Murder Case** — A classic 1935 re-telling of the assassination by Wallace Irwin that's much more fun than the Shakespeare version

**West Texas War and Other Western Stories** — by Gary Lovisi

**The Contested Earth and Other SF Stories** — A never-before published space opera and seven short stories by Jim Harmon.

**Tales of the Macabre and Ordinary** — Modern twisted horror by Chris Mikul, author of the *Bizarrism* series.

**The Gold Star Line** — Seaboard adventure from L.T. Reade and Robert Eustace.

**The Werewolf vs the Vampire Woman** — Hard to believe ultraviolence by either Arthur M. Scarm or Arthur M. Scram.

**Black Hogan Strikes Again** — Australia's Peter Renwick pens a tale of the outback.

**Don Diablo: Book of a Lost Film** — Two-volume treatment of a western by Paul Landres, with diagrams. Intro by Francis M. Nevins.

**The Charlie Chaplin Murder Mystery** — Movie hijinks by Wes D. Gehring

**The Koky Comics** — A collection of all of the 1978-1981 Sunday and daily comic strips by Richard O'Brien and Mort Gerberg, in two volumes.

**Suzy** — Another collection of comic strips from Richard O'Brien and Bob Vojtko

**Dime Novels: Ramble House's 10-Cent Books** — *Knife in the Dark* by Robert Leslie Bellem, *Hot Lead* and *Song of Death* by Ed Earl Repp, *A Hashish House in New York* by H.H. Kane, and five more.

**Blood in a Snap** — The *Finnegan's Wake* of the 21$^{st}$ century, by Jim Weiler and Al Gorithm

**Stakeout on Millennium Drive** — Award-winning Indianapolis Noir — Ian Woollen.

**Dope Tales #1** — Two dope-riddled classics; *Dope Runners* by Gerald Grantham and *Death Takes the Joystick* by Phillip Condé.

**Dope Tales #2** — Two more narco-classics; *The Invisible Hand* by Rex Dark and *The Smokers of Hashish* by Norman Berrow.

**Dope Tales #3** — Two enchanting novels of opium by the master, Sax Rohmer. *Dope* and *The Yellow Claw.*

**Tenebrae** — Ernest G. Henham's 1898 horror tale brought back.

**The Singular Problem of the Stygian House-Boat** — Two classic tales by John Kendrick Bangs about the denizens of Hades.

**Tiresias** — Psychotic modern horror novel by Jonathan M. Sweet.

**The One After Snelling** — Kickass modern noir from Richard O'Brien.

**The Sign of the Scorpion** — 1935 Edmund Snell tale of oriental evil.

**The House of the Vampire** — 1907 poetic thriller by George S. Viereck.

**An Angel in the Street** — Modern hardboiled noir by Peter Genovese.

**The Devil's Mistress** — Scottish gothic tale by J. W. Brodie-Innes.

**The Lord of Terror** — 1925 mystery with master-criminal, Fantômas.

**The Lady of the Terraces** — 1925 adventure by E. Charles Vivian.

**My Deadly Angel** — 1955 Cold War drama by John Chelton

**Prose Bowl** — Futuristic satire — Bill Pronzini & Barry N. Malzberg .

**Satan's Den Exposed** — True crime in Truth or Consequences New Mexico — Award-winning journalism by the *Desert Journal*.

**The Amorous Intrigues & Adventures of Aaron Burr** — by Anonymous — Hot historical action.

**I Stole $16,000,000** — A true story by cracksman Herbert E. Wilson.

**The Black Dark Murders** — Vintage 50s college murder yarn by Milt Ozaki, writing as Robert O. Saber.

**Sex Slave** — Potboiler of lust in the days of Cleopatra — Dion Leclerq.

**You'll Die Laughing** — Bruce Elliott's 1945 novel of murder at a practical joker's English countryside manor.

**The Private Journal & Diary of John H. Surratt** — The memoirs of the man who conspired to assassinate President Lincoln.

**Dead Man Talks Too Much** — Hollywood boozer by Weed Dickenson

**Red Light** — History of legal prostitution in Shreveport Louisiana by Eric Brock. Includes wonderful photos of the houses and the ladies.

**A Snark Selection** — Lewis Carroll's *The Hunting of the Snark* with two Snarkian chapters by Harry Stephen Keeler — Illustrated by Gavin L. O'Keefe.

**Ripped from the Headlines!** — The Jack the Ripper story as told in the newspaper articles in the *New York* and *London Times*.

**Geronimo** — S. M. Barrett's 1905 autobiography of a noble American.

**The White Peril in the Far East** — Sidney Lewis Gulick's 1905 indictment of the West and assurance that Japan would never attack the U.S.

**The Compleat Calhoon** — All of Fender Tucker's works: Includes *Totah Six-Pack, Weed, Women and Song* and *Tales from the Tower,* plus a CD of all of his songs.

**Totah Six-Pack** — Just Fender Tucker's six tales about Farmington in one sleek volume.

## RAMBLE HOUSE

Fender Tucker, Prop.

www.ramblehouse.com     fender@ramblehouse.com

228-826-1783   10329 Sheephead Drive, Vancleave MS 39565

Made in the USA
Las Vegas, NV
20 September 2022

55652068R00194